JUSTIFIABLE DECEIT

MIKAEL CARLSON

Danbury, Connecticut

Printed in the United States of America
First Edition
ISBN: 978-1-944972-00-4 (paperback)
978-1-944972-01-1 (ebook)
978-1-944972-12-7 (hardcover)

Book cover designed by JD&J

This book is a work of fiction. Names, characters, places, and incidents either are products of the author's imagination or are used fictitiously. Any resemblance to actual persons, living or dead, events, or locales is entirely coincidental.

Novels by Mikael Carlson:

– The Michael Bennit Series –

The iCandidate

The iCongressman

The iSpeaker

The iAmerican

– Tierra Campos Thrillers –

Justifiable Deceit

Devious Measures

Vital Targets

Revealed Secrets

Decisive Endgame

– Tierra Campos Thrillers Prequels –

Narrow Escape: The Summerville Massacre

– Watchtower Thrillers –

The Eyes of Others

The Eyes of Innocents

The Eyes of Victims

The Eyes of Addicts

– America, Inc. Saga –

The Black Swan Event

Bounded Rationality

Boiling the Ocean

– The Santa Trilogy –

Banning Santa

– The Dancing Trilogy –

The Dancing Life

For all the victims of school shootings and gun violence and the people who want to find a real solution

PROLOGUE

TIERRA CAMPOS

Summerville High School
Red Sands, Arizona

It can never happen to me. That's the mindset of every teenager who has ever lived. All of us have a false sense of security and an undying belief that bad things only happen to other people because we know everything. I won't get caught using drugs. I can still drive after drinking these beers. My parents are always wrong. I will know what to do in a crisis. I don't have to pay attention to this drill because a shooting will never happen here.

My complacency shatters with the first muffled pops coming from the hallway. It sounds like someone clapping textbooks together. Mr. Sassone ignores the interruption and continues his instructions to my class gathered in the school library.

The sound is more distinct now, like a string of firecrackers going off. I share concerned looks with my friends as my annoyed teacher walks toward the entrance to the library to investigate.

"That's gunfire," Josh says, his voice cracking.

"They haven't made an announcement," one of the students behind me says.

Denial is a powerful thing. We are conditioned to respond to the "code blue" command over the school's public address system, but there hasn't been one. My brain refuses to process what my eyes see when a figure materializes at the entrance to the library with a rifle in his hands.

Mr. Sassone rushes at the kid, and the scene plays out like a stop-motion video. The barrel of the weapon comes up as he's eight steps away...seven...six. The black-clad kid fires three shots into his chest. Mr. Sassone falls forward with his momentum and collapses onto the ground. Time seems to stop, and so does my breathing.

Everybody screams. Some start to run, but I can't move. I jump when the shooter fires his rifle at the fleeing students, and I watch in horror as several of them fall. Josh jerks me out of my seat and to the ground. Kids next to me tip their table over to shield them from the gunfire. It doesn't help. Bullets rip right through it.

I cover my head with my arms and squeeze my eyes shut. When I open them, the wide-open eyes of my best friend stare back at me, locked open after a bullet ripped through her head. This isn't happening. It can't be.

The firing stops. I know that's my chance to do something, anything, but I'm numb and can't force myself to move. Fear grips my body. All I can do is wait to die.

"Tierra, let's go!"

"No!"

"Tierra!"

I cover my head with my arms again and try to bury myself in the floor. I'm jerked to my feet and pulled deeper into the library by Josh and Diego. My legs feel like rubber, and I'm ready to collapse back to the ground when I hear shots fired behind me.

Diego veers right towards one of the storage closets along the back wall. A couple of students working at the computers at the far end of the room join us. I trip over a kid with a hole in his chest. The girl next to him is lying in a pool of blood. I'm hoisted back to my feet as I fight the urge to vomit.

A wave of panic surges through me. I know I'm going to die. The firing starts again in a deadly staccato rhythm. I look toward the shooter and see him staring right at us.

Josh opens the door, and we all pile in. Diego is the last one through and slams the storage room door shut. The oak does little to stifle the urgent screams silenced by loud pops from the shooter's rifle. Lives of people I know just ended. Waves of intense anger and sadness mix with the fear that we're next.

"We're going to die!" a girl who crawled into the room with us shouts between sobs.

"Help me," Diego says, dragging over a piece of steel shelving from the middle of the room to use as a barricade. Josh and another kid join him, positioning it against the wooden door that separates us from certain death. The shooter knows we're in here. I can only pray that he moves on.

The boys join us in the back of the room. We huddle on the ground when the shooting stops. All we can hear is our own heavy, panicked breathing. One of the girls pulls out her phone and tries to type a text with shaking hands.

"Call 9-1-1," Aiden whispers, his voice high and anxious.

"Someone is shooting in Summerville High School," her friend says, fighting to hold back her tears. She already dialed for help. "We're in a storage closet. In the library. Please hurry!"

The handle jiggles. I hold my breath as we clutch each other harder and stare at the door. We all fight to stifle our sobs and stay quiet. Aiden buries his head in the pile of arms and torsos. I press my eyes closed and grind my teeth together to stop them from chattering.

The jiggling becomes more determined. A few seconds later, a loud thud against the door causes us all to jump. Panic surges through me. He's hunting us, and it's terrifying. He's going to get in here. All I can do is wait for whatever happens next.

"The police are there," I hear the 9-1-1 dispatcher say over the cell phone. "They're right outside the library. Is the shooter still there?"

"He's outside our door," she whispers, putting it back up to her ear.

A moment later, the muzzle of the rifle points through the narrow opening between the door and the jamb. The gunman lets loose, and bullets pound the wall.

The noise is deafening. The sound of each shot pierces my eardrums. The smell of gunpowder permeates my nostrils. I break free of the huddle and get low to the floor. Josh does the same, draping his arm over me.

"Come on, come on…" I plead, quietly willing the police to intervene.

It may be too late. The gunman pushes against the door, then again, and again. Each time it moves the shelving and opens another inch. By the sixth or seventh push, he's forced it open another six inches.

The shooter sticks the barrel of the rifle through, this time aimed right at us. All he has to do is pull the trigger. I close my eyes for what I think is the final time.

"I am invisible. I am invisible. I am invisible," I whisper to myself, willing it to be true while I wait for the inevitable.

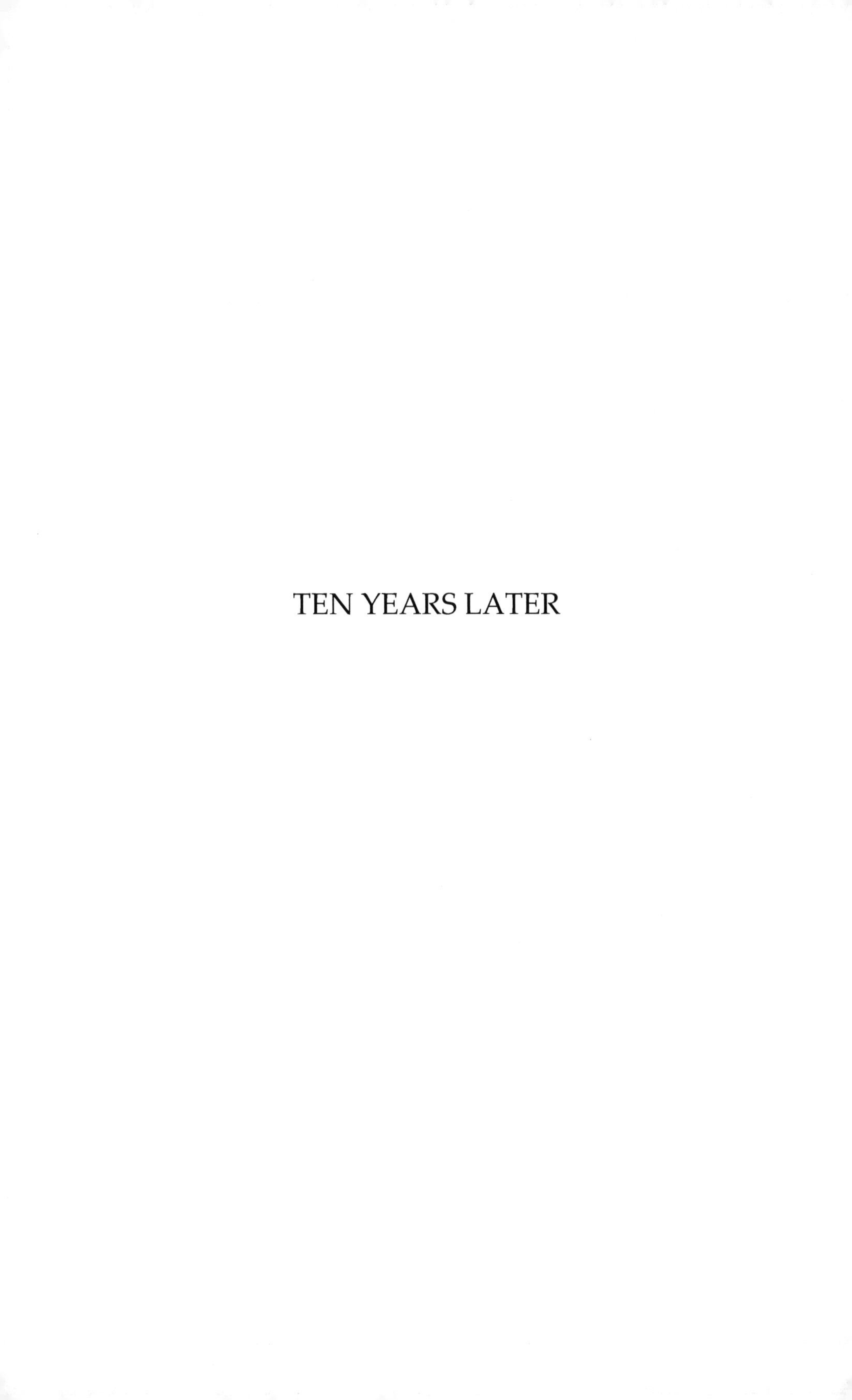

TEN YEARS LATER

CHAPTER ONE

CAPITOL BEAT

Cable News Studio
Washington, D.C.

The venerable Wilson Newman is one of America's most respected journalists. The aging anchor no longer crisscrosses the Capital chasing stories like the ones that made him a household name. Now the stories come to him. His no-nonsense interviews and hardball approach with prominent figures of both major parties make his program the single most successful political news hour in America.

"And now for tonight's final thought," he says, kicking off his closing monologue. "The shooting at Brockhampton High School in Massachusetts last year has resonated with the American people more than Parkland, Las Vegas, or even the murder of small children at Sandy Hook Elementary. Like the attack on Summerville High School in Arizona ten years ago, the trauma induced by the senseless violence is exceeded only by the lack of motive for it.

"The Brockhampton High shooter, eighteen-year-old Caleb Pratt, killed himself after murdering sixty-six fellow students and teachers. Whatever his reasons were for the heinous attack died with him. The only other person who may know – his friend Elizabeth Schwarzer – remains in a coma at MetroWest Massachusetts Medical Center after being assaulted at a vigil in the days after the massacre.

"The horror of what happened when Caleb walked into his school with a stolen AR-15 and opened fire may compel Congress to pass the first real gun control legislation since 1994. The Safe America Act, introduced by Democratic senator and presidential hopeful Alicia Standish, would ban all magazine-fed semi-automatic weapons, including handguns. The bill is a seismic shift in how Americans perceive gun ownership and will surely be challenged up to the Supreme Court.

"The bill still faces many obstacles to passage. The American Firearms Association is digging in for the fight of their lives. Their mishandling of the Brockhampton shooting has damaged the perception of them, but the progression of this bill in a Republican Congress has rallied their supporters and led to record donations to fund the fight.

"The AFA will have their hands full. Since the shooting at Marjorie Stoneman Douglas High in Parkland, Florida, the youth movement has tipped the scales in this debate. Leading the charge now is Ethan Harrington, the Brockhampton victim turned media sensation. He uses his massive social media following to spread his gun control message, and headlines huge rallies organized by the group Action Not Prayers. Both are applying significant pressure on elected representatives.

"There is only limited time for this debate to run its course before campaigning starts ahead of the next election. If the bill is brought to a vote this summer, the result is destined to have a profound impact on the race for the presidency and which political party occupies the White House. That's my final thought, and it's for the record."

Wilson's face changes from serious to something friendlier as he turns toward a different camera. It's the same move he's been using for over a decade and will live on in Internet memes and countless impersonations during reruns of *Saturday Night Live* long after he's gone.

"Thank you for watching *Capitol Beat*; I'm Wilson Newman. Good Night."

CHAPTER TWO

SENATOR ALICIA STANDISH

Capitol Hill
Washington, D.C.

Rush hour in Washington, D.C. is a misnomer. Rush "hours" is a far more appropriate description. Senator Alicia Standish starts her morning commute around six a.m. Politicians don't oversleep when Congress is in session. The business of governing is a never-ending grind that eventually wears down the most ardent and energetic people.

Alicia steps out onto the platform of the Capitol South station, determined to cut the seven-minute walk down by a third. Washington is divided into quadrants at the Capitol, and this spot on Pennsylvania Avenue Southeast is known for a different reason than the notorious residence that shares the street. Back to the Grind is the preferred coffee house for bureaucrats and political operatives on Capitol Hill. They get their morning jolt of caffeine with a dark roast blend that's out of this world. Daniel Wetzel, the senior senator from Arizona, is one of those people.

"Still taking the Metro to work?" he asks when Alicia steps in line alongside him. "You know we have reserved parking."

"Environmentalists love my small carbon footprint, and taking mass transit burnishes my working-class image."

"And that's what's propelled you to the top ranks of the Democratic Party and made you a frontrunner in the presidential primaries. I get it. Ambushing me here is a little brash, though, don't you think?"

"Isn't that the word on the Hill? That I'm the ruthless senator from Massachusetts who gets what she wants?"

"Something like that. What *do* you want, Alicia?"

"You know what."

He shakes his head without offering a word until they order large cups of java. Alicia slips the cashier her debit card, causing Daniel to scoff before shoving his wallet back into his jacket pocket. It was an overdramatic gesture. He knew she was going to pay.

"Thanks for the coffee," he says, sipping the brew as the pair head towards the Capitol. "I'm assuming you're here to browbeat me into doing something."

"I have the entire caucus lined up behind the Safe America Act. The entire caucus except you, that is."

"I saw the whip count. There are a few other holdouts. How do you walk so fast in those things?" he asks, staring down at her high heels as they walk. "I would break my ankles."

"I'm tougher than you. Don't change the subject. You need the progressive creds this bill offers to be relevant in the party. Not to mention being on the right side of history."

Daniel smirks. "I'm doing just fine, thank you. And remember how the last assault weapons ban worked out for Democrats."

The Federal Assault Weapons Ban was the colloquial name for a subsection of the Violent Crime Control and Law Enforcement Act passed by Congress in September of 1994 and signed into law the same day by President Bill Clinton. It placed restrictions on the number of military features on a gun and banned large-capacity magazines for consumer use.

"It cost Democrats at least forty of the fifty-three total seats we lost in rural areas during the 1994 midterms, and indirectly led to Clinton's impeachment," Alicia says. "A steep political price for a law that was allowed to expire in 2004 per its sunset provision if you ask me."

"This is different."

"That's what we always say. It doesn't make it true."

"Yes, it's a party line you should learn if you plan on keeping your career in politics," Alicia says, turning to a tried and true ploy as old as politics itself.

Political parties run on a merit-based system. Leadership expects a representative or senator to vote the way they want you to. There are times when they support rogues, especially when it involves seats in swing states. Alicia Standish hails from deep blue Massachusetts and doesn't have the luxury of defying them, not that she ever needs to.

Daniel Wetzel, on the other hand, represents one of those swing states. Although Arizona has gone blue the last couple of elections, the margins of victory were slim. He'll need financial help to get re-elected, and the money machines that power modern campaigns have no pause button. For a price, Alicia has the connections to fill his coffers with political action committee donations.

"The DSCC has its doubts about you. Word on the street is that the Republicans are going to run that Hispanic lieutenant governor against you. Wow, that's going to be an expensive race," Alicia says, emphasizing words for dramatic effect.

"I'll get my backing. We can't afford to lose my seat. You know that."

"There are other competitive seats we can afford to lose less. This election cycle is going to be the most expensive in American history. The Democrat Senate Campaign Committee only has so many resources they can spread around. They need to pick winners. Who do you think will help them do that?"

"You're making a lot of assumptions, Alicia," he says, stopping to let a group of school children unload from a bus in front of the Library of Congress. Some of them wave at the pair of legislators, who smile and wave back. Alicia wishes she didn't have to force hers.

"Daniel, I may be making assumptions, but I'm going to be the Democratic frontrunner going into the primaries. I'm articulate, passionate, and have policies that resonate with our base and independent voters. Would you bet against me in the general election?"

"It's a long time until then."

"Not that long," Alicia says, with a quick shake of her head. "I'm only going to get stronger, and you're going to need me at your side at rallies in Phoenix and Tucson if you want to have a chance at reelection."

"Is that the carrot?"

"Yes, now here's the stick: Do you want to be on the naughty list when I get sworn in on Inauguration Day?"

The only thing worse than being threatened is being threatened by someone who can follow through on it. Alicia is a master player in the great poker game that is American politics, and she wins without bluffing. If she's saying she'll hold a grudge, Daniel knows it's because she will.

"Be reasonable, Alicia. Arizona is a 'Constitutional Carry' state. Over a third of my constituents own firearms. Our state legislature is making it even easier to possess and carry them. It's not New England. If I go against them, what do you think my chances of reelection will be?"

"I know it's been a decade, but you remember the Summerville High shooting. You represent those families. What do you think your chances are if you don't support me?"

"I get it. I know this is personal for you because of what happened to your parents, but your bill passing this Congress is a long shot."

Alicia bites her lower lip. The mention of her mother and father causes her to feel a wave of sadness that she struggles to push aside. She gets emotional during interviews whenever they are brought up. This isn't the time for discussion of her motives.

"This is the best chance we've had in a generation to pass meaningful gun control legislation. We have a legion of young, vocal activists and a sympathetic public that has the American Firearms Association in full retreat. If this bill fails, it had better not be because a member of my party didn't support it."

"Let me give you a piece of unsolicited advice," Daniel says as they reach Constitution Avenue and prepare to go in separate directions. "You're a hammer, and everyone on the Hill looks like a nail to you. Sooner or later, you're going to swing and miss and smash your thumb. When you do, it will be the end of your presidential ambitions and probably your career in politics."

"Thanks for the tip. Now let me return the favor: Support this bill, or you'll be packing your office next year. If you think I'm bluffing, fine, call it. Otherwise, I'll expect an announcement of support by the end of the week. Enjoy your coffee."

Alicia checks the traffic on Constitution Avenue and crosses quickly. There's a bounce to her step. Every conversation she has brings her bill one step closer to passage. Some of her colleagues need to be charmed. Others need a less nuanced approach.

One of the first things politicians learn in Washington is when you know you're going to get your hands dirty, wear gloves. She needs his support and will apply as much pressure as necessary to get it. Hammer and nails, Alicia thinks, smiling as she turns her coat up to fight the biting wind outside the Hart Senate Office Building. She likes that analogy.

CHAPTER THREE

ETHAN HARRINGTON

National Mall
Washington, D.C.

Gun control supporters began filling the National Mall long before the first speaker took the podium. Thousands of people were bused in and handed signs by volunteers working for the event sponsor, Action Not Prayers. The electric atmosphere makes for great television, and that's what the organizers wanted.

The speakers sang, chanted, and challenged their parents' and grandparents' generations to be effective in eliminating gun violence from society. It was all a warmup for the main event – Ethan Harrington and his firebrand message that has mobilized and inspired an unstoppable movement.

"Yeah?" Brian Cooper says, answering his cell phone after it chirps.

"It's Rahul," his deputy chief of staff says. "We're getting great visibility on this rally. Clips of the speakers are getting social media saturation."

"What does Twitter look like?"

"Mostly supportive and energetic. The AFA will unleash their trolls, but their focus will be on a different hashtag. They don't want to keep ours trending."

"Good. Stay on it." Brian disconnects the call and turns to Ethan. "You're up, kid. Make us proud."

"Have I ever let you down?"

Brian watched him go from an angry teenager to an effective orator under the guidance of his mentor, Ryan Baino. Now the young activist waves to the crowd like a rock star as he walks onto the stage to enormous applause after the emcee announces his name. The energetic crowd responds to his every movement as he takes the microphone.

"On April third of last year, I joined a sad fraternity," Ethan says, kicking off his speech. "It wasn't one I had any interest in joining. That decision was made for me by a classmate who picked up a gun and decided to commit murder. It was made for me by politicians that refused to pass laws that would have prevented him from doing it.

"The pro-gun crowd and their sympathizers in the media like to call us victims. The real victims had their voices silenced that day. Now I speak for them, and I say do something. Do anything!"

The crowd reacts as if cued by a producer at a late-night talk show. The applause turns into a throaty chant of "Do something!" Ethan, acting as a veteran ringmaster of a thousand circus performances, lets it play out long enough for the cameras to capture the moment before he reasserts himself.

"One brave politician is. Senator Alicia Standish introduced a bill that will radically curtail the gun culture in this country. An assault weapons ban would have saved those students lost in all the shootings that have plagued our nation, but that doesn't go far enough. This legislation can't only be about mass shootings. We need to act to save the tens of thousands of victims of violent crime each year. Tragedies get all the coverage, but gun violence is a cancer that this country can no longer tolerate. Senator Standish's bill is the cure.

"We've waited too long for our country's leaders to act, and it's led only to disappointment. That ends with the passage of the Safe America Act. We won't tolerate parents burying their children because of senseless gun violence any longer. We won't tolerate our friends, siblings, and classmates dying while politicians attend fundraisers and fancy dinners with special interest groups. Anybody who doesn't support the Safe America Act needs to understand that their days in this town are numbered."

"Ethan has a natural feel for a crowd, doesn't he?" Ryan asks, coming up alongside Brian off to the side of the stage as the audience goes wild.

"Connecting with an audience is what a performer does best. He'd make a great political candidate."

"Only Ethan's not a performer. He was a kid who emerged from a school shooting covered in blood and made a statement that resonated with so many people it went viral in seconds. He has passion, and that's what makes him my greatest find."

"If you say so," Brian mumbles, turning his attention back to Ethan, who is getting the crowd amped up.

"Ninety-six people die every day from guns in our country. Is that okay with you?"

"No!" the crowd screams in unison.

"Do you think that should be okay with our politicians?"

"No!"

"Then I say no more! We are going to drag this country into the twenty-first century. Every legislator that fails to support it doesn't deserve to be called a representative. We'll ensure that this next election is their last!

"Now is the time to come together as Americans. This issue is no longer about red and blue, Republican or Democrat; it is about the kind of place we want to live. Those who take the gun lobby's money will fight to divide us but will fail. We will come together. We will unite and cry out for change. Together, we will all become the heroes that save lives!"

Brian sneaks a glance at Ryan out of the corner of his eye. He's smiling at his protégé like a proud father. The head of the Action Not Prayers spent months mentoring him with quotable statistics on gun violence to bolster his arguments. Ryan taught him how to work a crowd and manipulate the media. Together, they've forged a movement that is marching across America.

"This is the reason the senator's gun control bill will pass in Congress. Look at this," Ryan says, gesturing out at the audience. "This is why I brought Ethan and Senator Standish together."

"And here I thought that it was to raise money for more rallies," Brian sneers.

"You still don't get it, do you? Rallies are a means to an end. Your boss's bill won't make it out of committee without the public pressure Ethan gins up. With the media echoing the message and a frustrated public aligning with our cause, no moderate senator would dare vote against the Safe America Act."

"Let's hope it's enough," Brian says, shaking his head.

"I don't understand why you don't like me," Ryan says, still surveying the crowd from offstage. "We share the same goals."

"Do we?"

"I'll do whatever it takes to get more gun control in this country. You should be more willing to do what it takes to send your boss to the White House," he says, slapping Brian's shoulder.

Brian grabs the organizer's arm as he starts to head out on stage and returns the fierce glare he gets from him.

"Understand something, Ryan. Senator Standish is going to win the Democratic nomination and will likely win the general election. My job is to protect her from anyone seeking to take advantage of that. I won't let you do anything that puts her career in jeopardy."

"Of course you won't," he says, jerking his arm away.

Brian watches as Ryan embraces Ethan center stage and joins the crowd in a full-throated "no more" chant that they can probably hear in California. It's a moment custom-built for live television and will be hard for even the most ardent Second Amendment supporter to ignore. It's what Senator Standish was counting on to push her bill and what Action Not Prayers is great at delivering. Brian only worries about what the long-term cost of this alliance will be.

CHAPTER FOUR

TIERRA CAMPOS

WWDC TV Studio
Washington D.C.

The last century and a half gave birth to some of humanity's greatest inventions. Cars and airplanes were quantum leaps in transportation. Telephones revolutionized communications, though they also gave us telemarketers. We went to the moon, explored the depths of the oceans, and mapped the human genome. None of these advances were as transformative as the Internet. I can't think of another invention that you can use at your job that makes it look like you're doing work when you aren't.

"That doesn't look like any story I've assigned you, Tierra," Chet Flannigan says from behind me. Startled, I instinctively minimize the browser loaded with an article about the Brockhampton shooting faster than a boy looking at porn when his mother comes into the room. I'm usually invisible in this office, and now the executive producer of our flagship news broadcast is standing behind me. Talk about lousy timing.

"Hi, Chet. It's research."

"You cover local human interest stories. Why are you reading an article about Ethan Harrington?"

"This is Washington. We cover local news that has national interest. There was a huge rally that was local, and a gun control bill making its way through Congress has national interest. That is a human interest story."

Chet folds his arms across his chest. I wait for another lecture about how I should be focusing on the stories he gives me, not chasing the ones out of my reach. I'm about to get one when the horse's ass with perfectly styled hair and over-whitened teeth walks over.

"Hey, Chet. You wanted to see me?" Carl Brennan asks, prancing up to the two of us.

Carl is the prominent WWDC news anchor who fancies himself the next Sam Donaldson or Tom Brokaw. It's an opinion of himself that's highly inflated. I think he's a two-bit, no-talent hack who charmed his way into the evening news slot. Everybody knows it except him.

"Yes. Both of you follow me. We're heading upstairs."

We make our way through the bustling newsroom and take the elevator up to the top floor of our building, where all the brass is. I expected to head into one of the conference rooms when Chet veers into the news director's office. He's seated at his desk when we enter.

"Have a seat," he commands, gesturing to the two chairs in front of his desk.

Phillip Royce has had this job forever. There is rarely an issue or incident encountered that he hasn't run into once or twice before. Rumor has it that the only time anyone ever saw him display any emotion was during the 9/11 terrorist attacks. He's an able leader, but not the touchy-feely type.

Carl and I sit as instructed. Chet opts to stand along the wall next to the window.

"I have some exciting news to share with you. We've been working with Senator Standish's staff and Ryan Baino from Action Not Prayers for a couple of weeks now to land an interview with Ethan Harrington. I got a call today from the Velocity PR firm that represents him. They confirmed the in-studio live interview during Monday's broadcast."

"That's good news," I say, failing to see the reason for my being here.

"That is fantastic news. I already have a list of questions drafted. I'm happy to interview Ethan," Carl says, puffing his chest out.

"I'm sure you are, Carl, but that's why I wanted you here so I could tell you this personally. You're not getting the assignment. Tierra is."

"Me?"

I'm not sure that I heard him right. I didn't think Phillip even knew who I was. Anxiety causes my nerves to tingle. The WWDC news director is handing me the most significant interview our station has landed in ages. I have dreamt of getting my moment in the spotlight. The reality of it is terrifying.

"Chet told me you've been working here since graduating from college six years ago and have pleaded with him for tougher assignments. Now you're getting one. This is a huge opportunity for you."

"Uh, sir, no disrespect, but I'm the face of this station, and Ethan is an icon. I should conduct the interview."

No disrespect, my ass.

"Ethan Harrington has given a hundred interviews. We don't need to add another plain vanilla one to the list. I need an angle no one else has provided."

"I can come up with one," Carl pleads, as shocked about this development as I am.

"I'm sure you can, but not the one I have in mind."

"C'mon, Phil, what could she bring to an interview that I can't?"

The news director raises his eyebrows and waits for me to chime in. I know where he's going with this.

"He wants me because of who I am," I say in a near whisper.

"Really? And who are you, other than the local rape, fire, and murder reporter?"

The beginnings of a smirk cross the news director's lips. He glances over at Chet, who is staring impassively at me. He doesn't want to take sides against the station's premier talent. They have to work together closely. I take a deep breath.

"A school shooting survivor."

I never imagined that my big break would involve re-experiencing what happened that day in Summerville. I spent ten years trying to bury those memories while paying therapists to hand me a shovel to dig them out. This interview will force me to confront demons I'd rather not meet again.

"What difference does that make?" Carl asks.

"Tierra can relate to Ethan better than any other journalist because she's gone through what he did," Phillip says, leaning forward in his chair and interlacing his fingers below his chin. "They share a common experience, and that has the makings of a great interview."

"It's a mistake. It won't have the effect you think it will, Phil."

"You don't know what it was like being shot at," he fires back. "You don't know what it feels like not knowing whether you'll live or die. She does, and so does Ethan."

"A good journalist doesn't need to sympathize with a subject."

"That's true, but the most powerful interviews come from that type of connection. How do you feel about it, Tierra?"

I feel like I'm going to throw up, that's how. My mouth goes dry.

"Sir, I don't know if… This is… It was a traumatic moment in my life."

"I understand. The story is yours if you want it, Tierra. If you turn it down, you may not get another this big."

All eyes turn to me.

"I can relate to his trauma. Ethan will open up to me. It will be a great interview."

"I agree," the news director says with a smile. I must have sold it better than I thought I did.

"I can't believe this. It's a wasted opportunity."

"Thank you, Carl, but it's decided. You can show yourself out."

He rises from his chair and leaves in a huff, not trying to hide his annoyance. There is a fine line between closing a door with authority and slamming it. Carl came close to crossing it. Anyone else at this station would get reprimanded for that type of behavior. His close relationship with the news director will spare him.

"The interview will be live during Monday's six o'clock broadcast," Phillip says, ignoring Carl's behavior. "You have the A and B blocks with no commercial interruption in-between. Do a short intro, but skip rehashing the whole incident. Everybody knows what happened up in Brockhampton. Make this about Ethan."

"Yes, sir."

"Come up with some questions and run them through Chet. This station landing an interview with a national phenomenon like Ethan is a big deal, and I'm counting on you to do something extraordinary with it."

"I will."

"Carl will open the broadcast and immediately throw it over to you. The interview will be set up in the Living Room."

The Living Room is our nickname for the set furnished with a sofa and chairs, coffee table, and plants to give the space a comfortable feel to put our subjects at ease. With the multiple cameras, lighting, and all the microphones, I doubt anyone is.

"The two of you can work out the details," the news director says, rising from his chair and briefly glancing at Chet. "Congratulations, Tierra. You've worked hard here, and I know you're going to do a fantastic job."

I thank him and leave the office. My career trajectory just got the boost of my dreams, but I have to journey through my personal hell to realize it. All I have to do is not lose it on set – and not screw up an interview with the most recognizable activist in the country.

CHAPTER FIVE

SPECIAL AGENT VICTORIA LARSEN

Federal Bureau of Investigation Boston Field Office
Chelsea, Massachusetts

Federal agents don't get as much firearms training as people think. Television leads the American people to believe that graduating from the FBI Academy at Quantico turns agents into the reincarnation of Wild Bill Hickok. It doesn't. Trainees do spend a lot of time on the range before earning their badge, but shooting is a perishable skill that must be continuously practiced to prevent atrophy.

"Nice shot group," Victoria says, pulling off her hearing protection as her colleague pulls in his target. "You pulled a couple, though."

Special Agent Takara Nishimoto stares at his B-27 silhouette. Seven of the nine rounds are in the red and gray center bands. The two remaining shots found their way into the nine band closer to where the heart would be. They would be fatal, but he still jerked the trigger back instead of squeezing it on those two.

"You think you can do better?"

"I know I can. Don't be a cliché and ask me to demonstrate it."

"Fair enough," Takara says, reloading his magazine. "I know this isn't a social call. What can I do for you, Vic?"

Takara is well-regarded in the Bureau and gets assigned many of Boston's high-profile assignments. His range time is therapy as much as it is practice. Victoria almost feels bad about interrupting that.

"You led the Brockhampton School shooting investigation."

"And you conducted interviews and worked with the victims' families."

"I did, and they still don't have answers to their questions."

Takara stops loading but doesn't look back at her. "Are you sure you want to go down the rabbit hole?"

"If the Knave of Hearts didn't steal the tarts, I'm obligated to find out who did."

"How did that work out for Alice?"

"She woke up, so we'll never know," Victoria says, a smile creasing her lips.

Takara shakes his head and begins loading a second magazine. He's one of the rare agents unintimidated by a strong female, especially an educated one who's read the classics.

"The Brockhampton shooting is a political minefield now. You have a bright career ahead of you, Vic. Don't ruin it by sticking your nose where it's likely to get broken."

"Are you going to give me career advice or the information I'm looking for?"

"Everything is in my report."

"Eighth-grade book reports have more detail in them than that did. You watered it down. Tell me what you really think."

"What do I get out of this?" he asks.

"Not a date, if that's what you're asking. What's the pool on me up to, by the way?"

Takara shakes his head again. "Why am I not surprised you know about that?"

"Because I'm a good investigator and quiet whispering in the hallway doesn't make conversations private. I've been here for seven years. The prize money must be in the thousands."

"I don't know what it's up to."

"And you aren't going to find out by winning. Tell me what you think about the state police investigation."

Takara chuckles nervously, embarrassed. "Caleb was dead. Once they concluded nobody else was involved, the FBI got dismissed, and the investigation ended. Everyone was happy the case was closed, and here we are."

Victoria thinks about that as Takara uses binder clips to secure a fresh target to the frame. Pressing down on the small lever on the partition, he sends it careening down the range.

"Everyone? Does that include people in this building?"

"Here, the Hoover Building, even the DOJ. You know damn well that this case is radioactive now. None of the honchos will appreciate you asking questions. Why are you so interested in this? And don't say it's out of curiosity."

"Caleb Pratt committed suicide in the school. He didn't leave a manifesto behind. Elizabeth Schwarzer is the only person who may know his motive, and she was nearly beaten to death. You don't find that suspicious?"

"None of that explains why you're interested."

Victoria crosses her arms and narrows her eyes.

"Everybody wants to know the motive. There were no red flags for Caleb," Takara offers. "He was a social outcast, but never violent. As for Elizabeth, there's no reason to believe she knows anything."

"They went to the range at least twice a week, Takara. How much more of a violent tendency do you need? And speaking of that, how did he pay for it? Why wasn't any of that in your report?"

"State police investigators were handling that."

Takara slaps a magazine into his weapon. He pulls back on the slide and chambers a round. He sets the weapon down before putting on his eye protection.

"Police will get answers about Caleb's motive from Elizabeth when she comes out of her coma."

"If she comes out of it."

"It's not your problem, so drop it."

Takara turns and slides his muffs over his ears. Victoria is quicker. Donning her ear and eye protection, she shoulders him out of the way and picks up his weapon, firing it nine times in succession. The job done, she presses the catch and pulls out the empty magazine before returning the Glock to the ledge. He flips up the return switch and gawks when the target approaches. Only one shot was even close to the line. The rest found their mark dead center.

"Remind me to stand next to you in my next firefight."

"Who told you that the FBI was no longer needed to assist the investigation?"

"Detective Lieutenant Howard Spivey. He came in, thanked us for our hard work, and showed us the door. It came out of the blue."

"Did he decide that unilaterally?"

"I don't know."

"Then maybe it's time to find out. Thanks, Takara."

"You never answered my question, Vic," he calls out as she reaches the door leading out the range. "Why are you so interested?"

She turns and inhales deeply while scanning the empty range.

"I looked in the eyes of mothers, fathers, and siblings of sixty students and the spouses of six adults for weeks during those interviews. I felt the pain of their loss like it was my own. Sixty-six families lost people they loved who had no reason to die. I promised them answers to why they did, and I'm going to find those answers even if nobody else wants to."

The statement hangs in the air. Takara's mouth tries to form words, but none come out on the first couple of attempts.

"The case is closed, Victoria."

"Not for me, it isn't."

Victoria nods and slides through the half-opened door. Takara watches as she leaves. He can sympathize with her need for closure and knows she won't listen to his warnings. He found himself in a similar situation once. This is different, though. He hopes she figures out what she's getting herself into before someone ends her career.

CHAPTER SIX

TIERRA CAMPOS

Il Diplomatico Infuriata Ristorante
Washington, D.C.

The waiter finishes taking our order, thanks us in Italian, and heads off. Translated from Italian to English as "The Furious Diplomat," the upscale Italian Renaissance-themed restaurant near Dupont Circle caters to the political class of this city. It is renowned for its enormous Bistecca Fiorentina T-bone steak that causes my mouth to water every time one passes our table.

"I suppose a toast is in order," Josh says, raising his wine glass. "To opportunities and those who seize them when they come. Congratulations on landing your first big interview. Cheers!"

"Cheers to that," I say, clinking his glass and taking a sip of my Malbec.

I set the glass down and look around to see who I can find. This place has a reputation for always having a public figure dining in it. I'm disappointed that I don't recognize anyone here except the longtime friend with whom I'm sharing the table.

"What's on your mind, Tierra?"

"Why do you think anything is?"

"Because I've known you since elementary school. The Tierra I know would be home poring over other interviews, watching videos, and doing whatever she can to prepare for her big day tomorrow."

Our relationship is deeper than that. Josh was the one who pulled me off the floor and got me to the storage closet we hid in that fateful day at Summerville High. I owe him my life.

"Maybe I missed you."

"We hang out every two weeks. You don't miss me that much. Spill it."

"What do you remember about the shooting at our school?" It's a serious question, as dumb as it must sound to him.

"I don't know. Everything?"

"What was the scariest thing for you?"

Josh withdraws into his memories. It took a lot of therapy for both of us to be able to even talk about this — some things the mind naturally wants to wall off. The key for any survivor is to confront the trauma so it doesn't get pushed down into the subconscious, where it can do real damage.

"I remember being terrified when we were hiding. There was nothing we could do except wonder if we would be next. Then the gunman stuck his rifle through the door and pointed it right at us. I thought we were goners. What about you?"

"I remember seeing the bodies of our classmates when the police evacuated us from the building. I could only remember thinking that I was happy it wasn't me lying there. Then officers with rifles and handguns drawn ordered us to place our hands on our heads. It felt like such a ridiculous thing to do after what we went through."

"We were treated like criminals. I understand the rationale for it now, but I didn't at the time," Josh admits. "Are you sure this interview isn't too much for you? It's digging up old memories, none of them pleasant."

"Those feelings resurface every time there's another school shooting. They'll never go away. I've learned to deal with them."

Our food arrives, and the waiter offers to refill our wine glasses. I hadn't even realized I finished mine. We accept the offer and begin eating. After a few mouthfuls of his penne, he puts his fork down.

"Why did you ask about what happened to us?"

"Because something struck me when I was researching Ethan. He's never mentioned whether he's in counseling."

"Maybe he doesn't want to talk about it…or doesn't need it," Josh postulates.

"Ethan walked out of his school covered in blood. Believe me. He needs it."

"So, ask him."

"My producer won't let me. He told me what I would be asking." Josh clenches his teeth and tightens his lips. "What?" I ask.

"It's your interview, Tierra. They gave it to you because you're a great reporter."

"They gave it to me because of Summerville so they can market it as one shooting victim interviewing another. It has nothing to do with me."

He shakes his head. "Why do you put up with that? You're one of the most fiercely independent people I know. Why are you letting others call the shots?"

"I'm paying my dues."

"Psssh," he says, waving a dismissive hand. "I work as a junior analyst for the Commerce Department. I know about being the low man on the ladder. I also know there's a difference between paying dues and letting people run your life."

I slam my fork down onto my plate. The sound causes people at the tables near us to turn in our direction. Josh may be a close friend, but I don't need a lecture from him.

"What the hell is your problem?"

"Nothing."

"It doesn't sound like nothing," I argue.

"For six years, I've watched them take your talent for granted, and you be okay with it. You pay dues for two years, not six, Tierra. It's your interview. You need to fight to ask your questions."

"Listen to you judging me," I say as he starts to protest. "I make a local reporter's salary. I have the two shallowest roommates in America because I can't afford rent in Washington. Oh, and I'm paying off student loans that rival the national debt. I don't have the luxury of making demands to producers that can replace me in an hour."

"Only they can't replace you. I wish you'd recognize that. You're stuck where you are because you've never taken a risk. It's like you never came out of that closet we were hiding in. You're still in there waiting to die."

I close my eyes in a vain attempt to stop tears from pouring out of them.

"I can't do this right now," I say, dropping my napkin on my half-eaten dinner before standing. "Enjoy your dinner."

"Tierra? Tierra, wait! I'm sorry."

I rush to the foyer, fighting off competing waves of anger and anguish. Josh is one of the good guys. I owe him more than I can ever repay, but he crossed a line. I don't expect him to understand. He got past what happened to us at Summerville. As I turn in my coat check ticket and retrieve my jacket, I know I never have.

CHAPTER SEVEN

ETHAN HARRINGTON

The Illustrious Hotel
Washington, D.C.

Ethan passes the reception desk with his entourage following him closely. He swipes a key card in the elevator and punches the button for the top floor. The sleek and modern Illustrious is the most beautiful hotel Ethan has ever seen. Every ride up to his suite makes him feel like he's been transported to a luxury starship whipping between planets.

"We'll be down in the lobby," one of the bodyguards says after they step off the elevator to check the corridor. "Call us if you need to leave the building."

The two burly men don't engage in small talk, nor do they have any interest in Ethan other than keeping him safe. He can't go out in public in Washington without the two security guards flanking him. It's the one part of celebrity that the teenager loathes. The sheer number of death threats makes their constant presence a necessity but hampers the freedom he cherishes. Ethan escaped his parents' rules only to find new ones imposed on him.

"You guys want anything?" Ethan asks his remaining guests after they enter the suite. He immediately starts rummaging through the refrigerator.

"I'm fine," Ryan says, parking himself in a chair.

"Yes, I want to talk about the book," Tamara insists, taking a seat on the sofa and pulling out her iPad.

"I'm working on it," Ethan says, using the same automatic response he always does.

"I know you are. I get regular updates. What concerns me is what's in it and what isn't."

Ethan frowns. He doesn't like this ghostwriter any more than he did the first. Everything he wants to write is about the day of the shooting. Tamara is the one pushing him for the details, and it's the last thing Ethan wants to discuss.

"What do you mean?" Ethan asks, playing dumb.

"It's nothing more than your reciting gun control facts and making arguments against the Second Amendment!"

"My kind of book," Ryan muses, smirking.

"What's wrong with that?"

"Nothing, if you only want to sell ten copies. When you want to sell ten million, it needs to have more substance. You have a story that will connect with people. That's what you want, isn't it?"

"I've already told you that I won't talk about the shooting with you, a reporter, a ghostwriter, or anybody else."

"I need a real human moment out of you, Ethan. Your crusade and the senator's bill are important, but neither defines who you are. That's what people who are going to read this book want. I won't get a publisher to print it otherwise."

"I'm Ethan Harrington," he says, arms outstretched. "Someone will publish it."

Tamara frowns, wondering how she ended up representing a prima donna. He wasn't like this when they first met. Ethan needed help when the media demands for interviews were insatiable. Tamara's firm agreed to handle it at a significantly reduced price. Her ability to land him a book deal with a significant advance sealed the deal that is now in peril.

Ethan moves around the counter from the kitchen and plops on the sofa. He turns the massive television on and sips his Coke. Tamara bites her lower lip, trying to stifle her anger.

"Ethan, we need to –"

"Move on to something else," Ryan interrupts. "We can discuss this later."

Tamara isn't the type to back down. She didn't make it from the mean streets of Detroit to Velocity, the top PR firm in Boston, by being a pushover. She has navigated more accomplished clients through shark-infested waters. Unfortunately, Ethan is the flavor of the month, and nobody on earth is a hotter commodity right now.

"Fine, you're paying the bill."

"Yes, I am. Don't forget that."

"Let's talk about tomorrow's interviews," she says, ignoring Ryan's warning and bringing up Ethan's calendar. "We have you booked on two morning shows, CNN midday, and then you have a meet and greet with Senator Standish and some of her colleagues on Capitol Hill. The day ends with an interview at WWDC."

"A local station? That's a little beneath me, don't you think?"

"You make it sound like we're in Boise, Idaho, or something. WWDC is a large affiliate and very influential with the people who live and work in Washington. People you want on your side."

"It's still a local station. Cancel it."

"Ethan, this interview was arranged by Senator Standish herself."

"So what? I don't work for her. She should have asked me."

Tamara turns and stares at Ryan. The activist doesn't care about the book deal. Congress will vote on the bill long before it goes to print. An interview arranged by the Democratic frontrunner is another thing entirely.

"Ethan, United States Senators do not ask. They tell."

"Yeah, whatever."

"You'll do the interview then?" Tamara asks, hoping her client will be agreeable at least once today.

Ethan says nothing. He stares at the television on the wall and smirks at something amusing.

"Tamara, will you excuse us for a moment, please?" Ryan asks.

She doesn't need to be asked twice. "Send me a text and let me know the verdict. I'll be back here at six a.m., and we'll drive over to the morning shows together."

Ethan still doesn't respond. He continues to watch the television as Tamara lets herself out of the room. Ryan seizes the remote and turns off the TV, tossing the controller back down on the coffee table.

"I was watching that."

"I don't give a shit."

Ethan stands, picks the remote back up, and points it at the wall. Ryan slaps it hard out of his hand, sending it skittering across the floor toward the far side of the room. With both hands, he shoves the teenager back onto the couch and holds him there with one hand on his chest to dispel any notion Ethan has of climbing back to his feet.

"What's your problem, man?" Ethan says, glaring at his ally.

"I hate people who waste their lives."

"And I hate tofu. What's your point?"

"You survived a traumatic ordeal. You spoke with a passion that inspired millions of people."

"I think I know that."

"And that's your problem, Ethan. You're letting it go to your head, and it's clouding your thinking."

"Whatever you say, master."

Ryan reaches back and slaps Ethan hard across the face. Ethan is about to lash out when he sees his mentor only inches from his face.

"The only thing Americans like better than an underdog is a big shot who falls. You're going to do the WWDC interview tomorrow. Got it?"

Ethan rubs his cheek and glares at Ryan through angry eyes as he moves out of his personal space.

"And if I don't?" he asks, as Ryan starts his walk to the entrance of the suite.

"I've done a lot to realize this goal. Now that I'm in sight of it, I won't let anyone stop us. You know that better than anybody."

Ethan breaks eye contact.

"I made you, Ethan. I can destroy you just as easily. Always remember that. See you bright and early in the morning."

CHAPTER EIGHT

SENATOR ALICIA STANDISH

Hart Senate Office Building
Washington, D.C.

Few people have any idea how much work goes into getting anything done on Capitol Hill. Congress is a dysfunctional mess during the best of times. What the American public knows about the political wrangling and backroom deals is what can be boiled down to a series of soundbites and clickbait articles.

"They're here, and Ethan just arrived at the building," Brian announces from outside her office door.

"And the press?" Alicia asks, peeling her eyes from the roundtable panel discussing gun control.

"Well represented," Brian says. "Rahul has them gathered in the foyer."

The senator smiles. When CNN first broadcasted on June 1, 1980, nobody knew that the twenty-four-hour news cycle would transform how people interacted with the world. Television brought the Vietnam War into our living rooms, but CNN brought the Persian Gulf War to America in real-time. Now it's social media, the Internet, and smartphones that keep everyone informed everywhere, instantaneously. She's using all of those resources today.

Alicia greets the senators as Rahul guides the reporters to their positions along the back wall of her office. Ethan is the last to walk in, immediately introducing himself and posing for pictures. They're worth their weight in political gold given his celebrity status. Group shots also portray the bipartisan approach to the problem that appeases their constituents.

"First, I want to thank you all again for coming," Alicia opens once the press departs and everyone takes their seats around the conference table outside her office. "I understand that the Safe America Act is controversial and that there are political risks involved in supporting it. There are also good reasons why we need to summon the courage to do so. I asked Ethan to come here today to explain it from his perspective: a survivor from the worst school massacre in American history. Ethan?"

"Thank you, Senator. I was thrust into the national spotlight. I didn't choose it. I was comfortable just being Ethan, a teenager who preoccupied his time rooting for the Patriots and the Red Sox, talking about girls, and looking forward to college. My world changed the moment Caleb opened fire in my school. Once my shock subsided and grief set in, I realized that we needed to do something; that the old excuses for inaction no longer could be allowed to endure."

Alicia studies their reactions. She has been lobbying these three Democrats and two Republicans for months. Each has an upcoming election in the swing states they represent. This bill could make or break their reelection bids, and that's why they're on the fence. They are vanes at the mercy of the prevailing political winds. Right now, she knows it's pointing in her direction, but tomorrow is promised to no one.

The Democrats should be easier to sway since they're in her party. The Republicans will be a different story. Amanda Sheppard, the junior senator from New Mexico, and Joseph Velvick, the long-tenured senior senator from Iowa, have been open to her overtures. If she can get them to break ranks with their leadership, other dominoes may fall.

"I'm here because I don't want another student ever to have to experience what I did," Ethan continues. "If the political will had existed a year ago to make a change, I wouldn't be here. But it didn't, and I am, working with you all to ensure there never has to be another Ethan Harrington meeting with senators and pleading for action."

"I think we can speak for my colleagues when we say what you and many of your peers have gone through is a tragedy," Senator Velvick says, "but there are serious constitutional issues to consider."

"Yes, sir, there are. However, this isn't 1787, and if the framers of the Constitution had to deal with this level of violence day in and day out, they would have worded the Second Amendment differently. I don't advocate removing people's ability to bear arms, just restricting the kinds of arms they can use."

"And that's the problem, Ethan. As I have discussed with Senator Standish, the Safe America Act is too severe to appeal to my constituents," Senator Sheppard says. "Remove the restrictions to ownership and limit the ban to high-powered rifles with detachable magazines, and I can get behind it."

"Yes, that is the path of least resistance," Alicia says, leaning forward. "Unfortunately, we were sent here to solve problems, not take the easy way out."

"People have a right to defend themselves and their homes."

"Yes, senator, they do. And that can just as easily be done with a revolver and a shotgun. You don't need an assault rifle or semi-automatic handgun."

The five senators all grimace. Americans cherish their rights. Swing states or not, they know a buyback or confiscation of handguns is unpopular. The AFA knows it, too. They will spend millions in these senators' states to thwart their reelection if they vote for this.

To a politician, regardless of ideology or party, the essential issue to contend with is always reelection. It's why Ethan focused the rage of the American people on the politicians elected to serve them. The more they feel that their political careers are in peril, the more they listen.

"Children are dying," Ethan says, moving on to an emotional plea. "Americans are being murdered. They're taking their own lives in horrific numbers. Our society is enabling that. After every mass shooting, the percentage of Americans clamoring for the carnage to end shoots up and then retreats just as fast. Only this time, it didn't. Everyone is tired of the senseless deaths. You all have a chance to do something historic to prevent what happened to my peers and me from ever happening again."

Silence blankets the room. Each of the senators fidgets as they weigh what messages they would need to make to their constituents or recall their internal polling on the matter. It's not enough for a politician to vote their conscience anymore. It's a tough balancing act, but nobody ever said life in the Beltway was easy.

"I just don't know if I can get there," Senator Velvick states.

"Me neither. The handgun provision is too much," Senator Sheppard says in agreement. "We'll give it a hard look, Alicia, but your bill is very unpopular in our states."

Ethan's face flashes a hint of anger. Alicia moves quickly to cut him off before he can speak.

"I understand. Thank you all for meeting here today. It's rare enough to see both parties come together for a talk like this. That shows you how much times have changed from just a year ago, and how much America has changed with them."

The five senators exchange handshakes before her guests depart her office. Ethan and Alicia remain seated at the conference table after the room empties.

"Cowards," he mumbles.

"Opportunists," Alicia corrects. "What did we learn today?"

"That too many politicians won't do the right thing."

Alicia shakes her head. "The Republicans were always going to balk at the handguns provision. You knew that."

"Yeah, because they're cowards who hide behind nonsensical arguments about how acts of evil could still be committed using explosives or by ramming a truck into a group of people. As if any of that begins to reach the numbers killed from the rifles and handguns."

"They're not hiding behind them. Those senators are sitting on the fence until they get what they want."

"How do you know that?" Ethan asks.

"You have a lot to learn about politics," Alicia says, standing. "They didn't say 'no,' and anything that isn't a hard 'no' is a 'maybe' that can turn into a 'yes' for the right price."

"What price?"

Alicia smiles. "That's what I have to find out."

CHAPTER NINE

SPECIAL AGENT VICTORIA LARSEN

Federal Bureau of Investigation Boston Field Office
Chelsea, Massachusetts

Victoria smooths out the coat of her navy blue pantsuit for the fiftieth time while she waits seated in her boss' office. She has no reason to be nervous about this meeting, but she is. Fifteen minutes after their scheduled time, he finally comes in.

"Sorry I'm late, Agent Larsen. I got tied up on another matter."

"It's not a problem, sir."

She rises from her chair, and they shake hands. Special Agent in Charge Lance Fuller has been running the Boston Division for a year now and is known as a no-nonsense agent. He's respected, but the people who work under him also understand he's political and has his sights set on his next promotion. As a result, he views the world, and everyone in it, through the same prism.

"Very nice work on the Ramirez case. Prosecutors are telling me that the case is a slam dunk."

Victoria shakes her head. "If I have learned anything in my short career, it's that there is no such thing."

"Touché," Lance says with a smile. "Regardless, it was a tough case. You've done an exceptional job."

"Thank you, sir."

Five years removed from her Quantico graduation, Victoria's worked hard to develop professional relationships and make a name for herself as a special agent assigned to some of Boston's highest-profile crimes. It took months of long hours following the Brockhampton massacre to build the case against Jose Miguel Torres-Ramirez, a violent MS-13 gang member who went by the street name "Ranchero Diablo." He earned The Devil Rancher moniker by branding people who wronged him. Now he's facing multiple charges that will put him away for a long time.

"You're racking up an impressive list of investigations that lead to convictions, Victoria. Those are all rungs on a ladder that you can climb to run a division someday."

"Why do I detect a 'but' coming?" Victoria asks, sensing in his tone that this meeting is about to take an ominous turn.

"Because you're a good investigator. You also wouldn't be the first agent I've seen flame out when their career was burning brightest."

"Is that what you think is happening to me?"

"You're a maverick, Vic," he says, leaning forward in his chair and planting his elbows on his desk. "You don't set out to be one on purpose, but you despise rules when they get in your way. The FBI is one of the most bureaucratic organizations in the government. Constraints exist because we're constantly under a microscope. You have to learn to operate under them."

"I thought that's what I was doing."

"So did I until I heard you were questioning the results of the Brockhampton investigation."

Victoria knows she's busted. Despite being discreet, it was only a matter of time before word of her inquisitions made it back to Agent Fuller. She hadn't thought it would happen quite so quickly.

"What investigation? I hadn't realized there was one."

Fuller isn't amused. "We didn't run that investigation, the state did."

"From what I've seen, we never should have relinquished it."

"On what grounds? It wasn't terrorism, so it was out of our jurisdiction."

"It wasn't terrorism by a foreign actor, but domestic terrorism shouldn't have been ruled out," Victoria argues.

"Caleb Pratt wasn't associated with any domestic movements with extremist ideologies. You know about the urgency to rule whether something is terrorism or not. There was enormous public pressure in the wake of Brockhampton."

Victoria leans back in her chair. "And we made a definitive ruling without understanding the perpetrator's motive."

"Are you questioning the integrity of the agents who worked the case?"

"No, sir, I'm questioning whether the Massachusetts State Police did as thorough an investigation as we would have."

"That's not for us to determine. We assisted as we always do in these situations."

Victoria frowns. The FBI sought ways to assist law enforcement following the tragic 2012 shooting at Sandy Hook Elementary School in Newtown, Connecticut. The Bureau proactively supports first responders after an active shooter incident and supplements their activities with additional investigators and evidence response teams when requested.

"Would you have investigated Brockhampton differently if you were in charge?"

"Let it go, Agent Larsen," Lance snaps, reverting to formality. Victoria's question hit home, and he didn't like it one bit.

"What happened to the surveillance video inside the school?"

"What do you mean?"

"The school had cameras. That footage was pulled off the recorder and entered into evidence. A week later, it was gone. I want to know why. Don't you?"

"Victoria –"

"Then there's the range time, Elizabeth's coma, Caleb's erratic behavior in the school, the fact that he didn't start shooting right away –"

"Agent Larsen! When I say let it go, it's an order, not a suggestion. You have a caseload. Work on what you're assigned instead of groping in the dark for something that isn't there."

Little hairs stand on the back of Victoria's neck. There is no way after reading the report that he finds the conclusion convincing. This whole thing reeks of politics. Somebody is pressuring him, and now she wants to know why.

"Something is there."

"The Brockhampton case is closed. You have no authority to investigate it further. If you fail to heed that order, the next conversation we have in here will be far less cordial. There is no room for a rogue agent in this office. Do you understand?"

"Yes, sir."

"Good. That's the end of this discussion. I have to prepare for another meeting. You have done good work. Take some time off and get some perspective. Have a good day, Agent Larsen."

Victoria rises and leaves without another word. She makes her way back to her desk and crashes into her chair. If Lance's purpose was to steer her clear of questioning the accepted line of thinking, he failed. She has promises to keep. Maybe it's time for her to live up to her reputation. Mavericks don't tend to take no for an answer.

CHAPTER TEN

TIERRA CAMPOS

WWDC TV Studio
Washington, D.C.

The experience in the studio is much different than in the field, where I have a cameraman and not much more. Here, there are sound technicians, makeup, several cameramen, and staff buzzing around like mad. I sit in the chair on the Living Room set as a young kid puts on my wireless microphone. When he's finished, I put in my earpiece.

"*Can you hear me, Tierra?*"

"Loud and clear," I say, my voice shaky.

"*Good. Just relax. You'll do fine. We do have a slight change to the questions.*"

I tap on the earpiece. Did I hear him right?

"Which question changed?"

"*All of them. The new ones are loaded in the teleprompter. You should get the hard copy any second.*"

As promised, I'm handed a sheet of paper with the new questions. I scan them looking for subtle differences. I don't have to look hard. Chet can't be serious with this.

"These are all different!"

"*Calm down, Tierra. We had to scrap our questions and go with these instead. Don't ad-lib or go off-script. Just read what's on the prompter. You'll be fine.*"

As if the questions Chet was forcing me to ask weren't bad enough, these are horrible. They're all leading questions designed to elicit specific answers. This isn't an interview. It's propaganda.

"Two minutes out," one of the producers announces.

Ethan is escorted onto the set from the green room. I offer my hand and introduce myself. He shakes it briefly before taking his seat, acting like a patient waiting to see the dentist. I can understand his lack of enthusiasm considering he's a veteran of countless national interviews, but he doesn't need to be rude about it.

"Five…four…three…" the producer counts while silently showing the last two numbers of the countdown with his fingers before pointing at the anchors.

The broadcast's opening credits roll. Carl opens by welcoming the viewing audience and presenting the special live interview with Brockhampton shooting survivor and gun control activist Ethan Harrington.

I can't believe how nervous I am. My hands are shaking despite doing my best to calm them. After introducing me as the interviewer, Carl tosses it over. The red light over the camera glows, and I force my words out.

"Thank you for joining us tonight, Ethan."

"I was in the neighborhood," he says with a smug smile, reminding me, and everyone watching, that he thinks this is beneath him. At least that's how I interpret it. "I'm happy to be here."

"You've had a busy six months since the tragedy you experienced," I say, reading off the teleprompter and eliciting a nod. "Sometimes America forgets that you're only nineteen years old. You have the most recognizable face in the gun control movement and are a speaker at many of the Action Not Prayers rallies held in communities throughout the country. What have you learned from speaking at them?"

"That gun violence is pervasive. It's everywhere and affects everybody. This isn't just about massacres and school shootings. It's about families eating on the floor in Chicago so that they don't get hit by a stray bullet coming through their window. It's about veteran suicides at the rate of nine a day. It's about domestic violence. We have a plan to stop all that."

"You're referring to the Safe America Act."

"Yes, I am. I don't think older generations realize the impact that shootings and gun violence have on our nation. People are demanding that something gets done to prevent it, and we're working to ensure their voices get heard."

I scan the next two questions on the teleprompter as Ethan gives his answer. They are perfectly scripted to generate a specific answer. Were all his interviews conducted this way? The rehearsed answers are robotic. This can't be what Phillip was looking for when he chose me for this interview. Josh's words from dinner echo in my head. He was right. I can't do this.

"*Keep going, Tierra. You're doing great,*" I hear in my ear.

"We've heard a lot about your gun control activism," I say, starting the question before changing my mind, "but I want to go back to the day of the shooting and how it all began for you."

Ethan shifts uncomfortably in his seat. It's an interesting non-verbal response, but nobody wants to relive the trauma of a tragedy. I'm sure Ethan is no exception.

"Okay."

"I was in Summerville High School ten years ago when one of my peers walked in and opened fire. We both know what it's like thinking that we're going to a safe place only to have our worlds turned upside down. What were your first thoughts when you heard gunshots in the school? Did you know what was happening?"

"*What are you doing, Tierra?*"

"I knew exactly what it was," Ethan says, confidently.

"You did?"

"It was unmistakable. I remember thinking about what I would do to stop that shooter if he came my way."

Is he serious? I was hiding in a closet, terrified, and he's talking about confronting the shooter? He must be grandstanding. It's one thing to fight when retreat or hiding isn't an option, but no sane person thinks about putting themselves into harm's way unless it's the only option.

"That's very brave. What *would* you have done?"

The question had an edge to it. I didn't mean for it to be so obvious, but by the look on Ethan's face, it was.

"Whatever I could to save lives."

"*Get back to the script*," my EP demands.

"I think we both wish we could have. I spent a lot of time talking to a therapist to overcome my post-traumatic stress and have learned to deal with triggers like fireworks and sirens."

"They don't bother me," he says, shaking his head. "I mean, sometimes they do."

"You're lucky. I still don't like them. Have you talked to anyone about what you experienced during the shooting?"

"You mean massacre. I assume you mean a psychologist. I don't need to."

"Ethan, you went back into the library when the shooting stopped to try to save lives. All you saw were dead classmates. I can relate to that. You don't think you need help dealing with the emotional trauma of losing friends to that kind of violence?"

"You mean gun violence. People deal with things in different ways. You needed professional help. I don't. I honor them by focusing all my attention on passing gun control legislation so that it never happens again. The Safe America Act is a promise to America, and I'm pushing to ensure its passage."

It's a nice segue back to the canned questions he expects me to ask. I should do that before Chet blows his top, but I want an answer to a question first.

"*There's your opening, damn it. Get back to the questions!*"

"I understand your passion, but I've only ever heard you talk about gun control policy. Where do you draw your motivation? Were you close to any of the students who were killed?"

"The policy is what's important."

I blink a couple of times as I process what I just heard. I give him a moment to clarify his statement, but he doesn't.

"You don't think it's important to talk about the victims, only the politics?"

"That's not what I said."

"Okay, but I'm asking you because I lost a close friend in the Summerville shooting. Whose loss do you feel the most?"

"It's not about who was lost," Ethan says, his voice rising with his exasperation. "It's about the lax gun policies that made it possible, or we wouldn't even be having this conversation about a friend who killed sixty-six people."

Did he say, "friend?" I'm not sure I just heard him right. The statement isn't what I expected, so I take a deep breath without making it evident to the viewers.

"*Give him the chance to clean that up.*"

"Ethan, you just called the kid who murdered sixty-six of your classmates a friend."

"I misspoke," Ethan says. "I meant that I lost a friend."

"I understand. It must have been someone you were close to. I'll ask you again. Which victim had the greatest emotional impact on you?"

I watch as Ethan's throat tightens, and his cheeks redden. He shifts uncomfortably again before forcing a smile.

"I'm not going to answer that."

"Jesus, drop it, Tierra. If I have to tell you again, I'll pull the plug on this interview."

"It's not wrong to remember those we cared about and loved."

"I know that," Ethan says, his tone testy.

"So, you won't name any victims that you were close to?"

Ethan stares at me. Now I can feel my blood beginning to boil. He's dodging simple questions that any one of the students in Brockhampton could answer without thinking about it.

"Can you name even one of those who died at your school?" I ask.

"*Damn it, Tierra, I –*"

I remove the earpiece and hold it in my hand. I can still hear Chet screaming through the tiny speaker and clench it tighter in my fist.

"Of course I can," he says, not elaborating.

"Did you know Caleb well?"

The quick pivot catches him off guard.

"No."

"What about his friend? Did you know Elizabeth Schwarzer?"

Ethan's muscles tense, and he glares at me through hateful eyes. I watch him fighting to wrestle control of his emotions.

"No, not really."

"You never had any contact with her?"

"Look, I answered your question," Ethan protests, angrily leaning forward in his chair. "We're here to talk about gun control and getting lethal killing devices off the streets. That's what this interview should be about."

"And I think it's important for the American people to understand how the horrific shooting in Brockhampton shaped the leader of the gun control movement. Why are you evading those questions?"

"I'm not!'

I'm about to press further when the lights come up at the anchor desk.

"We'll be back with more from our special guest Ethan Harrington after these messages," I hear Carl announce after the cameras pointed at us click off.

An eerie silence grips the studio. Producers and camera operators all stare at me, not in anger but in disbelief. They all know I went off-script.

Ethan stands, rips off his microphone, and storms out of the Living Room. I'm about to follow when a door behind the cameras swings open, banging hard against the back wall.

"What the hell were you thinking, Tierra?" Chet screams, storming out of the hallway leading to the control room. It's not a question that requires an answer. "Get her off this set. Wait for me in my office until this broadcast is over!"

The technicians remove my microphone, and I make my way out of the studio. It's only now that I grasp what I've just done.

CHAPTER ELEVEN

ETHAN HARRINGTON

The Illustrious Hotel
Washington, D.C.

Tamara watched the interview from the studio and knew it was going to be a long night. Ethan has been a media darling for so long that he was ill-prepared for adversity. She immediately arranged for her colleague Xavier to join her and Ryan Baino at Ethan's hotel. She didn't care that it was the last place he wanted to be. Misery loves company.

"What right did she have even asking me those questions, let alone challenging my answers?" Ethan asks as he paces back and forth in his hotel suite.

"She's a reporter, Ethan. They ask questions. It's what they do."

"I've done hundreds of interviews with every major news outlet in the country. I've never been treated so bad!"

"Not by the national media, no," Tamara responds, almost bored. "She's regional and trying to make a name for herself."

Tamara's been in this business a long time. She's seen the press declare open season on her clients. If this is his idea of a slight, the kid is in for a rude awakening. Stars burn out, and she's watched the media turn on people overnight to earn viewers and clicks.

"This is your responsibility! You told me to do this interview."

"No, Senator Standish wanted –"

"I don't care what she wanted."

"You had better care," Ryan warns from the kitchenette. "Her bill gives our rallies purpose."

"Ethan, listen to me. You're a smart, eloquent young man who's passionate and fearless when it comes to communicating your beliefs. You had one bad interview. It will blow over."

Ethan sits in one of the chairs opposite the Velocity team. Tamara settles back into the sofa while her perturbed colleague stews in his chair. Both are relieved to stop following him back and forth with their eyes like it's a Wimbledon match. After a moment, Ethan looks up, sending a shiver down Tamara's spine. There is something hateful in his eyes.

"Tierra Campos humiliated me."

"You need to be cool, Ethan," Xavier says, engaging in the conversation for the first time since they arrived. "It wasn't that bad."

"Don't tell me to 'be cool.' Videos of the interview are already going viral."

"And we'll do any necessary damage control. That's what Ryan pays us for."

"What exactly does that 'damage control' entail? Are you going to release a statement? That's not good enough. She needs to be taught a lesson."

"Ethan, you're a public figure now," Tamara says, sensing the danger of where this is heading. "You can't –"

"We're done talking, Tamara. Get out. Take homeboy here with you."

Xavier doesn't take kindly to the comment but knows better than to say anything. Tamara also understands the futility of arguing. When temperamental clients get combative, there is little a PR representative can do to reel them in. Ethan needs a therapist more than he needs her. They'll just have to clean up any mess he makes.

"Let me talk to Ethan. We'll talk in the morning," Ryan says to the PR team as they collect their stuff and leave the suite.

"You gonna hit me again?"

"If that's what it takes to knock some sense into you."

"You don't think I should retaliate?"

Ryan stands in the middle of the room with his hands in his pockets.

"No. That's the kind of thing I take care of for you, remember?"

"I can take care of myself," Ethan argues.

"I need you to help get Standish's bill passed, not worry about getting vengeance on a reporter. Keep your eyes on the prize. I will take care of her."

"How?"

The corner of Ryan's mouth curls up. "Lay low for a couple of days. Let Velocity do their job. Understand?"

"Sure," Ethan says, turning on the television as Ryan shows himself out.

He spends the next fifteen minutes trying to relax and forget what happened. It doesn't work. The same fiery anger that had him pacing earlier still burns inside him. Justice is required, and he needs to administer it himself.

He reaches for his smartphone and navigates to Twitter to find that his debacle of an interview is still trending. The tweets are vicious. Tierra Campos, a nobody reporter, has given his political enemies the opening they've been searching for. They've wasted no time exploiting it.

Finding a comment from another "blue-checked" account, he closes his eyes and crafts his words. Verified accounts always get the most attention, and that's what Ethan is counting on. He doesn't care what Ryan says. This attack on him can't go unanswered.

CHAPTER TWELVE

SPECIAL AGENT VICTORIA LARSEN

Lead Rain Shooting Center
Brockhampton, MA

Brockhampton is a town under relentless siege by the media. They descended like vultures following the massacre to cover all the usual aspects of the story: the shooter's family, the victims and their families, the police, and the townspeople. The shooting tore at people's souls here. Reporters documented every ounce of their pain in glorious high-definition and beamed it around the world for everyone to see.

A year later, it's still a hotbed of media activity. Brockhampton is ground zero for Ethan Harrington's crusade, and satellite trucks will continue to park on the streets until he fades from the forefront of the American conscious.

Victoria isn't here for any of that. There is only one gun range located in this sleepy New England town, and it's still open. It can't be easy keeping your business afloat when everyone knows it's the place Caleb Pratt practiced murdering sixty-six people.

"Can I help you?" the aging clerk behind the desk asks with a cigar clenched in his teeth as Victoria approaches the counter.

"Are you the owner, Mark Wilkerson?"

"Yeah, why?"

"Were you in the Army?" Victoria asks.

"Hell no; Marine Corps gunnery sergeant. You here to shoot or ask questions?"

"I want to know about Caleb Pratt and Elizabeth Schwarzer."

"You need to leave now," he says, chomping down on his cigar as he stows the SIG Sauer he was cleaning.

"Not until you answer my questions, Gunny."

"I'm not answering questions for some slimy reporter digging for a story."

Victoria grins and steps back from the counter. She slides the bottom of her coat out of the way to reveal her gold FBI badge. Mark eyes it, unimpressed, but is slightly less annoyed at her presence.

"My name is Special Agent Victoria Larsen."

Mark folds his arms across his chest. His massive forearms are larger than her calf muscles. From his demeanor to his physical stature, there's nothing about this no-nonsense Marine that isn't intimidating.

"Good for you," he mumbles, obviously pissed she didn't introduce herself when she walked in. "I talked to you guys and every other investigator that traipsed through this town. I answered every question they asked."

"I know you did, Gunny. I read the report."

"Okay, then why are you here?"

"Because I want answers to questions they *didn't* ask," Victoria says, trying to build trust. She's not sure if it's working.

"They asked a lot of them."

"I have no doubt. I read that Caleb and Lizzie were here every week in the months before the shooting."

"Sometimes twice or three times a week," Mark says, correcting her. "But every Saturday morning for sure."

"How many rounds did he put downrange?"

"Three boxes of nine mil, minimum."

"So, range time plus the cost of ammo – that had to be expensive. How did Caleb pay?"

"Cash. Kids don't have credit cards or anything like that."

Victoria rubs her chin. Caleb didn't have a job, which was odd because most kids work part-time somewhere to earn spending money. How was he able to pay cash? State investigators never bothered answering that question.

"I told that to the cops, ya know. They didn't seem all that interested," Mark adds.

"Did Caleb and Elizabeth always come to the range alone?"

"Never with their parents, if that's what you're asking."

"No," Victoria says, "I mean other friends."

"Never. Caleb shot, and the girl either watched him or sat alone in the classroom."

"Doing what?"

"Stuff for school, I guess. The third kid never came in."

Victoria perks up, her eyes wide with surprise. "What third kid?"

"The one with the car. He would meet them in the parking lot on Saturday before Caleb came in and then drive off."

The state police would have investigated any notion of a third person to corroborate or dismiss any involvement. There was nothing ever mentioned about Caleb meeting someone with a car at the range.

"Did you mention this to the FBI?"

Mark's eyes narrow. "No, I remembered it later. I told that pain in the ass investigator the cops kept sending over here."

"Howard Spivey?"

"Yeah, that's him: one-hundred percent pure jackass, that one. I knew a guy like that when I was in the Corps. Everyone hated him."

"What did you guys end up doing to him?" Victoria asks with a smirk.

"Stuffed him in a seabag and hung him outside the barracks window by his belt. The first sergeant was pissed."

Victoria lets out a chuckle. Out of all the veterans she knows, Marines have the best stories. Army Paratroopers are a close second. Both will regale you with their tales when you get a couple of beers in them. There's no doubt they stretch the truth, but it's still entertaining to listen to.

"Do you know what this other kid looked like?"

"Nah. I never saw his face. I didn't give it much thought."

"How do you know it was a guy?" Victoria asks.

"I don't, actually, but his wheels didn't scream 'girl car.'"

"What was it?"

"An older, beat-up, white Ford Mustang. No, I don't have any video of it if that's your next question."

"I'll have to take your word for it, Gunny. Did Caleb ever bring a personal weapon to the range?"

"Never. He always shot the same weapon, though. This one," he says, pointing to the Smith & Wesson M&P 9mm.

Victoria nods. That checks out. The report says Caleb had that weapon with him along with the AR-15. He stole both from his father's two gun safes. He would never have had the opportunity to bring them here.

"What kind of shot was he?"

"A good one."

"Was he shooting for fun, or was he training?"

One of the theories being bantered around by pundits in the media was that bullying might have been his motive. Victoria initially thought that, too. The investigation into that was inconclusive.

"If you're asking whether he was practicing for revenge against his tormentors, I'd say no. Caleb liked to shoot. The girl was quiet and kept to herself. That's it. They were weird, dressed funny, had piercings, and any conversations I had with them were awkward. But they were always polite and respectful. Caleb did have an edge to him, though."

"You saw that firsthand?"

"He was in here firing a month before the shooting when a couple of guys from out of town started getting on Lizzie about her appearance. They were rude and making sexual comments, and he didn't like it one bit."

"What'd he do?" Victoria asks, intrigued.

"He packed his stuff up to leave, but before he did, he slapped a fresh mag in his weapon and walked over to their lane. He opened fire over their heads and scared the bejesus out of 'em. Don't you know he parked each one of those rounds in the center of their target? Carved out the middle of the damn thing. Then he cleared his weapon, grabbed his stuff, smiled at the boys staring dumbstruck at him, and left with Lizzie right behind him."

That doesn't jibe with Caleb's FBI profile. It took swagger to step in someone's lane and plug nine holes into their target. It's not something an introvert would do.

"Thank you for your time, Gunny."

"You got it, Agent Larsen."

Victoria heads for the door and stops. "One more thing. Why do you think Caleb shot up his school?"

"I've got no idea. I was shocked when I heard it was him. You know your way around a range, so I'm betting you've seen a lot. I've seen all sorts of people walk through those doors in my time here. Caleb and Lizzie weren't as crazy as half of 'em."

Victoria nods and heads out of the range to her car. She came here for answers and ended up with more questions. She stares out the windshield for a long time, hands on the wheel. Victoria knows what she has to do next. To hell with the consequences.

CHAPTER THIRTEEN

SENATOR ALICIA STANDISH

Hart Senate Office Building
Washington, D.C.

Alicia has spent much of the contentious eight o'clock strategy meeting listening to her trusted staff argue back and forth. Passions run deep in this office, but a consensus usually emerges when they don't agree on a policy measure or course of action. That's not the case this time.

She was surprised about Ethan's botched interview. He's done hundreds of them, and there was no reason to believe he'd get flustered at her questions. It's feeding the news cycle in all the wrong ways, and the staff is obsessing over its ramifications.

"The media will move off of the story. They sympathize with our agenda and –"

"This is too juicy to move off of, Rahul," Brian says, interrupting her deputy chief of staff. "The media like ratings. This is the kind of story that gets attention. They're eating this up with a soup ladle."

"Our supporters don't care. We won't win this battle on FOX News."

"No, but it could be lost there."

"And on social media," one of the senator's media specialists says. "It was trending for hours after the interview. The YouTube clip nearly set a record for views. The uproar was dying down when Ethan started tweeting about the reporter."

"Now the clips of the interview are everywhere," Brian says, still on the offensive. "Everyone wants to know why he dodged questions about the victims. People who wouldn't have seen it now can't miss it."

This is politics in the modern age. A tiny fraction of Americans watched live as Tierra Campos grilled Ethan. The media will ensure millions more see clips of it, much of it out of context. Sites like Facebook and Twitter serve as echo chambers that influence opinions. Americans pay scant attention to anything for long, so it pays to be aggressive and controversial. That's why Alicia is concerned. Ethan has proven to be an expert at using social media, but last night was a misstep.

"The AFA and other gun rights groups are screaming about it," Alicia's policy coordinator adds.

"When aren't they screaming?" Rahul says, disgusted.

"Fair point, but this time they have ammunition against Ethan. They're dragging him through the mud to slow down our momentum."

"And it's working," Brian confirms. "Networks are calling us for comment."

Alicia stares at her staff as they engage in arguments and side conversations. She takes a sip of her coffee and waits for the ruckus to die down. Right now, she needs to hear options, not pointless bantering.

"Ethan didn't represent himself well last night," she finally says, commanding everyone's attention. "That's all. Miss Campos rattled him, he misspoke, and she pressed him on it. Any decent reporter would have done the same thing. What's done is done. I want to hear the options about where we go from here."

"Shift the narrative back to the bill. Rise above the fray and get America to focus on what's important," the policy coordinator says.

"We should distance ourselves from Ethan," Brian offers. "He's a liability right now. He may return to being a spokesman for the cause when this blows over, but he shouldn't be directly associated with us."

"I like the opposite approach," Rahul argues. "We circle the wagons. An attack on one of us is an attack on all. I don't want the AFA thinking they can divide and conquer. We will need our allies behind us if we have any hope of passing the bill."

Hundreds of choices like this one are made in the office buildings on Capitol Hill every day. The media never learn of them, so neither does the American public. What they see are the consequences of those decisions, which can be severe.

"The American people are tired of burying children. They've channeled their anger against the obstructionists in Congress who line their pockets with the AFA's blood money. We've harnessed outrage but forgotten that our opponents are capable of doing the same."

"Senator, I --"

"Sixty-six people died in the Brockhampton school shooting, Brian," Alicia says, holding her hand up. "We wouldn't be where we are without Ethan. We're leading the charge to stop the bloodshed because he put us in a position to do so. What does it say if we abandon him now?"

Brian leans back in his chair. A good chief of staff knows better than to press the argument even if he doesn't like the direction the senator is heading.

"I know you don't like this, Brian. I also know you don't like Ryan Baino, but they are our allies. We need both of them. Ethan won't allow another media debacle to happen. And yes, his tweets last night were ill-advised. It happens to the best of us. Ryan can take care of that. I will not label him a liability and cast him off because he made a couple of bad decisions. Understood?"

"Yes, Senator," the group acknowledges.

"I will speak to Ethan. Brian, I need you to work with Rahul to get a statement out to the cable news outlets to help them pivot back to the bill. That's all."

The meeting adjourned, Alicia retreats into her office and dials a number. She wanted the WWDC interview, and they betrayed her.

"Phillip Royce," the voice says, picking up after the second ring.

"Good morning, Phillip. It's Alicia Standish. We need to talk."

CHAPTER FOURTEEN

ETHAN HARRINGTON

The Illustrious Hotel
Washington, D.C.

Ethan pounds on his pillow in frustration. This is the second straight night he hasn't slept worth a damn. He can't turn his mind off. The fallout from the interview still has him spun up. The quiet day away from the cameras and microphones did nothing to improve his mood.

His phone buzzes with another text alert on the nightstand. It's after two-thirty in the morning. He should have tossed the thing out the window hours ago. This message is from Harry Potter. That's unlikely, and the number isn't one he recognizes, but the content is.

01101101011001010110010101110100

"These guys need to get a life," he mumbles after moaning.

The numbers are binary for the word "meet." It's the language of computers, and that means only one thing. Ethan grabs his laptop and opens a connection via a VPN. The virtual private network creates an encrypted tunnel between a computer using it and a remote server, and routes Internet traffic through instead of relying on the hotel's wi-fi network security.

To prevent any other tracking, he enters the IP address for a secure chat room. The site comes up after he has the proper encryption key on his computer. It's the only thing that punk from Velocity has ever done for him that he appreciates.

The first chat comment pops up.

```
>Cyber0reo: H3y 3th4n
>Cyber0reo: h34rd y0u had tr0uble
```

"Yeah, you can say that," Ethan mumbles to himself after reading the ridiculously formatted message.

Leet, the short form of "elite," originated in the early 1980s in the hacker community. It was an elegant and simple way to prevent their websites and newsgroups from being found by keyword searches. L33tspeak replaces alphabetic characters with numbers or symbols that still convey the intended word.

Over time, it became popular in the gaming community as a way to suggest they were skilled. Encryption is common now, so only the lowest echelon of hackers still write like this. Ethan knows these guys are anything but novices. They use it to get under his skin.

```
>GunFreeE: some. handling it
>CyberOreo: 4nything we can d0
>GunFreeE: no. blasted her on twitter
>AnarchyBooster: ch1ldspl4y
>GunFreeE: maybe, but effective
>AnarchyBooster: wh4+3v3r
>GunFreeE: U got something else in mind?
>DialPirate: H4ck h3r
```

Ethan settles deeper into his pillow. He spent most of the day getting lectures from Tamara and Ryan. He even endured an uncomfortable chat with Senator Standish. She was less than thrilled about the interview but equally upset about his Twitter antics. Ethan said what she wanted to hear to get her off the phone.

The fervor over the interview has begun to die down, but only a little. Tamara and her minion claim they're doing damage control, but Ethan doesn't see it. He needs to do more. He stares at his laptop screen before typing.

```
>GunFreeE: can you do it?
>AnarchyBooster: psssh
>DialPirate: s|<1llz
```

"Yeah, I know you've got skills," Ethan says to his screen, smiling.

He was targeted by the American Firearms Association when he was rising into national prominence. They realized he was a threat to the money and message and sought to destroy him through a proxy group. Ryan said he was taking care of them, but Ethan had no means to fight back at the time.

That's when Xavier had one of these guys reach out to him. Ethan still doesn't know how a PR guy from Velocity became friends with hackers, but it must come in handy in our digital age. Dial Pirate provided him the IP address of this chat room, where the group offered their help. He never told Ryan about them and their collective sense of justice. Two weeks later, police arrested the men spearheading the public relations assault on him after finding child pornography on their computers.

The AFA guy who coordinated the attacks got it worse. The FBI discovered that he was siphoning money from the organization into a private shell corporation formed in the Caribbean. He vehemently denied the allegations of embezzlement and wire fraud but was still fired and is awaiting trial after a grand jury indicted him.

The hackers here never admitted anything. They take credit within their community without the general public ever finding out. In part because of their actions, Ethan has become a household name.

```
>GunFreeE: okay, prove it
>AnarchyBooster: You d4 m4n
```

>DialPirate: G4m3 On
>GunFreeE: when will I see results?
>AnarchyBooster: 8y m02n1n9

"By morning." Ethan smiles broader. It's nice to have powerful friends with questionable moral compasses and no fear of legal consequences. They will make sure Tierra Campos gets the punishment she deserves. The best part is, he'll avoid the lectures he got today. Nobody will ever know he was behind it.

CHAPTER FIFTEEN

TIERRA CAMPOS

WWDC TV Offices
Washington D.C.

There's nothing more unsettling than walking into a place and feeling every set of eyes on you. I was happy to get the call yesterday morning from one of the associate producers saying that I didn't need to come to the station. Things were so tense when I left after the interview that taking a day for everyone to cool off sounded like a good idea. Now I'm not so sure.

People I've known for years won't look at me, let alone talk to me. Co-workers duck into offices or change direction in the hall to avoid passing me. I get curt hellos from everyone else. That's my world right now, and it sucks.

I arrive at my desk to find its contents still there, undisturbed. That's a good sign, at least. I set my purse down but don't get the chance to sit before our hotshot anchor beelines across the office floor in my direction.

"I knew you would blow it," Brennan says, invading my personal space. He's as subtle as a chainsaw.

"I uncovered something that the FBI and Massachusetts police don't seem to know. I didn't –"

"You don't get it, do you? This is bigger than you or me."

"Nothing is bigger than you, Carl," I sneer, getting fired up over his combative attitude.

"You were wrong to keep pressing him."

"I didn't want to let him off the hook."

"I wouldn't have done it."

The arrogance of this man is astounding. "No, you would have pitched softballs and then thumped your chest about how great you are."

"You have some nerve!" he says, grabbing my upper arm. "I would have treated Ethan with the respect he deserves."

His voice is loud, and we now have the attention of the entire newsroom. Anyone tuning in at this point would see our senior anchor manhandling a young female reporter. It's not a good look.

"Get your hand off my arm," I demand.

I'm angry, but I keep my voice steady and firm. In almost any other situation, a lack of immediate compliance would result in a sharp kick in the balls. It's happened before. Unfortunately, at work in front of most of the staff, damaging our golden boy anchor isn't a career-enhancing move.

"What's going on here?" Chet demands as he strides toward us.

Carl's head snaps in surprise. He realizes that he's still holding my arm and quickly lets it go. I want to say, "the makings of a complaint to our Human Resources Department," but I keep my mouth shut. I'm not in a position to be snarky right now.

"I asked a question," Chet states, displaying more leadership than I have ever seen him exhibit.

"It's just a professional disagreement. Isn't that right, Carl?"

Carl is speechless. It's a phenomenon that ranks up there with Bigfoot sightings in terms of frequency. Chet stares at me and then back at Carl. The disappointed look on his face lets us both know that he's not buying it.

"Get back to work, Carl. Tierra, follow me."

His tone is only a few notches below overt hostility. Chet was the producer. He's getting the brunt of the blowback because I disregarded his instructions, and he's justifiably pissed about it.

"Good luck," Carl says, a small smile creasing his lips as he turns and walks away.

Chet and I make the trek up to the third floor in absolute silence. There's nothing to be said. We have different perceptions of what that interview was supposed to be. No amount of talking will change either of our minds.

Phillip Royce is waiting in his office when we arrive. I knew walking in this morning that a conversation with WWDC's news director was coming. I also know it won't be a pleasant experience.

"Close the door, Chet. Take a seat, Tierra. I wanted to have this meeting yesterday but thought it would be better to talk this morning to give myself the chance to calm down. Do you have any idea what you did on Monday?"

"Sir, I –"

"You grilled the leading gun control advocate in the country after you were told to drop it. Chet was pleading with you to stop. He's the EP. You should have listened."

"The people deserve answers –"

"You don't get to decide what the people hear! You knew this interview was important to this station. All you had to do was ask the questions. Instead, we embarrassed ourselves by cutting to commercial. Why didn't you end the interview when Chet told you to?"

The two men glare at me. There's no doubt that Chet told him every detail about what happened, so Phillip already knows the answer. He only wants to hear me say it.

"I removed my earpiece."

"That's right. You removed your earpiece. Chet should be thanking you for absolving him from any responsibility for your actions, or his ass would be in the seat next to yours. This catastrophe is now your responsibility."

"Sir, you gave me this interview because I could bring an angle that nobody else could. Because of that, I exposed a –"

"There is a reason we wanted you to stay on script, Tierra. This is Washington. The gun control bill is the most contentious piece of legislation I've seen introduced here in decades. Ethan Harrington is the public face of that movement. You can't begin to understand the political pressure surrounding this. People think we took sides against him."

I fight to hold my emotions in, clenching my hands to keep them from shaking. I want to speak up, but he's not here to listen to my side of the story. He's not listening to me at all. Phillip is concerned about the station's reputation, and now he wants an apology. I don't want to oblige. I don't think I did anything wrong, but he could end my future as a broadcast journalist.

"I'm sorry. I made a mistake. It won't happen again."

"I believe you," he says, putting me slightly at ease. "Unfortunately, you won't be here to find out. I have to let you go. Keeping you employed here… Well, this is best for everybody."

I don't register anything after "let you go." He waves a security guard holding a cardboard box filled with my belongings into his office. They must have started clearing out my desk the moment Chet and I got on the elevator. My heart sinks. My fate was sealed before I stepped into the room.

"We wish you the best of luck, Tierra," Chet says before security escorts me from the building.

There are no tearful goodbyes with coworkers, many of whom I considered friends. Most refuse to look at me as we walk through the lobby. Everyone is going on with their day as if I never existed.

People pass by paying me no attention as I stand outside the station, looking like a refugee. I'm invisible. I'm also broke, in debt, and have nothing to fall back on. There is nothing left for me in this city. No job, no opportunities, and no friends, not even Josh right now. I also have no means to leave it. I'm alone in this and have no idea what to do.

I pull my cell out of my pants pocket and stare at the notifications. There are over a hundred text messages and missed calls from numbers I don't recognize. They took the cell phone the company gave me, and very few people have this number. Who could all these people be?

I switch the phone off silent. It rings in my hand, causing me to jump out of my skin. I answer it out of habit.

"Hello?"

"Is this Tierra Campos?" The deep baritone voice of the caller sends a chill down my spine.

"Yes. Who's this?"

"You're a bitch for what you did to Ethan. I hope you burn in hell."

The call disconnects, and I feel the blood drain out of my face. All I can do is stare at the phone. More text messages arrive. My finger shakes as I open them.

Die, bitch.
You're a publicity whore. You'll get what you deserve.
You messed wit da wrong guy. You gonna pay.
Kill yourself.

My heart thunders, and I feel lightheaded. I struggle to power off the device through my teary vision when Josh's number pops up. I swipe to answer it.

"Josh!"

"Tierra, listen to me. You've been doxxed."

"Wh-what do you mean?"

"Your personal information is all over Twitter: your credit cards, bank accounts, personal email, even your phone number. Everything."

"This can't be happening."

"Tell the station that you –"

"I was just fired."

I hear Josh sigh, but he doesn't say anything. He must have thought it was a possibility.

"Tierra, you need to go to the police."

"Why?"

"You need to file a report. Your social security number was probably compromised. Your address is also on the Internet. It's not safe for you to go home. Do you have a place to stay?"

I know what he's going to offer. Things still aren't right between us following the restaurant, and I don't have the emotional energy to deal with that right now. I'm not sure I can deal with any of this.

"I'll be fine. I'll call you with my new number when I get it."

I end the call. Text messages keep pouring in, and the phone rings again with another anonymous caller. I fight to power down the device with a trembling hand, and I drop it on the sidewalk while trying to tuck it into my pocket. I squat down to pick it up and burst into tears, still invisible to the world around me.

CHAPTER SIXTEEN

SPECIAL AGENT VICTORIA LARSEN

Worcester State Police Detective Unit
Worchester, MA

The Massachusetts State Police is the largest and most bureaucratic law enforcement agency in New England. Eleven detective units work out of district attorneys' offices throughout the state. Worcester is one of the three cities with the authority to investigate homicides. Investigators there took the lead on the Brockhampton school shooting.

"I'll be right with you," the man says, not bothering to look up as Victoria is shown into the office.

Victoria takes a seat and folds her hands on her lap. Detective Lieutenant Howard Spivey has the reputation of being a conceited asshole. Victoria confirms that with one look around the office. Everything in it, from the awards to the pictures of him with dignitaries hanging on the walls, conveys a message that punches you in the face. He's not proud of his achievements while serving his community. This display is meant to show everyone to know how important he is.

"Sorry for making you wait. I had to finish that note."

"No problem. Thank you for seeing me. I'm Special Agent Victoria Larsen. I work out of the Chelsea office."

"Larsen…Larsen…you just finished the case against Jose Miguel Torres-Ramirez."

"I did. You're very well-informed."

"I heard from the DA that prosecutors in Boston are very pleased with your work. The Devil Rancher and his minions in MS-13 caused more than a few problems here."

Victoria isn't the least bit surprised about how Howard got his information. It's no secret that he's friends with Worcester's district attorney, who pushed to have him posted here when Spivey's predecessor landed a promotion. He's the veteran of a couple of hundred murder investigations and has earned praise from his superiors, so it wasn't a hard sell.

"I think everyone will benefit from locking that sadistic asshole up for the rest of his life."

Howard chuckles. "So, what can I do for you, Agent Larsen?"

"I'm hoping you can help me clarify a few things."

"Anything for our law enforcement partners in the FBI."

Victoria grins. She doubts he'll be so cooperative after hearing her first question.

"Did you uncover evidence of any other co-conspirators in the Brockhampton shooting investigation?"

On cue, the smile disappears from his face. "I'm confused. That investigation concluded. I'm sure you know that, so why did you come out here from Chelsea?"

"I'm just following up on some loose ends."

"There are no loose ends, Agent Larsen. Caleb Pratt killed sixty-six students, faculty, and staff in Brockhampton High School before putting a gun in his mouth and blowing his brains out. Case closed."

Victoria winces. Of all the expressions in the law enforcement and legal fields, that's her least favorite to hear. Howard is a thirty-year police veteran and the son of a New York City detective. He knows there is no such thing when a motive hasn't been established.

"Is it?"

"What is that supposed to mean?" Howard asks, now getting visibly angry.

"It means I'm wondering: Was any reason to believe that there were other parties involved?" Victoria asks, rephrasing her question.

"Why are you asking?"

"It's a simple question, Lieutenant."

"I'm not sure how the FBI operates, but if we had uncovered a shred of evidence that anyone else was involved, our investigation would still be open."

"I see," she says, ignoring the shade Spivey threw on the Bureau. "Who closed it then?"

"I don't think I like where you're going with these questions. I took this meeting out of respect for the FBI's outstanding support during our investigation. I didn't realize it would be an inquisition."

"There is no reason it has to be one. There is still no motive for Caleb shooting up his school. There is no explanation as to why he waited to start firing in the library or why his movements in the building were so erratic."

"We may never know, unfortunately."

"Somebody does."

Spivey steeples his fingers in front of his lips. "You're talking about Elizabeth Schwarzer. She might know something. She's also in a coma that she may never come out of."

"Yes, and it's not at all suspicious that the one person who might answer those questions was found nearly beaten to death without a single lead about who did it."

Victoria sees the hint of recognition in Spivey's eyes. There has been almost no discussion of that incident by the mainstream media or law enforcement. Only conspiracy theorists are barking about it on talk radio. She can sense that the comment spooked him.

"Is there anything else I can do for you, Special Agent?"

"You can tell me what happened to the video of the school's library and corridors."

"All surveillance was collected, but the recordings were corrupted and unusable. Our experts concluded that they couldn't save the video."

"That's convenient. Thank you for your time, Detective Lieutenant."

Victoria gets up to leave. She's not going to get anything out of Spivey. All she's managed to do is confirm her feeling that something isn't right.

"May I offer you a piece of advice?"

"Sure," she says, turning.

"Everybody wants to see justice. You're not going to find it by maligning the Brockhampton investigation. There's nothing to be gained by digging for gold in a pile of rocks."

Victoria walks over and plants her hands on his desk. She leans forward and looks him directly in the eyes.

"That's how you find gold, Lieutenant. Good day."

* * *

Howard watches Victoria leave and rubs his chin. Whatever this was, it's not right. He picks up his phone and punches in a number. It's one he never thought he'd ever use this long after the shooting.

"Hey, it's me. Yeah, I just had an FBI agent here asking questions about Brockhampton. No, I didn't tell her anything, but I think we may have a problem."

CHAPTER SEVENTEEN

CAPITOL BEAT

Cable News Studio
Washington, D.C.

"And now for tonight's final thought," Wilson Newman says, finishing the last segment and turning to the camera with the glowing red light. "Something despicable happened yesterday that should abhor every American. Something that, despite ideological leanings, should concern us all.

"Tierra Campos is a school shooting survivor from Summerville, Arizona. She overcame her trauma from the tragedy of that day to graduate with a degree in journalism from George Washington University and land a job at a prominent Washington, D.C. news station. She works hard, spends time with friends, and enjoys life in our nation's capital.

"Miss Campos was assigned a career opportunity to interview Ethan Harrington, a school shooting victim himself who became a prominent gun control spokesman and advocate for Senator Alicia Standish's controversial Safe America Act. The interview on Monday turned out to be a contentious one.

"Millions of Americans have now seen the exchange, and many did not like the tone of the questions. Even more have taken to social media to question her motives, forgetting what the press does in America is challenge the thinking and opinions of others.

"Yesterday, one of those critics crossed a line. Miss Campos's personal information was posted online for the world to see – a practice known as 'doxxing.' The perpetrators of this act may see it as a joke, or maybe feel it is justifiable retaliation against a journalist doing her job by asking difficult questions.

"It is neither. Doxxing is a vile and dishonorable attempt to humiliate and harass someone. Her identity will likely get stolen. Her life may be in danger. For anyone who believes she deserves this treatment: shame on you.

"We cannot afford to travel down this dark path. America was founded on disagreement. Only one-third of the colonists supported the revolution that would see us break away from British control. Sixteen delegates to the convention chose not to sign the Constitution in 1787. They had legitimate concerns about the direction of the country, and they voiced them.

"America is a different place today than it was at the end of the eighteenth century. The contempt Americans feel for those who don't think like they do has become a dangerous threat to our Republic. People vilified for their opinions is a violation of the bedrock principles of this nation."

Wilson pauses for effect to let his words set in.

"This invasion of privacy cannot go unpunished. We should not celebrate contempt toward our differences. This path cannot be traveled if we expect our democratic principles to stand the test of time. That's my final thought, and it's for the record.

"Thank you for watching our Thursday edition of *Capitol Beat*; I'm Wilson Newman. Good Night."

CHAPTER EIGHTEEN

TIERRA CAMPOS

Tierra's Apartment
Dupont Circle Neighborhood, Washington, D.C.

Today was just as long as yesterday was. Anyone who has been a victim of identity theft knows the process I'm enduring. New financial accounts and credit protection services are the tip of the iceberg after getting a new phone number, email address, and filing a police report. I haven't even begun to deal with not having any income or a job to provide it.

It's nearly eight o'clock by the time I reach my apartment in a quiet neighborhood that's only a short walk to popular areas like Adams Morgan and Dupont Circle. It's a great location to feel like I'm in the center of things without paying a fortune in rent.

I'm not surprised to find our lower-level apartment empty. My two roommates are also single and spend their free time scouring the city for Mr. Right. They're no closer to that goal than they were a year ago when I moved in.

I ensure the blinds are closed and pour myself a glass of wine. Content to crash on the couch and change out of my clothes later, I relish the feeling of being home and off my feet. Curled up under a blanket, I stop fighting my heavy eyelids.

Chatter outside my window jars me awake. I rub my eyes and listen as they talk. Annoyed that they're lingering, I kneel on the couch cushion and push the blinds apart to peek through. Two pairs of eyes stare at me, inches from my window.

I freeze in place. One of the guys has on a skull face shield and is wearing a black winter cap. The other has green hair and is wearing a face bandana that looks like the Joker. Both stare at me with hate in their eyes once the surprise wears off.

The men sprint back across the street to join a group of about ten people gathered on the sidewalk. One of them steps into the road and throws something toward me. I dive into the couch and cover my head as the window shatters. Razor-sharp shards rain down on me as I watch a brick skitter across the floor before bouncing off the far wall.

"Die, bitch!" I hear one of the voices outside yell over the cheers and hollering.

I slide onto the floor and grab my cell phone. My hands shake so hard that I misdial the numbers. I jerk my head toward the apartment door when someone jiggles the knob hard. A heavy bang follows it, then another. My heart begins to thunder in my chest. They're trying to get in.

My legs work faster than my head does. I flee the living room into the kitchen and open the door to the small back yard and stop cold. It's never this dark out here. The streetlight that illuminates the small area is out. They could be waiting to ambush me.

I change my mind and leave the door open as I retreat into the house and take refuge in a roommate's bedroom. Without better options, I curl up into a ball on her closet floor, close the door, and force my fingers to dial.

"9-1-1, where is your emergency?"

"Corner of 15th and T Northwest. People are trying to get into my house! Please send help!"

"How many people?"

"I don't know. They broke my window and are trying to break down the door. Hurry!"

"Okay, what's your name?"

"Tierra…Tierra Campos."

"Okay, Tierra. Can you find a place to hide?"

I force myself to calm down so I can speak. "I'm in a bedroom closet."

"Okay, police are on the way. Stay calm."

That's easy for her to say. The anxiety grips me like a vice. My palms begin to sweat, and I shake violently. This closet feels like a coffin; I'm fighting for my life in another dark, cramped space.

I hear a lamp crash on the floor and some furniture being tossed around. I know they're in the house.

"Find the bitch!"

"Where is she?"

"Damn! The back door is open."

"Go! Go!"

"She back there?" one of them asks, urgency in his voice.

"I don't know. I can't see a damn thing."

The faint sound of wailing sirens grows steadily louder. Help is coming. I begin to hyperventilate as I fight back my tears. Flashbacks of Summerville come streaming back, playing in my head like a sadistic movie. The darkness, the fear of not knowing what will happen next. Only this time, I'm alone.

"Check the bedrooms!" I hear one of the men shout.

The sound of those words causes me to stop breathing. I hear someone come into the room and I clamp my eyes shut just like I did once before. I try to make myself invisible.

"Cops are almost here. We gotta go, man!"

"The police are on the scene," the dispatcher says over the phone. "I will stay with you until they find you. Just stay where you are."

I want to respond but can't. A couple of minutes later, I see a flashlight searching the room through the slats on the closet door.

"Tierra Campos? Metro Police. We're going to open the door."

It creaks on its hinges before a bright light shines into my face. It took years of therapy to get over what happened in Summerville. In one night, the emotional scars have all been ripped open.

CHAPTER NINETEEN

SENATOR ALICIA STANDISH

Alicia's Apartment
Foggy Bottom, Washington, D.C.

Home invasions aren't ordinarily news. They are more commonplace here than politicians would ever want you to believe. The media attention isn't because of the crime in this case; it's because of who the victim is.

Alicia grinds her teeth as the on-scene reporter talks into his microphone in a perfectly framed shot that's complete with yellow police tape and the flashing red and blue strobes bouncing off houses on the residential street. Toss in the token interview with the ignorant neighbor who didn't see anything, and it has all the makings of a public relations fiasco for her.

The doorbell rings. Alicia knows there is only one person this could be. Sure enough, her disheveled chief of staff waits at the door holding a bottle of bourbon.

"I'm sorry for the intrusion, but I thought you might need some medicinal reinforcement tonight."

"I knew there was a good reason for hiring you. Come in."

"I see you've already started," Brian says, noticing the nearly empty bottle of bourbon on the end table next to the glass.

"It's been that kind of day. Please tell me you came here bearing some good news."

"Tierra Campos is fine."

"I think we're all happy about that, but how is that good news for *us*?"

"Because if she wasn't, what I'm about to tell you would be far worse."

"There's no way the kids who did that were Ethan's supporters," Alicia says, waving a dismissive hand.

"No, I'm sure they weren't. They were just thugs who saw her information online and decided to terrorize her, but it's still a bad look. That's far from the worst of it."

"I'm pretty sure I'm going to need another drink for this. Want one?"

"Absolutely."

Alicia fetches a second glass from the bar and pours them both drinks with the remainder of her bottle before opening his new one.

"Is this usually here?" Brian asks, picking up the framed picture of Alicia's parents.

"No, its spot is on the credenza. Sometimes I hold it when I need to be reminded of why I'm doing this. What do you have for me?" she asks, handing Brian his tumbler.

"Senators Velvick and Sheppard are back on the fence."

Alicia almost chokes on her bourbon. "You've got to be kidding me! You just told me yesterday that they were beginning to lean in our direction."

"They were. Now they're not."

"Does this have to do with the attack on Tierra Campos?"

"No, but I'm sure that won't help any. The chiefs of staff are claiming that their constituents back home –"

"Oh, please!" Alicia is as pissed as Brian's seen her in a while. "Who got to them?"

"I don't know. Maybe the AFA or their party leadership convinced them."

Alicia runs her hand through her hair. This setback could not come at a worse time with the committee vote on the cusp of getting scheduled. She could strangle the person who leaked that woman's private information, and Brian would be hiding a body tonight.

"If we can't even get the bill out of committee and then out of the Senate, we won't even make it to the House."

"We may have a problem there, too," Brian says, hanging his head to avoid the senator's glare. "The House Minority Leader says support there is softening, too."

Alicia frowns. She reaches over and grabs the picture of her parents. It was a happy time – one of the few they shared. They shared a heartbreaking life that ended tragically for both of them. She lets out a heavy sigh and forces herself to relax.

"You know, a Republican Congress considering such a radical gun control bill would have been impossible two years ago. It took Ethan channeling public outrage after Brockhampton to change that."

"Senator, you're not going to like what I'm about to say, but I'm going to say it anyway. I think it's time to get Ethan out of Washington."

"What are you talking about? Why would you want me to send away a media icon and the face of the gun control movement?"

"We need steady voices and a calm approach to get this bill passed. Ethan provides us neither of those. He's a great orator and advocate, and that makes him a lightning rod. The Campos interview was the first time he got challenged because she was a school shooting victim herself. It won't be the last. I'm suggesting we utilize Ethan for what he's good at – mustering public support."

"He can do both."

"There's no evidence of that. We're hemorrhaging support. This is a political fight that's going to be won by a professional politician and candidate for president. You're the one who is going to win votes in a Republican congress. Your arm needs to be around them when they defy their leadership. Ethan can't do that for you. Ryan Baino can't do that for you. Both of them may even be liabilities."

Alicia takes another sip of her bourbon, savoring the vanilla and caramel notes as she runs through possible courses of action in her head. Decisions have consequences, and she weighs all of them.

"He's going to think I'm cutting him loose. Worse, our political enemies will think we're divided. We need him, Brian."

"It doesn't need to be a public breakup captured on the front page of *Star Magazine*. I know you think Ethan is a good kid, but he's a narcissist. You know that. Promise to put him in front of a crowd or a camera, explain why it's important, and he'll do whatever you want."

Alicia swirls the remaining bourbon in her glass. "Thanks for coming over, Brian. I'll see you in the office in the morning. Tomorrow is going to be a long day."

Brian hangs his head and nods. He swallows the last of his bourbon and sets the glass down on the coffee table.

"Thank you, Senator."

Alicia shows him the door and locks it behind him. Brian has never liked Ethan or his mentor Ryan Baino. He has an ax to grind, but that doesn't make him wrong. She picks up the picture of her parents and replaces it on the credenza. Ethan has been an asset to this point, but this is about winning.

She can't lose any more support and must win back what she's lost. This bill would seal the Democratic nomination and pave a road for her right to the doorstep of 1600 Pennsylvania Avenue. A loss would make her quest for the nomination a bitter fight. If he is a problem, she needs to figure out how to solve it without turning him into an enemy.

CHAPTER TWENTY

TIERRA CAMPOS

Josh's Apartment
Georgetown, Washington, D.C.

Josh hands me a cup of tea. I don't bother asking whether it's decaffeinated. It's comforting to feel the warmth of the mug in my still-shaking hands.

"How are you doing?" Josh asks, sitting on the chair across from the sofa.

"Well, I've had my personal information broadcast to the world, been fired from my job, and was attacked by a mob in my apartment after they threw a brick with the words "die bitch" written on it through my window. Oh, and my roommates just evicted me. I'm doing great. Never better."

"Sorry, it was a dumb question."

"Yeah, it was," I say, allowing a slight smile before it disappears. "All I could think about in that closet was what happened to us. All those feelings came rushing back. I was just as petrified as I was ten years ago. I couldn't even breathe."

Josh was more than willing to welcome me into his tiny Georgetown basement apartment. It's a one-bedroom, but he has a sleeper sofa that will work just fine. The absence of windows is oddly comforting, considering what I just went through. I'm just grateful not to be alone right now.

"You're safe now."

"I stopped feeling safe a long time ago."

Josh is saying all the wrong things in search of the right one. It's like it was at the restaurant. I feel bad because he's only trying to help. The truth is, nothing will make me feel better about what's happened. I should stop penalizing him for that.

"It's all my fault."

"What?"

"Everything. I threw it all away. Everything. My job…my career…"

"None of this is your fault, Tierra."

"I asked the questions. I ignored my producer when he told me to stop. Nobody forced me to do that. I did it."

"Do you think you shouldn't have?" Josh asks, incredulous.

I stare down at my tea. "No, I shouldn't have. What has it gotten me other than fired from my job and attacked in my apartment? I was selfish. Now I'm paying the price. I've even placed you in danger."

The realization hits me like a hammer. If my attackers could find me at my house, they can find me here. When I was alone, I was the only one at risk. Now Josh is too. How could I have done that? I can feel myself begin to panic at the idea.

"I'm not in danger," he argues.

"I'm here, Josh. If someone finds me, you are. Do you think they won't kill you, too?"

"Calm down, Tierra. Nobody is going to come here looking for you."

"You don't know that."

"You're right; I don't. But if anybody comes, we'll face them together. You don't have to fight this battle alone."

I hear his words, but the thought of leaving consumes me. My heart rate accelerates, and small beads of sweat form on my forehead. I can feel the panic. Josh saved me once. I couldn't live with myself if anything happened to him because of me.

"I should go. I can't be here."

"Please, sit down," Josh pleads, as I get up and grab my coat.

"I can't. I need to go."

"I was suicidal after the attack at the school."

I had my hand on the door handle when he whispered the words so quietly that I almost didn't hear him. When they finally register, I turn around and look at him in awe. Why had he never told me this before?

"It's true," he says, his eyes welling up with tears. "I tried to be strong. I fought to convince myself that I wasn't bothered by what we experienced; what we saw. I spent the next couple of days pretending it was all a bad dream; that none of it ever happened.

"I bottled it all up inside. I couldn't talk to my parents because they wouldn't understand. Every loud noise I heard brought me right back to that closet. Right back to that fear that my life would end. I couldn't get it out of my head. Then one day, I decided it was too much to bear."

"What did you do?" I ask, managing only a whisper.

"I went into my mother's nightstand and found her old bottle of sleeping pills. I knew if I took enough of them, I would fall asleep and never have to wake up again. All the pain would be gone. So would the fear. So I got a glass of water and opened the pill container. I had the pills in my hand when the phone rang. It was you."

I slowly make my way back to the couch and sit on the edge. My panic and fear begin to subside. I'm caught up in the confession of my best friend – and a pain I never knew he'd hidden all these years.

"It was that night, wasn't it? The one when I was upset and called you. We talked for hours."

He nods. "I realized I wasn't alone in feeling vulnerable and scared. You were in pain just like I was. I realized a lot of us were. So, I put the pills back into her nightstand and poured the water down the bathroom sink. You gave me the strength to carry on when I no longer thought I could."

"I didn't know any of this."

"I never told anyone. Not you. Not my parents. Not even my therapist."

"Why are you telling me now?"

Josh wipes the tears from his eyes. He takes a deep, cleansing breath. I get the feeling that freeing himself from the weight of that baggage has given him a sense of relief. A decade is a long time to carry that around.

"Because you saved my life that night. You were there for me when I needed it most, and you didn't even know it. It's a gift I've never found a way to repay. Being here for you now is a good start."

I get up and hug him in his chair. It's a long embrace. He'd better not be lying about this because it's one hell of a guilt trip. I know he's not. Josh is a lot of things, but manipulative isn't one of them.

"Was Ethan behind your doxxing?" he asks when our hug finally ends.

"Maybe. He was angry at me, but I don't see how he's capable of that. It doesn't matter. It doesn't change anything."

"No, I suppose it doesn't. What are you going to do now?"

"I don't know."

"If I offer you advice, will you listen?" He offers an awkward smile.

"It depends on the advice."

"You thought Ethan was hiding something about the shooting in that interview, so you challenged him. If you think you're right, prove it."

"I don't think I'm cut out for that."

"You did it in college. You have more strength than you know, Tierra. I've seen it. It's about time you see it, too."

I close my eyes and shake my head. "You make it sound so easy, Josh. It isn't. I don't have a news organization backing me. I wouldn't even know where to start."

Josh points at the end table.

"You have a laptop, and I have wi-fi. That's where."

CHAPTER TWENTY-ONE

ETHAN HARRINGTON

Office of Action Not Prayers
Washington, D.C.

The rideshare drops Ethan off at Action Not Prayers' Wisconsin Avenue office located to the north of the Naval Observatory in Washington. It's a shared office building for small companies and entrepreneurs that is far less expensive than most of the commercial areas in the city. The space is optimized for collaboration. There are only a couple of assigned desks in the whole office. Everyone else engages in hot-desking – workspaces filled on a first-come-first-served basis. Ryan's workspace isn't one of them.

"You're an idiot."

"The bitch had it coming to her," Ethan says, taking a sip from his Coke.

Ryan glares at him. "Were you not listening when I told you I would handle it?"

"I don't need you to fight my battles."

"You want to back up and say that again? Because I've lost track of how many things I've fixed for you. I said I would handle it, and I did, just like everything else."

Ethan knows he won't win that battle. Ryan is right, even if it's not something his protégé will ever admit.

"Her doxxing is just a convenient excuse for the AFA to come after us, nothing more."

"It created sympathy for her, moron. I already have another problem in Brockhampton that I'm dealing with. I didn't need another. Whatever you were trying to accomplish, you failed and failed publicly. Perception is reality, Ethan."

"I'm winning people over. Isn't that what you want?"

"No. People's minds about this issue are already made up. At this point, they're either with us or against us. That isn't going to change by more than a percent or two in either direction."

Ethan blinks a few times in bewilderment as he stares at his mentor. He views Ryan as a dedicated knight in the gun control crusade who understands the endgame. Right now, Ethan feels like a general who doesn't know the battle plan.

"I don't understand. If we aren't convincing people that we're right, what are we trying to do?"

"Win."

"I thought that's what this was about."

"It is. It's what I'm doing. I have no idea what you're doing other than spending our money on swanky five-star hotels and walking around with security like you're a big shot."

Ethan's hands ball into fists as he feels his face turn hot.

"I don't need to listen to this," he says, standing.

"Sit your ass down, Ethan."

It wasn't a request. It was a threat. He plops back down in the chair and stares out the window.

"I think you're confused about how this works. Let me spell it out for you again. You deliver me results, and I clean up your messes. That's the deal we made. It never included you making new ones. I've taken care of Tierra Campos. Now it's your turn."

"Turn to do *what*?"

"Standish is losing support," Ryan continues. "If this bill is going to pass in a Republican Congress, it'll be because of what we do, not her political aptitude. She wants the credit so she can win the presidency. I want real change. It's time to apply pressure."

"What kind of pressure?" Ethan says through clenched teeth.

"The kind that comes from being louder and more energetic than our opponents. This is a political battle now, and selfish politicians have their self-interests in mind."

"So I've noticed."

"Good, then explaining this got easier. If we're loudest, we drown out the cries of the opposition. We dominate media reporting, saturate social media, and encourage grassroots efforts at rallies in every small town in America. With less dissent, it's easy for politicians to point to their districts to say it's what they wanted. You're going to ensure all that happens."

"Fine."

"One more thing. If you ever pull something like that again, you're going to have bigger problems than a PR issue. I don't care if a reporter claims to have pictures of you playing video games with Satan. You keep your mouth shut and don't post a damn thing on Twitter. You get me?"

"Yeah, I got it."

"Good. Get back to the hotel. I'll call when I need you."

Ryan watches Ethan leave in a huff. He starts to respond to an email on his laptop before slamming the lid in frustration and swinging his chair around to look out the window.

His cell phone rings with the number of the burner he gave Andre. He double-checks the caller ID, and connects the call.

"You in place?"

"Yeah."

"Any problems?"

"No. We got what we needed and are ready. Any news from down there?"

"Nothing. It's quiet. Let me worry about Campos. Do what you're up there to do. Ditch your burner and use the new one when it's over. Don't screw it up."

"We won't."

Ryan ends the call and tosses the phone onto his desk. He has to get ahead of this before things fall apart. He's spent a career eliminating the obstacles in his way. One of them is about to be taken off the board. He has no idea what he's going to do if Ethan becomes another.

CHAPTER TWENTY-TWO

SPECIAL AGENT VICTORIA LARSEN

Veni, Vidi, Vino Wine Bar
South End, Boston, Massachusetts

Many of the large port cities on the Eastern seaboard look a lot different now than they did two hundred years ago. Boston used to be connected to the rest of Massachusetts by a narrow isthmus called "Boston Neck." Over the decades, tidal marshes were filled in to create neighborhoods like Back Bay, South Bay, and the South End, which is home to the city's trendiest neighborhoods and best places for a night on the town.

Victoria got a text from her friend Denise after she finally broke up with her boyfriend over his commitment phobia. With some medicinal support necessary, they arranged to meet at a popular hot spot called Veni, Vidi, Vino to drown her tears.

"I'm sorry to keep going on like this," Denise slurs, after finishing her fourth glass of Shiraz.

"It's okay, hon. I know it was hard to break it off with him," Victoria says, clasping her hand as she starts to cry again.

She feels bad about lying. Victoria hasn't had a steady boyfriend since high school and couldn't imagine shedding a single tear over a guy. She's never met one who deserved it.

"I thought we had something special. We were always so great together," Denise whines as she starts to fall over out of her chair.

"Whoa, whoa, whoa, okay," Victoria says, catching her. "It's time to get you home."

Relationships are hard. Denise succeeded in making the pain of the break-up go away, if only for a little while. Good wine is better than therapy and often cheaper. The foremost concern for Victoria after paying the check is ensuring Denise makes it home okay. She's seen enough tragedy in her time at the FBI to know bad things can happen to intoxicated women.

"Whoa," one of the men outside the wine bar says as she guides Denise out the door onto the sidewalk.

The men gawk as Victoria orders up a ride from the app while supporting her drunk friend who can barely keep her legs underneath her. One of them is about to make a move before Victoria dissuades him with a harsh glare.

"Not tonight, boys," she chides.

Men are only courageous with her when they're drinking. Victoria is a strong, confident woman, and that can be intimidating. Liquid courage served in twelve-ounce bottles gives men grand notions of taking her home. It's annoying to her for the same reason it would annoy any woman: drunk men are anything but charming.

The squealing wheels of a black car catch Victoria's attention as it makes a left turn from a side street several hundred feet up the road and picks up speed. As the car approaches, engine whining, a man pokes his head out of the rear window. Victoria's heart rate throttles up when it passes under a streetlight and she notices the barrel of a rifle pointed in their direction.

"Everybody get down!"

Victoria shoves Denise to the ground and dives on top of her. The telltale signature of an AR-15 shatters the night as pedestrians scream and scramble for cover. The large window behind her shatters as the group of men crumple to the ground. She isn't sure if it was on purpose or if the inaccurate fire hits them.

The car slows as it grows closer. Bullets begin stitching the sidewalk, leaving gouges in the concrete only feet from her. Victoria breaks into a sweat and begins breathing heavily as her heart pumps the adrenaline dumped into her veins. She falls back on her training and draws her service weapon.

"Focus, Vic, focus," she says to herself, checking the backdrop behind the car for bystanders.

She pauses her breathing, lines up her sights, and squeezes off a couple of rounds. Her shots are accurate despite being in an awkward prone position atop her shrieking friend. They find their mark just below the rear window and cause the gunman with a skull face shield to retreat inside the car.

"Go! Go! Go!" the man in the back shouts at the driver.

Victoria adjusts her sight picture up slightly and is about to squeeze the trigger when the car accelerates violently. She jumps to her feet and levels her weapon as the black Audi speeds away. Not wanting to engage them as they flee up a street crowded with pedestrians, she holds her fire and pulls back her weapon.

Screams and wails of the injured pierce the night. People sense that the danger has passed and begin to emerge from the safety of the wine bar to investigate. One man recoils after seeing her with a weapon in her hand. She pulls back her coat, revealing the gold FBI badge clipped to her belt.

"I'm a federal agent. Call 9-1-1," she commands. "Tell them we need ambulances."

The man fumbles for his cell phone as Victoria rushes over to Denise and checks for injuries. Other than scraped knees and elbows, she's uninjured and suddenly sober. The men smoking cigarettes weren't as lucky. She checks the pulses of the first two and closes her eyes when she finds none. The third is bleeding profusely from his leg.

"We need to make a tourniquet," she tells a pair of men who emerge from the bar.

"Okay," one of them says, undoing his belt buckle and yanking the piece of leather out of the loops in his jeans in one violent pull.

"Good idea, but that won't work," Victoria explains. "The belt's too rigid. Give me your tie. You! Go find me a stick."

"A stick?" he asks, confused.

"Anything stiff, solid, and about a foot long that we can use as a windless rod."

"Okay!" he exclaims, rushing off.

"Do we need it?" the other man asks, shocked by the amount of blood as he hands her his tie.

"It's not a tourniquet without it."

Victoria keeps direct pressure on the man's wound, alarmed at the amount of blood he's losing. If she can't stop the bleeding and fast, he's smoked his last cigarette.

"Will this work?" the man asks, rushing back over to us with the broken spindle from one of the black lacquer chairs in the wine bar.

"Good enough."

Victoria wraps the necktie around the injured leg and ties a half knot. She places the piece of wood on top and ties a square knot over it. With a couple of twists, the volume of blood gushing out of his leg reduces to a trickle.

"Tie the loose ends around the wood," Victoria commands, careful to hold it in place to prevent the tourniquet from unwinding.

She begins to treat for shock as police vehicles scream to a stop up and down the street. The sirens cease their wailing, but the flashing strobes bathe the neighborhood in blue and red. Ambulances pull up three minutes later, and the arriving EMTs go to work. Victoria watches as they heft the wounded man onto a gurney, load him up and scream off towards the hospital. There was no need to do that for two of his friends.

Victoria shivers while a Boston Police sergeant takes her statement. The adrenaline surge is dissipating, leaving her vulnerable against the chill in the air. The uniformed men are keen to talk to her, especially since she discharged her firearm. She gives them the model and color of the Audi, but she didn't get the plate before it took off. Although she never saw any of the men inside, she did describe the skull face shield the gunman was wearing, for as much good as that will do.

"Everyone was lucky you were here. It could have been much worse if you weren't," the sergeant says.

"Yeah, lucky."

"Is there anything else you can tell us?"

"I, uh…" Victoria stops and shakes her head. "No, that's it."

He pats her on the shoulder and moves into the bar.

Victoria moves over to the bloodstain on the sidewalk and squats. The metallic smell of the drying blood fills her nostrils as she wonders if the man made it to the hospital. She looks down the street to the approximate spot the gunman began shooting. She was standing with Denise right in the path of the fire.

Drive-by shootings are not unheard of in Boston, but they aren't common either. The ones that happen are usually gang attacks against their rivals. Victoria can't think of a single instance where they've ever attacked a public place like this. It could have been a gang initiation, but that doesn't seem right.

This feels personal to her. She can't shake the feeling that she was the target of the men in the Audi. It could be retribution for The Devil Rancher's arrest, or it could be something else entirely. Either way, the men killed and wounded here tonight were collateral damage. She'll have to be on guard from now on. If she was targeted once, she can't help but feel it could happen again.

CHAPTER TWENTY-THREE

TIERRA CAMPOS

Josh's Apartment
Georgetown, Washington, D.C.

I lean back into the couch. I've read almost every article written about Ethan over the last three days and confirmed how little he talked about the shooting. It's an indictment of modern journalism. Most of the questions were versions of the ones my producer handed me to ask. Nobody has ever asked the questions I did. No wonder he reacted the way he did.

Just by the law of large numbers, some interviewer should have. If that isn't suspicious enough, I haven't seen more than cursory mentions of his experiences before he walked out of the school covered in blood. Not one story reports what he was doing during Caleb's rampage. That can't be an accident. His PR team is controlling that questioning, but why? I scribble a note on my legal pad before a series of knocks on the door causes me to jump.

"Tierra? Are you here?"

The creepiness of hearing my name makes my skin crawl. Josh is at work. Nobody else knows I'm here. My heart starts beating rapidly. Is another mob standing outside my door? Worst-case scenarios start playing through my head in high-definition. It fuels my building panic and thoughts of déjà vu.

"Tierra, my name is Austin Christos. I'm an editor at *Front Burner*. I'd like to talk to you."

The leader of a mob wouldn't use his name. I'm not about to answer the door, but that doesn't mean I can't do a quick check. The two pieces of information should be easy enough to confirm. I quietly start pecking at my laptop.

"Okay, I know me dropping in on you like this is pretty weird, but I'm asking you to trust me."

His profile comes up in the browser when I click on the link to *Front Burner*'s staff. His biography loads, and I scan it while remaining as quiet as possible.

"Oh, since you're checking my profile on our website, I should warn you that the picture is heavily photoshopped. I'm not really that devilishly handsome."

He's not banging relentlessly on the door or trying to force his way into the apartment. That doesn't stop me from staring at it like I have x-ray vision.

"This is a bad idea," I tell myself, moving to the door and pulling one of Josh's fat-headed drivers from the bag next to the closet before reaching for the knob.

After a deep inhale to steady my shot nerves, I crack the door open and get ready to whack him. The man is standing with his back towards me and is startled when he hears the hinges squeak.

"I was about to give up," he says, smiling.

"I didn't want to open this door."

"So, why did you?"

I don't have a good answer for that. I don't know why I did. "How did you know I'd check your profile?"

"It's what I would've done. May I come in?"

Nothing is threatening about him, or so I keep telling myself. I grip the club more tightly and step aside when he enters. He looks around Josh's living area before turning back to me and noticing the three wood I'm clutching.

"Do you golf, or were you planning to take off my head with that?"

"The latter. I still might. How did you find me here?"

"It wasn't easy. After we heard what happened at your apartment, we knew you would go to either a hotel or a friend's house. There was no way we were checking every hotel in the D.C. metro area, so we took a chance with friends. Once we found out that Joshua lived in the city, we knew you were here."

"We?"

"My staff and I at *Front Burner*."

I know *Front Burner* well. The twenty-four-hour news cycle and social media have made things nastier in America. Media organizations switched from reporting the news to shilling for one side of the ideological spectrum or the other. It's how they keep their core audience engaged, ratings up, and advertising dollars pouring in.

"You're an editor there."

"Senior editor…not that you care what my title is."

"Why was your staff looking for me?"

"Okay, yeah, that requires some explanation. We watched your interview with Ethan Harrington and then heard you were let go from WWDC."

"That's a polite way of putting it," I say, trying not to sound too bitter.

"No good deed goes unpunished. In your case, a good interview went uncelebrated, and that's a shame."

"You're an editor. Had you gone into television instead of online journalism, and I was one of your reporters, what would you have done after that interview?"

"Promoted you."

He says it with a straight face. There is no pearly white smile or hint that he's joking. I take him at his word.

"That doesn't explain why you're here now."

"I'm searching for talent to complete our team, which led me to you. Some people want affirmation of their political beliefs in what they watch and read. The rest of

America wants the news free of agendas, and that's what we deliver. You didn't attack Ethan Harrington. You did your job better than everyone else."

"You're here to ask me to interview for a position at *Front Burner*?"

"No, you misunderstood," he says, causing my heart to sink. "Your grilling of that brat was your interview. I'm here to offer you a job."

I slowly sit on the edge of Josh's chair. Not wanting to hover above me, Austin takes a seat on the sofa. I am instantly in love with the idea but don't see how I fit.

"I didn't think *Front Burner* had a broadcasting arm."

"We don't. We do have podcasts, though."

"Podcasts?" I make the word sound dirtier than it is. "That's not exactly what I do. I'm a television reporter."

"Yes, and the perfect one at that – attractive, engaging, articulate, and comfortable in front of the camera. It's a shame that an investigator with your instincts got assigned pedestrian stories at WWDC."

I smooth out my messy hair and look away. I'm wearing sweats, haven't showered, and am a general mess to go along with the bags under my eyes from the late nights and stress. I'm a far cry from attractive right now.

"You got that all from one interview?" I ask, looking down.

"Not exactly. Janey researched your exploits in college. You're a great writer. It took a lot of guts to go after those professors like you did. You're relentless, tenacious, and driven to find the truth." Austin glances at my computer and notepad and grins. "I rest my case."

"I haven't found anything."

"That's because you don't have our resources. My department models itself after the *Boston Globe's* Spotlight team. They're as driven and passionate as you are – and equally curious."

As intriguing as a job offer from him is, especially considering my current lack of employment or financial means, Austin's words are far more interesting. I lean forward, studying him.

"You found something on Ethan Harrington?"

He shrugs. "Let's just say we have more questions than answers."

"Are you going to share?"

"Not until you're an employee."

"You're a hell of a salesman. I think you forget that I don't have an offer."

Austin pulls out an envelope from his coat pocket and hands it to me. I lean forward and accept it. "You come prepared."

I pull the single sheet of paper out and scan it. My eyes deceive me. The salary is more than generous. It's obscene for what a reporter with my experience could ever make. Almost too good.

"If this is a joke –"

"We want you to be an investigative reporter for *Front Burner*, Tierra. You'll be based out of our offices here in Washington and will travel to assignments wherever you're needed."

"What if I say no?"

"I will wish you the best of luck in your career. We'll find someone else to fill the position."

"You're not going to say something campy like 'you have no other options?'"

"Do you?" he asks with a smirk. "This isn't charity, Tierra. We want you on our team, but the choice is yours."

I stare at the offer letter like it's the Magna Carta. This should be a no-brainer. After everything that's happened, I can't commit without thinking it over. I simply don't know how to explain any of that to Austin.

"I, uh…"

"You don't need to decide right now. You've been through a lot, and I don't handle rejection well. Take the day to think about it. If you choose to join us, here's my card. The address of our Washington office is on it. Be at work at nine a.m. tomorrow. One minute later, I'll know you chose a different path."

We both stand, and I walk him to the door.

"What if I'm late?" I call out, as he reaches the sidewalk.

"From everything I have learned about you, you won't be." He smiles and heads down the street.

Of all the things I expected to happen today, this wasn't one of them. I have a decision to make, even though I know deep down that I've already made it. Austin handed me the whole sundae, but it's the cherry that interests me. I need to know what he's learned about Ethan Harrington.

CHAPTER TWENTY-FOUR

ETHAN HARRINGTON

Cable News Television Studio
Washington, D.C.

Cameras, microphones, harried technicians and assistants, and a neurotic producer are mainstays in the studios of every cable news organization in the country. Ethan has spent so much time in green rooms waiting for interviews that he should have his mail forwarded to them. He knows the exact moment he'll be called in to makeup and when he'll be led to the set. It's all very routine now.

"We are joined with Ethan Harrington, one of the Brockhampton survivors and America's leading gun control advocate. Thank you for joining us this morning," the attractive host says.

"Thank you for having me."

"The American Firearms Association has gone on the offensive in recent days. They claim that the bill introduced by Senator Standish is a blatant attack on the Second Amendment and an affront to the rights of all Americans."

"They say a lot worse than that about me," Ethan adds, flashing a smile.

"Do you not support the Second Amendment?"

"I support its original intent. 'A well-regulated Militia, being necessary to the security of a free State, the right of the people to keep and bear Arms, shall not be infringed.' The framers saw the right to bear arms as a right of every law-abiding citizen to defend themselves against violence or tyranny.

"The significant words here are 'a well-regulated Militia.' It provides context for the actual meaning of the right to bear arms. A citizens' militia was needed before we had a large standing army and during a time when a union of sovereign states was an untested and dangerous concept. Those circumstances don't apply today."

"The AFA would argue that constitutional scholars and writings from our Founding Fathers refute that," the host says.

"Yes, and I've spoken to scholars who say the opposite. Both sides have strong opinions. I wonder if James Madison would have been more precise in his wording had he needed to deal with children getting massacred in schools across the new union."

"So, you reject the idea that it's a universal right?"

"The First Amendment isn't, so why should the Second Amendment be? We're not looking to ban firearms or take away people's right to defend themselves. The Safe America Act is intended to get deadly weapons of war off the streets."

"That has not been a popular sentiment in this country."

"No, but neither is burying the victims while we listen to politicians offer prayers for their families."

"What about the millions of legal gun owners who haven't committed a crime?" the host inquires.

These are the softball questions Ethan gets all the time. He has variations of the same answer that keeps him on message without sounding robotic or brainwashed. It's not as easy as it sounds. The media love soundbites. Complex ideas are challenging to convey in seven-word sentences.

"When the Safe America Act passes, there will still be millions of gun owners not committing crimes without semi-automatic rifles and handguns."

"The AFA also came out with a statement that says there are already hundreds of gun control laws on the books and that The Safe America Act is a liberal overreach."

"Yes, there are laws on the books, but what good are they doing? Waiting lists don't work. The assault weapons ban in the 1990s wasn't broad enough to make a difference. The only thing guaranteed to reduce gun violence is getting rid of firearms."

"What makes you think that will be more effective?"

"Ask the British and Australians."

The United Kingdom has some of the world's strictest gun-ownership laws. It's rare for civilians to possess any private firearms there. Australia had a similar awakening when thirty-five people were gunned down. The AFA likes to quote their own set of facts, but Ethan cites both as shining examples of what the United States could accomplish if our leaders had the political and moral courage to travel down that path.

"Ethan, if I may change the subject, you had a very contentious interview at a local Washington news channel last week that went viral."

"I did," Ethan says, nodding his head. "The interview was going to be with their anchor Carl Brennan. Tierra Campos replaced him, and it threw me off a little."

"She was a school shooting survivor as well."

"I guess. I mean, I responded the way I did because I felt like Miss Campos was grilling me to raise her public profile. I got flustered after I misunderstood a question she asked, and I apologize for that."

"So, you weren't friends with Caleb Pratt?"

Ethan suppresses a grin. It's a perfect leading question. It's nice to have allies in the media.

"Not at all. I barely knew him."

"The American Firearms Association is claiming otherwise."

"That shouldn't be surprising. Everyone knows that they are desperate. Our movement aims to make this country a safer place by removing the deadly firearms that kill tens of thousands every year. That's a threat to some people."

"It has been widely reported that Tierra Campos was doxxed following the interview. Do you think your supporters were behind that?"

"I don't. Things got heated between us, and my supporters are loyal, but they would never engage in that type of activity. Nobody deserves to have their personal information published online like that or be attacked in their home."

"So, you hold no ill will toward Miss Campos?"

"Of course not. I'm thankful that she wasn't hurt and hopeful that her doxxing doesn't adversely affect her life or career."

Ethan is thrilled that Tierra hasn't spoken publicly since the interview, leaving the media free to speculate on her motive. After a short time, America will forget the doxxing and the attack on her. The media will pivot their coverage to label her interview as a tactic by the AFA. She'll be forgotten in a month.

"You're courageous for speaking out like you have, Ethan. Do you fear for your safety from those who disagree with you and decide to turn that into action?"

"I get death threats all the time. I have to walk around with security to keep me safe from people who claim to love America. I'm grateful that those people who went after Tierra Campos weren't armed. I wonder what would happen if a mob coming after me was."

CHAPTER TWENTY-FIVE

SENATOR ALICIA STANDISH

U.S. Capitol Building
Washington, D.C.

The House minority leader, regardless of the political party, is the head of the "loyal opposition." That person is elected bi-annually via secret ballot by the party caucus or conference to exercise several essential institutional and party responsibilities. The first, and most important, is the creation and execution of a strategy to recapture majority control in the House of Representatives. That's Duncan Farnsworth's sole mission, much to Alicia's chagrin.

"Ethan didn't do you any favors last week," Duncan says, offering Alicia a seat in his office. "Was his transparent attempt at deflection in last night's interview his idea or yours?"

"He has a PR team. I assume they came up with it. And for the record, he didn't do *us* any favors."

"This is your bill, not mine, Senator."

Alicia has a good working relationship with Duncan. It doesn't mean they always see eye-to-eye. Her bill is both an opportunity and a liability for him. He has convinced Republicans to break ranks and support the Safe America Act while making Democrats from moderate swing districts in red states vulnerable in the next election.

"I know, you would have gone with something softer to attract more Republican support and appease the party moderates."

Duncan leans back in his chair. "Yes, I would have. They keep score in this town, Alicia. If we go all in and fail, our chances of recapturing Congress are gone."

"The GOP isn't voting on the bill for what it does or doesn't ban. They're scared to death about reelection and are using the prevailing winds to figure out how to vote. A softer bill wouldn't change that."

"The winds are changing. The outrage is subsiding. The American Firearms Association is running out the clock on you. The closer we get to the campaign season, the longer the chances are of this passing. Ethan Harrington isn't helping that."

Duncan isn't a fan of Ethan. While he likes the attention drawn to the gun control movement, the House minority leader considers him to be an entitled ambassador of Generation Z.

"We just won the committee vote in the Senate," Alicia says, defensively.

"Yes, because the Republican leadership on your side of the building thinks it won't pass a floor vote."

"We have the votes."

"Are you sure? The Senate majority leader may have idiotic beliefs, but he isn't stupid. The Republicans want to hand you a defeat to shore up their base."

Alicia glares at Duncan. He's scared of losing his position. She understands that, but leadership is about being willing to take risks. She is gambling with a presidential nomination. What does he have to lose that compares?

"I won't let that happen. There are several Republicans I can flip."

"They won't alienate their base by passing a bill that calls for a widespread ban of firearms. It's all lip service for the moderates. They won't vote for the bill when it hits the floor of either chamber."

Alicia leans back in her chair and stares out at the National Mall. She can feel her neck burning under the collar of her blouse. Duncan's pessimistic reading of the political crystal ball infuriates her.

"Can you get this done or not, Duncan?"

Alicia is in no mood to listen to excuses. She's been in Washington for longer than five minutes and knows there are deals to be made here. He only has to be more interested in winning than he is worried about losing.

"The bill wouldn't pass a vote in the House without changes."

"I'm not watering it down," Alicia snaps.

"Even if it costs you the nomination?"

"That's a big 'if.' My campaign is about much more than this bill."

"I know it is, but you have stepped up to deliver real gun reforms. Voters will expect you to deliver something. I'm not your enemy, Alicia. I want you to be successful, but you need to give me something I can work with. And you need to keep Ethan Harrington out of this building."

Alicia gives Duncan a puzzled look. "Why would I do that?"

"There is a growing number of my colleagues on both sides of the aisle that think he was involved in the doxxing of that reporter."

"You have to be kidding me," she says, her voice rising. "He wasn't involved in that. There isn't a shred of proof that he was."

"None of that matters. People on the Hill are going to believe whatever they want. He may be great at a rally, but he's damaged goods here."

"I am not going to muzzle the spokesman of the gun control movement," Alicia says, articulating every word clearly.

"Then you're making both our jobs harder," Duncan says, leaning forward. "I'm telling you plainly; I can't get this done in the House if Ethan's leading the charge in Washington."

Her eyes settle on the floor as she purses her lips in thought. Duncan has parroted the same basic message as her chief of staff. What do they see that she doesn't? The tension settles over her shoulders like a blanket. There's nothing more to be gained by talking about it here.

"Okay. Thank you for your time, Mister Leader."

"Of course, Senator," he says as they shake hands.

Alicia leaves and retreats to her hideaway on the other side of the building. Reserved for members of the Senate, these small offices are the real "undisclosed locations" of Washington. Hideaways are awarded according to seniority, so Alicia's isn't a luxurious space with sweeping views of the National Mall. None of that matters right now. It's a quiet place that lets her think in peace.

She makes herself a cup of tea and pops her heels off before settling into the comfortable chair. She bobs the tea bag through the hot water, watching as the liquid turns color. She takes the warnings about Ethan seriously but can't just cut him loose. He helped get her to this point and has a massive social media following. Banishment to the sidelines won't go over well with him, and she doubts Action Not Prayers will be enthusiastic about it either.

"Hey Brian," Alicia says, after picking up the phone and dialing the office.

"It sounds like you had a rough meeting on the other side of the Capitol," he observes after hearing the tone in her voice.

"Something like that. Get in touch with Ethan. Tell him I need to see him in my office this afternoon. Find a hole on my calendar and schedule it."

"Will do."

"Thanks. Don't mention the meeting to Ryan Baino."

Alicia hangs up and returns to her tea. American politics is part beauty pageant, part bar brawl. Both are about winning. The difference is the tactics used to get there. Alicia knows it's time to change hers.

CHAPTER TWENTY-SIX

SPECIAL AGENT VICTORIA LARSEN

Federal Bureau of Investigation Boston Field Office
Chelsea, Massachusetts

The Information Age has altered the process, but the lifeblood of all bureaucracies has remained steadfast: paperwork. Despite her unsanctioned focus on Ethan Harrington and the fact that she was almost gunned down, Victoria still has a job to do. Those duties entail writing countless reports and building cases against all sorts of evil people.

Needing to stretch her legs and caffeinate, Victoria grabs her mug and walks to the breakroom to pour a cup of abysmal coffee from the decanter that's been sitting on the warming plate for too long. She'd love to go out for a real brew, but every minute she's away is another minute she'll be here late tonight.

"I heard what happened Friday night. Are you okay?" Takara asks, entering the room after her.

"I'm thankful the guy in the back of the Audi couldn't aim for shit. Not that it worked out so well for the guys standing next to me."

"That tourniquet you tied saved one of them from bleeding out. That's something."

"I wonder if he would agree."

"Have you learned anything from the police?"

Victoria notices Takara's eyes shift to the floor when he asks the question. Takara is an excellent agent on a career trajectory that will lead him to higher leadership roles in the Bureau. In that respect, he's not unlike Lance Fuller.

"Are you asking as a friend or a curious colleague?" she asks.

"Are we friends?"

"Are you just a *curious* colleague?"

Takara grimaces, blaming himself for walking into that one. "I'm not sure –"

"I'll make this easy for you, Agent Nishimoto. A short time after our conversation at the range, you reported it to Fuller. At some point between when I got shot at and now, he asked you to find out if I think it was an MS-13 revenge hit for taking down The Devil Rancher. How am I doing so far?"

Victoria smiles at Takara as he puts his hands up in mock surrender.

"Okay, yeah, that's what we're asking. The Audi was stolen and found by the BPD torched in an East Boston alley. Forensics didn't recover any physical evidence, and there's no useful video of the occupants from any traffic or security cam in the city. It has all the makings of a revenge hit."

"Yes, it does, only you think it was MS-13, and I don't."

Victoria watches the relief disappear from his face after she drops that bombshell.

"What are you talking about, Vic?"

"MS-13 are brutal butchers. If they wanted to send me a message, it would be when I'm alone and vulnerable. They wouldn't execute an L.A. gangland-style drive-by."

"Assuming you were the target at all."

"I'm sorry, I keep forgetting you were standing right next to me…oh, that's right, you weren't there. I know who they were aiming at, Takara."

"Don't you think you might be losing your objectivity?"

"Let's walk through it. How did they know I was at that bar? A spotter? GPS tracker? That car came around the corner less than thirty seconds after I walked out with Denise. The timing was perfect. Does that sound like MS-13 to you?"

"Okay, let's assume you're right and it was someone else. Who?"

Victoria studies her colleague's face. She knows she's at an impasse. It's time to shake the tree and see if any fruit falls.

"Do you think it's a coincidence that this happened right after I marched into Howard Spivey's office and started asking questions about Ethan Harrington?"

"What? Are you wearing tin foil hats now?"

"Someone tried to silence me…permanently. What's so important to hide that it's worth gunning down a federal agent for?"

"I don't know."

"Me neither, but I'm going to find out."

She turns to leave, and Takara grabs her arm. "Vic, if I were you, I'd let this go."

Victoria brushes the top of his hand with her fingers like she's dusting off some lint. He takes the hint and lets go, looking at her sheepishly.

"If you were me, you'd understand why you couldn't."

Victoria heads back to her desk with her coffee to tackle the paperwork that awaits. That's the third time she's been told to back off from asking questions. Something is very wrong with all of this, and the FBI may be involved. She's going to need help putting it all together, but with Takara and Fuller working against her, she's running out of people she can trust for help.

CHAPTER TWENTY-SEVEN

TIERRA CAMPOS

Front Burner Washington Headquarters
Washington, D.C.

The first day of work is hard for everybody. Most new employees have at least visited their workplace during the interview process. I hadn't. There was nothing typical about my hiring, and I can't get over the feeling that I'm getting pranked.

"Good morning, can I help you?" the pleasant receptionist asks from behind the desk.

"Yes, hi. My name is Tierra Campos. I was just hired and –"

"And she's fifteen minutes early," Austin says, appearing from the elevator bank. "I'm impressed."

"You made it very clear what time the train pulls out of this station. I didn't want to miss it," I say, relaxing a little. Maybe this is for real.

"You'd be surprised to learn how many people starting jobs here didn't think I was serious about that. Welcome to *Front Burner*, Tierra. Let's go upstairs. We have some paperwork to do. Then I'll show you around."

After an hour of filling out forms and being issued an ID, Austin gives me the nickel tour. The architect must have been a Millennial designing this office for his or her generation. There are open concept floor plans, sit/stand desks, ergonomic chairs and computer peripherals, and relaxing décor. It feels lazy and uninspired to be the headquarters of the fastest-growing news source in the country.

"What do you think so far?"

"It's impressive."

"Psssh. No, it isn't," Austin says, with a smile. "You're a horrible liar. Let me show you where the real magic happens. That won't be impressive either."

We walk into the back of an office space with large windows and desks without cubicle walls in the middle. It has a modern, yet cozy feel to it. The atmosphere is anything but intimate. Austin's staff is consumed in a passionate discussion and doesn't even hear us walk in. He puts his finger over his mouth and eases the door closed.

"He's acting like a conquering hero and using that celebrity to tout his ridiculous belief that the Second Amendment is evil and the sole cause of all the county's problems."

"A growing number of Americans think it is. Don't their opinions matter, Logan, or are you turning into an elitist on us?"

"Sure, Olivia, if worrying about the mental health of people in any society who willingly gives up their rights is elitist, then I guess I am one."

"As much as it agonizes me to say it, Logan's right," a pretty young blonde in the room says. "Imagine if we applied his logic to the First Amendment instead of the Second? Would anyone restrict the freedom of the press because one news organization tells a lie?"

"They'd all be out of business today if that were true," a skinny brunette says without looking away from her computer screen.

"The ultimate price of freedom is living with the inherent danger of its abuse."

"Are you talking about politics or journalism, Tyler?"

"Neither. I'm talking about America. Penalizing the millions of lawful gun owners because a deranged psychopath steals a weapon and uses it makes no sense to me."

"The Safe America Act doesn't penalize gun owners. It just takes the deadliest weapons out of their hands."

"And who gets to decide what the deadliest weapons are? Politicians? Society in general?"

"And what happens when they expand that definition just because they can? Americans universally agree that their rights are disappearing. Why would anyone agree to forfeit more of them? If you don't want a gun, don't buy it."

I'm impressed by the conversation. It isn't nasty or personal. There's no name-calling or childish attacks. People are debating an issue the way they should. I never saw this kind of discussion at WWDC. I never even saw it in college.

Austin's staff is all on the younger side, not that I expected anything different. *Front Burner* is a new platform practicing old-fashioned, hard-nosed journalism. Their appeal is to anyone who thirsts for news, not opinions or agendas. They also don't worry much about their appearance in the office.

I'm wildly overdressed. It's never good to make assumptions, so I erred on the side of caution and dressed professionally. Everyone is in jeans. A woman wearing a skirt is the only exception to the rule.

"Are they always like this?" I whisper to Austin.

"Nah," he says, grimacing. "They're usually far worse."

"The purpose of government is to enact laws that prevent abuses without threatening freedom itself."

"The purpose of government is also to preserve life and the pursuit of happiness, according to Thomas Jefferson."

"Law-abiding citizens should never be forced to cede freedoms just because others take advantage of it. It's un-American to debase the bedrock of our Constitution."

"And yet politicians and the media do it all the time," Austin finally says, interrupting the conversation and stepping away from the back wall. I follow right behind him as the staff all turns in surprise.

"How long have you been standing there?"

"Long enough for Miss Campos to see how nuts you all are, but not long enough for her to run screaming for the door."

"I see you didn't tell her about the dress code?" one of the guys asks.

"I must have forgotten," Austin says with a grin.

"Don't let him fool you, Tierra. He did that to all of us. Logan showed up in a three-piece suit his first day. I'm Janey. I'm a researcher on this Island of Misfit Toys."

"It's nice to meet you."

Logan, Tyler, Madison, and Olivia also introduce themselves. I'm immediately struck by how personable they all are. It is much different than my experience at the television station where climbing the ladder meant knocking someone else off of it. This feels like a *real* team.

"Hi, I'm Jerome. I'm the token black guy."

"Please ignore him," Austin says, giving his subordinate a disapproving look.

"It's okay, Jerome. It looks like I'm the token Latina."

He laughs. "Oh, I like her already."

"We all saw your interview on WWDC," Madison says. "It was amazing."

"Thanks. I paid a hell of a price for it."

"You're going to be glad they fired you now that you're here."

"I hope so, but I was thinking more about the death threats, getting doxxed, having my identity stolen, and people breaking down my front door."

I tried saying it with a degree of levity, but the weight of it all made that impossible. The room falls silent.

"I've never gotten death threats. Can I see them?"

"Don't be rude, Logan!" Janey shrieks.

"We look at them a little like a badge of honor around here," Tyler explains, trying to break the ice. "Logan and Janey are researchers and the only ones here who haven't gotten at least one."

"Assuming you don't count the one Logan sent to himself," Jerome says.

"It was a joke."

"Sure it was, buddy."

I haven't checked any of my social media accounts since I was on the sidewalk outside the station. I switched them all to private later in the day to stop the posts but didn't read any of them.

"Got a computer I can use?" I ask.

I open Twitter on Janey's desktop and show everyone the tweets. Some are words, some are graphic pictures, and most are a mix of the two. I want to believe these are fake accounts, but they're legitimate users parroting the same theme: they hate me and think my life isn't worth anything.

Kill yourself and walk to the light.
I hope you and your family get gunned down in the street.
I'm going to kill you and your father and rape your mother and sister.

You should have died in that school.
I hope someone kills you with one of those guns you love so much.
You're evil and need to be erased from this planet in the worst way imaginable.
I'm gonna slice your throat and watch you bleed out Nazi scum.

"Oh my God," Olivia whispers.

"This is crazy," Logan says, shaking his head. Tyler muscles him out of the way so he can read.

"I'm sorry this happened to you, Tierra," Austin says. He looks like he wants to hug me. I could use one.

"Thanks. Austin, not to sound ungrateful, but I'm a little confused about why you hired me. I don't have any real-world investigative experience."

"I thought you might ask. Jerome, play her the news report."

He punches a couple of buttons on the remote, and the clip starts in the middle of an on-scene report. "Two are dead, one seriously injured, and two other people had what police were calling non-life-threatening injuries. Police said a woman is being credited for saving the life of one of the injured in an attack that they are labeling gang violence. From Boston's South Side, this is –"

"I don't understand," I say when the video freezes.

"The media never tells the full story. The woman fired two rounds at the gunmen, forcing them to speed off. She saved a man's life by applying a makeshift tourniquet made out of a tie and piece of a chair to his leg."

"That's a great story. Why wasn't it included in the report?"

"Because of who she is," Tyler explains. "Her name is Victoria Larsen, and she's a special agent in the FBI."

"Police are quietly claiming it was retribution for the arrest of a prominent member of MS-13. Agent Larsen led the task force that took him down," Janey adds.

"That makes sense."

"Yeah, except every expert on MS-13 that we've talked to has said they're not behind this," Logan says. "It's not their M.O."

"Which means it may be something else," Tyler interjects. "I have a source in the DOJ who told me that an agent is poking around the Brockhampton shooting without authorization. She dropped in on the Massachusetts State Police lieutenant who ran the investigation. This drive-by happened not long after that meeting."

"It's a bit of a stretch to think he's involved, don't you think?" From the sober looks on their faces, they don't. "Okay, so, you need me to find this woman and find out what she knows?"

"That's the plan, yes."

"Guys, no offense, but this sounds like a wild goose chase."

"Yeah, it does," Austin says, getting off his stool. "Until you piece events together. Caleb shoots up his school, and a video of Ethan goes viral. Three days later, he begins working for Action Not Prayers, a gun control lobbying group headed by a guy named Ryan Baino. Two days after that, Elizabeth Schwarzer, the only source who may know

Caleb's motive, lands in a coma. Police recovered no usable video from the library despite all the cameras, and the investigation suddenly closes. Ethan speaks at rallies and conducts interviews where questions about the shooting aren't allowed."

"You broke that unwritten rule and got doxxed and fired. An FBI agent in Boston asks questions, and she gets shot at," Madison interjects.

"By a guy described as wearing a skull face shield."

My mouth hangs open. Austin nods. "I'm sorry, but that's too many coincidences."

"It also doesn't make it a conspiracy," I say, wondering what I signed up for.

"You're right. It doesn't. We've been looking at this for a while but could never answer the million-dollar question," Olivia says. "Why?"

"We have a five-cent guess after watching your interview," Logan says, Janey nodding alongside him.

"Which is?"

"Ethan didn't misspeak during your interview. We think he was friends with Caleb and that the people around him are protecting a secret."

"What secret?"

The group takes turns looking at each other. Austin finally smirks and looks me in the eyes.

"That he knew there would be a shooting at his school that day."

My mouth hangs open as I sit down in a chair. I don't know what to say to that. Austin's implying the existence of a conspiracy and cover-up that would shake the country to its foundation in the middle of a divisive gun control debate. I stare at my hands, not wanting to look up. This is too big for me.

"Austin, you need an experienced investigator for this, not me."

"I put this team together to uncover the truth and have the guts to tell the people. 'Experienced investigators' with reputations to protect would never chase this story."

"Or risk the inevitable public attacks that will come with it," Madison adds.

The team's previous comments about death threats get put into context. They must have no fear. Fanatics pilloried me for asking questions at an interview. The blowback from collapsing the whole movement would define our lives. I wonder if they realize what that could mean and if I want to be a part of it.

"I don't know. I doubt this FBI agent will tell me anything."

"The only way to find out is for you to track her down and ask. This is all speculation. We're hoping you can find pieces to the puzzle for us up there."

"No pressure. When do I leave?"

"That depends," Austin says, smiling. "How fast can you pack?"

CHAPTER TWENTY-EIGHT

SENATOR ALICIA STANDISH

Hart Senate Office Building
Washington, D.C.

Ethan was the perfect foil to wield against the pro-gun crowd. Americans respond to him. He was unpolished but effective in his pleas after the attack at his school. People connected with him on an emotional level because of his passion. He later came to understand that people don't want an honest conversation about guns.

The AFA spews factually incorrect opinions that the masses eagerly recite. The gun control crowd isn't any better. Every mass shooting leads to social media outrage and people screaming about government intervention without articulating what they wanted their representatives to do. When asked, the response is always either "something" or "anything." That's not how the government operates.

Alicia introduced her bill because the time for inaction was over. She partnered with Ethan and Ryan, and together, they've brought the most stringent gun control measures in the history of the Republic within a few votes from becoming law. That's what has made this conversation so difficult.

"We've come this far, and now you're dismissing me?" he asks after Alicia delivers the news to him.

"It's not like that, Ethan."

"Then what is it like?"

"We're losing support in the House and Senate."

"Then let me help you bring them back into the fold," he pleads.

"That's precisely what I need you to do. These Republicans are worried about their reelection and the support they'd lose from their party. Public pressure is the key to winning, and that's what you're good at. It's what I need you to go back to doing."

Ethan leans back in his chair and folds his arms across his chest. "Is this about the WWDC interview?"

"No. We've all had bad interviews before."

"Is it about the doxxing? Do you think I had something to do with it?"

"Did you?" Alicia asks, cocking her head.

"Hell, no!"

Alicia shares a quick look with Brian standing in his usual spot at the back of her office. Ethan's reaction was overkill, and his denial didn't convince her chief of staff.

"Then it's not about that, either."

"You need my help to pass this bill," Ethan concludes.

"Yes, I do, but not in Washington. You have incredible energy, Ethan. I need America to keep feeling the electricity you generate when you're in front of the people."

"I can walk and chew gum at the same time."

"Yes, I know you can, but our message won't feel authentic if you're shuttling back and forth to Washington. The AFA will characterize you as a lobbyist."

"Who cares what they say?"

"Don't underestimate our opposition, Ethan," Alicia says, beginning to lose her temper at his insolence. "The media may be on our side, but they love conflict. Don't hand them some on a silver platter."

Ethan stands and points his finger at the senator. "You're making a mistake, but if you want me out of Washington, I'm gone. Good luck, Senator. You'll need it if you don't get the bill passed."

Ethan storms out of Alicia's office. She hears him stomp down the hall and sighs as Brian closes the door behind him.

"That didn't go well."

Alicia watches as Brian takes a seat in the chair Ethan was occupying. He straightens his suit and brushes off some lint.

"Ethan lied about the doxxing. Either he did it, or Baino did."

"You don't know that."

"Senator, he had the same reaction my four-year-old does after I ask him if he raided the cookie jar when I catch him holding the lid."

"You wanted him out of Washington and got your wish."

"No, ma'am. The House Minority Leader wanted Ethan out of the city. I want you to cut ties with both of them."

"And I heard you the first time," she snaps. "Like it or not, we need Action Not Prayers and Ethan. Understood?"

Brian looks at her for a long moment without speaking. Alicia squints at him, waiting for an acknowledgment.

"Yes, ma'am."

"Good. Send a press release about Ethan leaving D.C. to help Action Not Prayers organize the Brockhampton rally."

Brian nods and leaves her office. Alicia begins writing a note before slamming the pen on the desk. None of this is going as she'd hoped. It was her idea to ask Ryan Baino to bring Ethan to Washington. Now that he's gone, she'd better see dividends from it.

CHAPTER TWENTY-NINE

CAPITOL BEAT

Cable News Studio
Washington, D.C.

"And now for tonight's final thought," Wilson says, staring into the camera as he announces the beginning of his final segment. "As Americans enjoy the increased temperatures that come with late spring, thermometers are spiking around the country for an entirely different reason.

"The Safe America Act is heading for an eventual vote on the Senate floor, and supporters and detractors are gearing up for a fight. Nationwide protests have been a daily occurrence since the Brockhampton massacre, but now it's the pro-Second Amendment advocates voicing their opinions on the bill. The American Firearms Association, cowed into ineffectiveness by the forces behind the gun control movement, has returned to the political playing field with a vengeance.

"They have mobilized supporters to show up to counter-protest in every town that gun control advocates have received permits to rally in, often in very close proximity. The protests and counter-protests are calm for now, but, my fellow Americans, this is a powder keg. Sparks will fly as we edge closer to a vote on this contentious bill. Demonstrations allowed to exist in such proximity heighten the risk of a disastrous conflagration, and here's why.

"Both sides have much to lose when Congress casts their votes. Consideration of a gun control bill of this magnitude in a Republican Congress is unthinkable had the massacre at Brockhampton not occurred. The public pressure to act has been enormous, but the question has always been whether that pressure was sustainable. We are now beginning to see the answer.

"Politics has a natural ebb and flow to it, and support in Congress is dropping for the Safe America Act. The RealClearPolitics aggregate average of public polls conducted on the topic is showing a steady decline for gun control over the past couple of weeks, possibly due to Ethan Harrington's interview with former WWDC reporter Tierra Campos and her subsequent doxxing."

Wilson's head moves when the camera changes. The tight shot brings his face closer to the people in every living room in America who are tuned in. It's a psychological cue that what he is about to say is very important.

"The battle waged over the Safe America Act has nothing to do with the contents of the bill. Pugilists on both sides need to win. That supplants honest discussions on this vital issue. Intellectual evaluation of legislation has morphed into an existential struggle between divergent ideologies. The merits of gun control and the Second Amendment are not being debated in the marble halls of Congress. It is a digital street fight using snarky memes and viral videos in an all-out fight for your attention.

"If this is how our democracy lives moving forward, then it is how it will die. Serious issues like gun violence require serious conversations by leaders with an unwavering dedication to solving a problem, not scoring points with an electorate. That is not what's happening in Washington or around the country, and none of it is healthy for our Republic."

The emphatic delivery of the last phrase of the sentence resonates with the focus group the network brings in every night to gauge Wilson's performance. Focus group members are equipped with a dial they can turn left or right whether they like or dislike something, and the producers get real-time data about their show, their guests, and what subjects the producers should explore more in-depth. The meter spikes in the production room at the end of the monologue, and the producer whispers the result into the aging anchor's ear during the short pause.

"That's my final thought, and it's for the record."

"*You nailed it*," his producer says through his earpiece.

Wilson's face brightens before he launches his signature signoff. "Thank you for watching *Capitol Beat*; I'm Wilson Newman. Good Night."

CHAPTER THIRTY

SPECIAL AGENT VICTORIA LARSEN

Elijah Hampton Recreational Park
Brockhampton, Massachusetts

Very few investigations land an FBI agent on a basketball court talking to a teenager in suburban Massachusetts. Then again, she remembers that what she's doing isn't officially investigating. The Brockhampton High seniors graduated and went off to college or the workforce after the shooting, but many of them are back home for summer break. What she didn't expect is how resistant they'd be to her questions. Nobody wants to talk about that day, Ethan Harrington, or his crusade. Bryce is one of the few exceptions.

"Why did you agree to talk to me?" she asks, as he pulls up and launches a jump shot from behind the three-point arc.

Bryce Minnick is a good-looking kid, but not much of an athlete. At a minimum, basketball is not his sport. The ball clanks hard off the rim and skips away, forcing him past half court to retrieve it. Victoria smirks, getting the feeling that happens to him often.

"You're hot."

It's a sexist remark that she would resent coming out of the mouth of a mature man if there were such a thing. It's the expected answer from a hormonal teenager with an underdeveloped brain-mouth filter. Victoria will let him ogle her like a fat kid eyeing a Twinkie so long as he talks.

"Thanks. I only have a few questions. You were in the school's library when Caleb opened fire?"

"I was," Bryce says, firing off an absentminded three-point shot when Victoria rips the scab off that memory. "I was working on an essay. Caleb walked in and looked around for a while. I went back to writing when I heard the first shot."

"Do you know what he was looking for?"

"No clue."

"How long was he in there before he started shooting?"

"A minute. Maybe two. I don't remember."

Victoria nods. "What did you do then?"

"He was gunning down everyone he could, so I hid."

"You didn't think about trying to take him on?"

The question annoys Bryce. He tucks the ball under his arm and takes a deep breath before answering. "It wasn't a movie. I didn't know if he was alone. All I knew is he had a gun and I didn't, so I hid, just like I did during every drill I ever endured in that school. Doing anything else would have gotten me killed."

Victoria knows that's true. What caught her so off guard about the Tierra Campos interview with Ethan was his bravado about taking on the shooter. The typical reaction would have been more like what Bryce just described.

"Did you know Caleb?"

"Nobody knew him," he says, dribbling to avoid eye contact. "Not really."

"What do you mean?"

"He was a weirdo. Nobody talked to him except Lizzie."

"I see. Is there a lot of bullying that goes on at Brockhampton High?"

"It's high school. What do you think?" Bryce asks, offering a look to reinforce the stupidity of that question.

The theory that Caleb lashed out because of bullying was one of the first ones floated and dismissed by investigators. Victoria doesn't think the investigation explored that adequately. Out of the two people who know for sure, one is dead, and the other is in a coma.

"Touché. Were Caleb and Lizzie bullied?"

He stops, mid-shot. He pounds the ball hard to the ground twice before snatching it on the second bounce. "I wouldn't know."

"Did they ever sit with anyone at lunch?"

"Never," Bryce says with a chuckle. "They were recluses. Nobody associated with them or wanted to. He was always wearing headphones, and she was always writing."

"Writing what?"

"Poetry, I guess. She wrote a lot of really dark stuff. Lizzie always had a notebook with her."

"What kind of notebook? One for school?" Victoria asks as he bricks another shot.

The rebound comes to her beyond the three-point arc. She tucks the ball under her arm and waits for an answer. This kid isn't going to the NBA. He can spare a minute or two of undistracted adult conversation.

"No, one of those black and white composition ones, I guess."

That piques Victoria's interest. "Did either Caleb or Lizzie have any social media accounts?"

"They weren't the type of kids I Snapchatted. I don't even think either of them owned a smartphone. Why are you asking all these questions? Cops have already asked me all this."

"I'm searching for Caleb's motive," Victoria says. Bryce shakes his head. "Don't you want to know why he did it?"

"Nope. My friends are dead. Knowing why isn't going to bring them back. We're done here. Throw me the rock."

In one fluid motion, Victoria squares to the basket using her left foot as a pivot and fires. There's plenty of air under the shot, maybe too much as she tracks its trajectory. It turns out to be right on target. The ball slides through the hoop with a sweet, satisfying swish as it passes through the net. She turns and looks at Bryce, whose mouth is agape.

"You're not following through when you shoot. That's why you keep clanking the ball off the rim."

"Okay, you're even hotter now," he says.

"One more question, if you don't mind. Did Caleb ever own a white Ford Mustang?"

"No. He had some gray beater car."

"Did Lizzie?"

"I never saw her drive."

"Do you know of anybody in your school that drove one?"

Bryce cocks his head and looks skyward. "There were a couple of kids in school with Mustangs, but none of them were white."

Victoria bites her lower lip. The answer doesn't mean anything. The owner could have been someone he knew from another school with the means to fund their range time, but that doesn't feel right to her either.

The only way to know for sure is to get into the DMV database, search for white Mustangs, and track them down one by one. That could take months.

"Thanks for your time, Bryce."

"Anytime," he says, bricking another shot off the rim and sending the ball thirty feet in the other direction.

She shakes her head as she heads for her car. Teenagers never listen.

CHAPTER THIRTY-ONE

ETHAN HARRINGTON

Mayfield Estate
Brockhampton, Massachusetts

Ethan pulls his car off the street and past the dual stone columns at the entrance of the driveway. Wrought-iron gates are the only thing that could make Connor Mayfield's house more ostentatious. He accelerates up the long, tree-lined asphalt strip to the house. While not quite a mansion, the large house looks more like a Tuscan villa than something you would find in New England. It is flashy and ornate, just like Connor's father. There is no sign of his old man's Maserati in the garage as Ethan parks his car. Some things never change.

He lets himself into the house and is enthusiastically greeted by friends who haven't seen him for well over a month. These are the kids who rallied to his cause following his first statement to the press minutes after the massacre that devastated their school. Some of them he barely knew before the tragedy. A couple of others barely escaped Caleb's rampage with their lives. Now they are among his closest friends.

"You're late," Connor says, rounding the corner from the kitchen.

"Tardiness is the sign of a busy man."

"I speak from experience when I say that excuse never worked when we were in school."

"Yet you still managed to graduate. What's going on, Brother?"

The two young men share a hug. Ethan and Connor spent much of their time here without much parental supervision. A string of ineffectual nannies barely managed to keep them in line.

"How was your trip home?"

"I was stuffed into economy class. Need I say more?"

"How was Washington?" Prudence, the social media maven of the group, asks.

"Ridiculous."

"I heard they put you up in some swanky hotel."

"Yeah, the Imperial was nice. I would have traded all of it for some progress."

"You seemed convinced that it would be different this time," Connor reminds him.

"It is for some of them, but too many are still playing games. Politicians are all the same: they talk a lot and lie when their lips move."

"Including Senator Standish?"

Ethan squints at his friend. Connor believes all politicians are corrupt. Much of that is firsthand knowledge of his father's dealings. He wasn't a fan of working with Alicia Standish, regardless of the promises she made to Ethan. Now he's rubbing it in.

"She sent me out of Washington to get people reengaged. I think she didn't want me in there anymore because she's losing votes."

"You did botch that interview pretty bad."

"I got flustered and misspoke. Everyone made a big deal about nothing. It was bound to happen sooner or later. Politicians are just using it as an excuse to bail on the bill."

"I hate Boomers," Connor says.

"Right? They just don't get it, do they?" Prudence asks. She detests anyone over the age of twenty-five.

"Be fair. We can't blame them for everything. They've only ruined the environment, racked up trillions in debt, made everything from health care to college unaffordable…"

Connor grins as he lets his sarcastic analysis hang in the air for a moment. He can't stand anything about Baby Boomers or Generation X, from the music they listened to growing up to the mentality that landed America in its current predicament. The current company working in his family room won't refute any of that.

"Don't forget leaving us open to getting gunned down in our schools," Prudence adds, eliciting solemn nods from the assembled activists.

"I can't control what happens in D.C. If Standish wants me to come home and ramp up the pressure, I'm happy to do it. I want them to get off their asses and do something."

"Well, we've got a ton of planning to do before then," she says, excited but lamenting the amount of work ahead of them.

Ryan Baino and his group of dedicated volunteers at Action Not Prayers provide much of the logistical support for rallies, but there is a lot of legwork ahead of that. The activists sitting here arrange the lineup of speakers. It's tedious and time-consuming, but the price that needs to be paid to bring their message to the public.

"Why don't you guys get started. I need to talk to my man here for a minute," Connor says, putting Ethan in a friendly headlock.

The two boys walk through the enormous kitchen and out the French doors to the back patio. Joseph Mayfield spends a small fortune on pool maintenance and landscaping despite never spending more than a few hours here. He hates the outdoors, but Connor considers this his favorite place to think.

"I see your Dad isn't around," Ethan says, opening the conversation as they circle to the backside of the pool.

"He's still pissed at us. He's home even less than usual."

Ethan studies his usually carefree friend. His tone is grave and face even more serious than usual. Something is up.

"Are we okay?" Ethan asks as Connor flops into a lounge chair overlooking the pool. He follows suit in the adjacent one.

"You said you were friends with Caleb. That was an interesting development."

"I got ambushed, Connor. She went off-script, and I wasn't ready for it. I flubbed an answer. That's all," Ethan says, doing his best to dismiss the concern.

"Since when aren't you ready for questions?"

"Could you have done any better?"

"I don't do interviews. That's your schtick."

"It doesn't matter. The reporter's been taken care of. We're focused on getting back on message."

"You think doxxing her solved your problem?"

"No, that was for me. She got canned by the station. She won't be any more trouble."

"And if she gets rehired? Or if someone decides to run with the same playbook to get ahead?"

"Then Baino will take care of it."

"Good," Connor says, still not satisfied but no longer willing to argue about it. "The last thing we need is more questions."

"My turn. Any news about Lizzie?"

"Still in her coma."

"Are the police still looking into her?"

"Not according to my father."

Ethan stares out at the pool. If anyone can make good on a promise, it's Joseph Mayfield. While he and his son have a complicated relationship, he's never failed to come through for Connor.

"You know the stakes in all this," Ethan warns.

"Every bit as much as you do," Connor says, swinging his legs off the lounge chair and struggling to his feet. Ethan takes Connor's hand and gets hefted off his chair.

"Thanks."

"Let's get back to the team. We have to set up a rally that will let you rock Brockhampton, and I can't wait to see it."

CHAPTER THIRTY-TWO

TIERRA CAMPOS

Three Pines Park
Brockhampton, Massachusetts

Demonstrations in Brockhampton started days after the shooting. At first, it was grieving townspeople, shocked by what happened in their community and looking for a place to comfort each other and vent their anger. What I see here bears no resemblance to those early days.

The majority of these people are professional protesters, either being paid to be here or otherwise financially supported by one of a myriad of anti-gun groups. The early anguish was real. Special interests bought and paid for this outrage to achieve a specific end. The counter-protest being held only a couple of dozen yards away is no different.

One of the reasons I went into television reporting is that Americans are more likely to be compelled by images than persuaded by words. One photograph, whether it's a girl burned by napalm in Southeast Asia or a federal officer appearing to point his gun at a screaming Elian Gonzalez hiding in a closet, can frame the narrative of any issue.

News of the Japanese attack on Pearl Harbor was shocking in 1941, but Americans watched the horror in real-time as planes slammed into the World Trade Center and Pentagon. Two generations of Americans have been raised in the era of YouTube and social media sharing. Imagery has never been more salient than it is today, and both sides of this argument know that.

I walk along the edge of the town park. The two groups are divided only by police barriers and nervous local law enforcement officers. The town's decision to allow these opposing sides of a provocative issue to demonstrate next to each other is reckless.

None of what I see on either side contributes to the rational debate we need in this country on the issue. The pro-Second Amendment side, clad in red, white, and blue, are letting those colors make their statement. It's as if they believe they have a monopoly on patriotism.

The propaganda on the anti-gun side is sickening. The signs protesters are holding aloft are ludicrous. Some are clever, or even thoughtful, but those are the exception to the rule. Most are bitter, hateful, and pushing lies.

A woman shouting at the top of her lungs near the edge of the park is a perfect example. The sign she's carrying reads:

The only thing easier to buy than a gun in America is a Republican Senator

The man next to her stands quietly wielding a different message aloft:

I'm not against the 2nd Amendment. I'm against the AFA's disregard for common sense regulation

My favorite for the Captain Obvious award is:

Guns kill

After seeing both demonstrations in person, I'm struck by how small they are and how dishonest the media is in reporting them. Tight angles and opportune shots to make it seem like one protest is tiny while making the other appear huge. Fairness in reporting is no longer a distinguishable feature in most news organizations.

There's no sign of the FBI agent I'm looking for, despite Logan and Tyler insisting she's somewhere in town. I pull out my cell phone and point it at a trio of gun control advocates harassing pedestrians desperate to get away from them. I watch on the phone's display as one man yells at the protesters and is shouted down while police patiently observe nearby. It's only a matter of time before violence erupts when they pick on the wrong person. This is what polarization in America looks like.

I tuck my phone away and continue to skirt along the edge of the park, far enough away from both groups to avoid any interaction. Both crowds are energetic and vocal. I can only imagine what it will be like when Congress votes on Standish's bill. She is either the savior who is pushing her bill for the benefit of the country or the Antichrist trying to deliver a win for political reasons. It may not be a binary choice. There is no reason to believe she isn't doing it for both.

The FBI agent isn't here. Dismayed, I start to walk back towards my car parked in a municipal lot a couple of blocks away.

"Hey! Hey!" a man dressed in black with a bandana over his face shouts from down the sidewalk. He's dressed like he's ready for a riot. "Hey, you're Tierra Campos, right?"

I get the feeling this man's not a fan. A big part of me wants to lie. A bigger part of me refuses to. "Yeah."

"What are you doing here?"

"Walking."

"You think we're dumb?" the man asks, taking up a more aggressive posture.

"No, I think you're ignorant. I *know* you're dumb."

"Oh, you think you're funny. The bitch thinks she's funny," he says, turning to his friend.

"Yeah, a real comedian. I bet you think sixty-six dead kids is funny too. You must love school shootings so you can mock the victims."

I get the feeling these guys don't care about the victims at all. They're here to start trouble. I know I shouldn't engage.

"You want to start with us, fascist bitch?"

A shiver of fear runs through me. I turn to walk back towards the park and the police and bump into two guys standing right behind me. I look at their faces and recoil. One has a skull face shield and the other sports the Joker. It can't be.

"Remember us?" Skull Face says.

Joker pulls out pepper spray and scores a direct hit right to my face. My eyes begin to sting and water profusely. I double over.

"Die, bitch!"

A second later, I'm struck hard on the head. My vision bursts into a kaleidoscope of stars as I collapse to the ground.

I shield my head, waiting for the men to take their shots. They hover over me, appearing as blurry figures through my diminished vision. One of them kicks me in the stomach, causing me to gasp and cough violently. I want to be invisible again. A second kick lands on my ribs, causing a shock of pain to shoot through my body. I brace for another blow. It never comes.

Skull Face crashes to the ground next to me. He scuffles with a large man wearing a black leather jacket, and he's losing. I force myself to blink in a desperate attempt to clear my vision. It helps a little, and I cock my head to see a half-dozen men wearing biker jackets and American flag bandanas pummeling my attackers.

Shouts fill my ears as the boys tangle with the men who came to my rescue. Joker scores a hit with his pepper spray on one of the bikers, who drops to a knee, blinded by his tears. Another man crashes the pole carrying his American flag down on his arm. Joker drops the canister and gets rushed by two more men who make him pay with their fists.

I watch more people arrive through blurred vision as a melee erupts around me. The flashing strobes of squad cars announce the police arrival before I hear them barking orders as they desperately try to break it up. People scatter in all directions.

"Are you okay?" I hear an officer ask as he kneels next to me. My eyelids feel like sandpaper every time I blink. The excessive tearing does nothing to alleviate the pain.

"I can't see," I say, fighting the panic. Bile comes up to my mouth. I feel like throwing up.

"Are you hurt? Can you walk?"

I nod my head and feel myself get lifted to my feet. I'm wobbly, and my stomach turns as paramedics guide me towards an ambulance that just arrived. I look around the parking lot through my blurred vision. Police cars seem to be everywhere now.

EMTs work to flush out my eyes and advise me that the effects will dissipate with time. I lie down on the gurney for a trip to the hospital to get x-rays done on my ribs. They hurt like hell.

I can hear the commotion outside as I close my eyes and clutch the soft blanket that they draped over me. Skull Face and Joker were the same guys who were outside my apartment. They followed me up to Brockhampton and waited for me to return to the car. But why? All I can think about is wanting to go home, but I know I'm not safe there either. I'm not safe anywhere and may never be again.

CHAPTER THIRTY-THREE

SENATOR ALICIA STANDISH

Marquis de Lafayette Hotel Ballroom
Washington, D.C.

All glory is fleeting. The fundraising for the next election begins when the winner downs the last glass of champagne at a victory celebration. Politicians who do this well often have long careers in Washington. Those who don't give concession speeches.

Senator Standish is a decorated veteran of events that require a short speech, a lot of shaking hands, and even more photo ops. Not all of them are for her campaign. Tonight's gala is a non-partisan fundraiser for breast cancer research. Elected representatives from both sides of the aisle are here, mostly staring at each other warily through the bundles of pink balloons from across the room.

"I'm going to bring you with me every time I need another drink. Nobody clears the bar faster," Deputy Attorney General Conrad Williams says, watching a couple of GOP congressmen move off when Alicia steps up to order another glass of wine.

"It only works on Republicans," Alicia says, pointing at the Cabernet that the bartender dutifully pours.

"I'm not going to lie – it's odd seeing you at a bipartisan event."

"Everyone in America on the left and right agrees on the evil of cancer. It may be one of the few unifying things in the country."

"Fair enough. How have you been, Alicia? I haven't seen you for a while."

"That's because I do my best not to run afoul of the law. Spending time at the DOJ doesn't help you win elections."

"That's true, and you have a big one coming up."

"And that's the other reason you haven't seen me. I'm busy."

Conrad has been deputy attorney general for about three years now. A political appointee of the president and confirmed by the Senate when his predecessor returned to the private sector, he's the second-highest-ranking official in the United States Department of Justice and oversees its day-to-day operations.

An intelligent man and shrewd lawyer, many Democrats believe he should have his boss' job. Lisa Ehler is more than just a token female appointed to add diversity to the president's cabinet. She's a capable lawyer, trusted advisor, and has the president's loyalty. That hampers Conrad's upward mobility. Alicia wonders if this conversation is about Conrad's role in a future Standish administration.

"Yes, we're all watching to see if you can pass a landmark gun control bill through a Republican Congress."

"You don't think I can do it?" Alicia asks, sipping her drink. It was a direct challenge.

"I think you'll have to water it down and put a sunset provision on it like they did the Assault Weapons Ban of 1994."

Alicia swirls her wine and frowns. The Democrats still haven't learned that lesson.

"The AWB was flawed legislation riddled with loopholes. I'm not sure I would have voted for it without significant alterations that reduced exemptions. My bill will be more effective."

"You're that confident?"

The memories of her mother and father flash through her mind. She looks directly at Conrad and holds his stare.

"Yes."

"Then there's something you should know," Conrad says in a grave tone.

He nods towards a more isolated part of the ballroom's foyer, and she follows him there. He looks around before speaking to ensure nobody else is in earshot.

"Is this a state secret or something?"

"The AG asked me to relay some information to you."

"You could have dropped by the office," Alicia says, feeling a need to point out that there are more conventional ways to relay information than holding a secret meeting at a Washington fundraiser filled with partisan politicians.

"I wanted to avoid any scenario where people would ask questions. We have a bad history with that."

He's right about that. What happened in 2016 at Phoenix Sky Harbor airport when Bill Clinton met then-Attorney General Loretta Lynch is still subject to speculation. The encounter occurred just days before Hillary Rodham Clinton was to be interviewed by the FBI about her mishandling of classified emails. The former president intercepted the AG on her plane and provided fodder for conspiracy theories convinced that Clinton was attempting to get Lynch to go easy on his wife. Only the parties involved in the conversation know for sure, and the world never will.

"The AG heard rumors that there's an FBI agent in Boston poking into the Brockhampton investigation."

The attorney general supervises the administration and operation of critical federal agencies like the Federal Bureau of Investigation, Drug Enforcement Administration, Bureau of Alcohol, Tobacco, Firearms and Explosives, and U.S. Marshals Service. If anyone were in a position to know that, it would be her.

"The Bureau told her that?"

"No, it came from the governor's office via the state police, and that's the problem. Nobody in the Hoover Building has brought it to our attention."

Alicia clenches her teeth. Further politicization of the FBI will erode any public confidence they have left and make a tense debate over gun control that much worse.

They need to get control of their people, and if an agent has gone rogue, at least have the guts to let the DOJ know.

"The case is closed. Who's investigating and on what authority?"

"Some agent with an ax to grind, and with no authority that we know of."

Scenarios play through Alicia's head. It could be someone trying to undermine her gun control bill. It could also be an attempt to discredit Ethan because he misspoke during the Tierra Campos interview. Either way, it reeks of interference.

"I thought the DOJ was trying to steer the FBI out of politics."

The comment catches Conrad off guard. "We are."

"You're doing a lousy job. The FBI took a hit over the 2016 election from both parties. Perception is everything, and Americans viewing their principal federal investigative organization as biased is damaging to the nation."

Conrad wrings his hands and grimaces. "Lisa has already been in touch with the FBI director. We'll get to the bottom of it."

"I would hope so. I'd hate to see your work in restoring the FBI's tarnished reputation undone because of an unfortunate public disclosure."

Conrad's face changes at the insinuation. Words can be weapons, and their effectiveness is often dictated by how they get wielded. Alicia got the effect she wanted.

"You're not saying what I think you are," he says, his voice deeper and ominous. "We play for the same team."

"No, no, no, don't get me wrong, Conrad," she says, playing it off jovially. "I would never leak anything that damages the administration. But you know as well as I do that these things tend to get out. Someone in the media is sure to uncover it."

Alicia's words are one thing, and her tone is another. The great thing is that tone can be misconstrued, giving her plausible deniability should she be confronted by the president or attorney general about this conversation. The underlying threat is real despite her denials. She has no qualms about leaking anything to pass this bill, even if it means ruffling a few feathers. Successful passage is far from guaranteed, but Alicia will make damn sure it's not FBI meddling that dooms it. The deputy attorney general knows that as well, and he'll relay that to his boss.

"We'll keep the FBI under control."

"I know you will. This bill is important for the party and for the nation. I don't want to see the FBI caught in the crossfire when it gets a floor vote."

"I need a favor in return, Senator."

Alicia doesn't hide the disgusted look on her face. "I'm not going to entertain a quid pro quo on this, Conrad."

"I'm not asking for one. The AG wanted you to know this information in good faith. All I'm asking is for you to keep us and the FBI out of the press. Don't undo the work we are doing."

"I'm sure there will be nothing to worry about if you do your jobs."

Alicia pats him on the shoulder and heads back towards the bar for a final glass of wine. There is nothing to find in Brockhampton. This has to be politically motivated, and she's determined not to let that interfere with the passage of the Safe America Act.

CHAPTER THIRTY-FOUR

CAPITOL BEAT

Cable News Studio
Washington, D.C.

Wilson Newman broke onto the national scene reporting from Baghdad during the Persian Gulf War. He's reported on scandals from the Iran-Contra Affair through the FISA court abuses and Russian meddling during the 2016 presidential election. He has seen America at its best and its worst. There is no doubt how he feels about today's broadcast.

"And now for tonight's final thought," he says into the camera, with a disgusted tone. "Gun rights advocates marching to express their support for the rights enshrined to them by the Second Amendment were brutally attacked by thugs today in Texas. Across the country, gun control activists rallying in Minneapolis were pepper-sprayed and assaulted by a militia claiming to love America.

"A reporter has been doxxed and attacked in her home, and countless thousands of people have received death threats and all manner of disparaging comments on social media. This is the state of public discourse in America. It is what our Republic has become."

The teleprompter stops as Wilson pauses for a moment. He lets the silence speak to the viewing audience for him. He also uses the moment to get his own emotions under control.

"Passions run deep on this issue, and that should be no surprise to anybody. The United States has a centuries-old relationship with firearms and a short, yet deadly history of mass killings because of them. Americans have long celebrated and cherished the rights enshrined in the Constitution, and yet increasing numbers of them are willing to cede them for a greater sense of security in an age where weapons and words are more harmful than any time in history.

"Over the past decade, our political process has plummeted into an abyss of disparaging comments. Our elected representatives rely on ridiculous antics and eschew heady debates on the issues for snarky tweetstorms. There is no legislating, no leadership, and no civil discourse left in this country.

"Statesmanship is what will address and solve the critical issues facing our nation, gun control included. Soundbites and social media messages cannot resolve complex problems requiring detailed explanations and effective communication to the public.

Unfortunately, nobody is discussing whether the Safe America Act helps solve the country's problem with violence.

"Pundits speak in vague terms as supporters and detractors hurl insults at each other. One side claims gun confiscation will lead to a world modeled on Orwell's *1984*. The other side claims anyone who doesn't support this has blood on their hands and is personally responsible for thousands of gun-related deaths. It's divisive rhetoric that only widens the chasm between the two sides, and it's getting worse.

"Policy used to be determined through arguments using statistics and case studies. Now we decide it with insults, public shaming, and violence. The pendulum needs to swing back in the other direction. If this is our default way of governance in the future, our Republic will not survive. That's my final thought, and it's for the record."

Wilson's face doesn't change when he turns to a different camera. Unlike most broadcasts, he doesn't want to lighten the mood of the viewing audience before the next show. He wants them thinking about this. He wants them to find it depressing because he believes it is.

"Thank you for watching *Capitol Beat*; I'm Wilson Newman. Good Night."

CHAPTER THIRTY-FIVE

SPECIAL AGENT VICTORIA LARSEN

St. Elmo's Fryer
Revere, Massachusetts

Special Agent Audric LeClair looks around the diner, unimpressed. It may be close to the FBI office in Chelsea, but he knows there must be a healthier place to eat around here. Victoria always did like her fried food and is a regular here, based on the reception they got entering the diner. She is impeccably fit for a woman who still eats like a teenager.

He scans the menu across from his old friend. They've both come a long way since graduating from Quantico, although traveling in very different directions. They became friends despite being two different people with disparate career goals. Audric is chained to his desk in D.C., and Victoria rarely finds time to sit at hers. She was the one who loved the action that comes with fieldwork. He gets his action by watching it on television.

"The silence is killing me, Audie. It must be important if you came up here from your cozy office in D.C."

"Not really. I was in Boston and wanted to see you. What's good here?"

"Nothing if you're still health-conscious," Victoria says, earning a glare from a waitress who happened to be in earshot.

"They have salad," he says, studying the menu.

"I'm pretty sure they fry the lettuce, too."

Audie LeClair has the physique of a Tour de France cyclist. He's lean, stylish, and sticks out in a crowd. He's also never had a bacon cheeseburger in his life. He'd be the worst person in the Bureau to be on a stakeout with unless you like protein bars and smoothies.

"Stop bullshitting me. Why are you really here?"

He exhales deeply and sets the menu aside. He rubs the back of his neck and stares out the window. This is harder than he thought. Audric knows he wouldn't have made it through the academy without Victoria's help. It's a debt he'll never be able to repay but hopes today's visit is a start.

"You're in trouble, Vic."

"Aren't I always?"

"Not like this. Justice found out that you're asking questions about the Brockhampton investigation. They laid into the director, and he appeased them by referring you to the OIG."

Victoria winces. The Office of the Inspector General investigates allegations of serious misconduct against FBI personnel. They investigate improper behavior from using an FBI vehicle for non-official reasons to lying under oath. The penalties range from letters of censure and suspensions up to termination.

"That's it?" Victoria asks, trying to play it cool.

"This is as serious as it gets. They'll get what they want, and right now, that's your head."

"Why? Because I'm asking questions about a half-baked investigation?"

"No, because you're asking about Brockhampton and doing it outside of official channels."

Victoria watches a droplet of water run down her glass and soak into the napkin it's sitting on. She knew something like this could happen. It doesn't make her feel any better that she was right. All this for asking a few questions. She can't shake the feeling that it's overkill.

"So much for innocent until proven guilty."

"I know you're not that naïve when it comes to the bureaucracy. The guy assigned to adjudicate the referral thinks the best way to solve a rodent infestation is to burn the house down. It wouldn't matter to him that the homeowner would have no place to live. They're going to sideline you."

"How?"

"The Inspection Division is going to audit the Boston office for policy compliance and find something to use against Lance Fuller. He'll do whatever they ask."

Victoria has lost her appetite. She orders a ginger ale when the waitress returns and pulls out her pad. Audie does the same, knowing there is nothing he's willing to eat here.

"Why are you telling me this, Audie?"

"I don't want to see my friend ushered out of the Bureau."

"Is there a chance I won't get the ax at this point?"

"Yes. If you come clean, tell the brass that you found nothing and accept a suspension for abuse of investigative authority, they'll let you keep your job."

Victoria's heart sinks and her stomach twists into a knot, but not at her required penance. She stares at her close friend. He just lied to her face. Audie wouldn't have phrased it that way if it were an honest suggestion. The authoritative statement came from a man relaying demands made by a superior. He's here to leverage their friendship to get her to stand down.

"Why did you join the FBI, Audie?"

His eyes narrow. The question caught him off guard. "Same reasons you did. You know that."

"Do you love the work as much as I do?"

"Yeah, I do."

"Is that why you're selling me out? Does your career mean more than our friendship?"

"What are you –"

"Don't you dare lie to me again," Victoria demands. "Who put you up to this? What did they threaten you with?"

Audric leans back and takes a deep breath. He holds eye contact with Victoria, allowing her to study them. There isn't a hint of shame or guilt.

"Nobody. I volunteered to meet you when they explained the situation."

Victoria lets out a surprised laugh. "Wow. I didn't expect that from you."

"Did you sleep through the fallout from the 2016 election? This isn't about you, me, us, or even Brockhampton. There's no room for the FBI to interfere with the political process."

"I'm not."

"You are, even if you don't realize it. America will wake up a darker and more dangerous place than it is now if people believe we're derailing pending legislation. That's why the brass is reacting this way and why I'm here to talk some sense into you."

"Is that so?"

"It is. What's done is done in Brockhampton."

"There are unanswered questions."

"There always are. It's the state police's responsibility to answer them, not yours. If you keep going down this path, it'll cost you your career. End it now, and you get a slap on the wrist."

Victoria is sick to her stomach. Beyond Audric's personal betrayal, she's facing an impossible decision. She slides out of the booth to leave.

"What do you want me to tell them, Vic? They're going to want an answer," he says, refusing to make eye contact with her.

She promised the families answers but never considered it would come at such a personal cost. Every instinct tells her there's far more to learn about the Brockhampton shooting despite the lack of hard evidence. Victoria built her career on trusting that feeling. Now following it could mean throwing away everything she's worked for since the day she reported to Quantico.

"Tell them they win."

CHAPTER THIRTY-SIX

SENATOR ALICIA STANDISH

U.S. Capitol Building
Washington, D.C.

Senator Joseph Velvick's hideaway is about the only place Alicia could have this meeting. The public perception of Congress is a hyper-partisan divide among colleagues who hate each other. It's true that members of both parties once worked and socialized together far more than they do today, but there is not nearly as much animosity as people suspect. Bipartisanship does exist, not that the media shows any interest in covering it.

"We have a majority in both houses, Alicia. We don't have to pass this bill. It's political suicide for many of us if we do."

Velvick left Alicia the opening during their photo op with Ethan. That meeting was a publicity stunt to show constituents back home that the Senators are serious about finding a solution to gun violence. This discussion is not.

"It's political suicide for you if you don't. Why else are we having this conversation? Tell me your heart didn't ache while watching the memorial services in Massachusetts."

"Everyone's heart broke," he says, meaning it. "But you can't base policy on emotions."

"Tell that to the families. I went to many of those services. There were so many tears and so much pain."

"And you did a great job politicizing that."

"Guilty as charged," Alicia declares. "Families who lost their sons and daughters didn't want their deaths to be in vain. If positive change comes out of those tragedies, we're honoring them, not using them."

Joseph leans back in his chair, and Alicia follows suit. Gun violence in the United States has reached epidemic proportions. Shootings are not isolated tragedies but a plague on a civilized society. Alicia has used the media to remind the nation to see the forest and not the individual trees.

"My whole caucus thinks your bill is unconstitutional at best, and a stepping-stone to a full repeal of the Second Amendment at worst."

"Your caucus also knows that polls show that support for full repeal is minuscule, even among gun control supporters. Your colleagues want a watered-down bill, but where has that ever gotten us? We've been talking about gun control methods for decades. The ones enacted are ineffective, and the AFA won't accept the ones that work."

Alicia tries to stay calm and measured while delivering that line. She hates that organization with a burning passion hotter than a thousand suns. The American Firearms Association believes that the world hasn't changed since 1787. In their minds, the rise in mass shootings and gun violence doesn't warrant a solution. Protectors of the status quo have gotten their way for too long. Alicia is determined to end that.

"We have reasonable solutions. Alternative bills are being drafted to arm teachers, provide more safety measures, and add armed guards in schools."

"Joseph, only a coward would offer futile suggestions like arming teachers while the blood of our children flows through the hallways of their schools. Kids are no safer with a gun in the hands of a stressed-out, underpaid teacher."

"Senator, there's –"

"Does arming teachers address the number of suicides, robberies, and murders committed using firearms every year? Slapping a Band-Aid on this problem in the name of political expediency isn't going to save lives. The Safe America Act will."

"There is no evidence to show that your bill will make our schools any safer or have the impact you think it will. All you'll succeed in is creating a nation of criminals."

"Every life saved makes it worthwhile."

"Not if it tramples a right enshrined in the Constitution."

Senator Velvick plays hardball. He's a veteran of countless Senate battles as a member of the old guard. He's a wily politician who's lost in the new age of politics and is vulnerable in next year's election. Alicia knows he's here to make a deal and that this back and forth is just the opener for the main event.

"The right to own firearms is protected by the Bill of Rights because there was a real fear of a strong national government that was new and unproven. Rights that preserve free speech or spare us from unreasonable search and seizure are necessary today to protect us from government abuses. The right to bear arms using weapons far deadlier than a muzzle-loading musket is not."

"I'm sorry, Alicia. I'm not convinced, and I don't see how I can get there."

She's heard him say that before. Let the games begin.

"Easy. The polls show you the way."

"The national polls can say whatever they want. My base will turn on me. I will fight for my life in a primary."

Inevitably, every conversation turns to reelection in this town. It was the signal Alicia was waiting to get.

"Nobody in Iowa has your name recognition. A primary challenge is bound to fail. As for the general election, your base won't vote for the guy we'll put up against you."

That gets his attention. "Are you saying what I think you are?"

The advantage of being a frontrunner for the presidency is the strings she can pull with the party. If losing a seat in Iowa is the price for this bill getting passed, Democrats will pay it. The president gave her the leverage to make deals, and that's what she intends to do.

"I can find a likable woman of color to run against you that will win independents and moderates. You may win, or you may lose, but it will cost you a fortune either way. Or I can find someone even liberal Californians would find extremist that would never appeal to the good people of Iowa. The choice is yours."

"What assurances do I have that you'll do that if I give you my vote?"

"My word."

"That's worth nothing in Washington. You won't care about your promises if this bill passes and you start selecting curtains for the Oval Office."

"The bill still has to be brought to the floor, and that'll take time. Watch me move pieces around the board and then decide if I'm holding up my end of the bargain."

Alicia stands and heads for the door. He'll either take her up on that offer or not. There's no reason to stick around and debate it.

"What about Senator Sheppard? She's not up for reelection."

"Amanda wants federal funding for her education initiative in New Mexico. I can help her deliver on that campaign promise."

"You know, even if this passes the Senate, it's still a longshot getting this through the House."

"Yes, it is, but longshots always have the best payouts. Think about my offer."

National politics is high-stakes poker. You need to have nerves of steel, know what the right move is, and learn to bluff. Most importantly, you need a little luck when there's this much on the line. There is one fundamental truth that completes the metaphor: if you go all in, you had better win.

CHAPTER THIRTY-SEVEN

TIERRA CAMPOS

Veni, Vidi, Vino Wine Bar
South End, Boston, Massachusetts

Desperate times call for drastic measures. After not finding this FBI agent at the rally, and getting my ass kicked in the process, I try a different approach. The team caught a break tracking down Victoria. It turns out she likes wine as much as I do.

"This honestly would have been the last place I would have looked for you considering what happened outside," I say, taking a seat across the table from her.

"Who are you?" Victoria asks, annoyed.

"My name is Tierra. I work for *Front Burner*."

"I don't talk to reporters. I sure as hell don't share my table with one. So, if you don't mind."

"I don't blame you. We make for lousy company, always asking questions and all that."

"What happened to your head?"

I touch the spot where I got clubbed by Skull Face. It's still tender. Fortunately, there's no concussion or other permanent physical damage. The emotional impact is another story entirely.

"You're not the only one who dislikes reporters."

"Look, I don't know what you're looking for –"

"Who I'm looking for, actually. I'm here to talk to you."

Victoria leans back in her seat. Everything about this woman is no-nonsense. It's the type of attitude most females have when they have to survive in a male-dominated profession. I know the feeling.

"Why?"

"My editor has this crazy idea that you're investigating Brockhampton."

I watch as Victoria's face changes to something more remorseful. "The official investigation of Brockhampton is closed."

"Which is why yours is unofficial."

"Your editor is wrong."

"Maybe. I've only worked for *Front Burner* for like five minutes."

That piques her interest. "Where did you work before?"

"WWDC News in Washington."

"Washington? Wait," Victoria says, her eyes lighting up. "You're the reporter that interviewed Ethan Harrington."

If that's my claim to fame for the rest of my life, I'm going to throw up.

"And got fired, doxxed, victimized in a home invasion, and assaulted in a parking lot for my troubles."

"Sounds like you've had a rough stretch of luck."

"You have a gift for understatement, Agent Larsen."

Victoria picks up her glass of what I assume is either Cabernet Sauvignon or Malbec and takes a sip. The waiter shows up and asks what I'd like. She gives me a slight nod, so I order a Chardonnay.

"I know a little about retaliation myself," she says, flashing a half-smile, "especially recently. Nobody wants to ask questions about what happened in Brockhampton."

"Have you ever asked yourself why?"

"It's the question I ask most."

"And?"

Victoria starts to say something and stops. I don't press her. I thought it'd be a long shot that I'd keep my seat for ten seconds. She's armed and clearly in a lousy mood. I suppose that's why she's sitting alone. I don't want her to regret letting me order.

"I know you don't know me, Victoria. I'm a journalist, and we don't have the best reputation. But that's not the kind of journalist I am."

"I'm supposed to believe that?"

"God, no. I wouldn't."

The waiter shows up with my wine, and I take a long sip from the glass. It tastes like heaven. Of course, with what I've been through lately, even boxed wine would do the trick.

"There's a backstory to that interview with Ethan that makes this personal for me. My producer handed me a canned list of questions right before we went on air. Someone outside of the station wrote them. It defeated the purpose of letting me interview a fellow school shooting survivor. I was pissed, so I went off-script."

"They must not have liked that."

"My producer was screaming in my ear so loud that I took out my earpiece. Something was amiss when Ethan mentioned that Caleb was a friend, so I gave him the chance to clarify his statement. Then he couldn't even name a victim from the school. That was newsworthy. I couldn't understand why my EP got so upset."

Victoria's face softens. "He wanted you to shut up."

"Exactly. Nobody in that newsroom was interested in finding the truth. Nobody in this country asks the hard questions."

"Let me ask you a question, Tierra. Do you think there's more behind this?"

"Don't you?"

"I thought so. Now I'm not so sure. Either way, it isn't worth my career to bet it all on a hunch."

I lean forward. "What if it wasn't a hunch? Would you risk it then?"

Victoria's eyes narrow. They were aggressive questions to ask, but I have nothing to lose. I haven't begun to earn her trust, but she's intrigued. The fact that she hasn't told me to go pound sand is a step in the right direction.

"What are you proposing?"

"We trade notes."

"Why? Are you positioning yourself for a Pulitzer or something?"

"No more than you're trying to become FBI director."

Victoria crosses her arms. The FBI has every reason to hate the media, and I'm sure they engrain that distrust of reporters into their new agents. I have one shot at this.

"I first learned the five core principles of journalism when I was in high school. Truth and accuracy, independence, fairness and impartiality, humanity, and accountability should be as sacred to us as the Hippocratic Oath is to doctors. The difference between my peers and me is that I follow them."

"Nobody talks like that anymore."

"My father always said I was an idealist. I might not be able to change the world, but I can get this right. Maybe that will inspire others to do the same."

"Do you think that Ethan Harrington knows more than he's saying?"

"I think there are a lot of irregularities in the narrative and that people have a right to know the whole truth about what happened."

Victoria pushes her hair back off her forehead, smoothing it out. It looks like it was probably tied up in a bun before she came here. She doesn't strike me as the kind of woman who leaves it down very often.

I've done all I can do. The choice is hers to make. I only need to have the patience to endure the silence and await her decision, which isn't easy.

"Okay, but first, I have a ground rule: anything I tell you is off the record."

I shake my head. "I can't agree to that, Victoria. If something nefarious is going on, I'm going to tell the story. That includes anything you tell me. I will attribute anything we discuss to a source within the FBI familiar with the matter. That's it. Nothing will get traced back to you."

She didn't like that one bit. Again, it's a trust thing. "And if I say no?"

"It's still a free country…I think."

CHAPTER THIRTY-EIGHT

SPECIAL AGENT VICTORIA LARSEN

The Hotel Devereux at Copley Square
Boston, Massachusetts

Victoria was in awe when she arrived at the hotel room. She knew *Front Burner* is a money maker despite being so new, but the cash they're burning on this hotel must be ridiculous. She expected to meet Tierra at a Motel 6 or Red Roof Inn, not in one of Boston's top hotels.

Despite agreeing to this, it takes idle chatter over coffee for Victoria to gain enough trust in Tierra to move on to the business at hand. One of her cardinal rules is never to place her career in the hands of a journalist. It's not the first one she's broken in the last couple of weeks.

Tierra offers to go first to break the ice and explains all the questions they have and what her team has uncovered. There is nothing in terms of hard evidence, but it is intriguing. Victoria's discovery about the white car at the shooting range is her best lead, but nothing has come of it. It feels like a dead end but remains an unanswered question. There's nothing she hates more than that.

"You have no idea who owns the Mustang?" Tierra asks.

"I've been trying to track down a connection for two weeks. It doesn't belong to anyone associated with Caleb or Brockhampton High."

"Okay. How sure are you that the car is involved in this?"

Victoria rubs her neck in frustration. "Honestly, I'm not sure of anything. My gut tells me that whoever was driving that Mustang was paying for Caleb's range time."

"That's good enough for me."

"But not for my superiors. Look, Tierra, my career is already in jeopardy. The OIG is going to discipline me. I wouldn't flinch about fighting the bureaucrats if I had any evidence to go on, but I don't."

"So, let's find some."

"It's not that easy," Victoria says, shaking her head.

"No, it isn't. The investigation was shut down. I asked questions and was attacked twice in two different cities by the same guys. You asked questions and got shot at. Do you know what that sounds like?"

"A conspiracy. That's a stretch, Tierra."

"I doubt it's some backroom cabal that swears blood oaths never to utter their secret, but powerful people don't want anyone looking into Brockhampton."

Victoria stares at the granite countertop. She's thought about the conspiracy angle herself. It was strange hearing it from someone else, and that's the problem. She knows what her motives are. Can she say the same about a journalist she just met?

"What do you want to do?"

Tierra exhales deeply. "All we have are questions. The only thing I can think of to do is ask them publicly."

"Wait! You want to write an article?"

Victoria crosses her arms. It's the type of thing someone with an agenda or an eye on impressing her new boss would recommend.

"There's bound to be an overreaction when we ask questions and present what we know in the public sphere. We're not going to get anywhere doing a passive investigation. Someone has to make a mistake for us to learn anything."

"You're assuming someone will."

"You're the FBI investigator. If you have a better idea, I'm all ears."

Tierra has a point, and Victoria knows it. It could work. Lord knows that she employs a similar technique when interrogating suspects. Only this time, she's gambling with her career. She also knows that it's in equal peril by doing nothing.

Frustrated with the no-win situation, Victoria leaves the small kitchenette and paces around the room. Tierra lets her think it over without interruption. She's not lobbying for her approach, nor is she touting the merits of publishing the story.

"They'll accuse me of leaking to the press."

"It's not an official investigation, so there's nothing to leak."

"Tierra, if you screw me over…"

"Then, I imagine you'll put your gun to good use."

"Can I ask you a question? Why are you so sure about this? We don't have a smoking gun. It's all circumstantial."

"You're wondering if this is personal for me? I was doxxed and had my identity stolen. Thugs broke into my apartment and then attacked me in a parking lot four hundred miles away. Someone powerful called my news director and had me fired. Yeah, it is a little personal now."

"If you write an article, will your editor print it?"

"He will if it's a good one."

"Do I get to read it?"

"That's a violation of journalistic standards, but there is a workaround. You'll have to help write it."

The corner of Victoria's mouth curls up. She will never fully get over her trust issues, but this is an excellent place to start trying. The nation needs to know everything about the Brockhampton massacre. A warm feeling washes over her, and she enjoys that sensation. She's no longer in this alone.

"Okay," Victoria says. "We need more coffee first."

CHAPTER THIRTY-NINE

ETHAN HARRINGTON

Mayfield Estate
Brockhampton, Massachusetts

Connor summoned him to the house with an angry text message. Ethan doesn't like being treated like he's a servant but wants to know what the big emergency is this time. He grumbles about being up this early as he pulls into their driveway.

He parks in the usual spot and stops in the foyer after letting himself in. A couple of deep breaths help him keep control of his temper. Connor usually is in the back yard. Today he's leaning against the kitchen island, studying his laptop, and drinking a mug of coffee. Whatever this is must be serious.

"What's the big emergency?"

"Have you checked the news?" Connor asks, glancing up from the open laptop with accusatory eyes.

"Not recently, no. I was sleeping. What did I miss?"

"This."

He spins the device around. Ethan grins and expects to read something stupid, annoying, or both. He gets to the end of the headline and understands why his friend is in such a panic. His heart rate accelerates out of control after contemplating the impact.

"What the hell is this?"

"A problem. Read the byline."

The headline was jarring, but the name of the author is what hits him hardest. He shakes his head as he rereads it three times, feeling it can't be real. Typed in block letters underneath the article: By *TIERRA CAMPOS*

"You have *got* to be kidding me. She's an unknown television reporter! What the hell is she doing writing articles for *Front Burner*?"

"I thought you said this was handled," Connor seethes, the evenness of his voice masking a bubbling cauldron of anger.

Ethan doesn't answer. He reads the article to see if it matches the provocative headline. Few ever do in today's mainstream media. This one does. When he finishes, Connor looks like he's about to have an aneurism.

"There's nothing to this."

"Nothing? They're questioning the money for the shooting range. They mention the car, and you're seriously telling me it's nothing? How would they even know that?"

"She's fishing for a story. The whole article will get ignored. Other respected news organizations won't run with this."

"I guess you think that the AP and Reuters aren't respected news organizations," he says, nodding at the laptop.

Ethan checks the browser tabs loaded with articles from the two news organizations. They highlight unanswered questions about the Brockhampton shooting, and both reference Tierra's article. That was fast.

He should know better. *Front Burner* may be the newest member in the guild of news organizations, but their no-nonsense approach is exploding their readership and revenue growth. Tierra's article is a classic offering. There's no injection of opinion or speculation about a conclusion.

"The reporter you 'took care of' found herself a new gig. Nice job," Connor says, the sarcasm dripping from his lips.

"How is this my fault?"

"Because, idiot, you made her a martyr. This bullshit is getting picked up because of who she is now as much as what she wrote. She now has a platform that happens to have millions of readers."

"We can pass her off as bitter and looking for revenge," Ethan offers.

"Does that article read like she's either of those things? It doesn't seem so to me. She didn't even mention your name."

Ethan takes a deep breath. He's been here five minutes and is already tired of this conversation.

"What could she learn? The investigation is closed, and Lizzie is in a coma."

"I don't want to find out. Do you?"

"All right, so we have to stop this."

"Yeah, no shit. I'll talk to my father. You need to talk to Baino and focus on getting the bill passed."

"I don't control the congressional schedule, Connor."

"Then do what Standish wants and ramp up the public pressure starting with the rally here. Do something unexpected that will catch people's attention."

"Like what, a song and dance? It's a rally, not a Broadway musical."

"Do whatever it takes. Get creative. Damn, do I have to think of everything?"

Connor shakes his head as he heads out to the patio. Ethan's not about to follow. He doesn't need Connor barking in his ear, so he heads for the front door.

Baino can't fix all his problems. Another cyberattack on Tierra will draw suspicion, but the same doesn't go for her employer. If *Front Burner* wants to jump into this battle, then they're going to learn how it feels to be in the crosshairs. He needs to get home and fire up his laptop. He has a task for his friends.

CHAPTER FORTY

SENATOR ALICIA STANDISH

The National Mall
Washington, D.C.

Brian Cooper struggles to keep up with Alicia, even with her walking in heels on the gravel path that traverses the green space. She hasn't said much since they left the Hart Building. He's a veteran of several of these angry walks during his time as her chief of staff, a couple of them in snow and rain. He knows this is the calm before the storm. Alicia is a rumbling volcano. It's not a matter of if she erupts, it's when.

The National Mall spans almost two miles between the Capitol steps and the Lincoln Memorial. They've walked about half that distance as they approach the Washington Monument. She has usually blown her top by now. This meltdown is going to be a rough one.

"Have you settled down yet, Senator?" Brian asks as they cross Fifteenth Street and head for the concentric elliptical paths that circle the Washington Monument.

"I'm fine," Alicia responds, the sharp tone of anger resonating in her voice.

"Yeah, you sound fine."

Brian tries to enjoy the brisk walk while he can. It's a sunny day, and the scenery is beautiful. He loves the National Mall, with its tree-lined avenues and open space flanked on both sides by the treasured museums of the Smithsonian Institute and monuments celebrating American history and its remarkable figures. It's now a prominent part of the city and referred to as America's "front yard."

"I told Conrad to keep the FBI out of this," the senator finally says. "He looked me straight in the eye and said he would. The attorney general made the same promise to the president."

"There's no official investigation."

"There doesn't have to be. The *Front Burner* article referenced an FBI source close to the matter."

"Who is no doubt the rogue agent that Conrad warned you about at the fundraiser. The DOJ is more than capable of handling it. Let them."

"What are they going to do, fire her? It will raise even more eyebrows."

The senator is equal parts passion and logic. She relies on Brian to restore the equilibrium between the two on occasion. That is often the purpose of these walks. It's been a much harder task to accomplish over the past few weeks.

"All that article did was ask questions. That's it. They sounded like crazy conspiracy theorists, and you should dismiss them as such."

"Brian, you're being too cavalier, unless that's why you wanted Ethan out of Washington. Unless you think there is something to this," Alicia says, stopping in the middle of the sidewalk.

"Ethan has been a big help to the gun control cause. His value ends there. He's not going to push this over the finish line."

"So you've already said. I took your advice and sent him back up there."

"But you haven't divorced yourself from him or Action Not Prayers. You need to."

Brian can feel the tension radiating off his boss. Senator Standish is headstrong and loathes people telling her what she should and should not do. He usually has more tact in these situations, but the circumstances have changed, and so must the tactics.

"I know you think they had that reporter doxxed."

"I think they can't be trusted."

"Or you're wrong, and they can."

"You don't pay me to be wrong, Senator."

"No, I pay you to be my chief of staff, give me sound advice, and fix problems. This article is a problem."

"And my advice is that it's a problem for investigators, not us. I don't know if they'll find anything. All I know is that if you isolate yourself and the bill from them, it won't matter."

"You don't get it, Brian," Alicia says, walking again. "If we do that, it will look suspicious regardless of what happens. I am not going to risk this bill because of speculation. If you don't understand that, then I'm going to question why I hired you."

"And if you continue to come to their defense, I'm going to question why I accepted the job."

Alicia stops in her tracks and fires off the angriest look Brian has ever seen. He regrets his tone but not his words. She's the boss, but it was going to come to this. He knows he can't back down until she sees the truth. It's too late to take it back anyway.

"Do you have something to say?"

The senator knew Ethan was her guy from the moment he spoke into a camera. She never really vetted him, just like she didn't check out Action Not Prayers when Ryan approached her. Brian avoided criticizing the activists early on because they were useful. He didn't want to explain his misgivings to the senator.

That was a mistake he's desperate to rectify. His instincts scream that Ethan is hiding something. He knows that Ryan Baino is toxic. She is risking her career and her campaign for the presidency by associating with them.

"I do. You've been going through the motions since you introduced that bill. It was meant to be a starting point for bipartisan agreement, but now you treat it like the Holy Grail. In the meantime, the fire in the public's belly has burned out. Questions are getting asked. If you want –"

"That's not true!" she shouts, directing her anger at him while garnering the attention of some camera-wielding tourists around them.

"Respectfully, Senator, it is true. The media don't care about a factual debate. They care about ratings and advertising dollars. There is a controversy brewing about Brockhampton, and you'll regret wading into it. You'll lose the momentum you need."

"America is with us."

Brian shakes his head. "Americans are obsessed with reality television because they like peering into the lives of other people. News divisions cover the world using the same formula because they need drama and division to increase their ratings."

"The media wants my bill almost as badly as I do," the senator counters.

"Senator, everyone likes to watch big shots fall. If Ethan or Ryan is the least bit shady and you get involved, all the change you're pushing for will get lost in the noise."

"Your constant prattling about my relationship with Action Not Prayers is getting tiring."

"And what happens if I'm right? I have no idea what Tierra Campos's agenda is, and I don't care. Where there's smoke, there's fire. You need to get the Safe America Act passed before the country finds out for sure, and you can't get Republican support if you're linked with Ethan and Ryan."

"I'm working as fast as I can."

"No, you're not. Senator, you have primary debates coming up. You need the win. Make a deal with the Republicans on a softer measure."

"You mean you want me to sell out to them?"

"I mean secure the victory. A softer bill is better than no bill."

"Tell that to my parents," Alicia says, clenching her teeth.

Brian takes a deep breath. "What happened to your parents was tragic, but a better way of honoring them is to become president of the United States. The Safe America Act will guarantee the nomination but will kill you in the general election with moderates and independents. Not passing any bill will cost you both. That's the political reality. A deal is the best option you have."

"I appreciate your opinion, Brian, but I've already decided. I'm not abandoning my allies, and I'm not compromising on the bill. Since you can't accept that, I have no choice but to go forward without you. You're fired."

Brian rubs his forehead as he watches her walk back up the National Mall towards the Capitol. That gamble didn't pay off. He thought she would listen to reason, but she's fixated on her path. He can only hope she can live with the consequences.

CHAPTER FORTY-ONE

SPECIAL AGENT VICTORIA LARSEN

Victoria's Apartment
South Boston, Massachusetts

South Boston is one of the best neighborhoods in the city for anyone uninterested in spending an excessive amount of time commuting to work. The area has abundant shopping and dining options, bars, and recreation to go with easy access to public transportation. It's also safe.

Victoria unlocks the door and enters the apartment. She locks it behind her and drops her keys in the dish on the small, beat-up table that was here when she moved in three years ago. Her hand is reaching for the light switch before she freezes. The hair on the back of her neck rises as she scans the dimly lit apartment. Something feels off.

She quietly slides her weapon out of its holster and removes her heels, not wanting the clicking sound they make on the hardwood floor to give away her location. Her eyes adjust to the darkness as she pauses her breathing to listen.

The kitchen is empty, so she trains her weapon on the living area. The ambient light coming through the windows is just enough to let her make out the furniture in the room. There aren't a lot of places to hide except for the upstairs loft and the small bathroom. She quietly creeps over and peers through the partially open door for signs of an ambush. There are none.

Victoria takes a deep breath and rechecks the grip on her weapon. She does a quick analysis: someone could be behind the door. She pushes on it, crouching low. It bangs hard against the wall. The bathroom is empty.

She wheels, pivoting on her feet to point her gun at the black, wrought-iron spiral staircase that leads up to the loft bedroom. Quietly, Victoria creeps over to the far wall and glances at the latches of the small double-hung windows. Both are locked and secured. She takes a long, deep breath and exhales slowly. That leaves the loft left to check.

Stairwells are "fatal funnels" in building-clearing operations. They are narrow, confining, and offer no cover or concealment. Her stairs twist, making it even more harrowing.

Victoria lowers the temperature on the thermostat, causing the old air conditioner to crank up. It rattles and is generally loud, much to her usual annoyance. Now she hopes it will help mask the noise of her movements up to the second level.

She ascends the stairs at a quick, even pace as the air conditioner clangs to life. Near the top, she scans the loft that doubles as her bedroom for movement. What she can't see is the other side of her bed or inside the master bathroom.

There is no subtle way to do this. Victoria charges around the end of the bed, leaning to the right, weapon canted, ready to fire. Nothing. She jerks her weapon into the direction of the bathroom and lets out a couple of sharp breaths.

The door is wide open, as it always is, but nothing is visible in the darkness. Victoria opens the nightstand drawer and retrieves the emergency flashlight. Holding it next to her sidearm, she slides her finger to the trigger and clicks on the light.

The white beam bathes the master bath in light. It's empty. Victoria edges forward, shining the light through the glass shower door, expecting a figure to be hiding in there. There isn't one. She exhales deeply and switches off the flashlight, relieved that she's the only one here. She returns downstairs and turns on every light in the apartment before holstering her gun. Her neck is still tingling. It could be paranoia, but the initial feeling she had walking in hasn't left her.

Victoria looks around. She has lived on her own for a long time and is particular about the way she likes things. There is no laundry on the floor. The remote is put in the same spot on the end table after the channel is changed. Her small desk in the living room is always neatly arranged…except for now. She stares hard at her laptop computer on the desk. Her palms begin to sweat as the adrenaline pumps again. The lid is open, and the device is off-center.

Someone tried to access the computer. That's unnerving enough, but she's also aware that the apartment could be bugged with audio or video surveillance. She could sweep it herself or have colleagues do it to know for sure. Unfortunately, it's not inconceivable whoever was here also works in her building.

There's no point in sticking around to find out. Victoria heads upstairs, packs a bag, and heads out of the apartment. She double-checks that she locked the door behind her. Not that it matters. Locks only keep honest people out.

Victoria settles behind the wheel and starts the car, certain that Tierra's article had the desired effect. Someone doesn't want them asking questions, and she needs to learn who before things get dangerous. What scares her most is that someone risked shooting at and breaking into the home of a federal agent. What else are they willing to do?

She wants to call and warn Tierra, but she left her phone in the apartment since it might also be compromised. There's no point in risking the internal GPS giving away her position when she can pay cash for a burner phone. She'll give Tierra the number tomorrow.

Victoria drives a few miles away and checks into a mid-priced hotel room with good security and a twenty-four-hour front desk. The deadbolt and doorstop engaged, she drops her bag on a chair and pulls the window shade down. Content that the room is secure as possible, Victoria crashes on the bed without bothering to turn on the television.

No judge would have issued a warrant for surveillance on her. If this is the FBI watching her, they violated her rights as a sovereign citizen. Their incursion into her apartment was a crime perpetrated against her by an agency to whom she swore an oath. Whoever gave the order to break into her place took this too far.

She stares at the ceiling before closing her eyes. This is about more than her being a rogue agent. She was shot at. Tierra was doxxed and assaulted twice. Someone doesn't want them asking questions, and that someone may be in the FBI. Even if it costs her everything, she is going to pull back the covers and expose whatever they are hiding. She made a promise to those families, and she's even more determined now to fulfill it.

* * *

The black car is parked on the far side of the hotel's small lot, between an SUV from Pennsylvania with a stick figure family of four affixed to the rear window and a 3-series BMW probably belonging to some businessman cheating on his wife. The driver faced his vehicle away from Victoria's window to avoid being visible through the windshield. He adjusts the rearview mirror to keep an eye on the room. There's been no movement since she closed the shades, and that was the first thing she did upon entering.

He's never stalked a federal agent before. All but the most paranoid people stumble through life oblivious to his presence. They have their faces stuffed in their mobile phones, checking social media while listening to music on their headphones. They have no situational awareness whatsoever. This woman will be different, and he likes the challenge.

Content that his assignment is in for the night, he hits redial on the burner phone and listens as the call is picked up immediately at the other end. Neither party bothers with greetings.

"It's quiet."

"Did you get anything from her computer?" the voice on the line asks.

"I copied her hard drive. Nothing obvious on it so far."

"Is surveillance in place?"

"Yes, but she left her apartment in a rush."

"Where is she?" he asks, after a sharp sigh.

"A hotel near Longwood Medical."

"Okay. Continue to report her movements."

The line goes dead. The man grimaces, setting his phone down in the console. He checks the scan of the cloned hard drive running on the seat next to him. No results have popped up, so he settles in for the long wait until morning.

CHAPTER FORTY-TWO

TIERRA CAMPOS

Brockhampton High School
Brockhampton, Massachusetts

The warning I received this morning from Victoria has rattled me. She urged me to take appropriate precautions without specifying what that even means. Since I didn't have a clue, I called down to Washington and asked the team for some advice – for as much good as that did.

Any elation Austin had over my convincing Victoria to work together has morphed into dark fears that we're in danger. The attack on me in the parking lot shocked everyone. Tyler and Jerome volunteered to come up here. Even if I wanted help, what could they do? They are nice guys, but hardly warriors. Their fear over what happened to me had just started to subside before I called with this news.

I steer my rental car into the parking lot of Brockhampton High School. Everything about it makes me believe it's a typical American high school. Maybe it was once, but not anymore.

"Well, this is different," I mumble, after parking the car and walking toward the entrance to the school. This place is a fortress. There is less security guarding Area 51. The town and the State of Massachusetts must be paying a fortune for all this manpower to be here.

If this is the new reality of school for this generation, no wonder kids are scared of their shadows. The district wasn't joking when they warned parents and students to expect "enhanced security measures" after the shooting. A year later, all the barking about keeping kids safe has resulted in a horde of humanity pooling at the entrance of the school as they wait to enter. A shooter interested in inflicting mass casualties would drool at this. It's a killing field.

It wasn't like this at my school after the attack. All we got was a week off. There was a higher police presence when we returned, but this is insane. Students wait behind metal barricades while officers check their clear backpacks. This is a show to appease parents, townspeople, and the media who stoke their outrage. These measures are overkill and meaningless. Anybody wanting to sneak a gun or bomb into the school still can. All that the magnetometers and invasive searches are accomplishing is making students even more distraught.

Massachusetts State Police officers stand off to the side with a watchful eye as each student gets scanned like they were attending a concert or sporting event. I wonder if things would have been different had they been here the day of the shooting. One of the officers approaches me, sensing that I'm not supposed to be here.

"Can I help you?" he asks, extending his hand in the universal gesture that means stop where you are.

"Yes sir, my name is Tierra Campos. I'm here to see Principal Nebbich."

"Is he expecting you?"

"Yes, I called him yesterday to arrange it," I explain, meaning I called but never got past his secretary.

"Do you have identification?"

I pull my wallet out of my purse and hand him my D.C. driver's license. A glint of recognition precedes a grimace when he sees my name. Celebrity isn't all it's cracked up to be, especially when you're a journalist. People despise the media.

"Wait here, please," he says, turning away to talk into his radio. Five seconds later, two burly men swing the front doors open and stand watch over me as he disappears into the foyer.

A couple of minutes go by. The Main Office has windows overlooking the entrance to the school, and I see blinds part briefly. A moment later, the door opens, and the officer strides out alone.

"The principal isn't interested in meeting with you. I'm going to have to ask you to leave." One of his fellow troopers takes a couple of steps closer to me. They have experience dealing with prying reporters trespassing here in search of a story.

"I thought he might say that."

"Leave now, ma'am, or we'll physically escort you off the grounds."

"I'm not here to cause trouble, officer. Could you please give this to him? He's going to want to hear me out, even if he doesn't know it yet."

The trooper stares at me, measuring my resolve and determining how much of a problem I'll be. From a physical standpoint, not much. However, these men don't want to end up in a confrontation with a journalist in front of teenagers armed with cameras on their smartphones. That's my superpower.

"Sir, I can imagine you're tired of dealing with the media. I don't blame you. Trust me when I tell you that Principal Nebbich is going to want to read what's on that paper. Please give it to him, and if he still doesn't want to meet, I'll leave without a fuss."

He stares at the thin envelope like it contains anthrax. "Don't move."

I do as he says, not wanting to provoke any of the men watching me. There is a chance that this may work, but it's more likely not to. Those odds change dramatically when the principal comes storming out of the building.

"What the hell is this?" Nebbich demands, waving the paper in front of my face.

"An article scheduled for publication on *Front Burner* within the next two hours."

"Nothing in this is true! It's slander, and you know it."

"It's called libel when it's in print. You can scream that it's untrue, but my sources say otherwise," I argue.

The red-faced principal reminds me of an angry cartoon character minus the smoke coming out of his ears. My pleasant smile masks the smirk of knowing not a word of my last statement is valid. I didn't like having to resort to this, but I wasn't going to get to talk to him based on charm.

"It's a hit piece! Get her out of my sight!"

"Come with us, ma'am," the state trooper orders.

He grasps my arm firmly, but not aggressively. A local cop also joins the group of men. I don't resist, but I'm not finished talking.

"That's fine, Mister Nebbich. It's not going to ruin my career."

The principal stares down at the paper hard before looking up at the sky and shaking his head. I grin a little as the troopers begin to escort me back to the parking lot.

"Wait!" he says after we make it a third of the way down the sidewalk. "What exactly do you want, Miss Campos?"

"Answers to a few questions. If I can get five minutes of your valuable time, I will kill that article."

Nobody likes blackmail. People need to feel like they're in control of their destiny. I patronized him but also gave him an irresistible escape route.

"Give us a few minutes, please," he says to his guardians.

I'm happy to see the troopers move off, but I wish they'd wandered farther away. I don't want them possibly overhearing this. There's no telling who I can and can't trust in this town.

"Okay, you get three minutes. If I don't like your questions, I'm walking away, and you can print your article. My lawyers will handle the lawsuit against you."

"I know you've been through the wringer since what happened here. I'm not looking to do that."

"Get on with it, Miss Campos."

"Were Caleb and Elizabeth bullied in school?"

The question catches him off guard. Whatever reason he thought I was here, that wasn't it. And he's right. It's not why I'm here.

"Bullying is not tolerated here, period."

"Yes, I've read about the assemblies you've had, but what happens when someone reports bullying?"

He narrows his eyes at me. "We thoroughly investigate every complaint from a student or parent, but there aren't many of them."

"What about the ones not reported? What about the kids who take the abuse out of fear of what may happen if they do?"

"That doesn't happen in this building."

I frown. That's an ignorant statement. It happens everywhere.

"Did Elizabeth Schwarzer ever file a report?"

"No," Principal Nebbich states, with an emphatic tone and shake of his head. "She was quiet and unpopular. She kept to herself. My staff tried talking to her, and guidance counselors tried getting through –"

"I was told by a credible source that Elizabeth Schwarzer spent a lot of time writing in a black and white notebook. Did you know that?"

"I've never heard that, but it's not uncommon."

Does this guy know anything about kids today? "This is a digital generation, Principal Nebbich. They use devices, not notebooks. Believe me. It's uncommon. Was her locker cleared out?"

"That's a question for the police and would be documented in their reports."

I stare at him impatiently. "Did Caleb have any friends?"

Nebbich studies me for a moment, probably wondering if I'm circling back to the bullying question. If anyone asks him what we spoke about, it will be how he characterizes the conversation. The beginning and end of any discussion are always the most memorable.

"Are you asking whether I was surprised Ethan Harrington said that they were friends during your interview? Yeah, I was. He must have misspoken. I've never once seen them together."

"It's not at all what I was asking, but thank you for clarifying. What about after school?"

"I wouldn't know, would I?" Principal Nebbich asks, clamming up. "The only person I ever saw him with was Lizzie, and it was always on school grounds."

"Since you brought it up, Ethan is a leader. He must have been popular. Could he have bullied Caleb and said they were friends during my interview to cover it up?"

Principal Nebbich chuckles. "That's absurd. Ethan wasn't a leader or even popular before the shooting. He only spent time with Connor."

"Connor?"

"Connor Mayfield. The two have been best friends since middle school from what my staff has told me."

"Do you know if Connor and Ethan have remained friends since their graduation?"

"No, I don't. Is there anything else?"

"Yeah, one more thing. I know none of your students own one, but have you ever seen a white Ford Mustang in the parking lot? Maybe a car that was borrowed?"

Nebbich gives me a puzzled look. "I don't spend time learning what cars students drive, but I don't remember ever seeing one."

"That's what I figured. Okay, thank you for your insights on the bullying."

"If there was any bullying, I swear, I never saw it," the principal says, his tone quiet and sad. "I've asked myself if I missed anything… The truth is Caleb was pretty much invisible. I wish I had seen something…anything. Maybe I could have stopped it."

"I know that you would have, Principal Nebbich. Thank you for your time. I'll get out of your hair."

"Miss Campos? What about that article?"

I pull it from my pocket and rip it into small squares. "Completely off-base."

Nebbich nods and makes his way past the state troopers and back into the building. I feel sorry for him. He may be a bit of a jerk, but he's endured a horrible experience that I wouldn't wish on anybody.

The information about the car confirms what Victoria already learned, but it was worth asking. The principal was upfront with me, but I didn't learn anything outside of Connor Mayfield's name. Victoria never mentioned him either. I don't recall Ethan ever mentioning him in an interview. That's odd. Could Ethan have been confused by my question and meant Connor instead of Caleb? He wasn't a victim in the shooting, so it's unlikely.

I make my way off this hallowed ground with another question and no answers. Who Connor Mayfield is will be one more thing I'll have Janey and Logan track down. I hope Victoria is having more luck than I am.

CHAPTER FORTY-THREE

ETHAN HARRINGTON

Robert Treat Paine State Park
Brockhampton, Massachusetts

The darkness of this place is unnerving. Ethan zips up his jacket to fight that feeling as much as to combat the chill in the air. This park isn't the safest place for a meeting, which is probably why Baino chose it. It's secluded and empty enough where nobody would hear him scream. He shakes off the thought. He's been watching too much *Dateline*.

Like most eastern states, countless lakes and ponds dot the Massachusetts countryside. Just north of the Brockhampton town line is a popular park with a boat ramp, snack bar, and small strip of sand that counts as a beach for many of the locals. It's a fun place for families without a lot of disposable income to spend a day. His nights in this area were spent north of the beach in a spot that's a popular hangout for teenagers. One of the memorable nights he spent there led to this journey.

A pair of headlights rips down the drive from the main road. It's either the guy Ethan's waiting for, or it's a police car patrolling the park. He'd almost be okay with the latter right about now. This place is creeping him out.

The car pulls up behind Ethan's vehicle with his high beams on. After a moment that feels like an eternity to Ethan, the driver gets out and meets him between their cars.

"Are you Andre?" Ethan asks, eyeing him with some trepidation.

"Are you Ethan?"

Ethan gives him the "you can't be serious" look. He has the most recognizable face in America right now.

"This is a strange place to meet, don't ya think?"

"Would you rather discuss this at a Dunkin' Donuts where there are people, cops, and video cameras?"

Ethan frowns. There's nothing illegal about a conversation with this guy, but nobody wants to advertise the meeting. He's okay with not being seen with this punk.

"You don't look like Antifa."

"What does Antifa look like?"

"I don't know. Dressed in black with bandanas and cardboard shields, I guess."

"The black bloc only dresses like that during operations. Plus, I'm not Antifa."

"Sorry. I was told… Never mind."

"Antifa and my group are cousins of a sort. We believe in some of the same things but have different ways of getting results."

Ethan wants to ask but decides against it. Whatever this guy's into, it's not legal. It's best not to ask questions if you shouldn't know the answers. He'll ask Ryan if he gets any more curious.

"How do you know Ryan Baino?"

"We have a working relationship. Let's leave it at that."

"Did he tell you what we need?"

"He gave me the highlights and told me you could fill in the details, including providing the list of speakers and what order they're coming on stage."

Ethan hands him a sheet of paper with the names and approximate times of their speeches printed on it.

"What do you need that for?"

"It serves as cues for when we need to be in place. You want this to happen after your speech, right?"

"Yeah."

"Don't sound so enthusiastic. You sure you want to do this?" Andre asks when Ethan finishes.

"It needs to be done. It just has to be believable and not look staged."

"No problem."

"The police don't like any kind of disturbances at these rallies. Do you guys know you'll likely get arrested?"

Andre smirks. "Not a day goes by that we don't think about that. It wouldn't be the first time."

"Does anyone else know that you're meeting with me?"

"If you're wondering whether this can get traced back to you, no, it can't and won't."

Ethan wouldn't usually take that at face value. He has no way of knowing whether it's the truth, and it likely isn't. If this weren't necessary, he'd tell the guy to go pound sand. Unfortunately, like it or not, Ryan trusts him, and Ethan needs to.

"Any other instructions?" Andre asks, folding the paper and shoving it into the pocket of his jeans. "There won't be any more contact between us, including through Ryan."

"Yeah, don't screw it up."

Andre flashes a smug smile. "See you at the rally."

He climbs in his car and pulls out of the parking lot. Ethan watches the taillights wind up the drive before disappearing on the main road. He opens his car door, reassured by the dome light cracking through the darkness around him. See him at the rally indeed.

CHAPTER FORTY-FOUR

CAPITOL BEAT

Cable News Studio
Washington, D.C.

Wilson never goes through the motions, even on a news program that airs seven days a week. He always brings his A-game. The man known around journalistic circles for having boundless energy and an unmatched work ethic has dedicated his entire life to this job. He knows what good journalism is.

Maybe that's one of the reasons he's stayed in the game so long. Journalists have devolved from speaking truth to power to engaging in political punditry skewed to advance personal, often biased agendas. News reporting is more about the reporters than the events they are reporting.

Wilson also knows he's getting too old to keep up this tempo. Once he retires, his place among the pantheon of American journalists is guaranteed. However, before the lights go down on his long and distinguished career, he needs to find a successor willing to carry the torch he lit decades ago.

"Good Evening," he says, on cue from his set producer. "It is Monday, May twentieth; I am Wilson Newman and this…is…*Capitol Beat*."

The music plays as the opening graphics roll. It's the shortest opening of any television news broadcast. This show doesn't need much by way of introduction.

"America is consumed by the gun control debate raging in the nation. Tonight's story could be the latest on the controversial Safe America Act and its journey towards a floor vote in the Republican-held Senate. It could also be about the comments from the Senate Majority Leader or the bill's sponsor, Senator Alicia Standish of Massachusetts. We could even bring you more about the protests and counter-protests or the thoughts of people on Main Street, U.S.A.

"Instead, it will be none of those things. Tonight, we will focus on the Federal Bureau of Investigation. In 2016, the James Comey-led Bureau came under fire for its involvement in investigating possible collusion of the Trump campaign with the Russians during the presidential election cycle. How that investigation started, was conducted, and the evidence that initiated it came under incredible scrutiny during special prosecutor Robert Mueller's investigation and by Republicans in the Senate for years following it.

"When she was appointed, Attorney General Lisa Ehler promised to ensure the FBI remained a non-partisan entity. Safeguards were put in place to ensure the investigative powers entrusted to that critical organization were not abused to advance an agenda.

"Years later, it once again finds itself dragged into the middle of a partisan fight. But is that true, or is it mere speculation? Is the FBI injecting itself into the gun control debate, or are they being cast as foils for opponents to hinder efforts in Congress?

"The media have had their say. Since a *Front Burner* article in recent days began questioning the completeness of the Brockhampton investigation, both sides of the debate have initiated a war of finger-pointing. The American Firearms Association and Republican firebrands in Congress are using it to claim that the inquiry was flawed. Left-leaning politicians and news sites have accused the FBI of running a shadow investigation to sabotage the bill ahead of a Senate vote.

"Will the greatest chance for gun control reforms in a generation be lost because of forces outside the halls of Congress? Is the Safe America Act too controversial to pass a partisan legislature? Those are the questions we will pose tonight to a slate of guests, and let you, the viewer, decide."

Wilson shifts his view to a different camera when the red light above his blinks out. It's a visual cue that there is a shift to a new segment. With his introduction over, now he's ready to get into the meat of the subject.

"Joining us over the next hour is Deputy Attorney General Conrad Williams, spokesman for the American Firearms Association Oren Balshaw, Governor Landon Flynn of Massachusetts, along with congressmen from both sides of the aisle, our in-house political experts, and pollsters from the Marist Institute of Public Opinion who released some surprising results about America's view of the Safe America Act. My final thoughts will follow all of that.

"Before I introduce our first guest, let's see how we got to this point."

The lights in the studio dim. It's unnecessary since the video package is broadcast directly from the control room for the viewing audience. Wilson ordered it because he enjoys the short break from the white-hot lights when he can get one.

The pause also gives the crew a chance to get Conrad Williams settled in and make final adjustments to his makeup and microphone. The anchor shakes his hand warmly, but the men don't exchange pleasantries. It's something that Wilson has always found comical. Only first-timers are chatty on set. Program veterans are ready for battle when they are seated.

Wilson knows he needs to be careful in his approach tonight. He prides himself on his non-partisanship and is equally intense when going after both Republicans and Democrats. This is different. Shows like his are becoming extinct because the American public wants their preferred television programs to take sides. Honest debate and critical examination of the issues are going to join the dinosaurs in extinction.

The gray-haired goliath of the Beltway has been doing this for too long to change his ways, despite the direction that news directors and producers want him to go. His ratings are excellent, but that is never enough for them or their corporate masters. They demand more, even if that means sacrificing his journalistic integrity.

Wilson checks the timer of the video package as it counts down on the far wall. At five seconds, he takes a deep, cleansing breath as the studio lights come back up to full illumination. It's showtime, and his turn to play ringmaster in the circus that has become of this issue.

CHAPTER FORTY-FIVE

SPECIAL AGENT VICTORIA LARSEN

The Hotel Devereux at Copley Square
Boston, Massachusetts

The act should feel like a betrayal of her principles. "Thou shall not cooperate with the media" and "the media are an enemy never to be trusted" are two of the most prized and respected tenets of the law enforcement community. Although she'll never admit it publicly, Victoria is starting to enjoy these information-sharing sessions with Tierra.

She keeps telling herself that this is different. Tierra isn't a typical journalist by any real measure. She's curious and driven, but somehow also manages to be balanced and fair. The first article they worked on could have been a hit piece about Ethan penned only for the satisfaction of payback. Instead, it only questioned the investigation and highlighted everything that authorities still don't know.

Her account of the conversation with Nebbich was illuminating. The media have portrayed the man as a weasel, horrible administrator, sacrificial lamb, and God's gift to America's education system. Every news organization either sang his praises or thrashed him after the shooting. A week later, they would flip. Nobody knows what to believe now, which makes his reluctance to speak to any journalist understandable. It also makes Tierra's ability to break down that barrier and get a human moment out of him impressive.

"So nothing about the white Mustang?" Victoria asks when Tierra finishes reciting what little she learned.

"Did you expect him to know something?"

Victoria frowns. She didn't, but she hoped that lead would turn into something more than the dead end that it is.

"No, I guess not. I don't ever remember reading anything about Connor Mayfield."

"Are you sure the FBI report didn't mention him?" Tierra asks as Victoria begins leafing through the printout of the report.

"The names of all the students we contacted are on this list… His name's not here."

"Why would he be, though? The investigation focused on Caleb and what Lizzie may have known about his intentions."

"That's true, but the FBI took statements from every single student in that school, and even the ones who were absent that day."

"Did he fall through the cracks?"

"Maybe."

Victoria's response was half-hearted. Things like this don't get overlooked. There should have at least been a statement, even if it was only documenting that he didn't see or hear anything. There's no easy way to explain an omission of this magnitude.

The revelation hits Victoria with the force of a hammer. She flips open Tierra's laptop, who gives her a disapproving look. It's a relatable feeling. Victoria would break someone's hand for using her computer without permission.

"Are you going to log into your fancy FBI system?"

"No. Authentication issues aside, it could tip off my colleagues. I'm doing the next best thing: I'm consulting Special Agent Google."

"Special Agent Google? Are you serious?"

"The World Wide Web is the best source of information in the history of man. Agent Google knows everything," Victoria says, quoting one of her instructors from Quantico.

"He's also the best source of misinformation unless you believe everything you read on the Internet."

Victoria shrugs. "We take the good with the bad."

The results for "Connor Mayfield Brockhampton" reveal nothing. His father's name comes up instead. She opens a new browser tab and types his name and the town. It takes just over half a second for Google to blow up three hundred thousand results, most of them useless.

Victoria clicks on the profile done for a regional business magazine of a company called Urban Gables. There are no direct quotes in it other than the boilerplate language from a public relations executive, but there is a list of impressive projects and the name of the owner: Joseph Mayfield.

"Interesting."

"What is?" Tierra asks, moving around the counter. "Something about Connor?"

"No, his father. He's a prominent real estate developer responsible for high-end housing projects in and around Boston."

"Sounds classy."

"Not really. A lot of these results are about various accusations of bribery and corruption surrounding his company. This guy is shady as hell."

"I can have the team check his political connections."

"You can," Victoria says, checking the images tab on the browser, "but they won't find anything outside of pictures at the occasional charity benefit. Men like him stay in the shadows and control things behind a cloak of anonymity."

Joseph Mayfield may be crooked, but Victoria doubts even a two-year investigation loaded with enough warrants to turn his life upside down would find anything that could put him away. He'd use cutout companies or proxies to hide his illegal acts, providing him plausible deniability. She's seen it before.

Tierra exhales and collapses on the couch. "Do you think we have this all wrong?"

Victoria stares at Tierra over the laptop. That's not something she wants to hear after staking her career on this. The question is a reminder that Tierra can walk away from this any time she wants. Victoria can't.

"What do you mean?"

"We both think that Ethan is hiding something about what happened at Brockhampton. What if he's not the only one?"

"Connor Mayfield?"

"Maybe he's a chip off the old block. Like father, like son…always in the shadows. That's why there's no statement from him about the shooting."

"Maybe. It's a stretch."

"Yeah, it is," Tierra says, rubbing her eyes.

Victoria loads the next page, and a picture catches her eye. She leans in and squints. A shiver runs down her spine as she reads the caption.

"Uh…Tierra? You might want to come and take a look at this."

Tierra gets off the couch and joins Victoria at the small island, where she's given room to read what's underneath the photo of Joseph and a man in uniform. "Businessman Joseph Mayfield from Urban Gables Development joins Massachusetts State Police Lieutenant Detective Howard Spivey at the MetroWest Medical Center charity fundraiser… Is Spivey who I think he is?"

"If you mean the guy in charge of the Brockhampton shooting investigation, yes."

"It could be a chance encounter," Tierra says.

"Yeah, but they look pretty chummy to me."

Victoria stares at the picture. It's a coincidence. There's no reason a state police investigator wouldn't know a prominent developer. The only problem is that she doesn't believe in coincidences.

"Urban Gables…Urban Gables. I've seen that name before," Tierra mumbles.

"Where?"

"I don't… Can I have my computer back, please?"

Victoria slides it over and watches as Tierra opens up a spreadsheet. "What is that?"

"This is from Janey. She's one of our researchers at *Front Burner.* After you gave me the tip on the white Mustang, she got a list of all owners in the state with a car that fits the criteria. She then did records searches on the names and found addresses, occupations, and current…employers."

Victoria sees Urban Gables highlighted in yellow after Tierra does her search. The two women look at each other and then back at the screen.

"It might not mean anything," Tierra says, half-heartedly.

"You're right. I'm going to go find out for sure."

"You're not thinking of showing up at his house and asking him?"

Victoria grabs her things. "No, visiting the house is a bad idea. I was thinking about asking at his job site."

"You can't be serious."

"You're the reporter. What would you do to chase down a lead?"

"All right. Do you need me to go with you?"

"No, I'll do this alone. Do you think you can figure out where Joseph Mayfield is working today?"

"Probably. I can at least narrow it down."

"Okay, text me when you do. It might come in handy."

"Victoria?" Tierra says, causing her to stop at the door. "Please be careful."

CHAPTER FORTY-SIX

SENATOR ALICIA STANDISH

Vietnam War Memorial
Washington, D.C.

Alicia walks past the Three Soldiers Statue and follows the path to the Vietnam Veterans Memorial. She remembers how much criticism the sleek monument received when it was unveiled in 1982. It was a departure from the classic designs of the Lincoln and Jefferson Memorials, and purists decried the architectural heresy in a city known for its use of white granite and marble.

Yale University student Maya Lin designed it that way for a reason. The black granite's reflective nature allows visitors walking past the memorial to see their reflection amongst the names of the 58,000 servicemen and women who lost their lives in the Vietnam Conflict. Right now, she sees her own and can feel a connection to those who perished in that war.

"This is about the last place I'd have expected to find you," Conrad says, coming up alongside her as she stares at the names.

"Then you don't know anything about me," Alicia says, wiping away a tear. "My father was a first lieutenant in Vietnam."

"I thought he died… He's not on this, right?" Conrad asks, staring at the wall.

"No, but men from his unit are. Right there – panels Thirty-five and Thirty-six East. The Battle of Saigon during the Tet Offensive. My father was critically injured during fighting around the radio tower and came close to joining them. In hindsight, he should have died that day."

"How so?"

"Demons tormented him throughout my childhood. He lost a lot of friends during that horrible war and suffered from PTSD long before anybody knew what that was. The day after I graduated from college, he put a gun in his mouth and pulled the trigger. At least he lived to have a family when so many didn't."

"That must have been hard."

"Not as hard as mom's death. She was a public relations consultant who loved to spend her free time helping the downtrodden. She was a saint. Then, one day, one of those lost souls decided to take her life with a Smith & Wesson MP 9mm handgun for no particular reason."

"It sounds like it wasn't a crime as much as a tragic waste of a beautiful life."

"It was," she says, her eyes drifting across the names on the wall. "I should get the government to commission a work that memorializes every victim of gun violence in this country. It would take a mountainside, not a few granite slabs."

"I know the loss of your parents is why you're fighting so hard for your bill. And your bill is why you asked me to meet you here to revisit our talk at the charity benefit."

"Yes, the conversation where you promised that the FBI wouldn't get involved."

"And they didn't. I told you, it's a rogue agent –"

"How does that happen, exactly? Since when does an FBI agent have time to conduct a personal investigation? Is there not enough crime up in Boston to keep him busy?"

"Her."

"What?"

"Keep *her* busy," Conrad corrects her. "The agent's name is Victoria Larsen. She's an excellent inv–"

"Whatever," Alicia says, annoyed that the deputy attorney general felt that matters. "Answer the question."

"There are plenty of open cases, but she –"

"Is being permitted to run an unsanctioned investigation in her spare time? Come on."

"Not at all, Senator. We've taken appropriate action. Internal authorities are handling her referral, and her boss is being compelled to cooperate."

"Is he cooperating?"

"Yes."

"Then why is this agent still investigating?"

It is a question and an accusation, and one that puts Conrad back on his heels. He stares at the ground as he fidgets.

"Does the FBI think the investigation into Brockhampton needs to be reopened?" Alicia asks, staying on the offensive.

"I'm sorry?"

"The state police conducted a comprehensive investigation in Brockhampton after the massacre. The *Front Burner* article highlighted a lot of questions about that inquiry, alleging that it was incomplete. Are they right, or are they just trying to get clicks to boost their advertising?"

"The FBI offered support until it was no longer needed. We reviewed the report and were satisfied that they examined every lead. There are open questions about every shooting. Hopefully, we'll learn what Caleb's motive was someday. That article was largely speculative and focused only on rumor and innuendo."

"You're saying that the DOJ's position is that it's a false story? Fake news, as they say?"

He straightens up a little. "That's our belief, yes."

"Okay. Then this needs to end, Conrad. You have an FBI agent continuing to investigate for what I must assume are partisan purposes."

"We know. I've talked to Lisa about it, and she has had conversations with the FBI Director. It will be handled."

"I'm glad to hear that the attorney general is on the case, but I want to see action. It looks to me like this agent is trying to discredit the Safe America Act by alleging some vague conspiracy behind the massacre."

"We don't know –"

Alicia holds a finger up to silence him. "It doesn't matter if that's the truth. It's the appearance that matters. I refuse to let FBI interference cast a shadow over this bill."

"I understand. I promise you, Senator, we'll handle this quickly."

"Good. Then, don't waste time talking to me."

Conrad nods and walks back down the sidewalk that runs the length of the wall. Alicia takes one more look at the names forever etched in granite. So many have been lost in war. Many more have been lost in gun violence. She touches one of the names on the wall with her index finger. She may not be able to stop wars, but she'll do whatever possible to stop the senseless violence in her own country.

CHAPTER FORTY-SEVEN

CAPITOL BEAT

Cable News Studio
Washington, D.C.

The news broke fifteen minutes before the broadcast. It's too fresh and politically charged to ignore. It wouldn't be the first time Wilson has ordered the rundown tossed out and prepared the staff to improvise the show in front of a live national audience.

The direction of the program for the next hour is in the capable hands of the executive producer and the bookers who are furiously lining up interviews. There will be no time to prep questions for any of them. This is what live television should be about, and it's exhilarating to the old journalist. Wilson prefers the unscripted chaos over dry, carefully crafted productions. He gets to be one of the first to explain what happened and what it means to America.

"Good Evening, it is Thursday, May twenty-third, I am Wilson Newman and this…is…*Capitol Beat*."

The music plays as short opening graphics roll. Nothing appears on the teleprompter except the word "VAMP." Meaning 'improvise' by pianists and jazz musicians, the word made its way into theater through vaudeville and then into the world of live television. It's one of Wilson's favorites to see, as uncommon as it is.

"We start tonight with some breaking news today coming out of Massachusetts. Elizabeth Schwarzer, the eighteen-year-old friend of Brockhampton High School shooter Caleb Pratt, emerged from her year-long coma today. Days after the shooting, Miss Schwarzer was found severely beaten outside a vigil being held for the victims. Doctors questioned if she would ever recover from that trauma, and that has been answered today.

"We are waiting for statements from Elizabeth's doctors and the family attorney Preston Swain. When we receive them, we will bring them to you. We will start tonight with Boston affiliate WBOS reporter Patrick O'Shea, who has the latest from outside MetroWest Medical Center in Framingham, Massachusetts."

The lights dim, and Wilson checks the timer for the segment. Patrick's report is going to take around ninety seconds.

"What's next?"

"*We just received the statement from Elizabeth Schwarzer's attorney. Then we'll go with social media reaction to the news*," his producer says through his earpiece. "*Twitter is blowing up.*"

"I bet," he grumbles.

"*Graphics will be on your monitor. You'll have thirty seconds to comment before we put up the statement. Back in ten seconds.*"

Wilson glances at the clock and waits for the red light on the camera. When he reads the tweets on the screen, he's sick to his stomach. Social media turns rational people into scoundrels. Society would never tolerate the behavior widely accepted in the digital world, and nobody hates that more than he does.

"Thank you, Patrick."

"*We have the statement on Screen One,*" the producer says.

"Before we dive into America's response to the news, we have just received a statement from Preston Swain, attorney for the Schwarzer family. It reads:

We were blessed with a miracle today. After more than a year since the day Elizabeth Schwarzer sustained traumatic head injuries dispensed by unknown assailants, she has emerged from her coma. Miss Schwarzer is currently listed in guarded condition at MetroWest Medical Center. Her grandmother has joined her at her side as doctors and nurses continue to provide her excellent care.

The family continues to press authorities in state and local law enforcement to further investigate the egregious and despicable attack on her. We have received several requests from investigators to interview her and will entertain them only when progress has been made in uncovering the identity of her attackers and when she is medically able to participate in interviews.

Until then, we will continue to work toward her full recovery from this malicious assault.

"That statement was from Preston Swain, attorney for Elizabeth Schwarzer. The social media reaction to the news has been mixed. People are optimistic that she might provide long-sought-after answers to the motive behind the massacre, while some are spewing hate at a young woman because of her alleged involvement.

"Strong emotions about the Brockhampton shooting are understandable, but this rhetoric is not constructive. Many people were shocked at those who celebrated Elizabeth's beating a year ago. Social media was filled with messages of hate because they feel she deserved it just for being friends with Caleb. It was a mob mentality.

"Caleb was dead, and people wanted justice administered, regardless of whether Elizabeth knew anything or not. They didn't care that it was thugs who dispensed it or the fact that if she had died, anything she knows would have died with her. That's something America should want to hear.

"We will have more about this breaking story when we return after the break."

"*You're going to get a lot of hate mail over wanting to know who attacked her instead of her explaining what she knew about Caleb*," the EP says after the lights dim for commercial.

"I get hate mail every time I open my mouth. Why should today be different?"

"*Yeah, but this is different. Our audience won't be happy about it*."

"My audience tunes in for facts and objective analysis, not pandering. Law enforcement needs to answer both questions."

"*Yeah, but –*"

"What's next?" Wilson asks, cutting him off. He has a show to finish. The last thing he needs to worry about is how his words will be received by a public that's offended by everything these days.

CHAPTER FORTY-EIGHT

ETHAN HARRINGTON

Brockhampton Rally Planning Meeting
Brockhampton, Massachusetts

Few Americans know how much work goes into holding a rally. They can't appreciate what needs to happen before a speaker utters a word or attendees shout a slogan. Ethan never understood it until he met Ryan Baino and started organizing them with Action Not Prayers.

The Brockhampton Rally committee relocated from Connor's house to the cramped apartment of one of its members and the planning went well past dinner. Ethan didn't tell them why the change in venue was needed, although he had a lie ready in case any of them asked. Nobody did.

"I want to change the order of the speakers for the rally. What do you think?" Prudence asks, handing him a laptop.

Ethan grimaces and scans the screen. They've put together an impressive list of speakers, so finding the order that amplifies the message is an essential task that they need to get right. Unfortunately, it was already locked in at the moment he turned the list over to Andre.

"Why is the governor speaking first?"

"Isn't he supposed to because of like, protocol, or something?"

"That's like eating the meal before the appetizer. Move Flynn to the end," Ethan orders. "Just like it was on the original list."

"That means he'd be introducing you," Prudence observes.

Ethan smirks. "Exactly."

"I thought you'd want to have the Parkland gang introduce you."

Under ordinary circumstances, she'd be right. The kids from Marjory Stoneman Douglas High School are trailblazers. It would be an honor for them to handle the introduction. Ethan admired them long before the Brockhampton massacre, but the pull of being brought onto the stage by the governor of Massachusetts and one of Senator Standish's staunchest allies is irresistible.

"The Parkland gang can introduce the governor and remain on stage off to the side for his remarks. When he finishes, he will introduce me. I will enter from the left, shake his hand, and embrace each of them. Do it as we originally planned. It will be better visuals for the media."

"Okay."

The main goal is to get carried live by the cable news channels. The rally has to be good television. Speakers have to be quotable and available for follow-up interviews after the rally. The rally is about the message and its delivery. Prudence understands that better than most.

It sounds much simpler than it is. Most protests held across the country barely get mentioned on the news, even in today's twenty-four-hour multimedia news arena. The ones that get airtime either appeal to sympathetic news directors, or something spectacular happens at it that makes it newsworthy. Ethan is planning for both during his hometown rally.

A chyron on CNN catches his eye. He reads it and feels a sudden surge of anger.

"Hey, unmute that, will ya?"

The guy closest to the remote does as asked.

"Elizabeth Schwarzer awoke from her coma about two hours ago," a spokesman for MetroWest Medical Center says in response to a reporter's question.

"Was anyone in the room with her?"

"No. We were alerted at the nurses' station when her vitals changed."

"Have police questioned her?" another reporter shouts.

"Police are present in the building, but she is not yet strong or alert enough to be questioned at this time. We will permit it when she is medically fit to do so."

"Good. Now maybe they'll reinstate the death penalty and fry the bitch," one of the guys says from the other side of the small living room.

"The legislature will never bring that back, even for a monster like her," Prudence argues.

"Assuming she even knows anything," another chimes in.

"Lizzie went to the range with him every week. She knows something."

"Whatever. What do you think, Ethan?"

Ethan isn't listening. Oblivious to the other organizers in the room, he gets up and selects Baino's number from his cell. It rings as he heads to the bathroom and closes the door.

"I heard," Ryan says after the call connects.

"Now what?" Ethan asks, not wanting to say anything specific.

There's a long silence on the other end of the line. Ethan is about to start yelling at him.

"There's not much I can do."

"What do you mean? You said you would handle things for me. Do it again."

"It's not that simple. We'll talk about it later."

The line disconnects. Ethan plants his hands on the vanity and stares at himself in the mirror. Bags are forming under his eyes. He looks as weary as he feels. Shaking his head, he punches up another number and hits send.

"Hey, Bro. I just heard," Connor says on the other end of the line. "What's Baino going to do about it?"

"Nothing."

"What do you mean 'nothing?'"

"I mean he isn't going to do a damn thing. He says there isn't anything he can do."

"Shit."

Ethan shakes his head as he paces the bathroom. "There's only one option left. You have to talk to your father."

Connor exhales, sounding like a gust of wind muffling the line. "I don't know, Ethan. He isn't going to like that we didn't tell him."

"We have no choice, Connor. You know what's at stake."

"Yeah," he says, his voice quiet and resigned. "Swing by when you're through there."

"Will do."

Connor hangs up. Ethan's head starts pounding, and he massages his temples. Nobody can help them. Even if Connor's father does, it will come with a price. He balls his hands into fists as the helplessness overwhelms him. He picks up a heavy glass soap dispenser and smashes it against the mirror over the sink, shattering it into a thousand pieces. Not content with that, he pulls back his right hand, balls it into a fist, and punches it into the drywall, leaving a massive dent.

The door bursts open, and the guy who rents the apartment barges into the bathroom. His concern morphs into anger when he sees the damage.

"What the hell, man!"

"Sorry."

"Sorry? What the hell's wrong with you?"

"Nothing. I'm just a little stressed out."

The rest of the organizers gather in the small hallway outside. Prudence looks at the mirror and the busted wall before coaxing the owner back.

"It's okay; we'll get it fixed."

"This is bullshit."

"Relax, we can fix it. It won't cost you a thing."

Still unhappy, the kid retreats out of the bathroom as Prudence tells the others to give them a minute. When they move back into the living area, she closes the door.

"You okay?"

"Yeah."

"Who were you on the phone with?"

"Uh, nobody. One of my media contacts in Washington," Ethan says. "They aren't sending the reporter I hoped they would send to the rally."

"So you busted a wall, broke a mirror, and earned seven years bad luck? Come on, Ethan. Tell me what's going on."

Ethan considers it for a moment. He likes Prudence a lot. If Brockhampton had never happened and Ethan were in college, he'd ask her out. Now's not the time for that. He can't bring her into his confidence with this much at stake.

"It's nothing I can't deal with."

"This is you dealing with stuff?"

Ethan surveys the damage. He'll have to ask Ryan to pay for it.

"It is today. We have a lot of work to do. Let's get back to it."

Prudence wants to argue but decides against it. Whatever's haunting Ethan is for him to deal with, and she'll be there for him if needed. She returns to the group without another word, leaving him to contemplate this turn of events.

Ethan stares at his reflection in the shattered mirror. Elizabeth Schwarzer holds his life in her hands. If she talks, it's game over. For the first time since he embarked on this journey, the risks involved have become real.

CHAPTER FORTY-NINE

SPECIAL AGENT VICTORIA LARSEN

Urban Gables Development Site
Wellesley, MA

Wellesley is less than a half-hour drive from Copley Square. At least that's what her car's navigation system told her before the traffic congestion was factored in. Victoria knows some people who moved here last year. The town of thirty thousand is in the top five for median household and family incomes in all of Massachusetts, and ranks among the top ten wealthiest cities in the entire United States. That's why she doesn't live here.

She pulls her car into the street that leads into the development. Urban Gables builds nice houses. For their hefty asking price, they had better feature exquisite trim and moldings, modern kitchens, and all the conveniences a wealthy homeowner could ask for. She proceeds past them to the construction site, ignoring the signs warning her that she's trespassing.

Nobody pays her much attention, just like at the first site she visited. Workers go about their tasks, assuming she is just another homebuyer taking a peek at the progress. There are more trucks here than cars, and none of them are nice. She continues around the corner and scans the vehicles on both sides of the road. There are no Mustangs.

She exhales and shakes her head. Tierra said one of these two sites out of the six active developments was most likely. It looks like she was wrong. Victoria accelerates as she reaches the end of the construction and sees more finished units ahead. She catches something out of the corner of her eye and jams the brakes. Her heart rate quickens as she slams her car into reverse and looks into the unfinished garage.

"No way."

She pulls her car into the short, unpaved driveway and kills the engine while staring at the back of the car like it was a UFO. She climbs out and looks around like she's about to rob the place before taking a picture of the license plate with her phone.

"What are you doing?"

The voice startles her enough to where she reaches for her gun before stopping. A man in ratty clothes and a hardhat looks at her warily, and she relaxes a little.

"Good morning, sir. Is this your car?" He stares at her blankly, so she tries a different language. "Podemos hacerlo en inglés o español. Hablo ambos."

"Yes, I own this car."

Victoria is glad he chose English when given the option. Her Spanish sucks.

"And you work here?"

"Yes," he says nervously.

"As an employee of Urban Gables or a contractor?"

"Who are you?"

"Special Agent Victoria Larsen, FBI," she says, flashing her badge.

The man looks behind him like he's getting ready to run. Nobody likes getting questioned by a federal agent, especially immigrants, whether they have something to hide or not.

"I'm an employee. I'm here legally."

"I don't handle immigration matters, so I don't really care. What's your name?"

"Mateo. Mateo Morales."

"Where do you live, Mister Morales?"

"Worcester."

Victoria does the calculation in her head. Brockhampton is between Worcester and Wellesley. If he has been at this site since construction started a year and a half ago, it would be a quick and easy detour.

"Do you work on Saturdays?"

"Yes."

"Do you come straight to work in the morning?"

"Am I in trouble?" he asks, uneasy about the questions.

"Is there a reason to think you're in trouble?"

"No," he says after a short pause.

"Then, please answer my question, sir."

"Yes."

"You don't stop anywhere?" Victoria presses.

"No."

"Not for coffee, or a bagel, or maybe at a gun range in Brockhampton? Don't lie to me, Mister Morales. If you do that, you will be in trouble. Do you understand?"

His eyes give him away. Victoria's search is over. This is the car, Mateo is her guy, and this just got far more interesting. He looks around nervously, as if anxious that someone is watching them.

"I shouldn't be talking to you," he says, starting away from the garage.

"You're going to have a bigger problem than your employer if you don't. I can and will place you under arrest for conspiracy to commit multiple murders, and we will continue this conversation in an interrogation room."

"I didn't murder anybody!"

"I didn't say you did. You conspired with Caleb Pratt to commit them. Unless you're going to deny that you stopped by the Lead Rain Shooting Center once a week to meet him and Elizabeth Schwarzer there."

"I didn't… You can't prove I did anything."

"And yet we're standing here having this conversation. Are you willing to bet your freedom on that?"

Mateo is conflicted, and she knows he's more scared of talking than he is of Victoria. She's tempted to bring up what Mark Wilkerson told her, but doesn't want to give away too much.

"I'm going to level with you, Mateo. I have no interest in ruining your life. I don't think you were willingly involved in this. I think you were following orders. If I'm right, you need to tell me now."

"I was told to drop off an envelope to them once a week."

"What was in it?"

"I don't know. I never asked."

"What was in the envelope, Mateo?" Victoria demands.

He stares at the ground, kicking a rock with his boot. "Money."

"Who told you to deliver the money? Your boss?"

"No. The kid."

Victoria's eyes light up. "Connor?"

"Yes. He threatened to have his father fire me if I didn't do it. He said if I did as I was told and didn't ask questions, he'd arrange a bonus."

"Did you get the bonus?"

He nods quickly and then hangs his head in shame. "Five hundred dollars."

Victoria frowns. That's not much for a hush-money payment unless the person offering it was still in high school. It's also a fair amount for a man who works hard for long hours and probably has a family to feed. That's why Connor chose him.

"I don't want trouble. I need this job."

"I'm not looking to get you fired, Mateo," Victoria says, placing a hand on his shoulder. "I will take your statement when the time is right. Until then, this is between us. Here's my card. If anyone harasses you for talking to me, call the number on the back."

"Okay, okay," he says, wiping at the tears forming in his eyes.

"Now, get back to work before you get into trouble. If any of your friends ask what I wanted, tell them I'm thinking about buying and wanted to know about the construction quality."

He nods and moves off. Victoria climbs into her car and drives it out of the development. There is no doubt that a link exists between Caleb and Ethan. His best friend was paying for the range time. The question is, why?

She dials Tierra, who picks up on the first ring, and Victoria fills her in.

"That's amazing."

"We have a connection, but we need to understand what it means."

"Agreed," Tierra says. "So, what's the plan? Confront Connor?"

Victoria checks her rearview mirror and makes a mental note of the car behind her in the distance.

"No. I'm going to shake a couple of trees first. Text me the address of Urban Gables when you can."

"Will do. Be safe, Vic."

* * *

The man in the black car pulls out and follows Victoria at a distance as she heads towards the highway. A construction site is a strange place for her to come. He wanted to follow her into the development but thought better of it. If she suspected a tail, it would be the perfect place to find out for sure.

Whatever her reason for being here, it's something he needs to report. He picks up his cell phone and stops. What does he know that will appease the boss? He will ask why she was here, and he doesn't have an answer. She wasn't house hunting but could know someone who works here. He sets the phone down in the console. Maybe her next stop will shed some light on it.

The only option is to stick to the mission and make a report later. The road isn't well-traveled, so he hangs over a hundred yards back. This would be easier with a GPS unit affixed to her car. If Agent Larsen knows she's being followed, she hasn't let on. He thought this would be more of a challenge. He's losing respect for one of the FBI's best and brightest.

CHAPTER FIFTY

SENATOR ALICIA STANDISH

Hart Senate Office Building
Washington, D.C.

Some of Alicia's colleagues are cold, hard dictators who demand unconditional loyalty from their people and have chiefs of staff who run offices with an iron fist. Others treat their aides like a second family. She does neither and even kept her former chief of staff at arm's length. It's what made firing him easier.

"Settling in okay?" she asks, stopping by Rahul's office to find his face buried in his computer screen.

Alicia knows Rahul is a good man and a loyal soldier who is out of his element. He was a great deputy, but she's not sure he can successfully fill the role she needs him to. If he can't, she'll bring in outside help to advance her agenda. She's rooting for him; promoting from within is great for office morale.

"I'm still getting used to the job. Is there anything you need, Senator?"

"No, I've got things handled. What about you? Is anybody giving you problems?"

He takes his glasses off and sets them on his desk before rubbing his eyes. "Senator Wetzel is being difficult."

Alicia smirks. "I haven't talked to him in a while."

"He's nervous about the bill."

"He's nervous about his own shadow. I'll speak to him. What progress are you making with Velvick and Sheppard?"

"They're still on board after the deal you made with them. That could change if anything goes south."

"Then let's make sure nothing does."

Alicia is surprised her Republican colleagues are sticking with the program. The leadership must know their intentions by now. They'll have mobilized the caucus to apply immense pressure on them. The two senators will lose committee assignments and dollars needed for their campaigns. That's how the game is played. It's unfair, but a guarantee of reelection for Velvick and giving Sheppard something big to deliver for her constituents makes it a fair trade.

"Senator, you have a call from Governor Flynn," the reception says, after finding her in the hallway.

"Okay. Keep me in the loop, Rahul."

"Will do."

She retreats to her office and shuts the door.

"Hi, Landon. How's it going up in Boston?"

"Good afternoon, Senator. We're just fighting the usual battles. I imagine it's the same for you in Washington."

"It is. I meant to call you. You did a great job on *Capitol Beat* last night."

"Thanks," he says, his voice climbing a couple of octaves. "It isn't always easy dealing with a character like Wilson Newman."

"You mean the man who thinks he's the reincarnation of Edward R. Murrow?"

"Yeah, he does have a high opinion of himself. He's not the influencer that Murrow was by a long shot."

"No, he's a charlatan masquerading as an objective journalist. I despise his push to gain viewership and advertisers under the guise of nonpartisanship. Everyone has an agenda."

"I've dealt with worse, as I'm sure you have. I heard you wanted to speak to me about the Brockhampton investigation," the governor says.

"Yes, I did. There is an FBI agent poking around up there. The DOJ is handling the matter, but I wanted your opinion on the investigation the state police conducted."

"You want to know if I think they missed anything."

Alicia sits back in her chair. "Yes."

"Absolutely not," he says without hesitation. "I know the lead detective personally. Howard Spivey is as good as they come."

"And there's no chance he missed anything?"

"It would be out of character."

Alicia can't help but smile. Landon is a politician. Every statement he makes is a measured non-answer. He's decisive, yet his words are deniable. He has an eye on higher office someday.

"Are you afraid that this agent or some journalist is going to find something?" he asks.

"No. I'm afraid that they'll feed conspiracy theories that the Republicans will use to resist voting for the bill. Brockhampton is a focal point because of Ethan Harrington's involvement. I think they're trying to tarnish his reputation."

"Hmmm… Is that why you sent him out of Washington?"

Alicia starts playing with a pen on her desk. "He was doing more harm than good here, so I got him back in front of the people."

"That was smart. What are the chances your bill is going to make it through the Senate, let alone the House?"

"It's going to be close. That's why I asked Ethan to use his Brockhampton rally to ramp up the public pressure. I'd feel better about things if we could sway a few more moderate Republicans to join us."

"Did you know that I'm speaking at his rally?"

"Yes, and I thank you for that. Your support is greatly appreciated."

"It's the least I can do. Massachusetts was victimized by an unspeakable tragedy. The marathon bombing was bad, but we understood the motive, caught Tsarnaev, and got justice. Brockhampton was worse. Caleb Pratt may be dead, but we don't understand why he killed so many."

"Maybe Elizabeth Schwarzer can shed some light on it now."

"Maybe. I only hope your bill delivers some assurance to all Americans that we've taken the first steps to ensure this never happens to another community again. I'll do whatever I can to help you."

"I very much appreciate your support, Landon."

Alicia sets her pen down. She knows what this unconditional support is really about, and it isn't safeguarding the good people of Massachusetts. It's about landing a cabinet position in her administration to lay the groundwork for higher office, or maybe even a future run for president. Landon is young and ambitious, and Alicia will be more than happy to help his career along when she wins the White House.

"It looks like our party is putting a good lineup on the debate stage this summer. Are you ready for the primaries?" he asks, shifting to the election season that starts earlier and earlier in the modern age.

Alicia hasn't spent as much time in Iowa and New Hampshire as she otherwise would. Her advisors view the passage of the Safe America Act as her ticket to the nomination, so that's where her focus is. She lets her campaign staff handle enlisting volunteers and setting up a robust ground game to boost voter turnout. When the time is right, she can marry the two and ride into the convention like a conquering hero.

"We're building out our campaign infrastructure and fundraising. I think we're in a good position."

"I look forward to the opportunity to campaign for you."

"And I am eager to see you on the trail whenever I'm in New England. Let me know if anything changes up there. If I don't get the chance to talk to you beforehand, good luck at the Brockhampton rally."

"Thanks, I'm sure it will be an event to remember."

Alicia sets the phone back in the cradle. Brian Cooper's distrust of Ethan and Ryan has been gnawing at her since she fired him. She can now dismiss that as paranoia and relax. If Landon says the investigation is solid, she believes him.

CHAPTER FIFTY-ONE

TIERRA CAMPOS

The Hotel Devereux at Copley Square
Boston, Massachusetts

The phone at the office rings several times with no answer. That's odd. Austin is usually waiting at his desk for me to check in. His direct line leads to voicemail, but our team's main phone number sends a call to a hunt group that will bounce it around until someone picks up. I'm about to hang up and try that when the line connects.

"Hey, Tierra," Austin says, the stress in his voice evident. "This isn't a good time to talk."

"What's going on?"

"Our website is down."

"What? How often does that happen?"

"It's never happened. We have several layers of redundancy, including cloud hosting and backups synced in real-time in the event of a cyber or ransomware attack. Short of the Internet going down, our site never should."

I check for myself, typing *www.frontburner.com* into the browser. It returns 'ERROR 404 PAGE NOT FOUND'. I lean back from the laptop screen. This is bad. My news is going to have to wait.

"IT is working on it, but the outage started over twenty minutes ago, and there is no timetable to get the site back up."

"Is it a problem with the hosting company?"

"No. Our techs think it's a distributed denial-of-service attack. It means –"

"I know what a DDoS attack is. Any idea who's behind it?"

"No, everyone is more concerned about getting the site back online. Give your report to Logan and Tyler. I'll transfer you."

I sit down in the desk chair while he sends my call to their extensions. The guys pick up after the first ring.

"Hey, Tierra."

"Is this as bad as it sounds?"

"No, it's worse. We've never seen Austin like this."

"This can't be the first attack on *Front Burner*."

"Hell no, it happens all the time," Tyler says, "but this is the first successful one."

"I have a friend in IT," Logan adds. "She said the last time there was a cyberattack on this scale in the country, hackers exploited flaws in over a hundred thousand unpatched servers to overwhelm the bandwidth of the targeted web server."

I rub my face. If this was a deliberate and coordinated cyberattack, there's only one reason that Austin would be so stressed out about it. My stomach turns at the thought.

"Management thinks this is a reaction to my article, don't they?"

"Yup. They're demanding to know our sources, intentions, and the direction we're going in," Logan says.

"Austin is fighting them on it," Madison says, joining the conversation.

"Is he going to cave to their demands?"

They all laugh, clueing me in that the group listening in has gotten bigger.

"You don't know Austin very well," Jerome says, joining the party.

"All we did was ask questions. Why would someone do this?"

"That's a really good question," Tyler says. "It doesn't make much sense."

"Look, guys, we could be Ahab hunting the White Whale, but I think this goes far deeper than we thought. We found the white Mustang."

The team inhales so violently over the phone that it sounds like they sucked all the oxygen out of the room. I feel better now that I finally got to relay that, even if it wasn't to Austin.

"What? Who did it belong to?" Tyler asks.

"A guy named Mateo Morales. He's an employee of Urban Gables, the development company owned by –"

"Joseph Mayfield," Janey says. "The father of Ethan's best friend, Connor Mayfield."

"You got it. Remind me never to question your researching skills. Victoria confirmed that Connor had Mateo deliver money to Caleb at the range every Saturday morning. He never knew what it was for. Guys, this is a direct link between Ethan Harrington and Caleb Pratt."

The line goes quiet for a long moment. I stare blankly at the wall in front of me. It's a lot for them to take in.

"Maybe they were friends like he said during the interview," Madison suggests quietly.

"That's a stretch," Olivia argues.

"She's right. Ethan might not be involved at all," Logan says in agreement.

"So why don't we ask him?" Jerome asks.

"Because someone is going through a lot of trouble to cover up what's going on, and we think it could be the detective that was running the investigation."

"Howard Spivey?"

"There are photos online of him and Joseph Mayfield together. They're friends."

"That doesn't mean anything," Madison says.

"No, but Victoria was shot at and had her apartment broken into after meeting him. Evidence from the school was lost. Leads haven't been followed. He ended the investigation. What if he and Joseph Mayfield are protecting Connor and Ethan?"

"You think this is a conspiracy?"

"It sounds crazy, I know."

I'm annoyed that nobody says anything to refute that. They could at least assure me that I haven't gone completely off the deep end.

"Maybe it's just Connor. None of this points to Ethan," Olivia says, breaking the long silence. I was ready for that.

"They were best friends, Olivia. Ethan practically lived there in high school. If one of them is hiding something, I promise you, both are."

"You were assaulted twice. Do you think he's behind that too?"

I had already thought about that. It doesn't fit. There's no reason for a Massachusetts police detective to have a reporter attacked in Washington.

"I don't know."

"Then let's find out," Austin says, joining the conversation. "We might not have all the answers, but something about this still smells. All work on anything other than the Brockhampton investigation stops until we find out."

"The brass is okay with that?" Olivia asks.

"I don't care," Austin says with contempt in his voice. "They don't dictate what we investigate."

"Hey, I'm always down with sticking it to the man," Jerome says, "but what do you expect us to do?"

"I want to know everything there is to know about Howard Spivey, Joseph Mayfield, Senator Alicia Standish, and Action Not Prayers."

"Whoa. Where did that come from?" Tyler asks.

"They have the most to lose if there is something to uncover about the shooting," Austin clarifies.

While I appreciate his bravado, there's a danger in being so cavalier about this. Journalism isn't the same as it was when the *Washington Post* investigated Watergate, or the *Boston Globe's* Spotlight team brought the abuses of Catholic priests to light. It isn't even what it was five years ago.

"There's something we should consider before going down this path," Madison says, speaking up before I can. "The Safe America Act is coming up for a vote in the Senate. Won't we get accused of trying to sabotage it?"

"This isn't about the bill in Congress, Maddie. We follow leads and go where the facts take us. I'm not interested in opinions, speculation, or taking sides. Let them say what they want. So long as the facts are on our side, I'm content."

"What do you need me to do?" I ask.

"Elizabeth Schwarzer came out of her coma. See if you can find a way to get in to see her. Janey will send you the name of the family's legal counsel."

He can't be serious with that. I have a better chance at getting an audience with the pope than an interview with her. She hasn't even talked to the police yet.

"Any other miracles you want me to perform?"

"Start with that one. We'll talk about walking on water tomorrow," Austin says before hanging up the phone. Funny. Real funny.

CHAPTER FIFTY-TWO

SPECIAL AGENT VICTORIA LARSEN

Quincy Market
Boston, Massachusetts

Boston is chaos. Driving in a city whose oldest streets were laid out during Colonial times is not for the faint of heart. It'd be easy to think they followed random old cow paths, and Victoria knows that some of them were. Cars, bicycles, and pedestrians who embrace a culture of jaywalking all vie for space on city streets often while going in different directions.

Right now, she appreciates the chaos – there's nothing better when you're trying to get rid of someone tailing you. She picked him up right after leaving the Urban Gables development and getting on Interstate 95. He hung far enough back to avoid detection, but she'd seen the black sedan before. Victoria needed to be sure, so she took a circuitous route through the downtown. When her tail struggled to stay behind her, it left no doubt.

FBI agents are the hunters, not the prey, but time is of the essence. A plan forms in Victoria's head as she guides her car into the Dock Square Garage near Faneuil Hall. This plan is going to eat up time but may accomplish two goals at once. She finds a spot and parks, hurrying out of the parking structure without looking like she's in a rush.

Faneuil Hall is one of the main tourist meccas in Boston but remains a popular lunchtime spot with locals. The world-famous Food Colonnade at Quincy Market has thirty food merchants serving up cuisine from around the globe and is a sea of people at noon. Her tail will have to find parking and then manage to keep up with her through the mass of humanity. It'd be an incredible feat if he pulls it off.

Victoria eyes the man standing on the sidewalk as she heads toward the market. The glimpse was a brief one, but he's not anyone she recognizes. He casually follows her into the two-story granite structure, looking around and taking in the sights like a tourist. That's smart but not as impressive as his ability to find parking before she did.

Victoria enters the east side and begins weaving her way through the crowd. She stops abruptly to check out the menu of a rice and noodle place, forcing her tail to do the same. She continues forward, scanning menus hung over counters and on walls, gauging how close he's willing to get as they move deeper into the market.

He's about twenty yards back when she reaches the rotunda. Victoria makes her move. She turns right through the south canopy and picks up her pace when she exits the building. She hustles across the walkway toward a Christmas shop in the South Market, pulling off her jacket in the process. The display of ornaments on an artificial tree is woefully out of season but makes the perfect place to spy the plaza. She watches the man rush into the crowd of people, desperately searching for her.

Victoria zooms in the camera of her cell and snaps a picture. The man grows frustrated, picks a direction, and starts walking until he disappears back under the South Canopy. She heads in the opposite direction towards Faneuil Hall, letting her hair down to blend in more. The glass structure that houses the Government Center subway station looms just across Congress Street. Checking behind her, she sees the man running in her direction at a dead sprint.

"You've got to be kidding me," she breathes to herself before racing to the station and down the stairs to the platform just as the green line train pulls into the station. The timing is perfect. Victoria hops on and watches the doors close as the man races down the steps.

"How the hell did you catch up to me so fast, buddy?" she mouths into the window as the train pulls out. She plans on asking him at some point. There is no way he is tracking her by GPS. He would have found her in the shop if that were the case.

Victoria stares at the picture saved on her cell phone and a pit forms in her stomach. She has no idea who this man is, but she doubts he's in the FBI. That's a problem. Even if the surveillance is off the books, they still play by a set of rules. Now she doesn't know who she's dealing with and can't shake the feeling that she may be in real danger.

She tucks the phone in her pocket, content being safe for now. Victoria tries to shift her focus on what comes next. The first stop on the train is the Park Street station, and from there it's a quick walk through the Common to Beacon Street and the offices of Urban Gables. She checks her watch and frowns, hoping the boss decided to take a long lunch today.

CHAPTER FIFTY-THREE

ETHAN HARRINGTON

Velocity PR Offices
Boston, Massachusetts

These meetings are tedious. This isn't the first he's had at Velocity's Boston office, but it may be the last. Ethan is sitting in his conference room chair with his arms crossed as he gets another lecture. Tamara and Xavier are responsible for managing his public image, not his personal life.

"This isn't what I pay you for."

"You don't pay us. Ryan Baino signs the check, and at a steeply discounted rate. We knew you needed us to handle the volume of interview requests you were getting and only wanted to help," Tamara says, clasping her hands in front of her on the table.

"It was an advertising move for you, not a charitable one. Let's not pretend otherwise. I captured the attention of the country, and Velocity wanted to burnish their image."

"Fair enough," Tamara says, "but that doesn't change anything. I know you want to blame *Front Burner* for questioning what happened up in Brockhampton and Tierra Campos for asking you hard questions, but that isn't your problem."

Ethan shakes his head. It has been open season on him since Tierra Campos's article that questioned closing the investigation with so many unanswered questions. Worse, she brought up the missing videos and possible leads that haven't been chased down. It was a gift to the AFA.

"And what exactly do you think my problem is?"

"Others are following her lead. They've fixated on the story, and it's having an impact. You need to lay low for a while."

"Lay low? That's your expert advice?"

"It's the best course of action," Xavier says, leaning back slightly in his chair as he anticipates the blowback from their volatile client.

"Maybe it's time for a second opinion."

"Every crisis manager in the world will tell you the same thing," Tamara says, not as willing to hide her disdain. "We have a plan and need time to execute it. That can't happen if you're undermining everything we're doing."

"What exactly are you doing? It's not fighting for me."

"Not everything requires a confrontation, Ethan."

"Really? Confrontation is how I got this far. It's why you're working for me."

"A recent poll shows your trust factor at an all-time low. That's the real reason Senator Standish sent you out of Washington. Your negative mentions on social media are up tenfold since the Campos interview. It's not your positions they're attacking, Ethan, it's *you*."

"How would you know, Xavier? Do you work for the Geek Squad in your spare time? I know you aren't Genius Bar material."

"We have tools that monitor mentions and tweets across all social media platforms. Everything said about you online can be tracked. I showed you once so you could monitor it yourself, but I guess you weren't paying attention."

"Why would I? That's what I hired you for."

"Then let us do our job, Ethan," Tamara says, trying to take the heat off Xavier before he flips out on their client.

"I will when you actually start doing it. Here's some breaking news for you: we're getting ready to push through the strictest gun control legislation the country has ever seen. I won't let the AFA force me to hide because they launched a smear campaign."

"This isn't all because of the AFA, Ethan."

"What makes you think that?"

"Two decades of experience, for starters," Tamara says, losing her patience much like Xavier has.

"Is that it?"

"Ethan, you don't live under a rock. You see how heated the rhetoric is. That kind of thing happens when people are divided on an issue."

"I know you think you're worldly and all-knowing, Xavier, but you really aren't. Trust me. This is an organized attack meant to silence me."

"You're right. I forgot that you know a little about organizing attacks, don't you?"

Ethan's head shoots around. "What the hell is that supposed to mean?"

"Tierra Campos's doxxing. The DDoS attack on *Front Burner*. Pick one. You arranged both, and don't tell us you didn't."

Tamara stares at her associate but doesn't say anything. If it's a bluff, it's a damn good one. She's going to be pissed if Xavier held out on her. Ethan was one of her easier clients until he went to Washington. He was a kid who witnessed an unspeakable tragedy and was trying to make a better world when they first started working together. She hopes that Ethan wouldn't be that reckless, but celebrity changed him, and the Tierra Campos interview brought out an ugly side that Tamara had never seen.

"How dare you accuse me of that!"

"We can't help you if we don't know the truth," Tamara says, playing along. "Did you do it?"

"I'm flattered you think my hacking skills are that good."

"You know people whose are," Xavier answers. "Did you arrange it?"

"I don't need to listen to this," Ethan says, sending his chair careening backward after abruptly rising from the conference table.

"You're going to need our help to navigate this."

"I have a rally to plan. I don't have time to answer these ridiculous accusations. You were hired to help me. Stop interrogating me like I'm a criminal and do your jobs."

"We don't chase ghosts," Tamara says.

"Then what good are either of you? You're both fired."

Ethan storms out. He barrels past the glass windows and nearly knocks over one of their colleagues just before he disappears from view. Neither Tamara nor Xavier budges from their seats as several long moments pass.

"I wish I could say I wasn't sorry to see him go," Tamara says, breaking the silence.

"I can say it."

"That's because you don't have to answer to the boss. He isn't going to be happy about losing Ethan as a client."

"Trust me," Xavier says, "we just saved Velocity a whole lot of heartache. Something's not right with this guy."

"You don't really believe he's involved in something shady?"

"He went after Tierra Campos. I know that for sure. Why would he bother doing that unless he has something to hide?"

Tamara shrugs. He could be right. He could be wrong. Either way, Xavier isn't going to have to explain their getting fired to the honchos. It's not a conversation she's looking forward to.

CHAPTER FIFTY-FOUR

SPECIAL AGENT VICTORIA LARSEN

Urban Gables Beacon Street Office
Boston, Massachusetts

Victoria hates stakeouts. Her escapade at Quincy Market cost her too much time. She missed her opportunity to catch Joseph Mayfield at lunch and spent the last several hours stewing over it. She thought about waltzing into the office and pulling the fire alarm, then she dismissed it as a horrible idea.

Left with no other option but to wait, Victoria did whatever she could to fight the boredom while staying alert for her quarry. It's a relief when he emerges from the entrance to the building. She wastes no time crossing the street to catch him.

"Good afternoon, Mr. Mayfield."

He turns at the sound of her voice and gives her a look up and down while grinning. Victoria has looks that are bound to turn heads. That doesn't mean she appreciates being ogled. She can add being a scumbag to Joseph Mayfield's character flaws.

"Can I help you?"

"I hope so. Special Agent Victoria Larsen, FBI," she says, flashing her badge and watching the stupid grin disappear from his face. He turns and starts walking away.

"Am I under arrest for something, Agent Larsen?" he asks when she pulls up alongside him.

"Should you be?"

"You can talk to my attorney about whatever you want to discuss with me. Good day."

Joseph has the "talk to my lawyer" defense down pat. He must use that a lot.

"I can do that if you wish, but aren't you the least bit curious why I came to your workplace and ambushed you on the sidewalk? We both know you'll spend the next few hours obsessing over it."

"I'm assuming you're investigating my business for some reason."

"And you'd be wrong. I'm not interested in your shady development deals, although I am curious why state and local authorities aren't."

"Because they know that my business dealings are legitimate. What's this about then?" he asks, stopping to face her.

"I'm investigating the Brockhampton shooting."

Victoria spots the brief flicker in his eye at the unexpected reference. Microexpressions are impossible to fake or hide. She spent a lot of time at Quantico learning the technique to identify truth or deception without the aid of a polygraph machine.

"What does that have to do with me?"

"Nothing. Well, maybe nothing. It has everything to do with your son."

"You people are unbelievable. Connor was a victim. He was in that school when that psycho opened fire. I hope Caleb burns in hell."

"We agree on that, but I can't help but wonder if it's the whole story. What if there was evidence that Lizzie Schwarzer wasn't the only one helping Caleb Pratt?"

"You have some set of balls, don't you? That has nothing to do with Connor. If you come near my family or me, I'll destroy you."

Victoria is caught off-guard by the aggressive response. She didn't overtly accuse him or his son of anything that warranted a threat, especially from a man who spends each day dodging inquiries into his business dealings. She touched a nerve.

"Mr. Mayfield, did you just threaten a federal agent?"

"What if I did? Are you going to slap on the cuffs and haul me off? You don't know who you're dealing with, Agent Larsen. With one phone call, I'll be out of jail, and you'll be having an uncomfortable conversation with your boss."

Victoria stares hard into his eyes. "You're a very confident man. Did your son know Caleb or Lizzie?"

"My son had nothing to do with any of this!"

"That's a strong denial. I only asked if your son *knew* them."

Joseph glares at her. He knows he made a mistake and is angry at himself for it.

"If you question Connor without my permission, the only thing you'll get out of it is a lawsuit and embarrassing press. As if the Bureau needs any more of that."

"No, we certainly don't. Connor is nineteen now. I don't require your permission to speak with him. Let me ask you directly, Mr. Mayfield: was your son in contact with Elizabeth Schwarzer or Caleb Pratt at any time before the shooting at Brockhampton High School?"

"I wouldn't know."

"Would Howard Spivey know?"

Joseph's pupils dilate, and his breathing changes slightly. He won't answer the question because he'd be committing a federal crime. You have the right to remain silent or consult with an attorney when speaking with federal agents, but the U.S. Code makes it illegal to lie to one. There's no doubt in Victoria's mind that he knows that, considering his history.

"You would have to ask him."

"I intend to. How well do you know Detective Spivey?"

Joseph shifts his weight. He's not so cocky with his answers now.

"Our paths have crossed."

Victoria's eye's narrow. "Are you sure that's all?"

"Is there anything more, Agent Larsen?"

"Yes. Tell Connor I will be seeing him soon. Have a nice day, sir."

Victoria walks away, checking over her shoulder as she crosses the street to ensure he isn't following. She rattled him and confirmed that there's a connection between Joseph Mayfield and Howard Spivey in the process. Now she has to figure out what it is and how deep it goes.

CHAPTER FIFTY-FIVE

SENATOR ALICIA STANDISH

Office of Action Not Prayers
Washington, D.C.

Alicia drops down in the seat opposite Ryan's desk. She hates everything about this office and its collaborative design. Conference rooms and traditional office furniture work just as well as this crap, if not better. At least the head of Action Not Prayers has an appropriate place for her to sit and not a beanbag chair.

"You're honestly the last person I expected to walk into my office at seven in the morning, Senator."

"Less likely than someone from the AFA?"

"Not by much," Ryan says, leaning back in his chair. "What can I do for you?"

"You're holding an important rally next week in Brockhampton. You thought I wouldn't check in with you?"

"No, I assumed that you'd summon me to the Hill."

Alicia chuckles. "Capitol Hill is a nightmare right now. Advocates from both sides are laying siege to the Congressional office buildings. There's no hiding from them. It's best if you stay away."

"If you're afraid they'll start asking questions, they already are," Ryan says, pointing at his computer. "The *Front Burner* article opened the floodgates. A lot of media are now asking some of the same questions, and many are still wondering what Ethan meant during that interview. It's gaining traction."

"The DOJ will take care of the rogue agent feeding this garbage to *Front Burner*. I have bigger issues to worry about."

"Like problems getting votes?"

"Persuading politicians is like herding cats. Even if you round them up, it's hard keeping them penned in."

"You don't need my help with that," Ryan concludes.

"No. I need Ethan's."

Ryan leans further back in his chair and folds his hands over his chest. It was satisfying for him to hear this arrogant politician say she needs his help.

"I thought you sent him away because you could handle it yourself. If you need Ethan's help, talk to him. What do you need me for?"

"You're his mentor. You approached me with the idea of using him as a spokesman. Most importantly, Ethan respects and admires you. You can ensure Ethan conveys the proper message on Saturday."

Ryan gets angry. "You mean *your* message."

"I mean *our* message. We created this partnership because the Safe America Act benefits both of us."

"So, let me get this straight. Ethan's sacrifice to the cause is silence?"

"No, it's restraint. We're at a critical time, Ryan. Ethan's star isn't shining like it once was. If he starts attacking people, he'll damage his own reputation more than the AFA could hope to. He needs to focus on bringing more people under our tent, not shunning them."

"Attack politics works," Ryan argues. "His vitriolic words bring people to rallies."

"Setting attendance records in the NFL doesn't win you the Super Bowl. You've fought long and hard for this cause. This bill would be a huge win. Maybe that's why you're scared. Are you afraid you won't have a purpose if I'm successful?"

"That's ridiculous."

"It is ridiculous. I'm running for president. My campaign could use talented people like you experienced in organizing energetic gatherings."

"I have a job, Senator, and you don't have the nomination yet," Ryan says.

"You said it – I don't have it 'yet.' I'm also the frontrunner by a mile. As for your job, I don't think anyone will dispute how successful you've been with Action Not Prayers. The gun control movement owes you a debt of gratitude, but I won't apologize for wanting to make your position irrelevant before I even take office."

Ryan ponders the offer for a few moments. Alicia patiently waits for him to accept it. He would be crazy to refuse.

"What happens when your campaign ends and you don't need me to organize rallies for you anymore?"

"There is always a need for someone to mobilize grassroots efforts to advance the progressive agenda. Whether you are working for one of them or for me, I'll make sure you're gainfully employed."

Ryan mulls it over. It's an offer that would be difficult to refuse. Action Not Prayers won't be around forever. Success hastens his demise, and he understands that. This offer could be the golden parachute he was looking for, assuming Senator Standish delivers on her promises.

"You're a remarkable negotiator, Senator. I'll have a conversation with Ethan."

"That's all I can ask. I'll see you when you come back from Massachusetts."

"Will you be attending the rally?"

"I'll be up there, but I'm staying away from Brockhampton to keep the focus on Ethan. I'll be watching, though," Alicia says, rising from her seat. "Good luck up there. I'm expecting a great show."

Ryan spins his chair around and stares out the corner windows after the senator leaves. He hates knowing a powerful politician is watching his every move. It would have been better if she were going to the rally. It's too bad. A quick tweak of his Brockhampton plan would have paid huge dividends for the movement.

CHAPTER FIFTY-SIX

ETHAN HARRINGTON

Mayfield Residence
Brockhampton, Massachusetts

The feeling that something is different is confirmed when he spots the silver Maserati parked in its perpetually empty spot. Connor must have gotten in touch with his father. Now the lord has returned to the manor.

Ethan parks his car, enters through the front door, and makes his way into the kitchen. Connor is sitting on a stool at the kitchen island, staring blankly at the wall. He doesn't acknowledge Ethan's presence at all when he enters the room.

"Connor?"

"Ethan! Good to see you, my boy," Joseph Mayfield says, emerging from the dining room and slapping him on the shoulder. "Connor and I have been waiting for you."

He's caught off guard by the enthusiastic greeting. It's out of character for Connor's father.

"Good to see you, Mr. Mayfield."

"Oh, I doubt that."

"Sir?"

"Drop the act, son. However brilliant a liar you think you are, trust me, I'm better. I can see through your lies before the words leave your mouth."

Ethan feels a wave of tension course through him. He remains silent, not knowing what to say. Connor still hasn't moved or even looked at him. He's left to withstand the withering glare from Joseph Mayfield on his own.

"I wouldn't lie to you, Mister Mayfield," Ethan croaks.

Joseph's mouth forms an instant smile, albeit a devilish one. "Good, good! Let's test that, shall we? First, coffee."

He pours a mug, dumps in some cream and a spoonful of sugar, and hands it to his guest. Ethan stares at it like he's allergic to caffeine.

"It's not poisoned, Ethan," he says, pouring himself a mug and taking a sip. "Here we are – three men gathered in the kitchen over cups of coffee. Three men with secrets. What are your secrets, Ethan?"

"What?"

"What…are…your…secrets?"

"I don't have any," Ethan stutters.

Joseph sets down his coffee, nods his head, and smirks. He swipes Ethan's coffee mug off the island with his right hand. It crashes against the cabinet behind him, the porcelain breaking into shards that skitter across the tile flooring.

"Don't lie, son," he says in a menacingly calm voice. "You said you wouldn't."

Ethan's uneasiness turns into panic. He has no idea what Connor told his father. Instead of intervening, he's immobile, unflinching, and unresponsive. He wants to shake him out of it to help deal with his old man.

"You look confused, so let me help you out. My son trusted me with your dark secret after the shooting. I kept it because he was honest about needing my help with the mess the two of you made. Despite his bad judgment, I needed to protect my family. Now I understand there may be more secrets that neither of you told me. I think it's time you did."

"I'm not sure what you want to know."

"I want to know why an FBI agent accosted me after I left work yesterday. I want to know why that same agent was seen at one of my construction sites talking to an employee of mine – one who happens to own a white Ford Mustang."

Ethan's face goes pale. A lump forms in his throat. Every nerve in his body begins screaming at once as tension seizes total control.

"I… I…"

"You what? You know how she tracked that down? Because Connor doesn't seem to have figured that out."

"No."

"So you don't know?" Joseph asks, closing the distance between him and Ethan. "Why is she asking about my friendship with Howard Spivey?"

"Uh, I don't know that either."

"Good, a truthful answer. Now give me another. What does Elizabeth Schwarzer know about the shooting?"

"Everything we told you. That's it," Ethan says, trying to be brave in the face of the imposing figure looming over him.

"So, she doesn't know what you two idiots had planned?"

"No."

The left jab comes out of nowhere and hits Ethan square in the cheek. His vision explodes into stars, leaving him shaky. The second punch hits him like an anvil, connecting with Ethan's jaw with enough force to bounce him off the cabinets and send him crashing to the floor.

A powerful hand lifts him by the front of his shirt to his feet and holds him steady as he's punched a few more times. The final hit causes Ethan to almost black out. Joseph grabs him by his throat and pins him against the countertop. He struggles against it to no effect. The man's hand is like a vise.

Joseph squeezes tighter while reaching into the block and pulling out a long chef's knife. He presses it against Ethan's cheek, the tip only a centimeter from his eye. Ethan sees it through his blurry vision and stops resisting.

"I've seen you on TV, Ethan. You like to talk. Talk to me. If you lie even once, I will cut out your tongue. It will get worse for you from there. Nod if you understand."

Ethan stares at him, frozen with terror. He's heard stories from Connor about his father's rage but always assumed that he was embellishing the truth to look tougher. He knows now that the stories were all true, and manages a couple of short bobs of his head.

"You think I'm bluffing, don't you?" Joseph asks. "There is nothing I'm not willing to do to protect myself and my family. I will eliminate anyone who stands in my way, whether it's a reporter, a federal agent, or a teenage punk that's friends with my idiot son. Tell me that you understand."

Ethan's mouth has gone dry. "I understand," he rasps.

"Good. Now, I can handle the FBI agent. She can't prove anything. I need to know what Elizabeth Schwarzer is going to say to the police."

"I…I don't know."

Joseph presses the knife against his cheek harder. Ethan lets out a little shriek.

"Bullshit. Connor told me you know her better than anybody. Don't make me ask again. What does she know?"

"Everything."

"The thugs who attacked her should have finished the job. Is there anything else I need to know?" Ethan averts his eyes. "Don't make me ask again."

"Journals."

"What?"

"Lizzie…kept journals. She wrote them in school. Notebooks…like a diary."

"What's in them about the shooting?" Joseph demands.

"I…I don't know. She never let anyone read them."

"Are you saying that she may have kept a log of everything, and neither of you two clowns bothered telling me?"

"She was in a coma. We thought she'd die."

"Thinking was your first mistake. Where are the journals?"

"I don't know."

"You say that a lot. I'm tired of hearing it."

"She kept them hidden. I don't know where."

Joseph removes the knife and steadies Ethan on his feet before walking back across the kitchen. Ethan gasps for air, his hands rubbing his throat. He throws Ethan a dishrag to wipe away the blood oozing from his cheek.

"Caleb knew, but he won't be talking to anyone. Once she talks to the police, the world will know."

The realization annoys Joseph more than the delectable Agent Larsen did. He rinses off the knife and replaces it in the block before turning to his still-catatonic son.

"You two made one hell of a mess. I'm ashamed to call you my son."

Connor still doesn't move. He still hasn't emotionally recovered from whatever transpired before Ethan's arrival. Joseph scoffs, before turning back to Ethan.

"That had better be the whole story, son, or the next thing Tierra Campos writes will be your obituary. Get the hell out of my house and don't come back. I'll show you how you handle a problem like Lizzie Schwarzer."

CHAPTER FIFTY-SEVEN

TIERRA CAMPOS

The Hotel Devereux at Copley Square
Boston, Massachusetts

I sink into the sofa and rub my temples. Yesterday's conversation was tense, but this is worse. I know that newsrooms can be pressure cookers. Deadlines always loom, and the fear of getting scooped is omnipresent. The DDoS attack on *Front Burner* and fallout from management are taking a toll on Austin. I'm glad I'm in Boston right now.

"I'm coming up there and bringing help with me."

I drop my hands and stare at the phone with my mouth open, desperately trying not to be offended. It's not working.

"I don't need help, Austin."

"It's not all about that, and yes, you do. I should have come up there when you were assaulted in the parking lot. Now you tell me that Victoria was being followed –"

"I shouldn't have told you."

"I would have fired you if you didn't. Your safety isn't the only reason for us coming to Boston. This story is getting bigger by the moment. You can't do it all by yourself."

"I can."

"You can't. Trust me, I've tried before and know where it ends up."

"Austin, you entrusted me with this. It's why you said you hired me."

"That hasn't changed. I'm accelerating the investigative process, not taking over. Daily check-ins aren't going to get this done with the speed it needs to. You need us to track down information in real-time."

I can't argue with his logic. That doesn't mean I like the idea of my editor hovering over me while I work. It feels like I failed him.

"There's a huge gun control rally in Brockhampton coming up. It may be hard to find a room."

Austin laughs. "I don't think many attendees are staying at the Devereaux."

"Fair point. When will you be here?"

"I'll let you know."

I've only known Austin for a short time, but he's never been anything but confident and decisive. He seems to have a plan for everything. Why doesn't he know when he's coming? What is going on?

"Austin, level with me. How bad is it there?"

"You watch the news, Tierra."

"I don't care what snarky comments our competitors make. I want to know what management is saying."

There's a long pause before he speaks. "They are my concern, not yours."

"I started this, Austin. It's my responsibility," I say, ready to take full responsibility for the barbarians gathering at *Front Burner's* digital gate.

"What you did at WWDC was courageous. That's why I hired you, end of the discussion."

At least he found his decisiveness, just not in the way I wanted. I'm about to argue but someone knocks at the door.

"That's Victoria. I need to go."

"Okay. We'll see you soon."

Guilt sets in almost immediately. I shouldn't feel relieved to have Austin off the phone. I don't do awkward well, and that's what the call was. The completion of my check-in buys me twenty-four hours of not having to deal with whatever drama is going on in Washington. Whatever happiness I felt at that prospect disappears when I swing open the door and find Victoria fighting back tears.

"What's wrong? Is it Joseph Mayfield?" I ask, after letting her in and locking the door behind her.

"No," she says, dabbing at her eyes with a tissue. "Mateo Morales was killed in a construction accident this morning."

I cover my mouth with my hands. "Oh my God! How did –"

"He fell off a roof at the job site."

I was expecting her to say, "car accident" or "medical issue." That wasn't the case. While a tumble off a roof in his line of work is not an unexpected occupational hazard, the timing is damn suspicious.

"I'm so sorry," I say, as Victoria stares blankly at a spot on the floor. "How did you find out?"

"An ER doctor called me. I gave Mateo my card when I met him, and he still had it in his pocket."

Victoria has never struck me as the emotional type. She's hardcore in a way that comes from dealing with criminals and the tragedy they leave in their wake. She might have only known the man for a few moments, but here she is, mourning his loss.

"He had a wife and kids, Tierra. All he wanted was to make a better life for them. Now he's dead because he committed the mortal sin of speaking to me."

I don't dare refute her conclusion. It could have been an actual accident. As slimy as Joseph Mayfield is, it's hard to believe he would risk killing someone. Not that it matters. Mateo is dead, and Victoria blames herself.

"What about his car?"

"Funny thing about that. The Wellesley Police said he got a ride into work this morning. His vehicle wasn't at the worksite, nor was it at his home when the police informed his family. They're checking commuter lots to see if he met someone, but we both know he didn't."

"Do you think they'll find it?" I ask, already knowing the answer.

"No. It's gone."

My mind starts racing. If it was towed either from Mateo's house or the construction site, there might be a video of it. It'd be tough to track down and may not do us much good anyway. Our best lead has evaporated, adding to the tragedy of Mateo's death.

"Okay. What do we do now?"

"I want you to write an article about Mateo."

"And say what? That he died falling off a roof?"

"It was more than that."

"We both know that no employees will go on record about what happened. I'm sure there's no surveillance or proof of a crime. Unless you have evidence that anything nefarious happened at all, there's nothing to write about."

"He was murdered for talking to me," Victoria says, hurt and anger in her voice. She's not going to let this go.

"You don't know that for sure. It's speculation, and you know it."

"Since when has that ever stopped you?"

I recoil at the comment. It's not something I would have expected Victoria to say, and I don't like the implication.

"What's that supposed to mean?"

"Nothing," she says, turning away from me.

"No, say it."

"Your interview. You didn't have evidence that Ethan did anything wrong. He misspoke, but you had an instinct and ran with it. Why won't you do that now? Are you being handcuffed by your editor?"

"Why would you ask that?"

"I'm not blind, Tierra. I know what's happening to *Front Burner*. It's not a stretch to think they'll pull the plug on this investigation."

"You're hurting, Victoria. I get it. For the record, *Front Burner* isn't pulling the plug on anything. Austin is coming up here with members of our team to help us. He's determined to get to the truth, and so am I. We'll do it for the sixty-six people who died in Brockhampton High School. We'll do it for the people that buried them and for Americans who cried along with them. We'll do it for Mateo."

Victoria hangs her head, and a tense silence grows between us. She closes her eyes and presses her lips together. When she finally looks at me, her eyes are even sadder than when she walked in.

"I'm sorry, I –"

"Don't apologize, Victoria. We've both been through hell to get where we are."

"Yeah, we have. It's not about to get easier for me. My boss summoned me to Chelsea."

"What does he want?"

"I'm already under investigation. It can only mean one thing."

A single tear runs from the corner of her eye before she beats it away with her finger. I know what it's like being fired, but my job at WWDC didn't mean half as much to me as the Bureau means to her. It's a hell of a sacrifice.

"I'm sorry, Vic. You don't deserve this."

"I chose this path. I have to live with where it leads. I'm just going to make damn sure we reach the end of it, wherever it takes us."

CHAPTER FIFTY-EIGHT

SENATOR ALICIA STANDISH

Reagan National Airport
Arlington, Virginia

Senator Daniel Wetzel is always among the first to flee the city after a recess. No legislator wants to waste time getting out of this town the first opportunity they get. The direct flight from Reagan National to Phoenix at this time of day means he'll be home in time for dinner. Alicia's vindictive side would love to cause him to miss his plane.

"You know that the Senate is still in session, right?" Alicia asks, her heels clicking on the tile floor as she comes up alongside him at the large windows.

"No important votes are scheduled," Wetzel says, admiring the view. "I wanted to get a jump on the weekend. I'm guessing you aren't leaving town yet?"

"I have too much left to do in Washington to leave early."

"Your loss."

"In fairness, my flight's shorter. I don't expect to see this airport until late tomorrow morning," Alicia says, pointing out the inconvenience of having to track him down here.

Many in Congress use Reagan National for convenience, Alicia included. It's only about an eight-minute drive from Capitol Hill if traffic cooperates. When you're eager to get home, every minute counts.

"Your staff said this was urgent, Alicia, but I have a flight to catch."

"Then I'll get to the point. My chief of staff tells me you're back on the fence on the Safe America Act."

"I was never off it."

She cocks her head at him. "I thought we worked that out."

"No, I listened to you threaten me. I never agreed to your demands."

"You made a statement of support."

"You should probably read what I said instead of staffing it out."

The comment smarted because he's right – that's what she did. With so many Republicans in need of wooing and hand-holding, she hasn't devoted much energy courting members of her own party. Now Alicia's kicking herself for not being more attentive and is angry that she needs to be.

"Who's pressuring you? The AFA?"

He shakes his head and stares out the window. "They are pressuring everyone, but that's not why I haven't unconditionally thrown my support behind you."

"Then, why? Why is it I have to constantly convince Democrats when I should be spending my time convincing moderate Republicans?"

Wetzel snorts. "It's not that simple."

"Isn't it?"

"No. Gun control isn't a fight between parties; it's a fight between extremes. You would love nothing more than to shred the Second Amendment and confiscate every weapon in America right down to squirt guns. The AFA would arm every citizen with machine guns and have government programs to hand out free ammo."

"Which would you prefer?"

"It's not about what I want; it's what my constituents want."

"Don't bore me with your 'man of the people' schtick again. We've been down that road once already."

"I won't, as long as you don't say that this gun control quest doesn't have anything to do with running for president."

Alicia has been fighting to contain her anger throughout this conversation. For the first time, she lets it show. If he doesn't understand by now that her bill has more to do with her parents' legacy than her campaign, she won't convince him now.

"We're Democrats. We've been fighting this battle for decades. Now that we finally have a chance to enact gun control reforms, you're going to bail?"

"We shout at the wind every time there's a mass shooting and then offer policies too extreme to pass. The Republicans are willing to deal, but the legislation has to be sensible and measured. You could win this fight with a bill that takes those steps."

"It's not enough," Alicia says, dismissively.

"How do you know? There would still be mass killings and violence even if you melted down every firearm in America and cast them into a giant peace statue. It might even make things worse."

"Are you sure you're a Democrat?"

"I represent a state where people cherish the rights they have left. That includes the Second Amendment."

"What about the rights of Brockhampton kids who never went home from school that day?"

"We don't even know the real story up there."

Daniel didn't want to go there. The only thing those words could result in is more anger from a woman who is more honey badger than skilled negotiator. He looks at his watch, checking to see how much longer he can endure this conversation before the results are irreversible.

"Don't tell me you're buying into that right-wing propaganda?" Alicia asks, practically spitting the question out.

"*The New York Times* and *Washington Post* are asking questions now. Are they right-wing?"

"Do you want to go twelve rounds with me?"

"No, I want to get on my flight." Without another word, he walks away from her.

"Daniel, you don't want to be the only Democrat that doesn't vote for this bill."

That gets his attention. He stops and looks back over his shoulder. The expected expression was one of recognition or fear. Instead, it's amusement.

"What makes you think I'm the only one? Enjoy your trip home, Alicia. I'll see you when we get back."

Alicia watches him head for the security line. Most of the people elected to serve in this town are born liars. Not in this case. Wetzel knows something.

She pulls out her cell as she walks back through the steel and glass terminal toward the passenger drop-off area. A few taps brings up the contact for the Senate minority whip in her address book. He picks up her call on the second ring.

"Hey, Alicia. What's up?"

"When was the last time you did a count on the Safe America Act?"

"Uh, a couple of weeks ago. Why?"

"I need you to do another. I want to know if we're losing party support."

The request is met with a long silence as her colleague tries to figure out why she'd make the urgent request right before a recess.

"I haven't heard anything."

"Just do the count," she says, disconnecting the call.

CHAPTER FIFTY-NINE

SPECIAL AGENT VICTORIA LARSEN

Federal Bureau of Investigation Boston Field Office
Chelsea, Massachusetts

Victoria has been watching the second hand do laps around the wall clock since she arrived. She was told to report at three p.m. sharp for her meeting with Lance Fuller. Forty-five minutes later, she's still waiting in his outer office for him.

He may be on the phone with other government officials. He may be receiving a classified briefing about a terrorism ring suspected of operating out of Boston. Most likely, he's making her sweat it out because that's what vindictive bastards do.

Lance finally opens the door to his office. He glares at Victoria for a long moment. It's not accusatory or hostile; it's how an exterminator looks at a cockroach.

"Come in, Agent Larsen."

Victoria follows him into the office and shuts the door behind her. She takes the seat in front of his desk as Lance eases into his high-backed leather executive chair. He makes a show of arranging files on his desk before flipping one open. It's the kind of theater you'd expect in a crime drama, not a real FBI office.

"I assume you know why you're here."

Victoria plays dumb. "I'm afraid I don't, sir."

"You were referred to the Office of the Inspector General. They opened an investigation into you for alleged misconduct."

He studies Victoria for a reaction and gets none. The FBI's disciplinary system has five phases: reporting of alleged misconduct, investigation, adjudication, appeal, and implementation of discipline. She's in the second phase, and from the sound of it, about to move into the third.

"Who filed the report?"

"Does it matter? Under official FBI policy, employees are obligated to report allegations of misconduct to appropriate officials, who then pass them on to the OIG. Everyone in this building knows you're asking questions about Brockhampton, Victoria. They know you're talking to the press. Given the circumstances, I have no choice but to place you on administrative leave until the matter is adjudicated."

"You have no choice because the Inspection Division is auditing you."

Fuller's eyes open wide. He clears his throat as he looks down at his desk.

"How do you know that?"

"I'm an excellent investigator, remember?"

"The audit has nothing to do with the inquiry into your alleged misconduct. Serious allegations, I might add."

"It has everything to do with it, or we would have had this conversation a week ago. And are the allegations against me that serious? I'm not dealing drugs or drinking and driving. I haven't violated anyone's civil liberties. I haven't even leaked notes about privileged conversations with the president of the United States to the media. Not that there's a penalty for that if memory serves."

"Enough! What exactly is your relationship with Tierra Campos?"

Victoria smiles. "Tierra who?"

"You've been in contact with Tierra Campos from *Front Burner*. Go ahead and deny it."

"How exactly do you know that? Are you having me followed? Maybe even bugged my apartment?"

"We don't do that to our agents."

"Right. Well, someone is."

Victoria pulls out her phone and opens the jpeg picture of the man following her that she snapped outside Quincy Market. Lance stares at it and then back at her. She watches him intently for a hint of recognition – and doesn't get it. Lance's face remains completely impassive.

"I don't know who that is. What I do know is that you're wading into deep waters, Victoria. Fortunately, I think you're an excellent agent, and so do my superiors."

Lance opens his desk drawer and pulls out a plain white envelope. He holds it just far enough away that she has to get up to reach for it.

"I took the liberty of printing this for you."

"What is it?"

"Your 'get out of jail free' card."

Victoria opens the sealed envelope and scans the contents of the single sheet of Bureau letterhead from the Hoover Building. Her eyes open wide. It's not at all what she expected.

"A transfer request?"

"It's been pre-approved by Human Resources Division. Endorse it, and you'll report to the FBI Field Office in San Diego. Warm weather, nice beaches…"

"I didn't think transfers are authorized for agents placed on administrative leave."

"There are exceptions to every rule, Victoria. This is a one-time offer. Take it, and even if the OIG suspends you, the paperwork will likely never end up in your file. If you don't, they will find that you violated FBI protocols and dismiss you from the Bureau."

Victoria stares at the letter. She jumped on the interstate that leads to the end of her career the moment she started working with Tierra. Now she's being shown an exit ramp. Both paths require a sacrifice she isn't sure she can bear. Her thoughts drift back to her conversations with Tierra. She was so worried about *Front Burner* pulling the plug that she never questioned her own dedication to finding the truth.

Something is bothering her, though. Victoria should never have received this deal. Deep down, even Lance Fuller knows that. It came from the highest level, and they both know it isn't because anyone admires her investigative skills.

"If the allegations against me are so serious, why would anyone authorize my transfer?"

Victoria isn't a fool. The question answers itself. Someone with a lot of clout doesn't want her anywhere near Brockhampton. San Diego is about as far away as they can get her.

"The Bureau doesn't want to lose a talented agent like you over a mistake," he says, using a well-rehearsed line.

"Sir, we both know that nobody in the Hoover Building knew who I was before this."

"Take the deal, Victoria. It's the best outcome you can hope for."

She stares at the paper for a long time, weighed down by a crushing decision that she has no time to consider. That's by design. Special Agent Victoria Larsen closes her eyes, exhales deeply, and makes her decision. All that's left for her is to hope she can forgive herself for what she's about to do.

CHAPTER SIXTY

ETHAN HARRINGTON

Liberty Park
Brockhampton, MA

Ethan rubs his forehead in frustration, wondering how many times he has to go over this with them. They've been planning this event for weeks. Eventually, he hopes they'll get it.

"You can't put the stage there. Speakers will have the morning sun in their eyes, including me. You need to face the stage this way," Ethan says, using his hands to demonstrate the orientation to the north.

"That changes the whole setup."

"Then work it out. I'm not dealing with sun glare when I'm talking to thousands of people."

The team begrudgingly heads off to figure out a new configuration for the park. Ethan stays put and surveys the expansive site. Over fifty thousand people will cram into this colonial grazing area on Saturday. Add that to the 40,000 residents and Brockhampton will be the fourth largest city in Massachusetts during the event.

"You're not leaving any detail to chance, are you?" Ryan asks, coming up alongside Ethan.

"You're going to ruin your shoes," he responds, watching Ryan's feet sink into the muddy ground.

"I don't care. I bought them at Walmart. What the hell happened to your face?"

"Nothing. I fell."

"Into someone's fist?"

"Just drop it, okay? Why did you agree to let me organize this?"

"You said it'd be easy," Ryan says, grinning.

"I was wrong."

"I know. That's why I brought reinforcements up from Washington to help."

Ryan points over his shoulder. Ethan turns to see some of the Action Not Prayers volunteers heading over to Ethan's crew. A wave of relief sweeps over him. As dedicated as his team is, they're amateurs at this.

"Good. We could use the help."

"So could Senator Standish. She stopped by my office the other day to offer me a bribe."

Ethan looks at his mentor with surprised eyes. "A bribe for what?"

"To turn you into a robot. The senator wants you on message and not railing against the pro-gun crowd. She thinks I can get you to do that. She even offered me a job organizing events for her campaign if I agree."

"Is that what you're here to do? Convince me to tone it down so she can pass her bill and you can get another job?"

"I have no interest in working for Alicia Standish. I'm not an event coordinator. I founded Action Not Prayers because I hate the gun culture. I resent people who think owning a weapon of mass destruction is a right. Guns do nothing but create havoc. I have no intention of packing my tent and doing something else just because she passes her weak ass legislation."

"Weak legislation?"

"The Safe America Act doesn't go far enough. I want every gun off the streets and criminal prosecution of anyone who doesn't comply with confiscation."

"That's not realistic," Ethan says, shaking his head.

"Why not? Who would have thought a decade ago that public sentiment would have become so anti-gun? That's the problem with you, Ethan. Standish has you brainwashed."

"She does not!"

Ryan wanted to get him fired up. Ethan is better when he's acting on his behalf and not doing Standish's bidding. He needs him to get back to that.

"Please. If Standish asked you to drink the grape Kool-Aid, you'd ask for a bigger cup."

"That's BS, and you know it! I don't work for her. I work for the cause."

"Then prove it. I need you to be an advocate, not Alicia Standish's errand boy. She's using you to help deliver a bill that will only succeed in making her president."

Ethan was angry when the senator dismissed him from Washington. He's even more pissed that Ryan thinks he's a stooge. If he must choose sides, it's an easy decision.

"Tell me what you want me to do."

Ryan smirks and points over at the raised platform. "When you take that stage on Saturday, don't try to convince people to join our side - shame them into it. We're making inroads because we've demonized gun owners and made the Second Amendment unpopular. We need to double down on that, not back off of it."

"I can do that."

"I'm counting on it." Ryan drapes his arm over his protégé's shoulders. "This rally is going to be an event nobody will ever forget. I can't wait to see it."

CHAPTER SIXTY-ONE

SPECIAL AGENT VICTORIA LARSEN

Old North Church
Boston, Massachusetts

Victoria woke up this morning knowing she could be in San Diego right now. The weekend was spent taking long runs to come to terms with her choice. Tierra has been ringing her cell incessantly for days. It was a call she wasn't ready to take until she took care of some things. She's tired of playing defense. It's time to bait a trap and start taking the fight to them.

She strides past the Paul Revere statue on the tree-lined brick pathway and crosses Unity Street, keenly aware of the man trailing her. The wrought-iron gate marks the entrance to the campus of the Christ Church in the City of Boston. Better known as the Old North Church, it's the city's most visited historical site, hosting a half million visitors a year.

"In 1775, Robert Newman joined Captain John Pulling, Jr. in lighting two lanterns to signal Paul Revere that the British were crossing the Charles River and not traveling by land," a teacher tells her class in the courtyard as Victoria purchases a ticket. "The resulting skirmishes between the British and colonial militia on Lexington Common and in Concord ignited the American Revolution."

Victoria isn't here for the nostalgia of American history. It's an ideal location to meet up with someone for a handoff or conduct a dead drop. At least, that's what she wants her tail to think as she enters the gleaming white interior of the church.

She's amazed that the beautiful sanctuary is empty. With no time to waste, she plots her ambush. The stairwells in the back give her an advantage, so she climbs one up to the second level to wait. It isn't a long wait.

"Keep your hands where I can see them," Victoria says, descending the stairs after surprising her quarry from behind.

"It's about time, Agent Larsen," the man says, without turning.

"Are you armed?"

"Of course."

"Toss it in the box pew next to you."

"I'm not going to do that."

The man slowly faces Victoria. She tightens the grip on her weapon and lines up her sights. She's not eager to shoot somebody in a church, much less the Old North Church, but her finger is ready to move to the trigger to do just that.

The man slowly pulls aside his jacket, revealing a badge. "Detective Seth Chambers, Massachusetts State Police."

Victoria can't stop her mouth from hanging open for a moment. That explains why she didn't recognize him. It also puts Lance Fuller's lack of reaction to the photo into context. He's not an agent, after all.

"I think you have some explaining to do," she says, keeping her weapon trained on him.

"Agreed."

A small group of tourists enters through the doors behind them, adding some life and quiet chatter to the formerly empty sanctum. Victoria tucks her weapon under her light jacket and nods at the box pew.

"Sit," she commands.

Seth does as he's told. Victoria climbs into the pew behind him and leans forward to whisper in his ear.

"You're lousy at tailing people. You strolled right in here."

"I am actually very good at it. What I'm lousy at is getting caught."

"All evidence to the contrary."

"I was hoping you were finally going to confront me. I've been waiting for this moment since your Houdini act at Faneuil Hall. Nice job with that, by the way."

"Likely story. Hand me your identification."

Seth does as instructed, and she studies it. It's real, or an expensive forgery. She hands them back to him.

"Okay Detective, why are you following me?"

"I was ordered to watch your movements and report them."

"Report them to…?"

Seth cocks his head toward her. "I think you know the answer to that question."

"Humor me."

"Howard Spivey."

Victoria leans back. The Massachusetts State Police lead detective for the Brockhampton massacre is having her tailed. Tierra is going to love this development.

"Why?"

"I don't know. What I do know is it's off the books and without a warrant."

"That's a gutsy thing to order, don't you think?"

He shrugs his shoulders slightly. "Reckless is a better description."

"How did you get caught up in this?"

"As I said, I was ordered to. I didn't question it because it's the only way I could ensure your safety."

Victoria scoffs. "Ensure my safety? You don't expect me to believe that, do you?"

"Not really, but it's the truth. I got this assignment right after the South End shooting. There's no doubt in my mind that someone arranged to ambush you at the wine bar and frame MS-13 for it. Whoever is capable of that can do far worse. I wanted to be close in case that happens."

"Are you saying Spivey ordered my assassination?"

"He wouldn't have the balls. Spivey's a desk jockey. Somebody else is pulling his strings."

The pair turn to see a woman in colonial garb stomping down the center aisle. There is usually a guide present in the eighteenth-century church to educate and occasionally admonish visitors.

"You can't sit in the box pews!" she bellows.

"I'm very sorry," Victoria says, making her way with Seth up the aisle and out the double doors. She isn't as concerned about getting to her weapon as she was but touches it under her jacket to ensure it's still at the ready. The two turn right and head through the entry into the Washington Garden. The high brick walls and single access point give them a modicum of privacy.

"Is Spivey getting his orders from a higher level in the Massachusetts State Police?"

"No. It could be the governor's office. It could be something else. All I know is that he was pissed when I lost you at Quincy Market. He said he would 'pass it on.'"

"What are your intentions now?"

Seth presses his lips together and surveys the park. "I'm going to continue to observe and report. If I stop, Spivey will know something is up. At that point, I can't help you."

"Are you the only one tailing me?"

"You already know the answer to that, too," he says, smiling. He's right. Victoria knows he's the only one.

"I'm going to ditch you again if I don't want you to report something I'm doing."

"Please don't. If you're meeting somebody and don't want me to report it, signal me. I'll never be far behind you."

"If you can keep up with me, Detective."

Victoria walks back down through the church campus and into Paul Revere Park. As promised, her shadow is about fifty yards back. She doesn't know if he's telling the truth, but her instincts tell her he is. Still, a little research is in order. Luckily, she has a few friends she can call on for that.

CHAPTER SIXTY-TWO

TIERRA CAMPOS

U.S.S. Constitution
Charlestown Navy Yard, Massachusetts

I had never visited Boston before this assignment. This isn't a sightseeing trip, but that doesn't mean I can't visit some historical places. This strange request for a clandestine meeting provides one of those opportunities.

The U.S.S. Constitution is the oldest commissioned ship in the United States Navy. Active duty Naval officers and crew still serve aboard her in cooperation with the National Park Service. Visitors are required to pass through a security screening and show photo identification to board her. That's the reason I chose this site. If anyone is tailing him or me, they will be unarmed and conspicuous.

I wait on the gun deck in the bow of the ship. Families take pictures with the cannons, and children peer out the gun ports. Ten minutes later, a man dressed in khakis and a light jacket descends the ladder and makes his way over to me.

"This is a strange place to meet, Miss Campos," Brian Cooper says, looking around.

"It's easy to spot anyone who isn't a tourist. The only thing strange about this is Senator Standish's former chief of staff wanting to meet with a reporter, especially this one."

"Paranoid?"

"I was doxxed, my identity stolen, attacked in my home, assaulted in a parking lot, and I'm probably being followed. Yeah, a little."

"Fair enough. I've spent my career working in Washington. I appreciate the need for secrecy. Plus, I love this place. They built this ship in the North End of Boston in the late 1700s. The 'Old Ironsides' nickname came during the War of 1812 after defeating four British frigates during three separate engagements. Cannon fire from enemy ships couldn't penetrate her oak hull."

"I like a good history lesson, Mr. Cooper, but now's not the time. You went through a lot of trouble arranging to meet me. What do you want?"

"The same thing you do. Answers."

"I find that hard to believe. You work for Senator Standish."

Brian frowns and shakes his head. "Worked – as in past tense. The senator fired me, remember?"

"So, this is a revenge thing?"

"No. I want to save her candidacy."

I peer out the gun port at the water while processing that. It doesn't make a lot of sense. I want to heed Austin's warning about getting manipulated by this slick political operative.

"Most jilted former employees want to screw over their bosses, not defend them."

"That's true. I poured my heart and soul into that job. I should want to destroy Alicia, but I don't. I got fired for voicing my concerns about Ethan and Ryan Baino. I want you to find out if I was right."

"Justification for your beliefs?"

"Something like that."

"What are those, exactly?"

"That Ethan Harrington is hiding something, and Ryan Baino is covering for him."

"How long have you known that?" I ask, with a little too much excitement in my voice.

"I became suspicious of Ethan after your interview. I haven't trusted Baino for a while."

"Why not?"

"Because he was Antifa."

My heart flutters as the image of Skull Face and Joker pop into my head. They attacked me in Washington and Brockhampton. Could Ryan Baino have arranged it as payback for my Ethan interview?

"That in and of itself isn't a crime," I say, trying to extract more.

"No, unless you take their methods and apply them to intimidate gun rights advocates and young reporters into silence so you can push an agenda. Ryan Baino is a fanatic. If he is protecting Ethan for something, he'll stop at nothing to do it."

"Did you tell Senator Standish that?"

"Alicia never would have believed me. She doesn't know what her allies may be involved in. I want that printed for the record."

"I'm not interested in spreading your propaganda."

"Even if I can prove Ethan arranged your doxxing and the DDoS attack on *Front Burner*?"

Brian Cooper is the consummate political animal. He knew that would get my attention, and he was right. I feel like I'm getting played, but I can't tamp down my curiosity.

"You're a lousy source," I counter, fighting not to take the bait.

"I agree, but I'm not the one who will provide the details. Ethan fired his PR team last week. One of his former reps can tell you everything you need to know."

"What makes you think anyone at Velocity is a good source?"

"Judge for yourself," he says, handing me a card with two phone numbers written on the back. "This kid Xavier introduced Ethan to the hackers that had you doxxed.

Now he has a vendetta against Ethan and will tell you everything he knows. The top number is his cell."

"What about Ryan Baino?"

"I'm still collecting information on him. I will give it to you once I know I can trust you."

The problem with feeling like things are too good to be true is that they often are. Brian is telling me exactly what he thinks I need to hear to do his bidding. He may have even convinced Velocity to go along with the charade in return for something. It's too convenient, and I don't like it.

"Okay, Mr. Cooper. Let's assume you aren't lying through your teeth. What do you want in return?"

"Simple. I want you to prove that Alicia didn't know about any of this. Then I want you to publish that on *Front Burner* so everybody will know. I need someone in the media to give her a fair shake if I'm right. You're an honest broker that people listen to."

I understand the appeal to my ego for what it is. Despite the questionable motives and real possibility that Brian is still working for Standish, he'd make a valuable source. There's no harm in playing along.

"Senator Standish is pressuring the FBI to stop a friend of mine from asking questions."

"Victoria Larsen. Yes, I know."

The admission is surprising. "Is she having her followed?"

"I don't know anything about that. She talks to Conrad Williams at the DOJ. I suppose he could be involved."

"What's the bottom number on this?" I ask, holding up the card.

"An untraceable burner phone. If you need anything from me, call it."

"What if I find that she did know about Ryan Baino's Antifa ties or what Ethan is hiding? What if she knew that he arranged for hackers to come after me?"

Brian exhales and shakes his head. "Then I'm not the judge of character I thought I was. I'll be in touch, Miss Campos."

After a moment, I follow Brian up the ladder and watch as he exits the ship portside. I spend some time wandering around the main deck, searching for any eavesdroppers. There are none, and nobody appears to follow him off the pier.

Content that I gave him a long enough head start, I leave, eager to relay what I've learned to Austin. If Brian Cooper is lying, it's an elaborate ruse meant to convince us that Alicia Standish is a saint. If he's telling the truth, then the leading candidate for president could go down in flames because of her alliance with a nefarious teenage shooting victim. Now I need to figure out which one it is.

CHAPTER SIXTY-THREE

SENATOR ALICIA STANDISH

Standish Campaign Headquarters
Boston, Massachusetts

With things under control at her district office, Alicia decided to spend the rest of the day in her campaign office. There are some exceptions, but official resources must be used for government business and not political purposes. Alicia supports the principle that government funds shouldn't be spent to help incumbents gain reelection. She adheres to that tenet even if many of her colleagues only pay it lip service.

"I have news," her campaign manager says, walking into her small office and sitting in the chair across from her desk.

Angela Mays was a gift from heaven. She has decades of experience in gubernatorial and House races but has never had the opportunity to run a national campaign. Alicia made her an offer to run hers long before anyone else even declared their candidacy. She accepted immediately.

"I hope it's good."

"I wish I could say it is. We just received the internal polling data. You're not going to like it."

Angela hands her the printout of the results. She's right; it isn't great news. Support for her bill dropped five points, and her overall favorable rating followed it down. Alicia sifts through the rest of the data and frowns. The AFA's incessant barking is having an impact.

"We're off message," Alicia says, dropping the packet on her desk. "The AFA went on a social media blitz, and Elizabeth Schwarzer coming out of her coma sucked all the oxygen out of the news cycle."

"It's more than that, Senator. I think you're missing the point of this poll," Angela says, pausing for a breath. "I agreed to run your campaign because we agree on most policy issues. You're strong, capable, and can navigate this nation through whatever challenges it faces, foreign and domestic."

Alicia knows there's more. "But?"

"But outside of gun control, everybody has forgotten what you stand for. You've become a one-trick pony. People don't vote for a single issue in elections, not even the economy."

"Poll after poll puts gun control at the top of everyone's list of concerns."

"Yes, but it's still a long list. People care about things that affect them personally. Yes, gun control is a big issue, but not the only one."

"And I have talked about foreign policy, education, the environment, the economy, equal rights, abortion…"

Alicia stops when Angela opens her leather portfolio. She flips through some paperwork until she finds what she's looking for and hands the senator another sheet of paper.

"What's this?"

"A correlation of your polling data to those taken on the topic of gun control. Notice anything?"

It's impossible for Alicia to miss on the graph. The lines go up and down as all polls do, and her poll numbers move in parallel with the gun control ones.

"Senator, you're linked to this single issue," Angela warns. "It's a good thing if you pull off a win, but –"

"*When* I pull off a win."

"I appreciate your optimism, Senator, but you pay me to strategize. In this case, I have to plan for you to fail. If you do, this data shows it will drag down your numbers and be fatal to your candidacy."

Alicia rubs her neck. This is what a campaign manager gets paid to do. It doesn't mean she has to like it.

"Before I fired Brian, he said I should entertain passing a softer bill that Republicans could vote for. Do you agree with him?"

"I don't formulate policy, Senator. That's your decision. I only show you what those policies mean to your campaign."

"Presidential support is contingent on passing the Safe America Act."

"He's posturing. The president will support whoever the nominee is," Angela argues.

"I'm sure he will, but I have to win the primary for that to happen. His support will go a long way in securing the early states."

"And primary voters have to know what impact the future chief executive has beyond gun control. They need to know who you are and where you stand. Right now, they know that you hate guns. They've forgotten the rest."

Alicia glances at the article she was reading online about public support for gun control being the highest in American history despite the flagging support in Congress. It's a golden opportunity that she doesn't want to waste.

"I know this is a risk. I also know that both my mother and father were killed with handguns, and a softer bill would do nothing to address that. I don't want to win with a watered-down bill that does nothing to fix the problem because it's the easy thing to do."

Angela stares at her boss. Reluctantly, she nods. "I understand."

"The primaries are eight months away. There will be plenty of time to deal with other issues, including at the debates. In the meantime, my focus needs to be on the

Safe America Act. We have the Brockhampton rally this weekend. The bump from it could help propel us to victory."

"Then let's hope it goes as planned, Senator. Thank you."

Angela leaves and closes the door behind her. Alicia leans back in her chair and taps the article closed in her browser. She has had a great political career, but never have the stakes been so high.

CHAPTER SIXTY-FOUR

VICTORIA LARSEN

The Hotel Devereux at Copley Square
Boston, Massachusetts

Victoria raps on Tierra's door again. She would have heard the knocking one of the first three times she did it if she were here. No shower takes that long.

It's been a week since they last talked, and Victoria's feeling guilty she hasn't at least texted. Tierra could have gone back to Washington or checked into a different hotel. She could also be out investigating. Victoria pulls her phone out of her pocket to find out.

"She's not there," a handsome man holding an ice bucket says, coming down the hall.

"Who are you?"

"Who are you?" he parrots back.

"A friend."

"So am I. Wait, you're Agent Larsen, right?"

"Just call me Victoria," she says, trying to get used to not having that title anymore.

"I'm Tyler. I work at *Front Burner* with Tierra. She's in our suite. I can take you to see her."

They walk to the end of the long corridor, where he taps his key card on the panel next to the door. The light on the box turns green, followed by a clicking sound when the lock deactivates. Tyler opens the door and gestures her in. She stops cold a few steps into the suite. There are a lot more people here than she thought there would be. All eyes turn to her.

"Victoria?" Tierra asks, in genuine surprise. "I wasn't sure I was going to hear from you again."

"I know, and I'm sorry about that. It was touch and go for a little while," Victoria says, setting down her purse on the countertop.

"I guess some introductions are in order. Victoria, that's Logan, Jerome, and Olivia. Madison and Jáney are on speakerphone from Washington."

"Hi, Victoria," they say over the phone.

"It looks like you've met Tyler here, and this is my editor, Austin Christos."

The handsome man with sharp eyes and a warm smile shakes Victoria's hand with the perfect amount of pressure – firm, but not crushing. "It's nice to finally meet you."

Victoria offers a sheepish smile and feels herself blush a little.

"Everyone, this is Special Agent Victoria Larsen."

"Former special agent," Victoria interjects.

"I'm sorry, Vic. Is that why you fell off the planet?"

"Not exactly. I was given a choice. Lance Fuller offered me a transfer to San Diego and a promise to make my referral disappear. I turned him down, so he suspended me while the OIG makes arrangements to dismiss me from the FBI."

The words are more emotionally tinged than she planned. Tierra walks over and hugs her. It's not something the agent is used to, but she appreciates the support.

"The week wasn't a total loss. I found out who was tailing me and why."

"Are you serious?" Tierra asks. "Who was it?"

"You might want to sit down for this."

Victoria explains how she lured Seth Chambers to the Old North Church and ambushed him. Austin is clearly impressed, but nothing could prepare the group for her recounting of what he said.

"Whoa. The lead state investigator in Brockhampton was having you followed?" Jerome asks.

"That's a massive story," Logan adds.

"We have some news of our own," Tierra informs her, before breaking down the meeting with Brian Cooper.

"Is it just me? It seems like the more we learn, the less things make sense," Olivia says.

"She's right," Madison says over the phone. "Ethan, Connor, Joseph Mayfield, Howard Spivey, Ryan Baino, Alicia Standish, Brian Cooper… How are all these people related to each other?"

"There are links between some but not all of them," Jerome says.

Austin grabs a dry erase marker and wipes the whiteboard clean with the eraser. He draws boxes around names of all the key players and then begins connecting Alicia Standish, Brian Cooper, Ryan Baino, the Mayfields, Ethan, the hackers, Velocity, Howard Spivey, Seth Chambers, and finally Elizabeth and Caleb. It's an interesting graphic, especially when the group notices what's missing. Austin punctuates the thought when he draws a thick box at the top of the web of relationships and writes a question mark in it.

"It has to be Standish," Logan says, offering up the first opinion.

"Her former chief of staff would vehemently disagree with you."

"And you believe him, Tierra?" Olivia asks.

She looks at everyone in the room. "I do until I find a shred of evidence that proves otherwise."

"Or that's what he wants us to believe. It could be misdirection," Tyler says.

The team begins arguing. It's not a passionate or emotional debate. It's more like point-counterpoint. It's how Victoria imagines the Supreme Court conducts its deliberations.

"Are they always like this?" she leans over and asks Tierra, in a whisper.

"I don't know. I left to come up here the day after I met them, but it seems typical."

Victoria stares at the empty box at the top of the board. Someone needs to tie this together, but nobody fits. There could be a mystery player pulling all the strings, but it's nobody they've identified. Standish is the best fit, but it's not a perfect one.

She watches the team argue when a thought occurs to her. She walks over and picks up a marker and presses it against her lips. Everyone falls silent and turns their attention to her.

"What are you thinking, Victoria?" Logan asks.

"We're looking at this as a traditional conspiracy with one person at the top. What if it's more complicated than that?"

"How?" Austin asks.

"Conspiracy theories are conjured up out of a need for understanding. They're about asking questions and finding answers, regardless of the truth of those answers. Maybe we're trying to make the pieces fit into what we think we know."

"I don't think we're doing that," Tyler says, not following.

"Sure we are. We're looking for the man behind the curtain; the architect of the Matrix; the bearer of the one ring that controls them all."

"That is so sexy," Jerome says, appreciating the movie references and earning a slap on the chest from Olivia.

"Where are you going with this, Vic?" Tierra asks.

"There's only one thing tying this all together, and it's not a person."

Victoria uncaps the marker and writes two words at the top. When finished, she tosses it to Logan and rejoins Tierra next to the suite's kitchen counter. Nobody says a word. They're all lost in thought, staring at the two words they've been looking for: GUN CONTROL.

"Interesting theory. Let's walk through it," Austin says. "First, the political. Alicia wants the bill because she's running for president. She begins working with Ryan Baino and Ethan Harrington to push it to the American public. Everything is fine until Victoria starts asking questions and Tierra interviews Ethan."

"So Baino intervenes. He has some goons attack Tierra, and Ethan has her doxxed," Olivia says.

"Don't forget that those same goons try to gun down Victoria."

"Yeah, but that could be a coincidence. It might not have been the same guys," Logan argues.

"Assume they were the same. Why take things that far for asking questions?" Tyler asks. "It's too extreme."

"Let's set that aside for a moment and keep going. Let's assume Brian Cooper isn't lying and Senator Standish doesn't know any of this is happening. She thinks that the FBI is interfering with her bill, so she independently puts pressure on the DOJ to get Victoria to back off."

"They agree with her. When the threat of investigation doesn't work, they offer to transfer me and end the inquiry."

"Okay, that's the political side. Where does Howard Spivey come into this? We know he has a relationship with Joseph Mayfield."

"Connor was giving range money to Caleb for some reason. His father tries to hide his involvement by appealing to his friend, Howard Spivey."

"So Spivey maybe hides some evidence and prematurely wraps up the investigation …this isn't fixing a parking ticket," Tyler argues. "It's a huge risk to take as a favor for a friend. Then he orders Seth Chambers to break into Victoria's apartment and follow her? Why would he do any of that?"

"He could be getting paid. He could be getting blackmailed. Either way, Spivey could have been reporting what he learned from Seth to Joseph Mayfield."

"That would explain how he knew I was at the development site. The only reason for me to be there was the white mustang. To cover his tracks, Mayfield arranged for Mateo's 'accident,'" Victoria says, adding air quotes for emphasis.

"Okay, let's assume for a second that all of this is true. We don't have the link between Connor and Caleb."

"Yes, we do," Tierra says, getting excited. "It's Ethan. He might not be the mastermind of a conspiracy, but he's the catalyst. All of this is happening because of something that they don't want people knowing about."

"Like what?"

Tierra shrugs. She doesn't have an answer for that. The group shares looks with each other. It's a big leap to get there, but it is plausible given what they know. Austin taps at the top of the board.

"Maybe he wanted Caleb to do it so he could push for gun control."

"Yeah, but Ethan wasn't political before this happened. There's nothing that indicated he cared at all about that or any other issue before the shooting," Janey says, killing that line of thinking.

"What if it was a psychological need?" Olivia asks. "We all saw what happened after the Parkland shooting. What if popularity was Ethan's motivation? His principal said he wasn't popular in school. He becomes a survivor and then uses that to vault into the spotlight as a revered public figure."

"Unlikely. He didn't know that would happen."

"What about Connor? What's his motive?" Madison asks.

The team is at a loss for that one.

"I have a headache," Jerome mutters.

"Not one conspiracy, three of them: the shooting, the coverup, and the political fallout. The players are acting independently, but they all need the same thing."

"What?"

"Nobody willing to ask hard questions about what really happened up here," Tierra concludes. "So they all try to shut it down any way they can."

The group falls silent. Victoria may have inadvertently played a pivotal role in all this by pointing out inconsistencies and the lack of completeness of the official investigation. Tierra asked Ethan a question he couldn't handle. They have set the wheels in motion to uncover a scandal of epic proportions.

"It all fits, but can we prove any of this?" Logan says, bursting everyone's bubble.

"Not yet, but now we have a place to start. It's time to start flipping over stones and seeing what's underneath, starting with how Ethan knew Caleb and Lizzie. There has to be a link."

"She's not doing media interviews. Her lawyer was very clear," Tierra says.

"Hell, she won't even talk to the police," Jerome adds. "And we know neither Ethan nor Connor will talk."

"I will work on Elizabeth," Austin says, before spending the next few minutes divvying out assignments for the team. There are a lot of people to talk to and research that needs to be done.

"Tierra, that leaves you to talk to Ethan and Ryan."

"Are you crazy? One of them had me doxxed, and the other may have had me attacked twice. I don't think they're going to want to meet me, and I'm not crazy about seeing them myself."

"I understand, and if you say no, I get it. You're the best person for what I have in mind, but you'll need to bring some muscle."

"I'll go," Tyler volunteers.

"He said muscle, bro," Logan says, earning a glare.

"Thanks, Tyler, but I was thinking more along the lines of somebody who can handle themselves when things get ugly. Are you up for it, Victoria?"

Everyone snickers at Tyler and nods their approval. Victoria appreciates the vote of confidence from Tierra's boss.

"What do you have in mind, Austin?"

"Well, you were an FBI agent, and Tierra's a school shooting victim. Have either of you ever been to a gun control rally?"

CHAPTER SIXTY-FIVE

TIERRA CAMPOS

Liberty Park
Brockhampton, Massachusetts

The rally is half over, and people are still streaming to the park. Cars were parked outside of town because there is no space. Shuttle buses run back and forth on a continuous loop, disgorging hordes of people with each pass. It's an impressive logistical effort. There has to be eighty thousand people here.

Tyler, Austin, Victoria, and I hang out on the fringes of the crowd. We're only a hundred yards away from the stage, but it feels like half a mile. Speakers and a gigantic video screen next to the stage ensure everyone won't miss a single moment.

"More than 64,000 people were murdered with handguns in the United States since 2007," a speaker I don't recognize says. "Eighty percent of firearm homicides and an annual average of 737,360 violent crimes are committed with a handgun. Much of that violence is directed towards women. Handguns are responsible for seventy-one percent of female homicides in America. All that is before we factor in suicides.

"An assault weapons ban may have saved the students we lost in Brockhampton, Sandy Hook, and Parkland. It won't save the tens of thousands of victims of violent crime each year. The problem isn't only mass shootings. They're tragedies that get all the coverage, but gun violence is an epidemic that this country can no longer tolerate. Senator Standish's bill is the cure."

The line gets the people in the rally worked up. There is a sizable counter-protest at Three Pines Park in the center of town, where speakers are doing the same thing to an audience waving American flags. It's up to the police to keep the two groups as separate as possible when the events end. It's not a job I would want to have.

"You can call it a bill. I call it a solution. I would ask critics what they're doing to save our countrymen. When was the last time the AFA made a suggestion that would make a difference? We all know they have enough politicians in their pocket to pass something that could save lives if they wanted to.

"They need to understand that we will not be silent. We will not be ignored. We've waited for our country's leaders to act for too long and have been disappointed. That ends today. We won't tolerate parents burying their children because of senseless gun violence any longer. We won't tolerate Americans dying while politicians attend fundraisers and fancy dinners with special interest groups.

"I want the attack on this school to be the last one. I want the murders with handguns in Chicago, New York, and Baltimore to be the last ones. I want to see a day when we don't have to hold rallies and marches anymore because we finally rose up and demanded a solution to the problem."

"All right, boss, we're here. What's the plan?" I ask, turning to Austin.

"Ethan and Ryan will be meeting the press along with the governor once the rally ends. Not surprisingly, they wouldn't provide us credentials to be there."

"Okay, so what are we doing here?"

"We're going to crash it."

"I hope you're not expecting one of us to climb up on stage," Tyler muses.

"As entertaining as that would be, I doubt it would end well. Security backstage is tight. We just have to get close."

I wish I could be optimistic about this, but the odds of this working are only slightly better than walking into Baino's office.

"What about Victoria?"

"I'm going to hang back and see if I can find any of my colleagues. You don't need me for this."

"All right. Let's go."

We head off in separate directions, skirting along the flanks of the rally. The crowd gets denser the closer to the stage we get, so it may take me twenty minutes to reach it. People give me dirty looks as I jostle them trying to snake my way closer as the governor of Massachusetts gets introduced on stage.

CHAPTER SIXTY-SIX

SENATOR ALICIA STANDISH

Standish Residence
West Cambridge, Massachusetts

Ethan nailed his pre-rally media interview. His message set the narrative for the event better than Alicia could have expected. The various pundits sitting on cable news panels used the talking points emailed by her office and his interview to reinforce the message before the first speaker took the stage. Her decision to get Ethan back in front of crowds was a good one.

The overhead shots show the park filling up with tens of thousands of supporters brought there by a fleet of school buses. Ground shots focus on the signs provided by various gun control groups and homemade ones that create an authentic, grassroots feel to the rally. The optics of the event are amazing, and tight camera angles from the news choppers above make the crowd appear even more impressive.

The high-powered lineup includes school shooting survivors and young victims of gun violence who take turns at the podium. The speakers sing, chant, and challenge their parents' and grandparents' generations to eliminate gun violence from society. They reward the media covering the event with compelling images and countless soundbites.

Alicia's cell phone chirps. She fishes it off the couch cushion and glances at the screen to see that it's her chief of staff calling from the office. "Talk to me, Rahul."

"We're getting great visibility on Ethan's pre-rally interview. News organizations across the country aired clips of it, and we're getting dense social media saturation. The event is trending on Twitter, but we figured that would be the case. The tweets are mostly positive and energetic."

"Good. What about television coverage?"

"It's being carried live on all cable networks except FOX News, but they are talking about it."

"We have joined a sad fraternity," Governor Flynn says into the microphone, as his speech gets underway. "The pro-gun crowd and their sympathizers in the media like to call shooting survivors 'victims.' The real victims were the boys and girls whose voices were silenced that day just a couple of miles from here."

"Okay, stay on it. I want to listen to Landon's speech," Alicia says, hanging up and turning her attention back to her television.

"Following the attack on Parkland, our youngest generation pledged to take the fight for gun control to the ballot box. They swore to combat the long legacy of inaction. They called elected leaders out, challenging them to take the actions necessary to guarantee the safety of those they represent. If leaders continued to fail the American people, they pledged to elect someone who wouldn't. I'm the result of that promise."

The cheer from the crowd is enthusiastic, but not as electric as Alicia wanted. Governor Flynn pulls the microphone from its stand and moves to the edge of the stage. He knows he needs to get them fired up.

"I am not here for votes. I am here because ninety-six people die every day from guns in our country. Are their deaths okay with you?"

"No!" the crowd screams in unison.

"Do you think that should be okay with the politicians you elect to lead you?"

"No!"

"Then I say no more! The Safe America Act will bring this country into the twenty-first century. Every legislator that fails to support it doesn't deserve to be called a representative. Make every senator who stonewalls or says no pay for the lives they fail to save!"

A single rally is like dropping a stone in a pond. It makes a splash and ripples out before fading away. Multiple rallies drop more stones in the same pond. They amplify each other but still fade away. An effective call to action motivates people to keep dropping stones of their own in the pond. While the splashes might not be large, the ripples never stop. Politicians respond to those making the most waves in the pond. That's what Landon is stirring up, and he's good at it.

"Now is the time to come together, not as Democrats or Republicans, but as Americans. Solutions to gun violence are not about red and blue, or conservatives and liberals; it's about the kind of place we want to live. The AFA will fight to divide us. They will fail. We will unite and will cry out in one voice for change. Together, we will become the heroes who save lives!"

Alicia couldn't be prouder. Landon is connecting with the crowd in a way that only the best speakers can. The people are responding to him, and the media must be eating this up.

The chanting starts, a full-throated "no more" that sounds like it can be heard in Washington. It's a moment custom-built for live television.

CHAPTER SIXTY-SEVEN

ETHAN HARRINGTON

Liberty Park
Brockhampton, Massachusetts

"We are all Americans, and I believe placing the lives of our countrymen should always come first. This nation has a long and storied history of solving our problems. Sometimes those struggles are bloody. In the fight for the safety of all people and an end to gun violence, a bloody struggle is what we're trying to avoid. This battle will be hard, but we can and must endure!

"So, let's begin. It is my distinct honor to introduce a man who has done more to advance the cause of gun control than any other person in America. I am proud to call him a constituent and privileged to call him a friend. He is an advocate, he is a survivor, and he is going to make America a better place. Ladies and gentlemen, Ethan Harrington!"

Ethan gives a wave as he walks onto the stage to massive and enthusiastic applause. He understands why everyone wants to be a rock star. This is the closest he'll ever become. The feeling of adoration is exhilarating.

The governor embraces him when he reaches him at the center front of the stage. "I got them warmed up for you. Bring it home," Landon says, into his ear.

"I will."

"I have no doubt."

The governor grabs his hand and holds it aloft for the crowd and cameras. He lets it go and then steps aside to continue his applause. Ethan is soaking up the love when he catches something out of the corner of his eye. When he realizes what, it's too late to react.

Pop, pop, pop…pop, pop.

The roaring of the crowd muffles the sound. When the governor collapses and everyone suddenly crashes to the stage, the cheering turns into blood-curdling screams. Panicked people trample each other as they flee from the area in front of the stage. A lone figure remains standing there, staring right at Ethan.

A man rushes toward the gunman, who notices the movement to his left. He turns and fires, hitting the good Samaritan in the abdomen and sending him tumbling to the ground. The distraction gives those on the stage time to find cover. Ethan joins them.

The gunman wheels his weapon toward the fleeing teenager. A state police officer responds to the danger and hurls his body at Ethan. The pair crash onto the stage floor. He struggles to get him off, feeling claustrophobic.

"No, stay down!" the man commands.

Two more shots are fired. The officer suddenly rolls off Ethan and rushes over to his comrades checking on the governor. Ethan turns his head to see the shooter lying on the ground, surrounded by five men with guns drawn. He's not moving.

Sirens and agonizing wails punctuate the shouts of people fleeing the park. Ethan watches the panic unfold in complete shock. This isn't what was meant to happen. Nobody was supposed to get shot.

The officers move away from the governor, despondent. Ethan sits up when EMTs rush to his side. He's checked quickly by one of them and is lifted to his feet. His legs are wobbly under him as he watches the other paramedics lose their sense of urgency. When they step back from the governor, he takes in a sight that he'll never forget.

The man who introduced and embraced him moments earlier is lying motionless on the stage. He stares at Ethan with hollow eyes that will never close. What has Andre done? Governor Landon Flynn, a champion of the gun control cause, is dead.

CHAPTER SIXTY-EIGHT

TIERRA CAMPOS

Main Street
Brockhampton, Massachusetts

It's not a great distance between Three Pines Park and Liberty Park. When people fled the shooting, the town center was the obvious place to go. Most of the off-site parking for the event is just south of there. Scared, but far angrier about what happened, the gun control crowd ran right into the pro-Second Amendment rally. The result was predictable — all hell broke loose.

The shooting created a combustible atmosphere that has now ignited. Emotions are running high, and the police are spread thin. Even with reinforcements from the state and surrounding towns being called in for assistance, they have no chance of stopping the rioting from spiraling out of control. Downtown Brockhampton is a bad place to be.

A group of men starts ravaging a car parked down the street, breaking the windows with metal bats likely looted from the sporting goods store I passed. I duck into the entrance of a small boutique when I feel my phone vibrate and fight with shaking hands to retrieve it from my jeans pocket.

"Austin! Where are you?"

"Still at the park," he shouts into the phone. "Tyler's hurt. Where are you?"

I don't focus on the question. My thoughts lock onto the news about Tyler and my concern for his well-being. "How bad?"

"Bad enough. He got caught up in the stampede of people leaving the park. I'm staying here while we wait for ambulances. Nothing is getting through. Where are you?"

"In town trying to get back to the car. It's bad here. People are rioting."

"Get to the car and get out of Brockhampton. Where's Victoria?"

"I don't know. I haven't seen her since we split up."

"I'll try to reach her. Call me when you get someplace safe."

That's easier said than done. The car getting pummeled is now fully engulfed in fire as the marauders move on to the next. People up and down the street are fighting while others break store windows and start fires. This quiet, sleepy New England town has tragically become a battlefield.

The violence is everywhere — the sound of glass breaking and people shouting echo off the buildings lining the once-peaceful street. Gunshots pierce the cacophony, way too close for comfort. I shake my head at the irony.

There is no place to run and no safe refuge to hide in. Left with no better option, I push aside my fear and stay close to the buildings as I travel down Main Street. I need to make it to the car, hoping it's still in one piece. I don't get far.

Two groups of men clash in front of me, throwing rocks at each other. I don't know which side is which. I'm not sure they do either, or if it even matters at this point. Desperate to escape the havoc, I slip into the nook of a restaurant that had the good sense not to open today. It's only a matter of time before its sizeable front window finds itself in a million tiny pieces.

"Hey, guys, check this out," a man says, after noticing me cowering in the alcove.

Three men approach me. I retrieve the pepper spray from my purse and hold it tightly in my hand as I ready myself for a fight. The prospect is terrifying. The self-defense course I took in college won't help against three of them.

"Well, well, hello, sweetheart. Wanna have a little fun?"

"Looks like little kitty here wants to fight," the second kid says, noticing the pepper spray.

"Good, I like it rough."

I want to scream for help, but my mouth goes dry. It will only urge the young men on anyway. I'm frozen in fear and at the same time, angry for feeling that way.

I knock away the arm of the first guy who reaches for me. It feels good to be defiant and not helpless. Unfortunately, they're more amused than deterred. I ready myself for him to come again.

"Oh, this is going to be a good ti –"

A fist comes at him in a blur, and the punk hits the sidewalk hard. Before his friends can react, six guys in jeans and t-shirts jump them. One of the thugs gets cracked in the head by a pipe and crumples to the ground in a heap. The others try to protect their faces as they get punched and kicked.

"Like breaking windows and assaulting people, do ya?" one of the burly men asks.

I'm not waiting to see what happens next. These six guys could be worse than the other three. I slip out of the restaurant entrance and flee down the side street. Police are engaging with agitators at the next intersection, so I duck behind the restaurant's dumpsters and desperately try to stop the oncoming panic attack.

The acrid smell of smoke and a faint scent of tear gas fill my nostrils. I close my eyes and wonder if I'm in America or some unstable Third World cesspool of a country. This chaos is unlike anything I have ever experienced or would ever want to.

I need a plan of action. The route back to my car is risky, if not futile even to try. If the police are moving in to restore order, I can try to wait it out until they arrive. If they're busy quelling the violence, that may be equally pointless. Calling 9-1-1 certainly won't do me any good.

My phone vibrates again. I almost drop it when I see who it is. "Victoria!"

"Tierra? Where are you?"

"Scared out of my wits behind the dumpsters next to some cute little Italian restaurant on Main Street. Where are you?"

"I'm dodging some thugs on Elm Street."

"Are you okay?" I ask.

"I'll be fine. Stay put and out of sight. I'm three blocks away. I'm coming to get you. Then we're going to get the hell out of here."

I tuck the phone back into my pocket and peer around the dumpsters. Getting out of here is the best thing I've ever heard uttered. I'm safe for now, but that won't last forever. If there was a time for me to be invisible again, it's now.

CHAPTER SIXTY-NINE

VICTORIA LARSEN

Main Street
Brockhampton, Massachusetts

Victoria is a highly trained FBI agent who excelled at Quantico, is an expert marksman, and has hand-to-hand combat training. She can handle herself in dangerous situations like this. Outside of Marines or paratroopers, one would be hard-pressed to find someone more qualified to be on this street than her. It's still the last place she wants to be.

If she's uneasy about being here, Victoria knows Tierra must be terrified. She moves as swiftly as possible down Elm Street, making herself as inconspicuous and non-threatening as possible. Twice she was forced to duck into a store to lie low. The regular five-minute walk through a peaceful Brockhampton takes three times that.

She finds the restaurant Tierra was talking about with three bodies in the street in front. It isn't a good sign. Victoria sprints across Main Street and down the one-way road that leads off it. There is a small parking lot behind the building with two dumpsters tucked away in a corner.

"Tierra?"

"Over here."

The women hug after Victoria turns the corner. She expected the worst, but Tierra seems to be weathering the storm okay. Something is satisfying about her strength. She is a civilian and a trauma victim, yet she is persevering.

"Are you okay?"

"I'll be better after a glass of wine and a long, hot bath."

"Ditto. Let's roll."

Victoria and Tierra are leaving the relative safety of the dumpsters when a group of men dressed in black run down the road from Main Street.

"She went this way!"

It's too late to retreat once they emerge from the corner of the restaurant. Victoria looks around and grimaces. They're caught right in the middle of the small parking lot.

"There!" one of the men shouts, pointing at them.

The men start walking towards them. They are wearing face shields and bandanas. Tierra tenses up when she recognizes them. One has a skull face, and the other is the Joker.

"This must be our lucky day. It's a two-for-one deal."

"Those are the guys," Tierra whispers.

"FBI! Stay back!" Victoria commands, pulling her badge. They don't comply.

"That badge didn't stop us last time, bitch," Skull Face says.

"Oh, you both gonna get it good," Joker adds, both still approaching with the others behind them.

Victoria draws her gun and levels it at him. They stop coming toward the women, more amused than scared.

"Stop where you are, or I will defend myself. Who are you?" she demands.

"Pest control," Skull Face says, an ominous tone in his voice.

The five men fan out and form a semi-circle around them. Three of them are armed with bats and knives. Victoria eyes Joker and Skull Face. They aren't carrying weapons that she can see.

"Stop now, or I will fire."

"No, you won't," one of the men says, raising his spiked bat.

"Yes, I will. It wouldn't be the first time." She turns to Skull Face. "Remember?"

His eyes narrow. He nods at the man with the bat, who takes a couple of steps toward them. She notices Skull Face's movement out of the corner of her eye. She was expecting it. Nobody is this calm with a gun trained on them unless…

He reaches behind his back and retrieves the gun from his waistband but isn't quick enough. Victoria swings her weapon over and moves her finger to the trigger. She quickly lines her sights on him and squeezes. The shot rings out, hitting Skull Face in the chest below his right shoulder. Joker retrieves his weapon as the other thugs tighten the half-circle around Victoria and Tierra.

"You can't get all of us. Quit while you're ahead, bitch," Joker says, as Skull Face squirms on the ground.

"My thoughts exactly," Seth announces from the door at the rear of the restaurant. "Drop your weapons."

The four remaining men turn their heads to look at him. Joker doesn't move.

"There are nine rounds in this magazine. There are eight in hers. What are the odds we'll miss with half our rounds at this distance between the two of us? Pick up your friend and get to a hospital before he dies. Now."

Despite the odds, they have to think about it. Seth shakes his head. He makes a show of cocking the hammer of his Glock.

"I'm not going to repeat myself."

The warning gets the point across. Joker drops his weapon and nods at the others. They pick Skull Face up and move out of the parking lot and down the street.

"Are you both okay?" Seth says, emerging from the doorway.

"Yeah, just pissed off. I'm glad you're here, Seth," Victoria says, holstering her weapon.

"Speak for yourself. I should be home watching the Sox."

"I didn't think you'd be following me today."

"Someone needs to keep you out of trouble. I wonder if those guys realized I just saved their lives." It's a moment of levity in a tense situation, and both women appreciate it.

"Seth, this is Tierra Campos from –"

"I know who she is. It's nice to meet you, Tierra. Let's get the hell out of here. The police have cleared Three Pines Park and set up a staging area there. They secured a route to the east out of town. Everywhere else is a war zone, but we should be okay if we can get there. Are you ready to run the gantlet?"

"Can I say no?" Tierra asks, not looking forward to this.

"We could stay here, but I think the kitchen's closed."

The three of them head back through the restaurant and out the front onto Main Street, where the upheaval has calmed a little. Much of the rioting has spilled down the side streets, and they make good progress toward Three Pines Park.

The police have set up their riot control line where Seth thought they would. The central location of the park is a commanding position that breaks the downtown into quadrants that they can pacify one at a time. The presence of a National Guard Humvee means units were mobilized to provide additional manpower. They are likely keeping an eye on residential areas to stop the rioting from spreading outside the town's center.

State troopers stop the trio as they reach the park. Victoria and Seth show their identification, and Tierra flashes her press credentials. After a few questions, the officer is satisfied. They are passed through and escorted out of town past guardsmen and state troopers in full riot gear.

Tierra calls Austin, who answers the call from the back of a pickup truck loaded with injured on the way up to the hospital in Framingham. Tyler is going to be okay, but still needs a trip to the ER. She promises to meet him up there as soon as she can.

A small explosion rocks the center of town. It could have been a propane tank exploding or a bomb. At this point, there's no way to know. People have completely lost their minds. It's going to be a long night in Brockhampton, and what is happening here is going to captivate the country for weeks.

CHAPTER SEVENTY

SENATOR ALICIA STANDISH

Standish Residence
West Cambridge, Massachusetts

The images on the screen are horrifying. Cameramen are risking their lives by following lines of police with helmets and shields as they move down streets. Tear gas is fired at throngs of people who hurl bricks at them in return. The Revolutionary War started in Massachusetts. It almost looks as if a second one is starting here now.

Alicia dabs at the corners of her eyes with a tissue when the footage shifts to a victim of the violence bleeding profusely from his head. He didn't look like a rioter. He was in the wrong place at the wrong time and hasn't been able to escape the melee until now.

America watched a governor get assassinated right in front of their eyes. The cable networks carrying the rally live had their cameras pointed at him when the center of his chest exploded, and he collapsed to the stage. They broke away temporarily but weren't shy about continuing to air footage until their satellite trucks at the park were destroyed at the beginning of the riot.

What started as outrage at the attack turned ugly when the participants in the two rallies met in the center of town. Anyone with common sense got out of the area as fast as they could. Local and state police, along with units of mobilized National Guardsmen, have fought to restore order. Exhausted news anchors have been live for hours explaining every action taken in Brockhampton as cameras document it for their viewers. America is riveted to their televisions, even at this late hour. Regular programs on the networks were preempted hours ago.

The doorbell rings, but Alicia doesn't move. Her husband answers the door, and she hears Angela Mays' voice echo in from the foyer. There's only one thing this could be about.

"Good Evening, Senator."

"There's nothing good about it, Angela."

"You're right. Sorry, that was a poor choice of words. Have you gotten any updates from the governor, uh, lieutenant governor?"

"I haven't talked to him since this afternoon. I'm sure he's busy."

"Rahul Patel called me after you spoke to him. Police informed him that at least four people are dead and dozens more injured. It looks like the people left in town are agitators."

Alicia was afraid of that. Chaos invites degenerates like moths to a flame. Once word of the unrest got out, anyone with a need to torch a car or loot a business flocked to Brockhampton before police could seal it off.

"You're not here because Rahul called you with an update. You think that I need to make a statement and politicize this."

"Not politicize it; respond to the rioting and the assassination."

"It's the same thing."

"It isn't, and you know it. Governor Flynn's assassination hurts. I know the two of you were political allies and became good friends. That's why you need to make a statement tonight. The president has spoken to the nation, and the acting governor has given three press conferences. Nobody has heard from you yet."

"My bill is the reason for that rally."

"The gun control movement is the reason for the rally, and the Democratic frontrunner needs to step up and lead. You need to act presidential if you want the job you're running for."

Alicia knows that Angela is right. She has to get out in front of this as a candidate. The politician in her knows it's not the right time to talk about her bill. She doesn't want to look opportunistic.

"I will draft something that will be released by the campaign with prayers for the wounded and dead and condemning the rioting in Brockhampton. Nothing is to be mentioned about the Safe America Act."

"Senator, a leading gun control governor was murdered with a gun. You have to address that."

"Not today. There will be plenty of people from both sides who make that point for me. Let them politicize it. I think the bill speaks for itself after what happened."

The bourbon is the only thing keeping Alicia's anger in check. Her friend and ally was killed. A peaceful rally expressing free thought and opinion, a hallmark of any functioning democracy, has descended into chaotic hell. Most of all, she's pissed at herself for not being there. Survivor's guilt is a bitch.

"Senator, I think you –"

"Is there anything else, Angela?"

She recoils. The senator has never cut her off like that before.

"No, ma'am. I'll call you tomorrow."

Angela leaves, and Jack puts his hand on Alicia's shoulder as she continues to watch the coverage of the rioting. It gets worse with every passing moment as cell phone videos uploaded to YouTube find their way to news broadcasts. Everything has changed. Support for her bill will double, but the price is unbearable. It's all she can do not to burst out in tears.

CHAPTER SEVENTY-ONE

VICTORIA LARSEN

Liberty Park
Brockhampton, Massachusetts

Victoria left Tierra and the *Front Burner* team at the hospital. There's someone that she needs to see here, and a journalist can't tag along. Brockhampton is one giant crime scene. Police are everywhere, collecting evidence and securing property. Men and women in uniform with badges have replaced mothers with strollers on the sidewalks. The once-charming little New England town resembles a battlefield from war-torn Iraq or a bombed-out city in Syria. Shattered windows, torched cars, gutted buildings, and debris-littered streets mar the entire downtown.

National Guardsmen clad in body armor manned checkpoints Victoria had to pass through to get into town. Now she's facing angry police officers patrolling the Liberty Park perimeter along the miles of yellow police tape cordoning it off. Victoria knows she'll need a convincing story to go with her badge and FBI windbreaker to get her through. That's how tightly this scene is secured. "Can I help you?" an enormous state police sergeant asks when she approaches.

"Special Agent Victoria Larsen, FBI." She flashes her credentials. "I'm looking for Special Agent in Charge Takara Nishimoto."

"Is this official business?"

"I wouldn't be here otherwise, Sergeant."

"He's over near the stage," the man says, pointing with a knife-hand. He spent time in the military.

That wasn't as bad as she thought it would be. "Thank you."

Victoria walks across the field, careful not to disturb anything lying on the ground. She finds Takara talking to several agents from her office who look at her and then back at him as she approaches.

"Jesus, Vic, you're suspended. What are you doing here?"

"I need to talk to you."

"I'm a little busy," Takara says, turning his back to her.

Victoria looks around. "Yeah, no shit."

"I don't have time to deal with –"

"This is important, Takara. I wouldn't be here otherwise."

Takara gives her a hard look. He knows Victoria wouldn't just drop in like this. She's not going to insert herself into the investigation, nor ask him questions about it. The fastest way to get her out of here is to listen, so that's what he opts to do.

"Keep processing the stage," he commands the other agents. "Has all the video from here and downtown been acquired?"

"Teams are collecting footage from businesses and running them through facial recognition to see if any rioters can be identified. We're reaching out for any cell phone videos that haven't already been uploaded to YouTube."

"Stay on it. I'll be right back."

He gestures Victoria away from the stage. They walk about a hundred feet away, and Takara scans the immediate area to ensure they are out of earshot.

"You have guts coming here, Vic. You're on suspension, and we have an assassinated governor, a dead gunman, and a riot to investigate."

"Any information on the shooter?"

"Here I was, thinking you weren't going to grill me on a case you have no business meddling in. What are you going to do, leak it to the press?"

Victoria would like nothing more than to punch his lights out for saying that. Instead, another idea comes to mind.

"Maybe later," she says, not willing to argue with him. "First, I'll tell you the tale of an active agent who once had a gambling debt he racked up from underground poker games. Fortunately, it managed to disappear when an ambitious female agent fresh out of Quantico arrested the game runner for raking the pot."

Takara gets the point. He owes Victoria a favor, and now she's collecting.

"The shooter was killed by police. He didn't have any identification, so we're still determining who he is. From the looks of it, a Second Amendment supporter who decided to turn this debate into a war."

"Is that your feeling or what your superiors are telling you to say?"

"You're about to make this a quick conversation."

"It was a simple question. Do you think that, or are you being led in that direction?"

"Since when did you become a conspiracy theorist? Maybe you've been hanging out with Tierra Campos too long."

"That's true. You might think the same thing if you finished your investigation of the shooting. Don't make that mistake twice. The state can't shut this one down."

"They can if they want to."

"Not if you label it terrorism."

Takara's face contorts into confusion, disbelief, and annoyance. "Are you kidding?"

"Everyone is assuming the same thing you are. I mean, it's the easy motive behind this assassination, right? Unless it isn't. You need to be sure, Takara. It's what we should have done after the school shooting."

"Caleb hated people. That's the motive. He didn't have an agenda."

"You don't *know* that. Only one person knows the motive, and Elizabeth Schwarzer isn't talking. What if his co-conspirators had an agenda?"

Victoria practically whispers the question. That infuriates Takara even more.

"There are no co-conspirators."

"Are you sure?"

Takara squints at her. "You know something."

"It's circumstantial but compelling enough that someone tried to kill me because of it. Don't let the state take this out of your hands and shut down the FBI investigation. Call it domestic terrorism."

Takara kicks at a stone on the ground while he mulls it over. There is enormous pressure after a high-profile crime like this to provide a label for it. It was worse during the marathon bombing. He raises his head as if stumbling on a revelation.

"How do you know they'll try?"

"Because they did it once before. Create a task force to investigate what happened here and why. When Howard Spivey moves in to take control, make the call. Don't let him take it away."

"I don't have that authority."

"Lance Fuller does and will do whatever you recommend. He's getting audited and won't make waves."

"How the hell do you know that?" Takara asks as she starts walking away.

"Do yourself a favor and listen to what I'm telling you," she says, not looking back.

CHAPTER SEVENTY-TWO

TIERRA CAMPOS

MetroWest Massachusetts Medical Center
Framingham, Massachusetts

MetroWest is like every other hospital I've ever visited. It's filled with doctors and nurses, has a bland paint color on the walls, and assaults my nostrils with a peculiar nauseating odor. I join Austin and Madison in Tyler's room. We share hugs, and I take his hand as he lies inclined in his bed. He looks better this afternoon than he did a day ago.

"How are you feeling?"

"Like I got hit by a bus," Tyler says between spoonfuls of Jell-O.

"Being run over by a couple of hundred people will have a lingering effect," Austin says from his spot on the window ledge. "Any news on Skull Face or Joker?"

"Victoria said Seth have been looking for them. He pulled prints off the guns they left in the parking lot, but nobody matching his description has been admitted with a gunshot wound."

"Do you think he died?" Madison asks.

"Or he was taken to a private doctor who wouldn't ask questions," Tyler says, shifting in his bed.

"Are you sure it was the guys who attacked you before?" Austin asks.

"Positive. They were outside my apartment in D.C. Joker was the one who pepper-sprayed me here. They were hunting for me after the rally."

"But why? They're going through a lot of trouble to harass you."

"Yeah, they are. I don't know why."

There is a knock on the wall behind me. We turn to see a balding man with glasses and wearing an ill-fitting three-piece suit standing there.

"I'm sorry to interrupt, but my client may be able to answer that question," he offers, his voice nasal and whiny.

"You look familiar. Who are you?" Austin asks.

"My name is Preston Swain. I'm the Schwarzer family attorney. Elizabeth is my client."

Austin, Madison, and Tyler stare at him like he's from another planet. The silence gets awkward, so I stand and face the lawyer.

"What brings you here, Mr. Swain?"

"You do, Miss Campos. May we talk in private?"

"This is private. The guy in the corner is my editor Austin Christos, next to him is Madison, and the guy in bed who tripped over his own feet is Tyler. They all work for *Front Burner.* Anything you say to me can be said in front of them."

Preston looks at each of them, lingering on Tyler, who's desperate to rebut my dig but can't find the words before the opportunity passes. I patiently wait for the lawyer to agree. It's not like he's peddling state secrets or the missing eighteen minutes from the Watergate tapes.

"Very well. Your editor called my office about an interview with Lizzie. Against the strong advice of counsel, she has granted your wish."

"Are you serious?"

"Unfortunately."

"You don't sound thrilled about that, Mr. Swain. Are you being blackmailed or something?" an astonished Austin asks.

"She told me she'd fire me if I didn't set it up, so yes, you could call it that. I called your office in Washington and spoke to a disagreeable woman named Janey. She told me you were here."

"Okay, let's go," Austin says.

"There are two conditions," he says, shaking his head and holding up two fingers. "The first is that the interview is only with Miss Campos. The second is that everything they discuss is off the record."

"No deal," Austin snaps, sitting back down.

"Those are my terms, and they aren't negotiable. The police are thinking about charging her as an accessory because she won't cooperate with them. It won't help my client's cause if they read what she says on *Front Burner.*"

"Which is why you don't want her talking to me at all," I say.

"Yes. Apparently, I need to protect Lizzie from herself as well as the authorities. What is your final answer?"

"Deal." I can feel Austin glaring at me before I dare to check for myself. "It'll be fine."

An interview with Lizzie is the scoop of the decade, so being off the record is a painful missed opportunity to make *Front Burner* the talk of the country. That's Austin's reason for wanting the interview. I have my own – she can give me insights nobody else has.

I follow Preston to the elevator bank and take a car up a couple of floors. Unlike the rest of the hospital, the entire floor is empty aside from a pair of duty nurses at their station. Elizabeth's room is devoid of cards or flowers outside of a single small bouquet in a vase with a ribbon that reads: "My Granddaughter."

She is lying inclined in her bed, much like Tyler was when I walked into his room. She looks like hell, not that anyone who spent almost a year in a coma would look fashion model fabulous. She's paler than any picture I've seen of her, her complexion accentuated by the messy raven mop of hair on her head.

"You must be Tierra Campos. I heard you wanted to talk to me."

"Everybody wants to talk to you, Elizabeth."

"I've noticed. Step outside, Preston," she commands, not bothering to look at him.

"That's not a good idea. I insist that I be present for this."

"Okay. Miss Campos, will you write an article for me? I want the world to know that my lawyer sexually assaulted me after I woke from my coma. He touched me and told me if I didn't perform oral sex on him –"

"Enough! I'm leaving," he says, understanding the threat and the ugliness of fighting that accusation.

"I'm happy to have such a brilliant attorney."

I can't suppress my smirk, earning his ire as he walks past me.

"You don't trust your lawyer?"

"I don't trust anybody," Lizzie says, once the door closes.

Elizabeth isn't at all what I expected. Everyone I spoke to described her as weird and introverted. It's why she only spent time with Caleb. Instead, the young woman lying in that bed is smart, and dare I say…engaging. Despite not living up to the portrait painted for me, there is still a dark edge to her.

"Do you know who did this to you?"

"No. I don't remember much. I was walking away from the vigil when I was hit from behind. Then men in masks started beating me. I don't know who they were."

"What kind of masks?"

"It wasn't like Halloween or anything. One had something over his mouth that looked like a skull. Another guy was a clown. That's all I remember."

I feel the blood drain out of my face.

"The skull was from the nose down, and the clown looked like the Joker?"

Her eyes narrow. "Yeah, do you know who they are?"

"I might. Do you know why they attacked you?"

She shrugs. "It doesn't matter. Everybody wants me dead – most because I won't talk and some because they're afraid I will."

"You could have asked for anyone to talk to you. Why me?"

"I saw your interview with Ethan. I couldn't stop laughing at the part when he said he was friends with Caleb."

"Why was it funny?"

"Because Caleb and Ethan hated each other."

That's not what I expected her to say. Ethan said he didn't really know Caleb.

"Why?"

"Because of me. Caleb always had a thing for me. He asked me out like a hundred times, but I never liked him that way. One night, we got into an argument about it at the lake. I didn't want to go to that stupid party in the first place. He got mad, went home, and left me there. I don't have any friends, and the people there were horrible to me, so I grabbed a bottle of vodka and went off into the woods to get drunk. Ethan found me and took care of me. He was nice to me, and I was lonely, so…we had sex."

My shock registers on many levels. My legs get weak. I sit down in the chair next to her bed before they buckle. Ethan never mentioned he had any relationship with Lizzie, much less a sexual one. Investigators looking into Lizzie following the shooting never made the connection.

"We hooked up several times after that. Long story short, I ended up telling Caleb, hoping that he would stop pursuing me. He didn't take it well."

"Did Ethan know that you told Caleb?"

"Yeah, I told him."

I stare down at my trembling hands and take a deep breath. "Did Ethan know that Caleb was planning to kill his classmates?"

"I told him that, too. I had to. He was the target."

My mouth hangs open. That makes no sense. Why would Connor have helped a kid bent on killing his best friend? He might not have known, but it wouldn't take a mathematician to solve for *x* in that equation. He had to know.

Either way, now I understand why Ethan never talked about the day of the shooting. He wasn't in the library because he knew Caleb was coming for him. That's also why Caleb didn't shoot right away and moved erratically around the building. Ethan wasn't there, so he went looking for him. But why let him come and shoot up the school at all? Ethan could have reported it any time.

"Did you want him to kill Ethan?" I ask, not understanding any of this.

"No. It's the last thing I wanted. We had a special connection," she whispers, her voice tinged with remorse.

"Did you help Caleb plan to shoot up the school?"

Elizabeth closes her eyes and shakes her head. "It wasn't…nobody was supposed to die."

"I don't understand."

"I don't expect you to. I don't expect anyone to."

"Is that why you won't talk to the police about it?"

"I don't trust the police. They want to protect Ethan. They won't believe me."

I can understand why she thinks that way. If our theories are accurate, there is more than an element of truth to the conclusion.

"You wrote some details down in your notebooks, didn't you?"

She looks at me in surprise. It was a shot in the dark, but I hit my mark. Nebbich confirmed what Victoria learned from the kid she interviewed. Now I know they exist.

"They weren't just notebooks. They were journals. I wrote everything in them."

"Then why won't you share them?" I ask, trying to tread lightly.

"Why should I? Do you think they'll give people closure? That's a joke. Besides, I still need them."

The coldness of her words and creepiness of her tone change the room. It's like the physical manifestation of evil has just pulled up a chair for our conversation and opened the gates of hell so they can watch it play out.

"They're leverage. You're using them as bait so that Ethan will come see you. That's why you didn't cooperate with the police."

Elizabeth shrugs. "Maybe."

"But he hasn't shown up because he doesn't love you like you love him."

She closes her eyes and turns her head away. The words hurt, but I get the feeling that it's the truth. When she turns back to me, tears are forming in her eyes.

"No, he doesn't. Now you want me to give them to you instead."

"Of course I do, but it's your choice to make, not mine."

"Since when do reporters respect boundaries?" Her tone has turned hostile. I'm losing my chance.

"Since when do you abide by stereotypes?" I fire back.

The anger that seizes her face quickly fades into a knowing smile.

"Every person I have ever met is so self-absorbed that they don't take the time to look for the deeper meaning in something right in front of their face. Words contain truth if you can break the code. Time will tell if you're worthy or pretending to be something you're not, just like Ethan and everyone else."

"I'm not naïve. People interpret things in a way that fits their view of the world. They never uncover truth because they don't dig deep enough."

Lizzie's eyes light up. It's the first time any glimmer of happiness has escaped them since I've been here. She stares at me for a long time. I don't want to interrupt her thoughts, as I'm curious about what she'll say next.

"People only hear every eighth word after you've said two paragraphs' worth of them."

It's an odd thing to say. I thought I had gotten through to her, but as fast as it appeared, the glimmer is gone.

"If they bother reading at all. If you don't trust the world to understand, then why did you invite me to talk to you?"

"I'm not going to leave this hospital. I wanted you to know what happened between me and Ethan."

"Lizzie, why don't you think you're leaving here?"

She turns her head away from me again. "It's best left unsaid."

I'm animated when thinking about something. I lost a lot of money playing poker in college because of all my tells. Lizzie is astute enough to notice them too.

"Please, tell me."

"I've told you everything you need to know."

The door to the room opens, and Preston strolls in. "Your time is up, Miss Campos."

I thank him and Elizabeth before he escorts me out. I make my way back down to Tyler's room to tell the team what I learned. Her answers went from straightforward to cryptic. There are still so many unanswered questions, but if her premonition becomes reality, I will never get to ask them.

CHAPTER SEVENTY-THREE

SENATOR ALICIA STANDISH

The White House
Washington, D.C.

This is not a meeting that Alicia expected. Her driver pulls into West Executive Drive and discharges her at the entrance to the West Wing. She's always in awe when she enters this building. Alicia is a prominent senator and is used to being shown into the Oval Office when she comes here. It's her first time visiting the office on the opposite side of the building belonging to the president's chief of staff, Robert Akerman.

"Hello, Robert."

"Senator Standish, it's good to see you. I appreciate you taking the time to meet with me. I know you're very busy."

The two shake hands before he offers her a seat on the sofa. He sits in one of the two high-back fabric chairs across from her and sets his cup of coffee on the table between them.

"You didn't accompany the president up to Massachusetts?" Alicia asks.

"No, I stayed in Washington. It was more important we have this chat. You need to know that the president not inviting you up there was not a slight."

"Thank you. I appreciate the sentiment, but your saying that doesn't make it true."

He recoils slightly at the remark. "It is true, and the president will tell you the same thing. Unless you're more concerned about what FOX News is saying about it."

"I don't care what FOX News has to say about anything, Robert. Voters do."

"People voting for you probably don't watch that station. You authored the Safe America Act, lined up the co-sponsors, and introduced it to the floor. It's an impressive accomplishment. That's why the president has supported you every step of the way."

"Then what's the problem with showing that support publicly?"

"A governor was assassinated. He believes this isn't a time for politics."

"It already is political. Governor Flynn was a good man. He was a trusted ally, and his loss hurts, both politically and personally. I should be up there with the president."

"You need to be here, making the governor's death worth something. The loss of every person who has perished from a firearm must be worth something. You understand that, and that's why your passion about gun control resonates with people more than a photo op does."

Alicia leans back into the sofa. She wants the optics, but he's also right. Her enemies will portray her as cashing in on a tragedy. That might hurt more than rubbing shoulders with the president helps.

"Have you talked to the new governor?" Robert asks, changing the subject.

"We spoke after the shooting. Lucas is just as committed to the gun control agenda as his boss was, if not more so. He said he'd do everything in his power to continue helping me."

"That's good. You know that the FBI labeled the assassination terrorism."

"So I heard. It was the right call. I have no doubt the guy was a right-wing nut job making a political statement."

"You may want to hold off on those pronouncements. The FBI isn't so sure. They identified the shooter but haven't made the information public as of yet. I'm told that there are inconsistencies in his background."

That's news to Alicia. She hasn't spoken to anyone at the Bureau, but Conrad didn't mention anything to her, and he's the number two guy at the DOJ.

"I don't understand."

"Senator, I know how bad you want this bill. I know what it means for you personally and your campaign. Is there any chance you may have engaged in any illegal activity while working on this?"

Now it's Alicia's turn to recoil at the question. "No, why?"

"It's something I needed to ask."

"Robert, I'm a United States Senator and the frontrunner for the party's nomination. Don't play games with me. Why are you asking?"

"I told you that the president's support was contingent on passing the bill. It's also contingent on how you get it passed. You've been making a lot of promises on the Hill."

"Have you ever served in Congress?"

"You know I haven't, but you also know that I've been the longest-serving chief of staff in decades. I know what it takes to get legislation passed. Just don't go too far."

"What is too far?" Alicia asks, seething. "The Republicans own Congress. Without making deals, do you think there's any chance of this bill passing?"

"No, not without public support, and a lot of it."

"Which is why I asked Ethan to help with that during his rallies."

"Is that all?"

"I didn't like the insinuation the first time you made it and like it even less now. If you have something to say, say it."

Robert leans back in his chair and takes off his glasses. "The assassin's name is Denis Lansing. His social media profiles indicate he was a devout gun rights advocate and a member of an ultra-right-wing militia group. They call for the death of any politician who doesn't support the Second Amendment."

"That makes sense."

"It does, but the FBI thinks it was crafted to look that way. They have evidence of Lansing's ties to left-wing groups, including Antifa."

"You're not thinking that the assassination was somehow staged by our supporters? Because that's ridiculous."

"The FBI is investigating. Either way, the president is concerned that this issue is turning violent. Nobody in this building wants a civil war over the Second Amendment. Americans don't respond well to the perception of losing their constitutional rights, and the media is pouring gasoline on that fire. Be careful not to help them."

"Understood."

"I hope so."

The two rise and shake hands. A staffer escorts Alicia out of the West Wing and to her waiting black town car. She settles into the back seat, reflecting on what just happened.

Brian Cooper didn't trust Ryan or Ethan. She dismissed his concerns as paranoia, but now she's the one feeling paranoid. Does the FBI suspect Ethan or Ryan was involved in the assassination of Landon Flynn? It seems absurd. She can't imagine a scenario where the leading gun control advocate and his mentor would be involved in a shooting.

Whatever the FBI presented to him, the president is spooked enough to order his chief of staff to hold this meeting. It could be another effort to torpedo the Safe America Act, but they know the president is a supporter of the legislation.

"Back to Capitol Hill, ma'am?" the driver asks after waiting patiently.

"Yes, please."

The car heads back out of West Executive Drive. Alicia admires the brilliant white marble building out the window as the driver heads toward the wrought-iron gate. Another nagging thought refuses to leave her mind: if she wants this building to be her home and office someday, she needs to get this bill passed before the clock runs out.

CHAPTER SEVENTY-FOUR

VICTORIA LARSEN

Bunker Hill Monument
Charlestown, Massachusetts

Victoria loves this place. On June 17, 1775, soldiers from Massachusetts, Connecticut, and New Hampshire faced the British army in the first major battle of the American Revolution. The bloody fighting raged through fenced pastures on the hilly landscape across the Charles River from Boston. Two thousand four hundred Redcoats took staggering casualties in the three assaults needed to dislodge the Colonial Militia manning a makeshift redoubt atop Breed's Hill.

Nearly two and a half centuries later, an obelisk stands high atop the hill commemorating the battle that took place here. The small marble lodge adjacent to it is a perfect spot to meet someone when you want to avoid prying eyes. Victoria has no doubt Seth will follow her in here. She's right.

"I love the fact that the confusion about the name of this hill goes back to the battle itself," he says, joining her in staring at the statue of Dr. Joseph Warren. "Orders to fortify Bunker's Hill were carried out on Breed's Hill instead. British maps reversed the two names. It's amazing how small things like that have such an impact on history."

"It's always the small things that make a difference. Are the state police trying to take control of the investigation into Flynn's assassination?" she asks, not interested in historical anecdotes right now.

"They're asking why the FBI labeled his assassination terrorism. They're arguing that he was a state official and that it should be a state investigation."

"Who is?"

"Howard Spivey and Lieutenant Governor Spencer...well, former lieutenant governor. You were smart to warn Agent Nishimoto."

"Did you report that meeting to him?"

"No. I told him that I lost you in town. I said that I didn't know why you were there when he asked."

"I bet he was pleased about that."

"He wasn't, so he got a warrant for your arrest. The Commonwealth of Massachusetts now wants you in custody."

"What? On what charge?"

"Unlawful discharge of a firearm, assault with a deadly weapon, and attempted murder. There might be a few I missed. The restaurant we were behind has a camera back there. There's footage of you shooting that kid in the parking lot."

Victoria shakes her head. "I was defending Tierra and myself. I ordered them to stop advancing, and they didn't comply. There was a real fear for my life."

"I know. I was there, remember?"

"Did you tell him that?"

"No. He knows you had help but didn't know it was me. It doesn't matter. Spivey doesn't see it that way."

"And the guy I shot? The same one who shot at me and attacked Tierra twice? Does he care about that?"

"No, but I do," Seth says, handing over a file to Victoria. "We got a hit on the fingerprints they left on their weapons. The guy you shot never went to a hospital. I don't know if he's alive or dead."

"Do the state police have this?" Victoria asks, scanning through the file.

"I kept this on the DL. Nobody on my side knows you have this information. I'll keep the weapons in a safe place as evidence for the time being."

"Thank you, Seth."

"There's one more thing, Victoria. Spivey ordered me to take you in."

Victoria stands a little straighter. "Are you?"

"It's all bullshit, but I can't ignore a warrant. I have a family and a career to think about. So yeah, I was going to, but my plan changed about an hour ago. I got a call from a buddy of mine who works over at MetroWest. Elizabeth Schwarzer is dead."

Victoria stares at him, stunned.

"What? How?"

"Suicide. At least, that's what the police are calling it." Victoria rewards him with a look of utter disbelief. "It happened sometime this morning. The news should break within the hour."

"Tierra interviewed her in the hospital. Did you know that?"

"No, I didn't. Did she say anything?"

"Yeah, she dropped a couple of bombshells and a lot of cryptic mumbo jumbo. You said your plan changed. Where does that leave us?"

Seth lowers his eyes. Victoria knows he's conflicted. Good cops never imagine themselves running afoul of the laws they swore to uphold. Seth's a man of integrity, but also believes in justice. He knows there's nothing just about the charges Spivey is bringing against her.

"You're going to leave here going one way, and I'm going another. Avoid public places and find a place to lay low. Don't use credit cards. You know the drill. I can't know where you are, so don't go anyplace I can find you. Stay away from Tierra's hotel. They'll be watching it. That may buy you a week. After that, all bets are off."

"Okay," Victoria says, more in acceptance of her situation than agreement with his advice.

"This is where we part company, Agent Larsen."

"I'm not an FBI agent anymore, Seth."

He extends his hand, which she takes. "You'll always be an agent to me. Get to the bottom of all this. I'm rooting for you."

Victoria nods. Thank you again, Seth."

"Victoria? One more thing. You get one shot at this. Don't fire until you see the whites of their eyes."

CHAPTER SEVENTY-FIVE

ETHAN HARRINGTON

Coffeechusetts Bean Brewery
Framingham, Massachusetts

There are plenty of coffee shops in Brockhampton, but few have hip music and a cozy atmosphere where someone can sit and enjoy a cup. The two Ethan usually frequented downtown are testaments to the destruction rioters left in their wake. Desperate for some quiet time away from the tumult in town, he drove up to Framingham to get his caffeine fix.

The Coffeechusetts Bean Brewery is easily the largest coffeehouse Ethan has ever seen. It features sacks of beans everywhere, plenty of seating on the first floor and balcony, and almost every flavor and strength of brewed coffee imaginable. Add in some good music pumped through an array of speakers, and it's everything a proper coffeehouse should be.

Ethan finds an empty spot in the corner and fires up his laptop. His first order of business is checking various social media sites. The rally was meant to give a push for the movement by stirring people's emotions with words. He got the attention he was looking for in all the wrong ways. Not a single word about that is written. It's all outrage over the assassination of the governor and riot that decimated his hometown.

Everyone has jumped to conclusions about the shooter and his motives. Conspiracy theorists are out in force with nobody to refute them because the shooter was killed by the police. Ethan searches for news of the event in his browser and scans the headlines:

FBI Labels Assassination in Brockhampton Terrorism
Investigation into the Brockhampton Shooter Yields Surprising Result
Conspiracy Theorists Speculate on Brockhampton Assassination Motives
Brockhampton Assassin Identity Still Not Released

He closes his eyes and rubs the back of his neck to ease the tension. Andre let them down. Ryan wanted something for the media to latch onto and drive coverage of the event. Ethan crafted his message so that his words would do the rest. He wants to believe that Andre defied Ryan and did this on his own. He didn't. Ryan instructed him to shoot and kill the governor of Massachusetts. He must have.

Ethan slams the laptop shut. Ryan used him. He must have arranged this with Andre before Ethan turned over the list of speakers. The cause means more to him than anything. He will sacrifice anything and anyone to get the level of outrage he wants, including murdering an elected official with Ethan standing right next to him.

To Ryan Baino, the ends always justify the means. He could have given the lineup to Andre. He had his own copy. The only reason he wanted the two of them to meet was to get Ethan's fingerprints on the assassination. If anyone talks, including him, he'll be implicated.

Ryan has him by the balls. Their fates are intertwined, and if he ever goes down, it's the end for both of them. Ethan selects a number from his contacts and waits for someone to pick up.

"Action Not Prayers. How may I direct your call?"

"It's Ethan Harrington. Is Ryan back in D.C. yet?"

"No, he's still in Boston but should be flying out soon. Can I take a message for you?"

"No, this can't wait," Ethan says. "Where's he staying?"

* * *

Ethan knocks again on the motel room door in Natick and hears rustling coming from inside. He's impatient, anxious, and angry – three emotions that affect rational judgment in profound ways. The door finally opens, and he wastes no time.

He's not a fighter. The last brawl he got into was in the third grade when another kid tripped him on the playground at recess. Still, throwing a punch is natural, even if he'll never have a career in mixed martial arts. His fist connects with Ryan's face, sending him staggering backward. Ethan lunges at him, and the two of them careen off the end of the bed.

Both spring back to their feet. Ethan lunges at him again. This time, Ryan is ready. He steps to the side and uses Ethan's momentum to send him crashing into a dresser, knocking the small flat screen television to the floor.

Ethan struggles to stand and takes a wild swing, missing his target completely. The miss leaves his right side completely exposed. Ryan lands a couple of punches to the gut before Ethan connects with an uppercut that doesn't have the muscle behind it that it needs to. Bloodied but unfazed, Ryan lands a crushing right to Ethan's temple.

His protégé drops to his hands and knees and gets a kick to his midsection that lays him out on the floor. Ryan is about to kick him again and stops only while Ethan coughs violently.

"Are you done?" Ryan asks, hovering over him. "You wanna tell me what that was all about, or do you want me to kick your ass some more?"

Ethan only scoffs before struggling to his feet and sitting on the edge of the bed. He shakes his head, trying to regain his equilibrium after the blow to his temple. Ryan sits in a chair and gingerly touches his face.

"You killed the governor on purpose," Ethan finally blurts out.

"Andre's guy killed him. I only arranged it. So what?"

"So wh…what's wrong with you? He was an ally!"

"He was a political hack currying favor with someone he thought would be president of the United States. He wanted everyone to think he believed in the cause, and now they do."

"And you think he had to die for that? What good does it do?"

"You still have a lot to learn, kid. People are sheep. They're easy to herd. Don't believe me? Open your eyes and see what's going on out there. People are joining us in droves. You did a great job mobilizing public pressure to get Standish's bill to the floor of the Senate. I just made sure it passes."

"I thought you hated her bill," Ethan sneers.

"I said it was weak, but it's a good start. The journey of a thousand miles starts with the first step."

"How many more people do you plan on killing to get there?"

"Far fewer than if guns are still legal, my friend."

"I wonder if Governor Flynn would agree," Ethan says, rubbing his ribs. They hurt like hell.

"He was a charlatan. He should thank me for cementing his legacy."

"You had him murdered, and for what? *Your* legacy?"

Ryan leans back in his chair, amused. "That's rich coming from you, Ethan. You are the king of dark secrets, remember? You could've gone to the authorities and stopped Caleb at any time. You didn't. You have to live with that, not me."

"You think I'm going to let you hold that over my head forever?"

"That's baked into the cake, buddy. I remember the day I approached you. What was it: two days after the shooting? You were doing all these interviews and basking in the attention. I made my pitch, and you said you had a problem. I had Andre solve it."

"He didn't solve it."

"It's solved now, isn't it? Sometimes things work themselves out. I've done everything I can to protect you. This is how you repay me?"

"I didn't need you for anything."

"Yeah, you did. You wanted to be bigger than the Parkland kids. It wasn't enough to be an activist. You wanted to be the face of the gun control movement so people would fawn over you. I made that happen. You're a household name. You should be thanking me, not hitting me in the face."

Ethan points a finger at Ryan. "Murdering Flynn wasn't needed to pass the bill."

Ryan shakes his head. "And that's where you're wrong. You don't incite people with words shouted through a megaphone or heady debates on television. You need to hit them with a hammer and make them feel it."

He shouldn't have expected a different answer. Ryan will do anything to force society to contort to his worldview.

"How long before you decide that it's time to sacrifice me?"

"You know, Ethan, you're brilliant on television. You look into reporters' eyes and lie right to them."

"Answer the question, Ryan."

"I am. You said in one of those interviews that you would gladly give your life to save others."

"Go to hell!"

"You first, buddy."

He realizes that this conversation is going nowhere. Ethan stands and edges closer to the door. There is no telling how Ryan will react to what he has to say.

"I could take this to the authorities."

"Nobody likes a tattletale, Ethan, but I can't stop you. Just know that we'll go down together. You'll become a pariah instead of a messiah. I'm ready to lose everything for this. The question is, are you?"

Ethan glares at Ryan. They both know the answer to that question.

His mentor shakes his head, walks over to the door, and opens it. "Get the hell out of my hotel room and think about it somewhere else. I need to clean up and get back to D.C. You do what you think you need to."

CHAPTER SEVENTY-SIX

CAPITOL BEAT

Cable News Studio
Washington, D.C.

The two sides had to be kept physically separated. Wilson has spent a career moderating contentious debates and refereeing arguments between people who legitimately hated each other. Never has he felt so much angst between two groups of people. They were anxious about being on the same set together.

To gun control advocates, Oren Balshaw might as well have cloven hooves, horns, and a tail. They believe the mouthpiece for the American Firearms Association is leading the sheep right off the cliff in this country. The AFA believes the same thing in reverse — the Second Amendment is how people preserve rights enshrined by the rest. To both sides, there is little room for conversation or compromise on the issue.

"Welcome back to our special extended Sunday edition of *Capitol Beat*," Wilson says, after returning from the commercial break. "This is our continuing coverage of the deadly attack on the rally and subsequent rioting in Brockhampton, Massachusetts yesterday. We've heard from both sides of the gun debate this evening, and this is my final thought.

"The conversation about guns in America has turned into a vicious argument that claimed its first high-profile victim. Unlike the violence that has erupted at rallies and marred marches, this was a deliberate hostile attack. Governor Landon Flynn of Massachusetts was not a bystander — he was the target. Of the fuzzy circumstances and conspiracy theories swirling around what happened in Brockhampton, that much is fact.

"Advocates claim that gun rights groups have drawn first blood in America's second civil war. The shooter's motivations may have died with him, but the FBI has labeled this an act of terrorism. America has heard the statistics: five are dead, including the alleged shooter, and countless injured in the melee that followed."

Wilson pauses and folds his hands in front of him.

"Americans should be coming together over these tragic events, but we instead find ourselves further divided. Collective mourning over the loss of a governor is impossible when people assign blame and point fingers. Whether this is an isolated incident by some deranged lunatic or a symptom of the heated rhetoric in today's society isn't important.

"Gun control advocates believe there is no reason for anyone to possess a firearm and regard owners as a menace to society. Second Amendment defenders argue that legislating away evil is impossible, and penalizing gun owners makes America more dangerous, not safer. These arguments have devolved into hatred for those with different opinions. Maybe that has manifested itself into an assassination, or perhaps it hasn't. Americans should agree to let the FBI do their jobs before concluding anything.

"This is not a zero-sum game where one side wins and one loses. Right now, it's bigger than that. Of all the questions surrounding what happened this weekend in Brockhampton, there is one conclusion we can draw: we are all losing. That is my final thought, and it's for the record.

"We will return tomorrow night with the latest developments of the assassination and rioting in Brockhampton. I'm Wilson Newman; goodnight."

CHAPTER SEVENTY-SEVEN

SENATOR ALICIA STANDISH

Hart Senate Office Building
Washington, D.C.

When a day starts with the alarm not going off, spilling coffee on yourself because you're walking too fast, and getting heckled on the Metro by some tourists from Texas, it's safe to assume it's going to be a long one. Alicia walks down the corridor and turns into her office to find her chief of staff waiting for her impatiently. Her assumption about the day is proving correct.

"Good morning, Senator."

"It's never a good sign when you're waiting by the door of the office first thing in the morning, Rahul."

"I have news."

"Fine. At least let me get to my office first."

Rahul is desperate to prove himself in his first shot at the big time. Under normal circumstances, the senator would have found a permanent replacement by now. With her bill on the Senate agenda and the rigors of a national campaign right around the corner, there isn't enough time to find a seasoned replacement for Brian Cooper. Fortunately, legislative needs will wane as they get closer to Election Day, so there isn't much he needs to do other than run the office. At least he's eager to please.

"What do you have?" Alicia asks, settling in at her desk.

"I spoke with Angela Mays. She says your poll numbers went through the roof. Congrats."

"We lost an ally in Landon Flynn and the lives of four other people in Brockhampton last weekend," she says, sternly. "I'm not celebrating a bump in the polls right now."

Rahul immediately regrets saying it. "Apologies, Senator."

"Was that your news, or is there something more?" she asks, logging in to her computer.

"Uh, yes, ma'am. I had a conversation with some of our friends in the media. They received a letter from Elizabeth Schwarzer this morning that was sent by her attorney."

"Oh, yeah? Which news organization?"

"All of them. Every major outlet in the country got the same one."

"She had access to a printer from her hospital bed?"

"Not exactly. There were two hundred letters – all the exact same and all handwritten. The news will break any time now."

Alicia looks at him like he's crazy. She doesn't even hand-write her Christmas cards. She'd almost be impressed with the effort if Elizabeth hadn't likely abetted a mass murder.

"Were they suicide notes?"

"No, they said it was mostly poetic rambling."

She closes her eyes and exhales. Elizabeth could have said anything. There's no limit to how much damage she could do to the passage of the Safe America Act with a few carefully chosen words. The fact that Rahul's contact says it's gibberish is a relief.

"Was there anything about Caleb's motive included in her poetic rambling?"

"No."

"Then tell me, really, why does anybody care what she said? Elizabeth Schwarzer abetted a mass murder. Nobody should care one iota about what she has to say."

"But everyone will. It's ratings and clicks for the media because America has a morbid fascination with Brockhampton."

Alicia leans back in her chair. He's right, but she doesn't have to like it. She'll never understand why America is captivated by a massacre.

"Get a copy before the world sees it. Anything else?"

Rahul looks down and shifts his weight. "Yes, ma'am. I have one more piece of troubling news. A mutual friend of ours told me that Brian Cooper is talking to the media."

"Brian is no longer in my employ," Alicia says, trying to mask her own concern. "He can speak to whomever he chooses. I'm sure he's looking to get a gig in some Washington news bureau."

"Senator, he's working with Tierra Campos."

Alicia rubs the bridge of her nose. The hits just keep on coming. She wanted to believe his past loyalty to her wouldn't cause him to seek revenge. Now she knows that she was wrong.

"I see. Did your friend happen to say what Brian is discussing with *Front Burner*?"

"Not specifically, no. I can try to find out."

"Do that. Thank you, Rahul."

He leaves, and Alicia immediately gives up trying to focus on anything else. Brian doesn't know anything damaging about her. She has never engaged in any activity that would jeopardize her run for the White House. That doesn't mean he won't make things up. Brian wouldn't be the first source to lie to a journalist for personal gain.

The stakes are going up another notch. She has a growing number of enemies trying to take her down. That list will only get longer through the primaries, the nomination, and the election. Welcome to American politics.

CHAPTER SEVENTY-EIGHT

TIERRA CAMPOS

JFK Presidential Library & Museum
Boston, Massachusetts

The John F. Kennedy Presidential Library and Museum sits on the Columbia Point waterfront site with views of Boston's skyline and the Harbor Islands. It's a unique glimpse into the 1960s and offers visitors a chance to experience Kennedy's thousand days in office.

I'm not here for political nostalgia any more than I was on the U.S.S. Constitution to experience nineteenth-century naval warfare. It's only coincidence that my meetings with Brian Cooper are taking on a historical flair.

"JFK was one of my favorites," he says, materializing next to me.

"Oh yeah? Are you most fond of the womanizing, the conspiracies, or the shady way he got elected in the first place?"

"I take it you're not a fan?"

"Actually, I am. JFK had a vision that few presidents exhibit. I'm just intellectually honest about his presidency. I wonder what his legacy would have been if Oswald hadn't assassinated him. Is that for me?"

Brian looks at the file under his arm, wondering how I noticed it without looking at him.

"It is, but first, you need to tell me why you want it."

"Were you at the rally this weekend?"

Brian shakes his head. "No."

"I was. I think the riot left more of an impression than the rally did, though."

"True for most Americans."

"I think that was the point," I say, turning toward him.

Brian's head shoots around. "You think Ryan Baino was behind it?"

"I don't know. I do think he was behind the attacks on me, Victoria's drive-by, and Elizabeth Schwarzer's coma. If he's capable of all that, why would he stop short of killing a politician?"

"How do you know about Elizabeth's attackers?"

"She gave me a description of them."

"Interesting. When the Senator started working with Ethan to help promote the Safe America Act, I learned Ryan was involved, so I checked him out. This is the list I compiled of his known associates."

"You never explained why you didn't share this with your boss."

"My job was to protect Senator Standish. Much of that involved advising her about the people she came into contact with. Baino has a fairly checkered past, but he was an asset to her. I thought it was better to just keep an eye on him."

"What do you think now?"

"That I should have done things differently."

Brian pulls the file out from under his arm and hands it to me. There isn't that much in it – mostly background information and a photo or two. I peel through the pages looking for something interesting. I stop when I find it.

"All these people are Antifa?"

"Most of them. Victoria can help find out what the FBI has on them."

"She can't. She was suspended by the FBI, and there's a state warrant out for her arrest."

"For what?"

I stare at one of the pictures and focus on the man's eyes. I imagine a skull face shield over his nose and mouth, and punch the picture with my index finger a couple of times.

"Shooting this guy during the riot," I say, turning the picture toward Brian so he can see it.

Brian shakes his head. "Andre Serrano. He has a rap sheet a mile long."

I stare hard at the picture of the man who assaulted me twice and was stopped from doing it a third time. Skull Face has a name now. He has a boss that was giving him orders. He also has a connection to one of the most powerful politicians in the country.

"Alicia Standish is a United States senator, Mister Cooper. You can't seriously be saying that she doesn't know that her staunchest ally was involved with people like this."

"And yet I am. The senator is an idealist. She's politically savvy but assumes people's motives are as pure as hers. That includes ideologues like Ryan Baino. I tried to protect her from people like that. My replacement isn't up to that task."

"Okay, I know we made a deal, but nothing I've seen exonerates Senator Standish from anything."

"I let it leak that I was talking to you."

So, that's his game. I should have known. He ultimately wants an article that clears the senator of wrongdoing. In the interim, he's trying to manipulate her by using me.

"You're something else."

"It only reflects on me, not you. The senator doesn't know what I'll say. I'm hoping she'll be careful because of that."

"Or she'll come after you."

"She has a mean streak, but revenge isn't her style." He hands me a thumb drive. "This has everything included in that file you're holding and a whole lot more."

Brian turns to walk out. There's one more thing we need to discuss before he goes.

"You heard about Elizabeth's letter?"

"Word travels fast at my level, Miss Campos. Outside of her attorney and her grandmother, you're the only person who spoke with her after she emerged from her coma. Maybe you can figure out what the nonsense she wrote means."

He grins, leaving the exhibit in the direction of the exit. I stare at the folder in my hand. Political operatives are purveyors of information. In that way, they aren't unlike the intelligence community. He was right about my chat with Lizzie. Could he be right about Senator Standish as well?

CHAPTER SEVENTY-NINE

CAPITOL BEAT

Cable News Studio
Washington, D.C.

The producer starts the count. The news cycle is moving so fast that Wilson isn't sure an hour-long show is enough anymore. With gun control dominating the broadcast every night, he wonders if he will ever be able to discuss any of the dozens of other issues facing the nation.

"Good Evening, it is Tuesday, June third; I'm Wilson Newman and this…is…*Capitol Beat*."

The opening sequence rolls, and Wilson prepares himself. He's been reading off a teleprompter his entire adult life and honed that skill to the point where he could read James Joyce on air without looking like a fool. This is different.

"On tonight's show, we have Attorney General Lisa Ehler and FBI Special Agent Lance Fuller here to discuss the latest on the assassination of Massachusetts Governor Landon Flynn. We also have pollsters from the Marist Institute of Public Opinion bringing us the latest gun control numbers, and reports from Brockhampton and Capitol Hill in Washington.

"But first, newsrooms across the country received a handwritten letter this morning from Elizabeth Schwarzer via her attorney, Preston Swain. In a statement given to the media this afternoon, he explained that his client instructed him to release the letters upon her death. A day later, she was found dead in her hospital room of an apparent suicide.

"Our panel will discuss that creepy premonition in a segment later in the show, but first, I'm going to read the letter she sent on the air. These are the final written words of Elizabeth Schwarzer," Wilson says as the words appear on the teleprompter.

He reminds himself to read them slowly and deliberately, not because he wants to drive the point home, but because they make no sense:

> Death comes to us all. No longer am I the movie of the week. I'm free of this novelty t-shirt world masquerading as Shakespeare and Socrates. Humorless animals shed crocodile tears for the fallen and celebrate the demise of those deemed irredeemable.

> The Enlightenment sought truth and found only corruption of spirit. Unanswerable questions deserve no answers. Those that seek them wander through the dark woods known only to a couple. The enlightened find truth where emotion and ecstasy first met.
>
> Acidic tears burn my cheeks for nobody. The morality of my soul weeps not for answers. Immoral societies burn witches at stakes and lie themselves. Souls, like water, find low ground in a sunken world falling ever deeper into the abyss.
>
> People walk in shoes made of lead as mankind slogs slowly through the pouring rain to their oblivion. My peers spend time training for futures devoid of happiness with no room for air or error. Happiness is illusion in a circus fun house. Life is not the novel you read and shelve in a bookcase; it is pain, and mine has ended.

"Freud would have had a field day with this young woman," Wilson says after the pause when he finished. "Her last words to the world were dark and poetic, just like how she was characterized in life. Whatever she knew about Caleb Pratt's motive in the Brockhampton massacre died with her. That may be the real tragedy behind her life and her death.

"We'll be back with the attorney general after this short break."

CHAPTER EIGHTY

VICTORIA LARSEN

The Hotel Devereux at Copley Square
Boston, Massachusetts

Forget the fancy security systems with high-definition cameras that cost thousands of dollars before installation fees. A quartet of twenty-dollar pet monitoring cameras does the same job at a fraction of the price. In this case, those cameras allow Victoria and the *Front Burner* team to watch a state police tactical unit bust down the door to Tierra's hotel room like they were Marines in Fallujah.

The men and one woman, who is working hard to look like one of the boys, fan out with assault weapons up and at the ready. They check every inch of the room. One of them checks the refrigerator as if it were a legitimate hiding spot.

"Keep searching, boys, we're not there," Victoria says, grinning.

Austin's room is relatively safe for her. If the police are doing this under the auspices of a warrant, as they likely are, his suite wouldn't be included in it. She doubts they know the journalists are here. Thank God for Seth Chambers.

He came through for Victoria in a big way, both with the heads-up on the arrest warrant and by warning her about the raid via text. The two-hour notice gave Jerome and Logan time to install the makeshift surveillance network in Tierra's room so they could all watch the show.

"Are they still looking for Victoria?" Logan asks.

"No, the warrant is an excuse. I'm not the primary target," Victoria says, watching them intently.

"How do you know?"

"Because they're searching the room."

The team leans in to see the officers ransacking the place. One of them brings out one of Tierra's bras from her bedroom and makes a comment that causes the others to laugh. She doesn't need audio to recognize its sexual nature. Even the woman with them gets a kick out of it. So much for professionalism.

Tierra isn't overly concerned about the men displaying her undergarments. After the hell she's been through with the doxxing, it's tame by comparison.

"They think we have Lizzie's journals."

"Why would they think that?" Tyler asks.

"I don't know, but maybe my chat with Joseph Mayfield had something to do with it," Victoria concludes.

"Hey guys, I know you're busy watching grown men act like teenagers at a Victoria's Secret, but I think I have something," Janey says over the phone.

"What's up?" Austin asks.

"I've spent the past hour comparing Elizabeth Schwarzer's death letter to her other writing. Something is off."

"Death letter" is what the media personalities call it since neither "suicide note" nor "manifesto" seems to fit. Tierra is trying to get the team to drop the term, but her pleas are falling on deaf ears. They like the ridiculous moniker.

"Other writing? You mean her poetry?"

"Yeah, the stuff her grandmother gave the press after she was hospitalized," Janey explains.

"Is the death letter a fake?" Olivia asks.

"No, I think she wrote it, but it's just…different."

"She just got out of a coma," Tyler offers. "Who knows how much brain damage she sustained."

"Or she was just plain crazy," Logan adds.

"I think Lizzie was much smarter than people know. As for her injuries, she was lucid enough when I spoke with her," Tierra interjects.

The group nods. Tierra was the only one of them to speak with her. They won't challenge her impression.

"Okay, so what are we missing?" Victoria asks.

"Nothing. I mean, there's nothing here," Jerome says. "It's just a bunch of meaningless words strung together."

"Not to her," Madison says. "The imagery is bizarre, but that's how she saw the world. If I've learned anything in my life, it's that people only see what they want to."

Tierra's back straightens like she was hit with a thousand volts of electricity. She closes her eyes, and her lips start to move.

"What is it?"

Tierra holds her hand up. "What did you say, Olivia?"

"People only –"

"Never mind, I heard you. Jerome, can you pull up the letter?"

Jerome does as requested and shares his computer screen with the television in the room. It would make it much easier for them all to see if Tierra moved away from the front of it.

"What is it?" Austin asks.

"I'm not sure. Lizzie said something at the hospital that didn't make sense at the time. 'Words contain truth if you can break the code.' It was out of context but felt like there was a deeper meaning to it. I think maybe it's in here."

"There's nothing here," Logan argues. "Unless you think we should take her literally about finding the answers in the 'dark woods known only to a couple.'"

"No. Lizzie was an enigma. She wouldn't be that obvious."

Tierra continues staring at the letter as she recalls her conversation in the hospital. The long silence grows longer as everyone stays quiet and gives her time to think.

"Every eighth word after the second paragraph," she finally mumbles. "Lizzie said 'nobody hears anything more than every eighth word after the second paragraph!'"

"Are you sure?"

"I've never listened to anything more attentively than her words in that hospital. I dismissed it as her being figurative, but what if it was literal? Count it out."

Everyone gathers around the television. Tyler takes up the task of writing the result on the second whiteboard as Olivia slowly reads the third and fourth paragraphs. Everyone counts on their fingers as she does. Halfway through, the pace picks up with the rise in excitement.

When Tyler's finished, he steps away from the whiteboard and sits on the edge of the bed. He lets out a deep breath as everyone sharply inhales. It's not figurative. It's not metaphorical. It isn't even philosophical. What they read is astounding.

CHAPTER EIGHTY-ONE

SENATOR ALICIA STANDISH

U.S. Capitol Building
Washington, D.C.

Alicia has put in long hours to get this far. Once a committee has reported a bill, as they have with the Safe America Act, it is placed on the Senate Calendar of Business pursuant to Senate Rule VIII. The calendar is not what most people think. It's more a to-do list of legislation eligible for consideration. Countless bills are never brought up during a two-year Congress.

To get a floor vote in the Senate, the majority leader makes a "motion to proceed." The Senate can begin consideration if it's agreed to by a majority vote. Alicia's problem is the Democrats aren't the majority party, so Republicans needed to agree to it. The public outcry following the assassination of Governor Flynn forced their hand. At least some good came from the tragedy.

"Pursuant to rule twenty-two, the Chair lays before the Senate the pending cloture motion, which the clerk will state," the presiding officer commands from the rostrum.

"Nervous?" one of her colleagues asks, as the clerk announces the motion and readies the chamber for the vote.

"Not as much as I will be after this motion passes and we have the actual vote."

Alicia made the cloture motion on the Safe America Act right after the motion to proceed succeeded. There is a built-in cooling-off period, and now that the quorum call is complete, it's time to vote on it. Alicia has exactly sixty votes, according to the last count by the minority whip. Just enough Republicans are crossing party lines to bring an end to the debate and get the bill an up or down vote.

"We, the undersigned Senators, in accordance with the provisions of rule twenty-two of the standing rules of the Senate, do hereby move to bring to a close debate on the Safe America Act," the senior assistant legislative clerk reads.

"I ask for the yeas and nays," Alicia announces, expressing her desire that a roll call vote be entered into the Congressional Record.

"Is there a sufficient second? There appears to be a sufficient second," the presiding officer announces after a few dozen hands go up. "The clerk will call the roll."

"It's game time," Alicia mutters to herself.

She scans the chamber. It looks like everyone is back in town for this, even the presidential candidates. Legislators running for the presidency routinely miss votes when campaign season starts. She will miss her fair share once this bill passes.

"You know the Republicans will filibuster this to death if this cloture motion fails," her colleague warns her.

"It won't fail."

"Filibuster" is a Dutch word meaning "pirate" and has a long history in blocking legislative action. Most Americans are familiar with Jimmy Stewart's filibuster as Senator Jefferson Smith in Frank Capra's *Mr. Smith Goes to Washington*. Most of them aren't that sexy in real life, although Senators Huey P. Long, Strom Thurmond, and Ted Cruz have had some memorable ones.

The clerk begins to call the names of all senators in alphabetical order, and each member is directed by rule twelve to declare assent or dissent to the question without debate.

"Abernathy."

"Yea."

"Adams."

"Yea."

"Archer."

"Nay."

Senators go to the rostrum to make their "yea" or "nay" responses after the clerk calls their names. The vote may take no longer than fifteen minutes, as was established by unanimous consent at the start of this Congress. Sometimes they are kept open beyond this limit to accommodate senators hurrying to the chamber to cast their vote, but that won't be a problem for this one.

"Baumann."

"Nay."

"Carpenter."

"Nay."

Cordova."

"Yea."

The House has screens installed over their rostrum that show the results of their electronic voting. She could use that right now. She's trying to keep count in her head. This vote is going to be tight.

The business of Congress is incredibly dull. It's the reason C-SPAN doesn't bring in huge ratings. This is a crucial vote only because it sets the stage for a more meaningful one. The American people don't care about this – they only want to know the result. It's one reason politics has become so sensationalized. Few Americans understand the process but love the drama it creates when politicians flock to cameras.

"Standish."

"Yea," Alicia says, moving back towards her small desk after the vote is cast.

"Talarico."

"Nay."

"Thomas."

"Yea."

There are no surprises. Everyone has voted as Alicia expected they would. Each vote gets entered into the Senate Legislative Information System. The government is tidy about their records, at least in Congress. The bureaucracy is another matter.

"Wainwright."

"Nay."

"Wetzel."

The Senator from Arizona gives her a nod as he approaches the rostrum. Alicia nods back and allows herself a small smile. His vote will do the trick and set the Safe America Act up for a dramatic floor vote in a few days. With the support she's earned in the House, successfully ending the debate right here and now paves the road for its passage.

"Nay."

Alicia's jaw slacks open as a buzz fills the chamber. With no remaining senators waiting to vote, the presiding officer announces the result.

"On this vote, the yeas are fifty-nine, the nays are sixty-one. The motion fails."

Alicia balls her hands into fists as they begin to shake. The debate will continue until she makes another cloture motion that passes. Daniel Wetzel has screwed her, their party, and the American people. The coward is fleeing the chamber now, but he can't hide from her for long. She stomps out after him before being ambushed by the press.

Wetzel heads for the subway that leads to the office buildings. Alicia stares at him as he flees. He can run, but he can't hide. He's going to answer for this.

CHAPTER EIGHTY-TWO

ETHAN HARRINGTON

Robert Treat Paine State Park
Brockhampton, Massachusetts

The spot isn't accessible by the parking lot that families use when they bring their children to play on the small beach. Ethan was thrilled that a cop didn't show up when he was meeting Andre there. Fortunately, he doesn't need to tempt fate twice.

After hours, high school kids parked on a dirt road leading to the hangout spot by the lake. That's where Ethan and Connor left the car and began to tromp down a path through the woods with a pair of flashlights.

"I can't believe I'm here doing this," Connor says, whining for the second time in thirty seconds as he carries the small gas can. Ethan isn't about to endure a third.

"Stop your bitching. It's the least you can do for sitting there while your father had a knife to my face."

"If he finds out about this, he'll have one to mine."

"Do you want to fix this or not?"

"It is fixed," Connor argues. "Lizzie is dead."

"Yeah, but her journals still exist. I don't want to spend the rest of my life worrying that some kid will stumble onto them."

"What makes you think they're here?"

Ethan doesn't respond immediately. They reach the rock that marks the center of the teenage gathering area. The grass is beaten down, and empty cans litter the ground. He points his beam to the north, trying to get his bearings.

"Because there's no other place left to look," he finally says.

"If I end up with Lyme disease or Zika, I'm going to be pissed."

"Mosquitos and ticks will be the least of your problems if you keep whining about it. Come on."

There's no path leading the way to the hidden place, which was the point the first time he was here. The pair trudge through the underbrush along the edge of the lake, careful not to get too close to the water.

"I hope you know where you're going."

"I do. We're here," Ethan says, spotting the large rock fifty feet into the woods and knowing that there's a natural depression in the ground next to it.

It's the perfect hiding spot. The sunken area is the size of a standard swimming pool and deep enough to obscure almost anyone ducked down in it. It's concealed by scrub brush, although the floor of the depression is nothing but pine needles.

"I didn't know this place was here," Connor says, swinging his flashlight around in an arc as he scans the depression.

"I didn't either until someone showed it to me."

"Wait a second. Did Lizzie show you? Is this the place you nailed her?"

"Shut up and look over there."

"Oh, man."

Ethan sighs and points his flashlight at the other side of the small rise. He knows he should never have told Connor what happened between him and Lizzie. It was the only way he could explain how he knew about Caleb's plan to shoot up their school. That was before being told that he was going to be the first victim.

"There's nothing here, bro."

"It's here somewhere. Check near those trees."

"How do you know it's here? Did you have a séance with your old flame?"

"What Lizzie said in the second paragraph was about us. She wanted me to know where the journals were."

"You're unbelievable."

He moves off and checks near the trees as Ethan stares up at the dark top of the rock. No way she would climb up there to hide them. He recalls the letter's message. "Where emotion and ecstasy first met." That can only mean one place, and he points the beam at the base of the rock where they first had sex.

Evergreen boughs and leaves cover an old Army ammo can with yellow writing stenciled on the side that indicates it used to hold 20mm rounds. It's big enough to cram notebooks in.

"Bingo."

"You found it?" Connor asks, almost tripping as he rushes over. "Damn. Where'd she get that from?"

"How the hell would I know?"

Ethan unlatches the box, pries the handle up, and opens it towards the hinged end. He shines the light inside. It's packed full of notebooks. He turns the ammo can upside down and dumps them on the ground in the middle of the depression as Connor keeps the light on him.

"Give me the gas can."

"Aren't you going to read them?" Connor asks.

"I already know what they say, same as you."

Ethan reaches for the gas can. Connor yanks it away. He tries again with the same result.

"What the hell are you doing?"

"My father wants to read them."

"Not a chance," Ethan says.

"It wasn't a suggestion," Connor says. "We owe him."

"We don't owe him shit. Once these are destroyed, all the evidence of what happened goes with it. Give me the gas."

Connor pops the cap off the spout and starts dumping the gasoline on the ground. Ethan slides his hand down towards the end of the Maglite and swings it. The sweeping arc ends with the satisfying crack of hitting Connor's face. His knees go weak, and he crumples to the ground. Ethan shines the light on him, amazed that the flashlight still works.

"What the hell, man!" Connor checks his cheek and sees the blood on it from the laceration.

"Anything more you want to say? Like last words?" Ethan says, menacingly.

"You've lost it!"

"Yeah, maybe."

Ethan seizes the gas can and dumps its contents over the notebooks. He pulls out a Zippo and sparks it after three attempts. He tosses the lighter onto the pile of notebooks and watches as they erupt in flames.

"Why did you bother telling me what Caleb was planning?" Connor asks as he climbs to his feet.

"Because you were a friend."

"I never should have listened to you."

Ethan stares back at the fire consuming the notebooks. The flames cause shadows to bounce off the rock and the scrub brush that line the edge of the depression.

"Nobody can hurt us now. Not even your father."

"We owe him everything, Ethan. Do you know what would have happened if he hadn't intervened?"

"He did it for himself more than for you or me. We're done here. Let's go."

"What do you want me to tell my father?" Connor whines.

"I don't really give a damn," Ethan says, feeling like a huge weight has been lifted off his shoulders as he watches the flames die down as the last of the paper is consumed. He feels invincible as he climbs the embankment out of the depression.

CHAPTER EIGHTY-THREE

VICTORIA LARSEN

Lead Rain Shooting Center
Brockhampton, Massachusetts

Victoria pulled into the parking lot with Tierra and Austin half an hour ago, but it feels like three hours. Austin waits impatiently in the driver's seat as Victoria keeps her head down in the back seat. Neither of them has said much. They only stare at the door, waiting for Mark Wilkerson to unlock it and open the range.

"Come on, Mark, open the damn shop," Victoria mutters.

"It could be worse, Vic. You could still be in the duffle bag."

"Haha."

None of them could be sure there was an unwatched exit at the hotel, so the team went full Hollywood to sneak her out without being seen. Tyler purchased a huge North Face duffle bag with wheels on it so they could drag it along the ground. The look on Victoria's face was priceless when they told her to climb in.

It was tight and uncomfortable, but she fit inside. They managed to wheel her down to the lobby and out to the car without anyone intervening. Once they were out of Boston, Austin freed her from the bag that he hefted into the trunk. She's less than thrilled with the experience.

"You know, we could be wrong about all this," Austin says from the driver's seat.

"Yeah," Tierra says, "but I don't think so. Lizzie wanted me to find her journals, but only if I was honest with her about listening to what she was saying. She was clever."

"Evil clever," Austin mutters.

"But still clever."

"Vic, how well do you know this guy?" Austin asks, staring in the rearview mirror.

"We met once."

"That doesn't mean he'll let you search his range."

"I think I can convince him."

"Well, here's your chance to find out. Good luck."

Mark comes to the door and fiddles with the lock from the inside. The two women climb out of the car and look around like they're casing the place. Mark is still standing at the entrance when Tierra and Victoria walk in. He grimaces when he sees them.

"Hello, Gunny," Victoria says, using the Marine's rank instead of his name.

"Agent Larsen. It can't be a good sign that you're here this early."

"Don't be like that, Gunny," she says, playfully. "I'm hoping to repay the favor you did for me the last time I was here by making your life easier."

Mark snorts, chomping down on his cigar stub. "Who's this? Another agent?"

"No, my name is Tierra Campos. I'm a journalist."

"Have a nice day, ladies."

Mark walks back to the counter and fans through the waivers on a clipboard. He has no interest in paying either of them any attention. Victoria looks at Tierra. It's her move.

"Gunny, I never served in uniform."

"Ya don't say?" he sneers, not looking up. Tierra isn't dissuaded.

"It wasn't my calling, but I do know something about duty, sacrifice, and courage."

"Yeah, sure you do."

"I was the victim of a school shooting ten years ago. I was hiding in a closet with the shooter right on the other side of the door. He was forcing his way in. He pointed his rifle at me. I thought I was going to die at that moment. I've never known that kind of fear."

Mark nods at her. There's no doubt that he's seen his share of action. He can relate to the fear, and it has his attention.

"What happened?"

"The police stormed in. They got into a shootout with the gunman and killed him. If they had come in ten seconds later, I wouldn't be standing here."

Victoria wishes she hadn't mentioned that. While it may appeal to Mark's sacrifice and oath to defend the innocent, he can construe it in a different way. The way his eyes narrow and mouth contorts, that's what has happened.

"Let me guess. You're on a crusade to violate everyone's Second Amendment rights now."

"Not really, no. I'm not here to advance an agenda. I'm here for the truth."

"That's what they all say."

"Fine. Come on, Vic. We'll let the police tear this place down to the foundation when they search for it. I can just as easily camp outside with every other reporter in the country when they do. I'm sure you'll love all the attention."

Victoria is about to protest but decides to trust her friend. Tierra is an expert at getting information from people, so she plays along. She tosses a shrug in Mark's direction and follows her to the door.

"Search for what?" Mark asks before they can leave.

"The biggest piece of the puzzle about what happened in Brockhampton High School," Victoria says.

Mark gives them a puzzled look.

"Lizzie Schwarzer kept journals," Tierra explains. "She stashed them at your range. If we find them, nobody will ever need to know where they were hidden."

"I saw her writing in those notebooks. What makes ya think they're here?"

Tierra hands him a printout of the letter to the media. He puts on his reading glasses and unfolds the paper. He starts to read before looking over his frames at her.

"I've seen this before in the paper. It's mumbo-jumbo."

"Yeah, it is unless you know how to read it. I met Lizzie in the hospital when she came out of her coma. While we were talking, she gave me a code that I didn't understand until this letter was released. Starting with the third paragraph, read every eighth word."

"The…answers lie…in…the…lead rain…training room…in…the…bookcase." Mark sighs, handing the article back to Tierra. "Shit."

The look on his face is a mixture of surprise and resignation. He's convinced. Veterans are a fickle bunch who are great Americans but distrust the bureaucracy. They respect law enforcement, but that only goes so far. There was no telling how he would react to this.

"She waited in the training room sometimes when Caleb was on the range. Follow me," he says, leading them down a hallway past the handgun range, several briefing rooms, and the armory.

The training room is nothing more than a makeshift classroom with long tables and chairs, a whiteboard at the front, and an old steel bookcase from the 1950s along the back wall. Victoria and Tierra walk up to it like it holds the Holy Grail. In some respects, it does.

Mark pulls out some dusty old binders and military manuals, starting with the top shelf and moving down. He checks behind the ones that remain. Tierra and Victoria want to help to speed the process up, but Mark doesn't ask for help or appear interested in accepting it. With one shelf left, both women are beginning to wonder if they made the wrong assumption.

"Had to be the bottom shelf, didn't it?"

The Marine kneels, his joints popping with the effort. With a hand on the side to steady himself, he pulls out old firing manuals and bends down to look.

"I'll be damned," he says, muscling out a thick accordion file.

He examines it before looking at the two anxious women. With one last chomp on his cigar, he hands the file to Tierra.

"Thank you, Mark."

"Aren't ya gonna open it?"

"I didn't think you… Don't you have a range to run?" Tierra asks.

"Sixty-six people were murdered in this town. The kid who did it shot at my range. I damn sure want to know why. Open it."

CHAPTER EIGHTY-FOUR

TIERRA CAMPOS

Lead Rain Shooting Center
Brockhampton, Massachusetts

I untie the accordion file and carefully peel back the flap. A dozen black and white composition notebooks are crammed inside. I select the most recent one, take a deep breath, and open it. The writing started in February of last year, a month and a half before the Brockhampton shooting. I flip through it and find the last entry is fifteen pages or so from the back. I look at the date and exhale.

This is beyond creepy. On these pages are the inner thoughts of a deceased young woman whose friend murdered sixty-six people. I brace myself for what I might find on the pages.

"Read it," Mark directs, thrusting his chin at the notebook in my hand.

I shift my eyes to Victoria, waiting for an objection. Instead, she nods. I take a breath and exhale before starting to read.

April 2nd

Tomorrow is Caleb's big day. It's weird knowing that everything will change; that our lives will never be the same; that Caleb will never see another sunrise or sunset.

Part of me feels guilty about Caleb. He's only ever wanted my love and attention. He could never understand that my heart belongs to Ethan. When he enters the school with his gun, Ethan and Connor will be waiting for him. They will stop him.

The world will react to what Caleb tried to do. They will assign blame and scream empty words about how life is precious as they lift Ethan and Connor on their shoulders like the heroes they are.

Living life isn't the priority anymore. Winning at it is.

Lizzie

Victoria and I stare at each other for a long time. The gravity of these words weighs on me. She must feel it too.

"He knew it was going to happen," Victoria whispers. "They were going to stop him so they could be heroes."

"Principal Nebbich said he wasn't a popular kid in school. This is how he was going to change that."

"What went wrong?" Mark asks, chomping down on his cigar again. "Because he didn't stop shit."

"I don't know. That was the last entry."

"Are there entries that mention Ethan?" Victoria asks.

I leaf through the pages. There is writing on every one of them. If the other eleven notebooks are the same, it will be an incredible insight into what happened and what was going through Lizzie's mind.

"Yeah, a lot of them, from the looks of it."

"Let's see if we can find out how this all started," Victoria says, pulling an earlier notebook. Mark folds his arms, not wanting to participate.

I begin scanning the first pages of the journal I have before Victoria starts reading.

January 11th

I told Ethan what Caleb was planning today. He was shocked that Caleb could be capable of that. He says we need to go to the police. People talk. That's all there is in the world. I told Ethan to wait until I could see if he was serious.

"He was going to go to the cops?" Mark asks.

"Apparently."

"But he didn't. What changed?"

Victoria flips through the pages of the notebook she's holding. "This one is from three days later."

Ethan talked to me today. It's so nice to be noticed. He said that we shouldn't go to the police. He and Connor said they can handle Caleb. I don't like the idea, but he put his arm around me and said to trust him. I got all warm and squishy inside. I didn't know a boy could have that effect on me. I do trust him.

"She told you that she knew Ethan was the target."

"That's what she said," I say, recalling the conversation in the hospital. "I'm sure that's in here somewhere. Check this out. It's from two weeks before the shooting."

I slept with Ethan again today. He's the most amazing guy. I told him I was worried for him. He said they would be ready and won't let Caleb hurt him. I believe him. He's so brave and strong. He will be a hero and I get to be with him. Unlike anything else in this world, he's perfect.

"He wasn't as brave and strong as she thought," Victoria says, scoffing.

"Or perfect. I think in her twisted mind, this was going to create a bond between her and Ethan that he couldn't ignore."

"That's crazy," Mark opines.

"That's love, Gunny. It's easy to confuse the two," I say, closing the notebook and sitting down at the table.

"What are you going to do now?" Mark asks, sticking the cigar stub back in his mouth. "Put them all online?"

I stare at a random spot on the floor. What to do with these journals is something that I've only just now begun to ponder. Even when I learned these existed, I never really thought we would find them. Maybe I should have.

"I don't work for WikiLeaks. Without context, publishing these might be worse than not knowing the motive at all. It'd be as irresponsible as broadcasting a gunman's name following a mass shooting and giving them the attention they crave. We need to walk people through this."

"Tierra, the FBI needs these journals. They are evidence."

"The FBI isn't looking for them. They're too busy looking for *you*."

"The state police are looking for me."

"What?" Mark asks, confused.

"It doesn't matter. *Front Burner* can't keep these."

It's not the first time I've been at odds with Victoria. If she thinks I'm just going to let her turn these over to the Feds who may be as likely to bury the truth as prosecutors were, she's certifiably nuts.

"I don't plan on keeping them, but we need to take some precautions. I've been attacked. You've been shot at and tailed. What do you think will happen if Mayfield or Spivey or Baino learns we have these? We have to ensure they're not lost forever."

"Okay," Victoria says, taking a seat of her own. "What do you have in mind?"

CHAPTER EIGHTY-FIVE

SENATOR ALICIA STANDISH

Russell Senate Office Building
Washington, D.C.

There are three Senate office buildings on Capitol Hill. Alicia's office is in the Hart Building, and she attends committee hearings in a room in Dirksen. She rarely goes to the Russell Building because there is no real reason to. This is a special occasion. After the stunt Daniel Wetzel pulled at the cloture vote, he's lucky she isn't bringing a flamethrower with her.

Alicia doesn't even acknowledge the receptionist in his office as she walks right past her. The woman protests but has no chance of catching up before the senator reaches the conference room.

"What to do with the scourge of gun violence in the United States is one of those problems," she hears Daniel say on the other side of the door. "It's a concern we all have, and the truth is, there are no simple solutions. If there were, even the politicians who work in the building behind us could have solved it by now."

"Some of us are trying," Alicia says, barging into the room without invitation or apology. She stands over Daniel with her arms crossed.

"Guys, can you excuse us?"

"No, let them stay. They work for you. Everyone here should understand the damage you did yesterday and the cowardice for not facing the music after you did it."

"Alicia, this isn't personal. It's about preserving our rights."

"And my bill isn't about banning all guns in the hope that it somehow makes us safer. It's about banning the ones that I know will."

"That's not going to solve the problem of gun violence in this country."

"It's a start. If I save one life with this bill, it's worth it."

"That's not how my constituents see it. It's a gun grab that will make many of them feel less safe. I can't get behind the Safe America Act as it's written."

"Fine. Then vote for the cloture motion and give the bill the up or down vote it deserves."

Alicia thought it would have been easy to make up for the vote she lost when Wetzel betrayed the party. It wasn't. No deal was rich enough to get a single senator to budge following the cloture vote, and she made some generous offers. The chamber is entrenched now, leaving Wetzel the key to success or failure.

"I agree, it does deserve a vote," he concedes. "Unfortunately, with all the deals you've made in both chambers, is anyone actually voting how their constituents demand?"

"We get to determine the kind of country we live in. It's not preordained, and it's not dictated to us. It's our future to make, and that starts with the bill you can't find the moral courage to support."

Wetzel shakes his head. "Senator, you're so focused on victory that you've forgotten the process. A bill of this magnitude deserves a rigorous debate. You sought to limit that right out of the gate. That's why I voted against cloture."

"The Republicans brought it to the floor. They wanted the cloture vote even though they couldn't be seen voting for it."

"They think you'll lose."

"That's not true."

"It is, and you'd know that if you spend a scintilla of time thinking about it. They're planning to flip their own before the vote by promising who knows what, but you're too blind to see that. You're campaigning, trying to do right by your constituents, doing your job, catering to your family, and trying to push through major legislation. It's enough to distract anyone."

"I'm managing just fine."

"You're off your game. The Alicia Standish who stormed into this town when she won would have known I wasn't going to vote for cloture. She would have remembered that I don't respond to threats or promises. Then she would have taken the time to convince me I was wrong."

"Did you sleep through the past two decades? Congress doesn't work that way anymore. Nobody cares about the debate or high-minded ideals anymore – not the media and definitely not the people."

"I care."

"I wonder if you'll think that way when the Democrats primary you before the next election because you're the only one in the party who didn't support this bill."

"Yes, I will. I serve at the pleasure of the people of Arizona. If they see fit to elect a new representative, then that is their will. Until then, I want to hear the floor debate. I want to hear from America. Maybe I'll be swayed, maybe I won't be, but I'm going to listen."

"I am going to get the extra vote for cloture I need," Alicia says, sounding as convincing as she can.

"I have no doubt that you will," Daniel says. "So why are you still here talking to me? Go get it."

Alicia storms out of Wetzel's office and leans against the wall in the corridor. She was just humiliated in there. She's losing her edge. Wetzel is a softie who should have been an easy mark for her. Instead, she ran into a man who suddenly thinks he has a backbone made of titanium. Damn him and his high-minded principles.

She needs to get it together and fast. There was some truth to what he said — she should have known about his vote. It was an oversight that cost her greatly. Mistakes like that on the campaign trail will cost her the Oval Office. With one ill-advised scream, Howard Dean killed his chance for the nomination in 2004. It happens that fast.

The clock is running out. She needs to close debate on the bill so it can get a vote before her momentum dies. She's so close. Something has to give. Something big needs to happen to bring this to a conclusion.

CHAPTER EIGHTY-SIX

ETHAN HARRINGTON

Coffeechusetts Bean Brewery
Framingham, Massachusetts

The center of Brockhampton may not look like it was hit by a tornado anymore, but most businesses still aren't open. Recovery will take time, although the psychological scars may never heal. Ethan journeyed north to Framingham to park himself in the corner of his new favorite coffee shop to kick back and relax.

"Hello, Ethan."

He looks up to see the smiling face of Tierra Campos hovering over him. Ethan leans back, folds his arms across his chest, and grins. Tierra cocks her head and shares a grin of her own.

"You have some nerve showing your face here," he says, his voice conveying his amusement.

"Of course I do. I'm a journalist, remember?"

"Yeah, I remember all too well. What do you want?"

"An interview," Tierra says, taking a seat. "This time without the cameras or the canned questions."

"Do you really think I'm going to talk to you?"

"No. I'll probably have to do all of the talking."

Ethan looks around the coffeehouse. There are about a dozen people seated here at tables and the coffee bar. He wants to know how loud and obnoxious he can get with her without the video of it ending up on YouTube.

"Unless you're apologizing, I'm not interested in anything you have to say."

"Oh? What am I supposed to apologize for?"

"Trying to embarrass me during an interview. Not letting me clarify when I misspoke before grilling me. Running around town and digging up dirt on me. Take your pick."

"You have an interesting take on history, Ethan."

"If you say so. It doesn't really matter anymore," he says, sipping his coffee.

"You're very smug today. I'm guessing it's because you visited the place where 'emotion and ecstasy first met.'"

Ethan grins, holds his hands out with his palms up, and shrugs. "The world will never know."

Tierra lets out a laugh. "That's very true, Ethan, only like everything else with you, it's not really the truth. You went to the spot by the lake where you first hooked up with Elizabeth and found her notebooks."

This time, Ethan doesn't look so smug as the smile disappears from his face.

"How could you know that?"

"The second paragraph of her letter, dummy. She wanted you to go there and find the ammo can with the notebooks in it. Did you?"

Ethan feels the blood drain out of his face as a rush of nervous energy races up and down his spine.

"That wasn't in her letter."

"No, it wasn't, was it? What did you do with the notebooks you found, Ethan?"

"I burned them. They're nothing more than a pile of ash. Happy?"

"Not really. You didn't read them before your little bonfire, did you?" Tierra says, leaning in and whispering to him. "I bet there was some good poetry in them. A little dark for my tastes, though."

"You're bluffing."

"I'm not. I have the journals. I know everything."

"Bullshit."

"I was surprised when Lizzie told me that you were Caleb's target. I was more shocked to learn that she told you what he was planning months before the shooting, and that you wanted to go to the authorities. Why did you change your mind? Or did Connor change it?"

Ethan's pulse quickens, and he breaks into a cold sweat.

"Where did you find her journals?"

"It's a long story. You can read about it."

"Give them to me, or I'll –"

"You'll what, have me doxxed? Go ahead, GunFreeE. Tell CyberOreo, AnarchyBooster, and DialPirate to do your dirty work again. You can even have them conduct another cyberattack against *Front Burner* for good measure."

Ethan's mouth hangs open. He knows she isn't speculating. She used their handles.

"You can't possibly…"

"Know that? One of your many problems, Ethan, is that you've never met a real journalist. The media was so enamored with you that they never bothered digging. I did and found all kinds of things. One of them was that Xavier from Velocity Public Relations got you in contact with hackers when you were looking for revenge against the American Firearms Association. By the way, GunFreeE is a dumb handle."

"I, uh…"

"Tell me what happened that day. I know you and Connor were supposed to stop Caleb as soon as he entered the school. Why didn't you? Did you chicken out, or did you just not care that much for your classmates?"

"Go to hell."

"You let sixty-six people die. You first."

Ethan starts to get out of his chair.

"This is your last chance to set the record straight, Ethan. On the record," Tierra says, starting the recorder on her smartphone. "How do you respond to what Elizabeth Schwarzer wrote in her journals about you knowing about Caleb's attack on Brockhampton High School months before it happened?"

Ethan glares at her.

"No comment."

"Very well. Ethan Harrington did not refute the allegations made in Elizabeth's journal. When asked, he would not provide a comment for this story."

Tierra switches off the recorder.

"If you print that, I will destroy you."

"You've already tried and failed, buddy. Your mentor had his goons attack me twice, but I'm still here. If it makes you feel any better, I don't have Elizabeth's journals anymore. I only have copies. The FBI probably has the originals by now."

Ethan stands and balls his hands into fists. He doesn't care who's here. He's ready to bash her face in. Tierra seems unconcerned about his aggressive posture. Ethan steps around the table, ready to pound her face.

"Lizzie loved you."

He shakes his head. "It was sex. That's all it was."

"Maybe for you. Not for her."

"You don't know anything about us."

"I know pretty much everything about the two of you. Let me give you some advice, Ethan: start looking for a good lawyer. You're not going to get softball questions like you did from reporters when you are on the stand at your trial."

She waits for a witty or arrogant reply and gets none. The kid who was never at a loss for words suddenly can't find any. Tierra stands and gives Ethan a slap on the shoulder.

"Let me know if you change your mind about the interview. See ya around, Ethan."

CHAPTER EIGHTY-SEVEN

VICTORIA LARSEN

Federal Bureau of Investigation Boston Field Office
Chelsea, Massachusetts

When the book closes on Victoria's life, this may go down as one of its dumbest chapters. People wanted by the authorities don't typically traipse into a building full of FBI agents. It doesn't matter that it's a state warrant or that she worked here. It's still a stupid thing to do.

Tierra handed over the journals after they made copies. Victoria insisted that she deliver the notebooks to her peers. Austin pleaded with her that it was unnecessary, but to no avail. For her, this is personal as much as professional. She wants her colleagues to know she was right.

Takara's task force is working in one of the large conference rooms. Building security escorts her there, and she walks into a room full of shocked faces. Victoria knows half the people here. The other half certainly know her.

"Victoria?

"Hello, Agent Nishimoto."

A state police detective springs from his chair and moves toward her, reaching for something on his belt. Two of his uniformed counterparts near the back of the room join him.

"Victoria Larsen, you are under arrest for –"

"Hold on a moment, detective," Lance Fuller says, holding a hand up in front of the determined state investigator.

"She shot a man during the riot. There's a warrant for her arrest."

"And this is my building. Agent Larsen came here of her own volition. Let's find out why first."

It was a sober moment for Victoria. The man who architected her departure is the first to come to her defense using her title. All eyes in the room turn to her as she unslings the satchel and opens the flap. She glances up, half expecting the state police to reach for their sidearms. They don't.

She pulls the accordion file out and places it on the conference room table. Everyone stares at it as if she just produced one of the Roswell aliens.

"What's this?" Fuller asks.

"The complete set of Elizabeth Schwarzer's personal journals. They provide Caleb's motive for the shooting at Brockhampton High School."

The gasps can be heard down the hall. Agents start conversations with each other as Takara pulls out one and flips through with Lance looking over his shoulder.

"How did you get these?" Takara asks.

"It was a team effort with Tierra Campos and *Front Burner*. They're fascinating reading. It turns out that Ethan Harrington knew in advance of Caleb's plan and even partnered with Connor Mayfield to help facilitate it."

"Whoa."

"Then there's what's happened since the attack," Victoria says, digging out a stack of papers bound with a clip from the satchel. "*Front Burner* has a source close to Ethan that provided them with compelling information that he coordinated the doxxing of Tierra Campos and the cyberattack against them. The perpetrators are elite hackers he regularly talked to in a secure chat room. I'm sure Cyber will be interested in that."

"Why would he do that?" one of the agents asks.

"He had a lot to hide. He also had a lot of people covering for him. One of them was Ryan Baino, the founder of Action Not Prayers. He arranged for Andre Noyer and Luke Walton, along with several unknown subjects, to attack Tierra Campos on two occasions. Their prints were pulled off the weapons they left behind in the parking lot after I shot one of them when they drew on us."

The agents look at the state police, who look unmoved. Victoria knows it wasn't the story they were told.

"According to information provided by Brian Cooper –"

"You got information from Alicia Standish's former chief of staff?" Takara asks.

"Actually, he was one of *Front Burner's* sources. He maintains that one of Baino's associates was the gunman in the Liberty Park rally shooting. He orchestrated the assassination of Landon Flynn. All the details are in the file."

"Anything else in your bag of tricks?" Lance asks, clearly impressed.

"I'm just getting started, sir," Victoria says, pulling out another stack. "Ryan Baino was aggressive in ensuring that nobody asked questions about what happened in Brockhampton. It wouldn't have been necessary had the state police conducted a complete investigation."

"Hey, wait a minute!" the officer closest to her protests.

Victoria slams the stack down on the table. He never takes his eyes off of her. She meets his stare.

"Joseph Mayfield is Connor's father. It turns out that he is close friends with Massachusetts State Police Detective Lieutenant Howard Spivey."

"That doesn't mean anything."

"You're right; it doesn't. This affidavit from a state police detective details how Spivey ordered surveillance on me without a warrant that included installing video and audio devices in my apartment and having me followed."

Victoria pauses to watch for Lance Fuller's reaction. He may have dismissed her the first time she mentioned it, but he isn't now. The state police detective in the room has a different response. He works for Spivey and doesn't appreciate seeing his boss's name dragged through the mud in front of the Boston FBI.

"Why is *Front Burner* sharing this with us instead of writing it?" Takara asks.

"Because most of these are criminal acts. I convinced them that the FBI should have these under investigation before the public reads about them first."

Takara grins, knowing why she wanted this task force opened – it forced their hand. *Front Burner* will cause them an embarrassment of epic proportions if the Bureau chooses not to investigate now. Even the attorney general or the DOJ cannot interfere. It's brilliant.

"If you've finished, there is still a warrant out for your arrest," the detective says, testing the waters.

"Was that at the direction of Howard Spivey?" Lance asks, not about to capitulate anything after what they just learned.

"I resent the implication of any wrongdoing in his office!"

"Do you know Seth Chambers, Detective?"

"Yes," he responds, looking at the other officers in the room.

"Is he a good man?" Victoria presses.

"Yes."

"Then why are you calling him a liar?"

The officer stares at her with a dumb look on his face. She unclips the affidavit from the stack and slides the document across the table.

"I can't speak to this," the detective says, regaining his footing after scanning the affidavit. "I only know that you're walking out of here in our custody."

"That's not going to happen," Lance says, as several other agents sense trouble and rise out of their chairs.

"It's okay, sir," Victoria says, holding out her hands.

"What are you doing, Agent Larsen?"

"I've been in law enforcement my entire adult life. Now it's time to trust the system that I have dedicated it to."

The detective cuffs her, hands to the front instead of behind her back. It was a gesture of courtesy.

"Are you sure about this, Vic?" Takara asks.

"I can see the whites of their eyes," she says.

"Victoria Larsen, you're under arrest for reckless endangerment, unlawful discharge of a firearm, and murder. You have the right to remain silent. Anything you say or do can be used against you in a court of law. You have the right to an attorney. If you cannot afford an attorney, one will be provided for you. Do you understand these rights as I have read them to you?"

"Absolutely."

CHAPTER EIGHTY-EIGHT

CAPITOL BEAT

Cable News Studio
Washington, D.C.

"And now for tonight's final thought," Wilson says into the camera. He has a lot to say and only hopes he can fit it in before the credits roll.

"We've focused this entire show on the bombshell report by Tierra Campos published on *Front Burner* that highlighted countless systemic failures in law enforcement. It's clear to everyone that the investigation into what transpired at Brockhampton High School, and in the days and months leading up to it, was incomplete and handled poorly. That a journalist could uncover what state and federal law enforcement did not should be disconcerting to every American.

"It reflects the need for good journalism and serves as a reminder of how hard it is to find. The media made Ethan Harrington a household name. Interview after interview, he offered his opinions, but we never asked hard questions – shame on us for that.

"Have reporters and journalists turned into pundits? Did everyone in the media fail to ask questions because they liked Ethan Harrington's politics? Tierra Campos did her job and was doxxed, attacked in her apartment, and assaulted at a riot for her troubles. Her partner, FBI Special Agent Victoria Larsen, was suspended and may be dismissed from the Bureau for the sin of asking questions. Her arrest by Massachusetts State Police on charges related to the rioting has been questioned by federal investigators who maintain it was self-defense.

"Critics have taken to the airwaves decrying the *Front Burner* article. They call it a smear campaign designed to derail the Safe America Act currently being debated in the Senate. Ultimately, the question is about what role this new information will play in the vote. It shouldn't be any.

"But this is the problem with elevating someone to be the face of a movement and then treating him like a demigod. Ethan Harrington will be investigated for his alleged crimes, but that shouldn't impact policy. Unfortunately, we know it will. Senators were affected by the public pressure Harrington worked to apply. America has learned through Elizabeth Schwarzer's journals that he could have stopped the Brockhampton massacre before Caleb Pratt fired a single shot. How many members of Congress will base their votes on a fraud?"

Wilson looks down at his paper. Sometimes his final thoughts are loaded into the teleprompter, and sometimes he wings it. Tonight was the latter. He didn't know what he wanted to say. He still isn't sure.

"Ethan Harrington may have dealt a severe blow to the gun control movement. It is also a blow to our democracy. Conspiracy theorists have labeled many shootings in this country 'false flag' operations. They claim that these incidents are manufactured by the government to strip away the Second Amendment rights of the citizenry.

"Their accusations have always been met with derision. They never offer evidence to support their conclusions. Now there is not one conspiracy in Brockhampton, but as many as three. How will we trust our investigators after this? How will we trust our media? Can we trust our elected officials? Can we even trust the victims?

"That may be the lasting legacy of the deadliest school shooting in American history. It may also be the worst part of that tragedy. That's my final thought, and it's for the record."

Wilson doesn't smile for his sign-off. The media needs to do some serious soul searching. He isn't sure they are up to the task. The *Front Burner* article was a painful recognition of his failures, too. Maybe the moment for him to sign off for the final time is here.

"Thank you for watching *Capitol Beat*; I'm Wilson Newman. Goodnight."

CHAPTER EIGHTY-NINE

TIERRA CAMPOS

Front Burner Washington Headquarters
Washington, D.C.

We worked on the article Friday night and all day Saturday in Austin's suite at the Deveraux. He made it clear that it was mine to write despite being new to *Front Burner*. It was a generous gesture considering this is the story of the decade. The rest of the team did their part to help. Much of the time was spent figuring out what we should and shouldn't divulge in the first of what may be hundreds of pieces.

Austin offered some suggestions for polishing it on Saturday night before submitting it for final proofreading in Washington. After that, it was beer, pizza, and some long-overdue relaxation. There was no celebrating. We only wrote an article. We didn't accomplish anything yet.

That changed Sunday morning when the article was published online. It spread across the country like wildfire. Cable news immediately started reporting on the piece, and political news shows changed their lineup to cover it. There were more hits on our website in one hour than in the past month, according to Tyler's "friend" in IT. The tech geeks thought it might have been another denial of service attack.

By afternoon, every news organization in the country was covering the story. It had all the hallmarks of a great scandal – influential players, shady dealings, and a compelling storyline about an event that resonates with the public. It's why conspiracies about the JFK assassination are still so salient in people's minds.

The team was beaming when they headed to Logan airport for the trip back to Washington. I wasn't. The news about Victoria's arrest made me nauseated. I shouldn't have agreed with her not to publish anything about her arrest.

I insisted on covering the statement the FBI made late Sunday afternoon. I wanted to hear what they had to say. The Bureau confirmed the existence of Lizzie's journals but would not respond to my article when asked. I stood in back, wanting to raise my hand and ask them if they were sure. They also confirmed that there were persons of interest in the assassination and riot. The final bombshell came when they claimed that new information compelled them to open a federal investigation into the Brockhampton school shooting.

None of that sat well with Howard Spivey. An hour after the presser ended in Chelsea, he made a statement to the cameras in his Worchester office defending his investigation. He was even bold enough to assert his belief that the FBI was being manipulated. My work completed, I decided to get the hell out of Boston and take Josh up on his offer of a late dinner. He wanted to hear all about the adventures that led to the article.

Despite the lack of sleep, I had no problem getting out of bed and ready for the beginning of the workweek. It's only the second time I have ever commuted to *Front Burner* and was a half-hour late arriving at the office. The main floor is a hive of activity. Phones ring off the hook as harried staffers rush through corridors and between cubicles. I expect the team room to be the same. It isn't.

The lights and computers are off. No phones are ringing, and not a soul is here. They all came back yesterday, so where are they? I check the nameplate next to the door to satisfy my paranoia about being in the wrong office. I may have only been here once, but my sense of direction is on point.

Did I miss a memo about this being a day off? I'm about to leave and find someone to ask when I check the conference room. The lights are off, and the smoked glass partition keeps me from looking in. I'm about to turn around when the lights come on.

"Surprise!" the team sings out in unison, scaring the crap out of me.

The entire team is wearing stupid party hats. They rush forward to offer their congratulations on the article. I'm not sure why I'm getting all the credit, considering they helped write it.

Senior managers and the managing editor of *Front Burner* come from the back of the room and share in the fun. They're appreciative of the excellent work we did. Austin is the only person missing.

"Where's the boss?" I ask Janey.

"Right behind you."

I turn to see him holding an enormous ice cream cake with "Congratulations Tierra" written on it in icing.

"Sorry, we had to keep this in a freezer on a different floor."

Austin sets it on the conference room table, and I hug him.

"You're late," he says, playfully. "Have you heard from Vic?"

"No. I'm worried about her."

"I spoke with Lance Fuller this morning. He said they would take care of her. They know the arrest is BS."

That doesn't do much to comfort me. The FBI wanted her head on a pike a week ago. The change of heart is just too convenient for me.

"Did he comment on the article?"

"Not on the record. Agent Fuller had a lot of questions about our sources and how we obtained the information we did, though."

"I bet he did. Did you answer?"

"Some of it."

The managing editor summons everyone's attention. The room falls silent.

"When we created *Front Burner*, we wanted an investigative arm that would operate with integrity and diligence that would be the envy of news organizations across the country. You rewarded that vision.

"I'll be honest; I wasn't sure you would. I trusted Austin to make personnel decisions but never understood them. Nobody in this room is a big name with decades of experience. If your work has taught me anything, it's that none of that matters when you find talented people. Each one of you brings valuable skills to *Front Burner*. Never has that been more evident as it is now.

"Miss Campos, I also owe you an apology. If not for Austin's staunch defense and blatant disregard for my authority, I may have fired you. It would have been the biggest mistake I've ever made. You have brought great credit to yourself and *Front Burner* in your handling of this investigation. I sincerely hope you're with us for a long time to come."

There is a lot of clapping, and then Logan cuts the cake. We share stories and enjoy the moment while it lasts. Over the coming months, we will have to deal with the consequences of our investigation. I have no doubt that the rollercoaster I've been on will start its trip down the track once again.

CHAPTER NINETY

ETHAN HARRINGTON

Law Offices of Galloway, Cramer & Shapiro
Boston, Massachusetts

There are three things in the world that defense attorney Dewitt Galloway loathes. The first is anyone who thinks giving up constitutional rights is a path to safety and security. The second is political correctness. The third is a lack of punctuality. When Dewitt tells a client to be at a place at a particular time, they'd best listen or start searching for new representation.

Dewitt is no fan of Ethan based on the first two criteria. The young spokesman for the gun control movement took care of the third when he was over a half-hour late for their first meeting. He decided to retain Ethan as a client despite all of that, along with his epically bad decision-making.

"Let me see if I have all this straight: Caleb tells Lizzie he wants to shoot up the school to get her attention. She tells you because she loved you. Connor comes up with the idea that the two of you can be heroes because he wants to impress his father, so you guys decide to help him by paying for the range time. Then you were going to turn him in until Lizzie told you that he just wants to kill you. So you decide to wait and intervene at the school. Did I get that right?"

"Yeah, that's about it."

"So, why did he start shooting kids in the library if you weren't there?"

"I don't know."

Dewitt shakes his head. "When do you plan on telling me the rest?"

"I've told you everything," Ethan says, slouched in his conference room chair.

"Not everything. I have pads full of notes from our sessions. Not one of them answers the question of why you and Connor didn't follow through on your plan."

Ethan looks out the window.

"Caleb's father had two gun safes in his house. He had the combination to one but not the other. Lizzie came and found me that morning and said he got into the second one."

"The first one had the handgun?" Dewitt asks. "And the second one –"

"Was the safe with the rifles. It had the AR-15. Connor didn't want to go through with it because he was scared, so he went back to class…and I hid in the bathroom."

"You knew he would go straight to the library looking for you."

Ethan hangs his head. "Yeah. I tried to convince myself that Caleb would chicken out. Then I worried that he might not. I was about to call 9-1-1 when I heard the shots. I will never forget that sound and the screams that came after them. By that time, everybody was calling for help."

Dewitt writes a quick note before looking up over his reading glasses.

"He walked around looking for you. That was why police said his movements were so erratic."

"He came into the bathroom I was hiding in but didn't check the stalls. I was standing on the toilet, trying not to make a sound."

"What happened after he left?"

"He went down the hall. A couple of minutes later, I heard cops shooting at him. That's when I went to the library and…"

Ethan closes his eyes and squeezes them hard. Dewitt waits patiently for him to speak again. Tierra Campos was right during her interview with him: he needs a lot of therapy to deal with this.

"I could smell the gunpowder in the room. There was blood everywhere. Bodies were lying on the ground…some huddled together. What I remember most was the eyes. They were all staring at me, staring through me."

"Did you try to help anyone?"

He shakes his head. "I didn't know what to do. I'm not sure anything could have been done."

"Instead, you covered yourself in blood and made yourself look like a victim."

"I panicked. I didn't want anyone to know what I'd done. I thought… Well, it doesn't matter."

"And everything you said to the camera when you left the school was for show."

"Yeah."

"And Connor went along with it."

"I told him that I would tell everyone it was his idea if he didn't. Connor told his father, and that's how we managed to keep it quiet. He had Spivey erase the video from the hallway and library and not follow up on leads. He closed the investigation the first chance he got."

"Do you know what Howard Spivey got in return?"

"Money. A lot of it. Joseph Mayfield has had an arrangement with him for years. It took a lot to buy his silence, from what Connor told me."

Dewitt takes off his reading glasses when one of his associates knocks on the door and enters the conference room. "They're here."

A ticking clock, from the sound it makes to the visual of numbers counting, is suspenseful. Television and movies use the concept well. Fox's hit show *24* perfected the idea. The timer in Ethan's head has been ticking down since he met Tierra in the coffee shop. It reaches zero as he watches the FBI climb out of their vehicles from the conference room window.

"You think there's enough of them?" Ethan asks, staring out the window.

"Trials are a pageant, but arrests are a sport. From now until your arraignment, everything that happens is geared to compel you to cooperate and plead guilty. Law enforcement and prosecutors will do anything they can to gain a psychological advantage. You need to prepare yourself for that. Do not breathe a word of anything we've discussed to the police or the FBI."

"They already know most of it courtesy of Tierra Campos."

"Yes, but you don't want to confirm any of it."

"Can you stop this?" Ethan asks, turning to plead with his attorney.

"What do you want me to do, barricade the door?"

"You're a lawyer. Isn't there some legal trick you can pull?"

Dewitt has been in this profession for even longer than his gray hair and beard would indicate. Countless clients have asked the same question. They think he's Matlock, not that Ethan has even heard of that show.

"They have a federal warrant, Ethan. We cannot interfere with law enforcement as they discharge their duties. All we can do is ensure that your rights aren't violated. Our work begins once you are arrested and booked. After that, I will work to get you the best deal I can."

Ethan continues to watch out the window, wondering if Connor is being hauled off to the sound of his father's protests. Joseph needs to join his son. If not, Ethan may be able to arrange something with prosecutors to help ensure he does.

"I have one more question before they get up here. Did you have any romantic interest in Elizabeth Schwarzer? I mean, something other than sex?"

"No. Why?"

"Because if you had visited her even once in the hospital, she never would have given Tierra a means to find the journals, and you wouldn't be standing in my conference room."

Ethan is about to ask what the point of that comment was when a federal agent knocks on the door of the conference room before a dozen agents pour in.

"My client is unarmed and –"

"Ethan Harrington?" the agent asks, cutting Galloway off.

"Yes."

"We have a federal warrant for your arrest. Face the wall and spread your feet apart."

Ethan does as commanded, and an agent cuffs him. He doesn't listen as his rights are read to him. With the clicking of the cuffs around his wrists, the crushing weight of reality settles on his shoulders. A single tear rolls down his cheek as he's led out of the conference room.

CHAPTER NINETY-ONE

SENATOR ALICIA STANDISH

Capitol Hill
Washington, D.C.

This vote has all the joy of dancing without music. On broken glass. Without shoes. Alicia's excitement about the prospects of passage yields to apprehension over the inevitable demise of the Safe America Act. Nobody wants to let the grim reaper in when he's knocking at the door.

The clerk completes the roll call vote. The result is a foregone conclusion. The only thing left to do is tally the final score.

"Are there any other senators in the chamber who wish to vote or to change their vote?" the presiding officer asks. "The yeas and nays are as follows: yeas thirty-four, nays sixty-one, with five voting 'present.' The motion fails."

Alicia looks around the chamber. There is no applause or celebration from the Republicans. It is a victory for the gun rights advocates who support them, but they don't want to aggravate the majority of Americans who still want some form of gun control in this country. It's bad form to celebrate a bill's demise that addresses that, no matter how unpalatable they find it.

Holding her head high, Alicia exits the Senate chamber and plunges into the teeth of the media. They're camped everywhere, looking to pounce on every senator they can in the aftermath of the vote. She hears some of her colleagues blaming her for the miscalculation. Others claim that the bill trounced the Second Amendment. A few say the fight over gun control is just beginning.

Her statement is short and predictable: talking points about how she's disappointed in the result and looks forward to continuing to pursue legislation that will curb gun violence. To anyone watching, it is an anemic performance that lacks passion and zeal.

She steps away from the media under a barrage of questions about her plummeting poll numbers and the inability to secure a victory on her signature bill. The media is angry about this failure and is taking it out on her. Her opponents in the primary are seizing the airtime she once monopolized. Her ascension to the nomination is no longer a guarantee.

She makes her way to the underground transport that connects the Capitol with the Senate office buildings. None of what happened is her fault, but she can't say that to the media. Americans like strong leadership. Alicia will be met with harsh criticism if she passes the defeat off on a teenage survivor of a mass shooting. The *Front Burner* articles implicating Ethan in the Brockhampton shooting were devastating. His arrest, captured by a local television affiliate as he was walked out of his attorney's office, was catastrophic. The face of the gun control movement indicted for the mass shooting that propelled him to stardom is damning on every level.

The news about her political career has only added to the angst. Republicans are pressing for an investigation into whether she knew about Ethan's involvement in the incident. It's not surprising – it's politics. She is, or at least was, a presidential frontrunner, and there are political points to be scored. Democrats would be doing the same thing if this happened to a Republican.

She makes her way to the office and collapses into her desk chair. The last twenty-four hours have been the most painful of her life. Nothing slows time like living through something that may change your life forever. It makes minutes feel like hours and hours, days.

Rahul knocks on the door jamb. "Senator, I'm sorry to interrupt, but there's someone here to see you."

"I don't want to see anyone."

Alicia expected certain things when she came in this morning. She knew this place would have the feel of a morgue. She also knew there would be a horde of media demanding statements about her failure. The one thing the senator never anticipated was her former chief of staff walking into her office to gloat.

"You."

"Senator," Brian Cooper says, in a conciliatory voice coupled with a respectful nod.

"You didn't wait long to drop in during your victory lap, did you?"

"I'm not taking a victory lap. The bill's defeat is the last thing I wanted to happen."

"That's hard to believe considering the damage you've done."

"I didn't do anything to kill the bill, Senator," he says, taking a seat in front of Alicia's desk.

"You were working with Tierra Campos. One of your friends ratted you out, so don't bother denying it."

"I can tell you exactly which friend it was because I wanted you to know that I was working with her."

Alicia glances up at Rahul, who stands quietly in the back of the office in Brian's old spot. He offers a slight shake of his head, not buying it either.

"Why?"

"I wanted you to pause and think things through. I thought you would if you heard I was talking to *Front Burner*."

"Do you expect me to believe that bullshit?"

"No, you believe what you want to, Senator. That's why you didn't move in with a softer bill and why you didn't listen to my warnings about Ethan and Ryan."

Alicia purses her lips. "Yeah, well, I guess none of that matters anymore."

"You can still honor your parents' memory by winning the presidency."

"You're not reading the recent polls if you think that."

"It's a year and a half until the election. The polls are going to change a few times between now and then."

He is right in that respect, not that Alicia will cede the point. Polls change, although not after a situation like this. A year and a half is an eternity in politics, but it's also a long time to have an albatross hanging around your neck.

"Brian, I've lost the president's support. My poll numbers are in freefall. Do you know what the worst part is? Fifty-seven percent. Fifty-seven percent of registered voters believe that I knew what Ethan was up to and didn't care. That number is only going to go up if the Republicans get their investigation."

"Tierra Campos knows you didn't know about any of this," Brian says.

"Who cares? She wanted this bill dead and won't lose sleep over me going down with it."

"Don't be so sure about that, Senator. She wanted the truth about Brockhampton. It ended up much deeper than she imagined; than any of us imagined."

Alicia frowns. "A journalist concerned about the truth. That will be the day."

"You will find out soon enough. My deal with Tierra was for her to find the truth about your involvement with Ethan and Ryan."

"I didn't know anything about what they did."

"I believe you. She will, too. You didn't trust my instincts about Ethan and Ryan, so please trust them now."

"Is there anything else, Brian?"

He understands a dismissal when he hears one.

"No, ma'am," Brian says, rising from his chair. "Good luck."

Brian leaves, and Rahul follows him out. Trust is a commodity Alicia can no longer afford to invest in. She has every reason to hate Tierra Campos, but what if Brian's right? As unrealistic as it sounds, maybe she is trying to do the right thing. One way or the other, she is going to find out.

ONE MONTH LATER

CHAPTER NINETY-TWO

SPECIAL AGENT VICTORIA LARSEN

Federal Bureau of Investigation Boston Field Office
Chelsea, Massachusetts

Victoria squeezes the trigger three times in succession. She pauses after a short inhale and fires three more shots. After she exhales, she fires the remaining three rounds in her magazine before the slide locks to the rear.

The shooting range isn't just a place to hone a skill; it's a retreat from the real world and a chance to focus on a single target with all of her concentration. There is no politics or drama here. The task is simple: make the weapon an extension of yourself and put a shot through a piece of paper.

"First week of your reinstatement and you're here on a Saturday," Takara says, leaning on the partition between shooting lanes.

"I'm shaking the rust off," Victoria deadpans, pulling in the target to reveal a tight group of holes right in the center.

"Yeah, I can see that you're getting sloppy. They're not in the same hole."

"This is a role reversal from the last time we were here. The word around the office is that you're staying busy."

"Yeah, I'm still unraveling the web of lies that is everything about Brockhampton. Thank you for that, by the way."

"Someone has to. Try doing it without a team working for you."

"But you did have one, didn't you?"

"I suppose that's true."

Front Burner was instrumental in getting the murder charges against her dropped by mustering incredible public and political pressure on state prosecutors to make things right. It took some time, but they finally saw it for the self-defense it was. Lance Fuller took care of getting the suspension expunged from her FBI record.

Victoria misses Tierra's friendship. She works in a man's world and has always had a hard time bonding with women. It was different while working with Tierra. She felt like she could be herself, maybe for the first time in her life.

"You know, I half expected you to be shaking me down for all the details," Takara says.

"I already know that you've issued enough arrest warrants to cause the printer to run out of toner. Everything else I see on television."

"Not all of it. Joseph Mayfield was on the roof with Mateo Morales, according to the crew on the worksite. Nobody saw it happen."

"I'm sure he's lawyered up and maintains it was a tragic accident."

There's no real justice in the world. Joseph Mayfield may land in prison, but that won't bring Mateo back to his wife and children. He is gone, and nothing can fill that void in their lives. Justice is nothing more than a balance sheet that never equals out.

"It hasn't hit the news yet, but Ethan is taking a plea deal.

Victoria smirks. "Of course he is."

"He told prosecutors everything he knows about Ryan Baino. I'm not sure if you know yet, but we confirmed that the guys who attacked Tierra twice were the same ones who shot at you outside Veni, Vidi, Vino. Ethan claims it was ordered when Ryan Baino heard that you were asking questions."

"Do you have any leads on finding them?"

"We're on the trail. The guy you shot is alive. He was taken to a private surgeon in New Hampshire. He's been arrested for a whole host of charges. They left there and went to Pennsylvania and then Ohio. We have an idea where they're going. We'll catch them."

Victoria bobs her head up and down as she processes the information. Tierra will sleep easier once she knows the guys that she called Skull Face and Joker are behind bars. Now that their names are out there, it's only a matter of time.

"What about Standish?"

"It looks like Tierra's *Front Burner* article was spot on. There's no evidence that she knew what any of them were doing."

Victoria hangs a target and runs it out to the end of the firing line.

"Vic, the brass here has taken every ounce of credit for this investigation. Why aren't you upstairs setting the record straight? Or why don't you have Tierra Campos write about it? If it wasn't for you –"

"I don't need the credit. This was never about enhancing my career or getting on television. I made a promise to people who were hurting. Knowing I kept it is all the reward I need."

She studies Takara's face. He doesn't understand. It's not that he's insensitive, he's just career-motivated. He likes basking in the limelight of a job well-done. Victoria is only interested in doing the work.

"That's a mistake. The honchos owe you a debt of gratitude. You should collect."

"I did my job and almost got crucified for it. There's nothing to be gained by stealing their thunder. It won't matter soon, anyway."

The comment catches Takara off-guard. "Are the rumors of you taking a job in the Hoover Building true?"

"That's ridiculous," she says, sliding her hearing protection on and emptying the magazine at the target downrange.

"Then you're leaving the FBI." Takara sighs after Victoria doesn't refute him. "You are, aren't you?"

Victoria recalls the target and gives a satisfied smile at the result. She pulls it down and tosses it in the trash behind her before starting to pack up her stuff.

"I'm not sure yet."

"You just worked your ass off to get back in. You're the most notorious federal agent since Eliot Ness. Why leave now?"

"Do you even need to ask?"

"Please don't do anything rash," Takara pleads. "There's a place for you here."

"If the last few months have taught me anything, it's that there probably isn't. Take care of yourself, Agent Nishimoto," she says, patting him on the arm.

"Where are you going?"

"I'm meeting the victims' families. The last time I saw them, I looked them in the eyes and made a promise. Now I'm going to look them in the eyes and deliver on it."

She makes her way out of the range and to the lobby of the building. Victoria stops when she reaches the exit. The metaphor isn't lost on her. Doors are a transition – leaving one place and entering another. That's where her head is right now. A few months ago, she wouldn't have thought of leaving the FBI. Now she has a hard time finding reasons to stay.

She takes a deep breath and starts walking. When Victoria passes through the doors, she isn't sure if it's for the last time.

CHAPTER NINETY-THREE

CAPITOL BEAT

Cable News Studio
Washington, D.C.

Wilson looks at Tierra as the technicians make final adjustments to her microphone and the last touches of powder are applied to her face. She's an impressive young woman. Of course, part of that composure comes from her being used to this.

"Nervous?" he asks, taking his seat.

"Not really. It's just that the last time I was on camera, I was asking questions, not answering them."

"Thirty seconds," the floor producer announces.

"You'd be surprised how similar those two things are. Do you miss it?"

"Part of me does, yes."

"Well, maybe you'll get your chance again someday."

"Ten seconds…nine…eight…"

"Good Evening," Wilson says when the count reaches zero. "It is Sunday, July fourteenth; I am Wilson Newman and this…is…*Capitol Beat*."

"It's been a month since the arrest of Ethan Harrington," he opens, following the playing of the title sequence. "The head of the non-profit Action Not Prayers, Ryan Baino, and several others in the group have been indicted. Connor Mayfield, a close friend of Ethan Harrington, was arrested along with his father, prominent Boston developer Joseph Mayfield, and Massachusetts State Police Detective-Lieutenant Howard Spivey.

"At the center of it all is Tierra Campos, an investigative journalist for the online news magazine *Front Burner* and someone who has become a household name over the past month. She's here with us tonight on this special broadcast of *Capitol Beat*. Thank you for speaking with us this evening, Tierra."

"Thank you for having me, Wilson."

"You've had a busy couple of months."

"It's been interesting, for sure."

"The story you published about how you uncovered Elizabeth Schwarzer's journals was riveting. Why do you think she wanted you to find them?"

"I ask myself that all the time. I just don't know. I listened to her in that hospital room. It may be that she felt connected to me at that moment. I think she wanted me to know the story."

"She could have just told you where the journals were."

"That would have been easier, for sure. Elizabeth was a complicated girl. She didn't trust anybody. Maybe it was her way of seeing if I was worthy of knowing the truth."

"A lot of people do question the timing of those revelations. You've come under fire from critics in the media who claim you torpedoed the Safe America Act on purpose. How do you respond to that?"

"The purpose of journalism is to present news important to the lives of people. It's how we stay informed of the events and issues that shape the outside world. I didn't willingly torpedo gun legislation. I provided information people need to be free and self-governing. The real question is, what would have been the consequences had I waited?"

Wilson leans in a little. He wants to see how she'll answer this. He's made up his mind, and that will frame his final thought at the end of the broadcast.

"Do you believe the mania surrounding Ethan Harrington was a reason behind that lack of scrutiny into his actions during the shooting?"

"It's not a secret that many in the media wanted the bill to pass. Maybe that's why nobody asked the hard questions, and that's the problem. Journalists must put their feelings aside in their reporting, but that's something happening less and less now. That line between opinion and reporting shouldn't be so blurry."

"What about you? Did you want the bill?" Wilson asks.

"I'm a school shooting victim. I have an opinion, but that exists separately from being a journalist. I don't get paid for my opinions. I'm paid to uncover facts and report them accurately."

"You also uncovered enough evidence to convince the FBI to investigate the laundry list of people arrested for their actions before and after the Brockhampton shooting. Did you ever think that was part of a grand conspiracy?"

"Initially we did, but the more we investigated, the less a conspiracy fit the facts. It turns out there was no shadowy figure pulling all the strings. Ethan Harrington, the Mayfields, and Ryan Baino were all defending their own interests."

"What about Senator Standish? Was she involved?"

"I know both the FBI and the Senate are investigating. As I said in my article, we haven't uncovered any information that she was aware of any wrongdoings by Ethan Harrington, Ryan Baino, or any other player."

"So, she wasn't involved?" Wilson asks, trying to get her to commit.

"I can't categorically state that yet. We haven't uncovered anything in the course of our reporting that leads us to believe Senator Standish knew."

Wilson smiles. Tierra is smart. She is relaying what she knows, nothing more and nothing less. *Front Burner* hasn't found anything. That's it. He decides to test her again.

"Senator Standish got beat up pretty badly in the first Democratic primary debate. She's way down in the polls. Would you vote for her for president if she was to win the nomination?"

"That's between me and my ballot," Tierra says, smiling back at him.

"The media isn't the only group criticizing the name you've made for yourself. Advocates claim Senator Standish's bill was the closest we've ever come to solving the gun violence epidemic in this country. Do you feel responsible for what happened to the bill?"

"I presented the truth about what happened in the months before the Brockhampton massacre. I exposed Ethan Harrington's complicity in it because the families of those who died deserve that truth. We uncovered how Joseph Mayfield and Howard Spivey suppressed the investigation; and how Ryan Baino tried to silence anyone asking questions, including me. Americans have a right to know all that."

"Do you think that this irreparably damaged the cause for gun reforms?"

"Ethan played on people's emotions when he perpetrated this fraud. Gun violence is a major problem that serious people need to find solutions to, and I hope both sides can find the courage to work on that together."

"You strongly condemned the American Firearms Association when they publicly thanked you on social media for your reporting. Why?"

"It was insulting. I didn't act on the AFA's behalf. There is no place for tribalism in a nation as great as America, and I will not contribute to it. That mentality leads to rioting. It leads to physical violence. It leads to personal attacks on social media. I've experienced all of that. That can't be the future of this country."

"So many people had different agendas before and after the Brockhampton massacre. They engaged in conspiracies and cover-ups to hide the truth about what happened there. How do you think they all explain their actions?"

"It's an impossible question for me to answer with any certainty. I will say this: they all believed in what they were doing. For them, it was justifiable deceit."

"We'll be back with more from Tierra Campos following this short break."

"We're out," the producer announces.

Tierra leans back as the makeup artist comes in to touch up the powder on her face. After decades of doing this, Wilson has developed a tolerance to the heat these lights throw off despite hating them. Most others aren't that lucky.

"That was very impressive, Miss Campos."

"Thank you, and it's Tierra. I was trying to be as honest as I could be. You did a good job trying to trip me up."

"I wanted to see if you could handle it, and you did. You should take my job when I retire."

"I've been watching you my whole life, Wilson. I hope you never retire. I could never be worthy of replacing you."

Wilson isn't so sure. As far as he's concerned, this is a job interview as much as it is a real one. There is no doubt that he could pass the torch to this young woman who has so much to offer. She's faced remarkable adversity and still managed to keep faith in herself. She could do any job she wanted, including this one. *Front Burner* won't want to let her go. She's almost guaranteed to win a Peabody and Pulitzer for her reporting in Brockhampton. If he offered, would she accept it? There is only one way to find out.

ACKNOWLEDGMENTS

I was asked a question a few months ago by a woman wondering why I write. That was a simple answer – I write because I enjoy it. She followed up by asking what was so rewarding about it. That answer was easy as well: that my readers enjoy it. The moment I decided to share my writing with the world, this became a journey with the thousands of people who invested their time and money to join me. You have my deepest gratitude and I hope you enjoyed this latest novel.

A very special thanks to the love of my life, Michele. This journey to publication was much longer than most, and she remained patient and supportive of me throughout the whole process. She is my cheerleader, sounding board, and a long-sufferer of having to repeat herself because I'm so involved pecking at a keyboard that I don't hear her talking to me. Thank you for being you, honey.

I broadened my number of beta readers for this novel. Their input was valuable, and I can't express how much I appreciate them taking the time to read the first draft and provide me with their opinions. Special thanks to Jenny, Kelly Greet, Dan Murphy, and Mark Mulvaney for their great feedback and support!

To my beloved mother, Nancy, and my sister, Kristina, and my brother-in-law, Ken: thank you for your incredible support. Family is everything and I am thrilled to have a close one.

Another big thank you to Derek Murphy at Creativindie for his guidance during the developmental edit. He went above and beyond with his work on *Justifiable Deceit* and pointed out flaws that I worked hard to fix. Thank you to Michael Waitz at Sticks and Stones Editing for doing some much-needed polishing for me and pointing out continuity errors and discrepancies that I never would have caught on my own.

Book covers are a tricky business. What I like isn't always the cover that gets the most attention. JD&J did a fantastic job taking the subject matter of the novel and turning it into a great cover.

ABOUT THE AUTHOR

Mikael Carlson is the award-winning author of the novel, *The iCandidate* and the Michael Bennit Series of political dramas. He is also the author of the Watchtower political thriller*s*. *Justifiable Deceit* is his tenth novel.

A retired veteran of the Rhode Island Army National Guard and Unites States Army, he deployed twice in support of military operations during the Global War on Terror. Mikael has served in the field artillery, infantry, and in support of special operations units during his career on active duty at Fort Bragg and in the Army National Guard.

A proud U.S. Army Paratrooper, he conducted over fifty airborne operations following the completion of jump school at Fort Benning in 1998. Since then, he has trained with the militaries of countless foreign nations.

Academically, Mikael has earned a Master of Arts in American History and graduated with a B.S. in International Business from Marist College in 1996.

He was raised in New Milford, Connecticut and currently lives in nearby Danbury.

Made in the USA
Columbia, SC
03 April 2025

85002c7d-3f7c-4b72-a3e4-8508c63c8466R01